Book 1

# THE VIEW FROM THREE WINDOWS:

## A Chicago Story

by
Elaine Jagier Mark Shaw

DREAMER'S PRESS-Shaw
740 St. Andrews Lane #41
Crystal Lake, IL 60014

Cover Illustration By Sherry VanSkyhawk

For information, address inquiries to:

Dreamers' Press
P.O. Box 223
Algonquin, IL 60102

First Printing December 1993
Printed in the USA

*Dedicated to my family...*
*each and every one*

*Special thanks to...*
*Mom & Dad for giving grist to my mill*
*My children, for being there all these years*
*My husband, for constant encouragement*

This is a work of fiction, a novel whose plot, though imaginary, uses Chicago as an authentic backdrop as it weaves bits of historical fact into a story set during the colorful World War I period.

*I hope you enjoy reading this book. May the characters, like real friends, help to reaffirm your Faith, inspire your Hope, and ignite your hearts with Love.*

Elaine Jagier Mark Shaw

## CHAPTER 1

Emilia's mother watched the scene from her perch on the edge of the only chair in the examining room. She felt like a cornered bird, appropriate for her plump, partridge-like figure. All through the examination her dark restless eyes absorbed various details in the room...gray walls...ominous instrument table... finally, Doctor and patient. Oh, poor patient, poor beautiful Emilia...weeping, pale Emilia... frightened...so frightened. Michalina half rose from the chair, wanting to comfort her Emilia, then fell back, knowing her time would come when Dr. Temple completed the examination.

He was tall and handsome, the Doctor, with silver-gray hair and piercing eyes. He loomed over the examining table like the shadow of death, shaking his head in disgust, as though dismissing the frail sixteen year old child-woman who clutched a white sheet to her breast and shrank from his touch.

"Take her home and keep her happy. There's nothing I can do. Six months, maybe…"

Emilia lay on the table feeling cold as the top of an iceberg; confusion numbing her brain. Tears spilled from her eyes. Dr. Temple spoke to her mother as if she hadn't been there. He said, "six months...maybe" as though he thought she would die. Surely something was wrong. She must have misunderstood his meaning. No doctor...no human being, would simply say...no hope...go home... die...not to Emilia... not to mama's baby. It couldn't be! Emilia looked at her mother, frightened eyes pleading.

Michalina knew – now it was her time to speak.

"Doctor, what you say?"

At fifty-six years of age, Michalina Kaszmierski had lived in America for thirty-five years, and still her English came softly, in the halting tones of a Polish immigrant, whose gentle voice found it easier to roll melodiously with the soft "sh" sounds of her native tongue. Surrounded in her neighborhood by others of like background, she had little need or desire to perfect her new language.

Now, she stared at Dr. Temple, waiting for some response, since she felt certain she had misunderstood his voice, his tone, his actions, but no, she could not now misunderstand the scornful look on his face.

He said, "What do you want? What do you people expect? You waited too long, and you probably don't even have the money for this examination."

Michalina's eyes widened. Emilia whimpered like a beaten puppy.

"Doctor, no, please, I haf money. Here. We pay...always, we pay."

Quickly, Michalina opened her black leather pocketbook, and pulled from it the small cowhide change purse which Emilia knew so well. Of course her mother had money in it. Somehow, her mother had always pulled pennies from its near empty bottom, enough to pay for the needs of their whole family...nine children...mother...father. It was a wonderfully magic change purse which wouldn't stop producing...ever...especially now...when Emilia was in trouble. She stared anxiously, through steadily spilling tears, watching her mother open one side, then the other, finally pulling two neatly folded dollar bills from its tiny, dark, gaping mouth. They would pay...they would pay, and Dr. Temple would begin to smile, and then he would cure her.

Michalina extended her hand. "Please. . .take."

Dr. Temple walked away...turned his back on them.

"Take your money. Take your daughter. I can't help her."

Hysterical sobs ripped from Emilia's throat as she jumped down from the examining table and rushed to Dr. Temple, grabbing at his stained white coat, pummeling his back with her fists, letting her protective white sheet drop to the floor, revealing her emaciated body.

He grabbed her shoulders and looked at her. Until today, he hadn't examined her in several years. Pitiful, he thought. Despite the sharpness and angularity of her frame, there was a delicacy about her that reminded him of a daffodil swaying in the sunlight...a pale, delicate beauty, shimmering as it changed. And those eyes! Swirling blue depths, rushing to the blackness of her dilated pupils, somehow seeming to encompass her world. Yes, he held a beauty in his hands, though she would never see fulfillment. Maybe if they'd come in more often... maybe...but he couldn't become involved in this problem. They were hopeful, helpless, indigent immigrants. He had to be rid of them! He mustn't allow himself to think of them any other way. The girl's sobbing, the mother's pleading, nothing would help. He had no magic. He led her back to the table and gave her a small dose of morphine, enough to calm her, forced her to lie there a bit longer, then helped her to sit. She was quiet.

"You may dress now."

That's how he left them. That's how he walked out of the examining room and out of their lives forever.

## CHAPTER 2

Michalina dressed Emilia as though she were a child of two once more. She buttoned her black cloth winter coat in anticipation of the sharp March wind outdoors - all the while whispering words of comfort to her.

"Momchu," Emilia sobbed, "Momchu."

Softly, in Polish, Michalina ordered her youngest child to stop crying. They would leave Dr. Temple's office and never come back. She knew he didn't care about them, that he didn't understand their problems...their difficulties...their beliefs...their hopes. He couldn't understand the conditions under which they came to this country...their desperate flight...the ship...the crowded cattle hold. Nor could he understand the conditions under which they'd first lived...three families in one small flat. He didn't know how they'd struggled...saved...bought a home, and raised nine children. He didn't know that this youngest child, now a young woman of sixteen, who spoke perfect English and had a fine office job, that she wanted to become an actress, and that they would help her and encourage her. He didn't know that they always paid their bills so their names would never stand out in any merchant's black ledger book. No, he knew nothing about them. Maybe...he didn't even care.

Michalina tucked Emilia's silky blond curls under her hat and dried her eyes for the last time. There would be no more tears. They could never come back here. They would find a good doctor, one who did care, one who could help Emilia to reach full womanhood. After all, this was Chicago...America...1917; her frail Emilia would not die. In Polish, Michalina commanded Emilia to stand straight, to her full five feet, four inches. In English, Emilia promised to try.

Once out on the street, Michalina tucked Emilia's feverish hands into her coat pockets, contrary to her usual practice of slapping the hands of anyone in her family who tried this, for she could not and would not continually sew new pockets in expensive coats. Michalina insisted they all own and wear warm gloves, but today she made a concession to this shivering child...gloves *and* pockets. Then she slipped her arm through Emilia's and together they tried to hurry to the corner where the trolley would stop.

It felt good in the streetcar...warm. The conductor walked up and down the aisle a few times, between the rows of gold cane seats, smiling sadly, knowingly, at them. He recognized Emilia's emaciated pallor accentuated by fever-bright eyes. A pity, too, he thought. She was a beauty...fair, blonde, blue-eyed... little features. He thought of his sister who died of it only last year, the "con" it was. He wanted to talk to them, but the woman sat with her eyes closed...sleeping or thinking...maybe just not wanting to talk. The girl stared, glassy-eyed. He walked past them and sat in the empty seat at the back of the car.

Michalina pretended to sleep, but her mind worked rapidly. She didn't want to talk to her daughter now, and there was no need. She didn't know what was in the doctor's medicine, but she did know it was something to make Emilia quiet. There was time enough for talk when it wore off and Emilia would realize the terrible meaning of the doctor's words...the death sentence. But now, why should it be so? Michalina knew some who had the TB. True, none were cured, but many lived...weak and pitiful...but they lived. She didn't want the sanitorium for Emilia...she didn't want pity...but surely, if others lived, then somewhere there must be a doctor who could cure the TB. After all, this was Chicago... America...1917. She sighed. How easy it was to think in Polish, but now the children were grown, perhaps she should go to night school and learn to speak properly in English, then maybe the doctors wouldn't look down on her. She would think more about that.

Emilia sat at her mother's side, feeling better than she had in months. The invisible heavy weight that seemed always to press down on her chest was gone for the first time in months. She was light-headed and giddy and her thoughts were scattered; they resisted organization, but it didn't matter. Mama would think of a way to help her, so she would think only about Frankie. He had been over last night, as he always came on Wednesday night and they held hands and walked to the movies. She tried not to cough. When Frankie came, Tata looked up from his newspaper, from the DZIENIK CHICAGOSKI, and he frowned.

Then he said, "What? Again you go with him? You are too much alone with him."

He grunted and lifted the paper in front of his eyes again, but he didn't say she couldn't go. Sometimes, she was afraid of Tata; he didn't talk much and she never knew what went on in his head, but he was good to her, gave her anything she wanted, and had never spanked her...ever. She loved Tata, in a distant sort of way, not at all the way she loved Frankie. Frankie wanted to marry her, she knew, he hadn't asked her yet, but he wanted to, she just felt it.

It was funny how they met. Her girlfriend, Florchak, said, "Mil, you have to come to the picnic."

"No, I can't, Florchak. I haven't got a beau. I'm not going to be the only one without a fella's arm to hang onto."

"Don't call me, Florchak. I'm Florence. This is America. And I know you haven't got a beau. If I hear you cry about your lost Benny anymore, I'll...I don't know what I'll do."

"You see? So don't remind me about Benny..."

"Forget Benny. My cousin Frankie's coming, but he's so shy he won't ask a girl."

"Oh, no...no stranger for me. I want to know my man."

"He's not a stranger. He's my cousin."

It was funny the way Florchak talked her into it, but it was the best thing that ever happened to her. Frankie was so handsome...older than she...seventeen...lean and broad shouldered, dark hair and eyes, not very tall, maybe only a little taller than she, but so kind and gentle, and he never took his eyes off her... an angel, he called her...a beautiful angel.

She felt Ma's nudge. She didn't want to stop thinking about Frankie, but she opened her eyes and saw their stop coming up. The tracks whistled while the red bricks in the street seemed to run along with the trolley to keep up, and the sun played hide and seek among the naked Poplar branches. Peter Poulis was standing outside his fruit market talking to some woman. They waved their arms in excitement about something...such a beautiful day...a happy day...she couldn't be thinking right. Dr. Temple didn't tell Mama she would die...that was crazy...she couldn't die.

The trolley screeched to its usual skidding halt and they lurched down the steps. Michalina put her arm through Emilia's again, and they crossed the street to the fruit market.

"Ah, Mrs. Kaszmierski, how are you today? And lovely Emilia, how are you?"

Peter's smile seemed to widen his thin, dark-skinned Greek face. The Poulis brothers were both small men with big hearts who made friends easily, partly because of the beautiful fresh produce which sparkled through the store windows in rainbow freshness.

The woman with whom Peter had been talking turned, narrowing her eyes in scrutiny as she saw Emilia. It was Mrs. Elinora Steech who lived on the next block. She was very big - and Emilia didn't like her, not because of her appearance, which was really quite handsome, but because she felt suspicious of her. She'd been married three times; Emilia thought there must be something wrong with a woman who couldn't make up her mind about a marriage partner. She'd heard people say that one man could never satisfy Elinora Steech. She'd always thought they were talking about simple boredom, but now she began to wonder. Her girlfriends said the neighborhood ladies were talking about something else entirely, and that she'd know what they meant when she got married. Emilia looked away and shuddered.

"Michalina!" the woman called loudly.

Emilia turned toward her again. There was something so open, honest, and happy about her voice, as though she had no problems or cares, a voice that seemed to say it loved life. She must be thirty, but she seemed ageless. She confused Emilia.

"Elinora..." Michalina forced her greeting manners, though not too convincingly. "Fine day...no?"

"Never mind the day. What are you doing to this child? She looks like the walking dead. Have you had her to a doctor?"

"Ya. Today we go. We come from Dr. Temple now."

"And what?"

"Emilia, you go with Mr. Poulis. Carrots, potatoes and onions, we need. Only good ones."

Emilia left, she didn't want to hear anyway. Mama and Mrs. Steech could talk. She didn't care what they said. She wouldn't believe Dr. Temple...she couldn't...yet, once inside the store, her shoulders began to shake with wild, silent sobs. Peter Poulis put his arms around her, and let her cry on his shoulder, never asking once what troubled her. Emilia saw Peter's brother, Marcus peer out at them from the back room, a sorrowful look on his face. Did they know? Probably. Everyone seemed to know. Anger stabbed Emilia's heart. Why hadn't Mama known? Maybe they could have done something. Then she felt guilty for blaming Mama. No, it wasn't right. There was no use in blaming. That wouldn't help her now.

When Michalina was certain that Emilia was safely inside, she told Elinora their story. It was hard, but she needed to confide in someone just then. She began to question herself about why they hadn't gone to the doctor sooner, to blame herself for this terrible thing that was happening to her youngest child...but she hadn't been sick long. It was very sudden. She'd had a cold on and off for a few months. Michalina gave her medicine and told her to dress warm. She would seem better then worse. She stayed up too late too often...with Frankie...with the girlfriends. She didn't get better. Lately, she had no appetite, lost weight, fevers came and went. Her eyes were too bright. Now...Dr. Temple said six months...maybe. Michalina's eyes filled with tears; she brushed them aside.

Elinora put her arm around Michalina's shoulders and squeezed.

She said, "No, you listen. Forget Dr. Temple. He's a fool. I know; I've had the TB, my brother's had the TB, and look at us now...big...fat...happy."

Michalina looked at Elinora, astonishment suddenly damming the flow of tears.

"But how you do this?"

"You take Emilia to see Dr. Noshkins...over on Ashland and North Avenue. You tell him Elinora sent you. Then you'll see. Everything will be all right."

"But Dr. Temple say six months... maybe..."

"So...maybe...I don't know. Who can say. But Noshkins is worth a try, no?"

"Ya. We go."

The two women parted company. Michalina joined her daughter in the fruit market, inspected the vegetables she gathered in brown paper bags, paid for them, and led Emilia out the door exchanging little conversation with Peter Poulis who seemed to understand her preoccupation.

She hurried Emilia as much as she could. It was getting very late and Tata would be home waiting for supper, wondering why it wasn't ready for him this evening. Then Emilia stopped abruptly while pulling on her mother's arm.

"Momchu, look."

They stood before the newspaper stand. Headlines jumped at them from the DAILY NEWS. "REVOLUTION OVERTHROWS RUSSIAN GOVERNMENT".

"Ach, Dziecko. We are lucky to be here...in this country. Is trouble everywhere now in Europe. Again, Poland be cut to pieces. Now, come. Hurry. Tata waits for supper."

Tata and the boys, Wladek and Harry, were probably home from work, complaining about a cold and empty stove. At least the other three boys had homes of their own and wives to cook for them. Emilia's three sisters were also married and in their own homes at this hour cooking for their husbands.

Wladek, who now insisted upon being called Walter, being his usual mischievous self, threw a damp dishtowel at Emilia the minute she came through the kitchen door.

"Hey, Mil," he teased, "did you take Mama shopping again?"

Harry lowered his evening paper and looked at his sister. "Cut it out, Walter, can't you see she doesn't feel good?"

"I'm sorry, Mil. Did you go to the doctor today? What did he say?"

Michalina interrupted. "Emilia, go to your room. Rest. We call you for supper."

She spoke in her customary at home fashion...half Polish...half broken English.

Tata came from the parlor, frowning, scraping his pipe bowl, blue eyes sharp as a lightning streak, fixed intently upon his wife. As always, his military bearing commanded peace.

"Nu, Mama? Co cie tam?"

Michalina covered her face with her hands and sank into the nearest chair. She said nothing, made no sound whatsoever, but tears forced their way through her fingers like flood waters through chinks in a dam.

Walter put his hand on her shoulder. "What Mama? What did the doctor say?"

"Six months...maybe..."

Harry threw his paper on the floor. "Dear Jesus Christ." Not being able to say anything more, he went to his own room, slamming the bedroom door behind himself. He and Emilia were the two youngest...seven years between them... they'd always been very close.

Tata stopped scraping and clutched the pipe bowl.

"Mama," he asked, "what *you* think? What Emilia says?"

She told them about the examination, the medicine, Elinora Steech, and Dr. Noshkins, finishing with, "Emilia doesn't know, but we go tomorrow."

## CHAPTER 3

Friday, March 16, was a cloudy day with intermittent showers and steely winds. Michalina and Emilia dressed warmly for their hour's trip to Dr. Noshkins' office. They had to travel by trolley car from their home on the northwest side to a neighborhood Michalina considered inferior. It was a two transfer trip and the wait in between was cold.

Emilia was quiet...exhausted, pale and puffy-eyed from sobbing through the night and much of the morning. Last night, long after Frankie left her, and her brothers and sisters went back to their own homes, she had walked the floor wringing her hands, beating her chest like some wounded animal...and sobbing. This morning she awoke crying. She wondered why God was punishing her. It didn't matter to her what her sister, Stasha, had said about God loving her very much because He was giving her such a big cross to carry. That didn't make sense. She loved Mama, so she wouldn't hurt Mama. If God loved Emilia, why was He hurting her? No, God must be mad at her, though she didn't know why. She'd tried to be good.

Now, she began to worry about this trip to a new doctor. What if this Dr. Noshkins said the same thing? She would have no choice, she would have to believe...six months...maybe. She couldn't believe. Frankie wouldn't let her. He told her so last night, after Harry called him to come over. It was all so terrible, but what Frankie said, oh that was good. The whole scene flew through her mind again.

Frankie stood at the door. She was so happy to see him! They sat in the parlor and everyone let them alone...this time. She didn't have to tell him much; he knew most of the story from Harry. She put her head on his shoulder and he held her hand.

"Mil, let's get married now...tomorrow..."

Mil looked up, surprised that he proposed so suddenly. In spite of everything, she had to smile at his burning red face...his soft brown eyes that couldn't seem to leave hers. Then, quickly as it came, her smile vanished.

"Married? But Frankie, I'm sick. What if you get sick?" What if Dr. Temple is right?"

Emilia remembered how she felt. The shock of the afternoon and the effect of the morphine had worn off. She was nervous and upset. She left Frankie's side, paced the floor and wrung her hands. She cried quietly, at first, then hysterically, and that's when it happened...the cough...soft...soon building to a hacking crescendo...sputum that would not be contained...and then blood...brilliant flecks on her handkerchief...and then, a small red stream.

"Oh, my God!" she screamed. "Frankie!"

He rushed to her side and put his own handkerchief to her mouth. "God Almighty, no! The doctor was wrong!" he said. "You're not gonna die!"

Michalina and Tata came alone from the kitchen, for the others had already left. They saw the death color on the handkerchief.

"Jesu, Marya" Michalina cried, as she rushed to Emilia's side and gently supported her to the sofa.

Tata hung back and prayed, Mil guessed. He always prayed to God in emergencies. What else could he do? He was not a demonstrative man, and he didn't believe it was proper to touch his children, especially the girls...that was for Mama to do. He worked hard everyday, sometimes even on Sunday, and he prayed...that was for him to do. But...why should she think of any of that now, she wondered.

Again, Mil began coughing and gagging into the handkerchiefs. Then, seized by panic, her eyes widened...darted wildly from one person to another... like those of a cornered mouse, seeking refuge. But, just as suddenly as it all started, it was over...she was quiet, breathing heavily, the coughing done. She whispered, "Momchu."

"Dziecko, tomorrow, we go to Noshkins...early, we go."

Frankie knelt at her feet, burying his head in her lap, then they heard his muffled words, "Mama...Tata...I wanta marry Mil...right away...tomorrow..."

Tata stared at Frankie, a flicker of softness shone in his eyes, then abruptly he turned away.

"We see," he said, "we see."

Tata left the room, and Mama hugged them both closely.

That's how it happened last night, and now they were almost there...North and Ashland...Dr. Noshkins' office...Frankie's neighborhood, but Mama didn't like it that Frankie lived here. How crazy it was that Mama resented Dr. Temple's attitude, and then felt nearly the same way herself about other, more recent Polish immigrants. Emilia wondered why. Someday, when everything was all right again...she would ask.

Oh, she worried, what would Noshkins say? Had Elinora Steech been this bad? What would she have to tell Frankie tonight?

## CHAPTER 4

They walked half a block, arm in arm, then stopped before a dark, narrow doorway wedged between the dime store and a flower shop. Michalina compared the number on the door with her scrap of paper, nodded, and gently pulled Emilia inside.

There was barely room enough for both of them to stand at the bottom of a seemingly endless wooden staircase, which curved at the top, making the door that had to be up there, invisible.

With every creak of the stairs, Emilia's heart pounded more violently and her breath was harder to catch. At last, they reached the top, and Michalina opened the plain oak door that ushered them into a spacious, bright waiting room, whose front wall was lined with great windows that viewed every bit of across-the-street-activity below.

No one waited and no one appeared. They sat down in wicker chairs facing the frosted glass door that read Harry Noshkins, M.D. On the other side stood another frosted glass door, lettered - Leonard Noshkins, D.D.S. Emilia decided they must be related. Everything was old, but clean and bright, and casually friendly. Only a few minutes passed, and then the frosted glass door opened. A short man in a white coat looked at them. He didn't appear to be as tall as Emilia. He wasn't fat, but rather rounded, especially in the middle. He had dark skin which was accentuated by a halo of graying dark hair...about forty maybe, and very pleasant...friendly...like the room. He looked dwarfish, Emilia thought.

He smiled at them. "Are you waiting for me...or my brother?" He motioned toward the opposite door.

Emilia burst into tears; Michalina shushed her. Dr. Noshkins went to them. He knew whom they wanted to see, it was obvious to his practiced eye; his was merely an introductory question.

"There, there," he said, patting her back as he led them beyond the door, past a great desk, through a short hall with doors on either side; and into the examining room. He took a long white tie gown from a hook and handed it to her.

"Remove your clothes and put this on. I'll be back shortly."

He bustled out of the room, not a motion wasted. Michalina helped her undress and she climbed onto the examining table. Soon, he returned, signaled by the creaking of the padded green leather examining table.

He smiled at them both and busied his hands...pressing, feeling, applying his stethoscope.

They were tense; the examination seemed long. Then, once more, he smiled at them warmly, calmly. There was no alarm in his face. Emilia felt everything must be all right. Dr. Temple was wrong after all...just a cruel, hateful man. Now, Dr. Noshkins would tell her everything was all right.

He said, "I think we must know your name."

She told him and introduced Michalina.

"How did you happen to come to me?"

"Elinora Steech recommended it."

He smiled broadly. "Ah, Elinora...her case went very well." He grasped Emilia's shoulders and looked at her intently...sympathetically. "You are very sick," he said.

She stared at him a moment, then jerked away from his touch. Frightened that he would confirm Dr. Temple's words, she cried, "No, I don't want to die...no..." After shouting the rebuttal to her own thoughts, she sobbed, and pounded her fists on her knees.

A firm knock at the door went unnoticed by the women, but Noshkins knew it would be his brother checking to see if everything was all right. Noshkins opened the door, and waved him away.

"Thank you, Leonard."

Michalina jumped to Emilia's side.

Dr. Noshkins sighed deeply and said, "I must tell you the truth if you are going to help me try to make you well."

Emilia allowed the words to run through her consciousness several times. Realizing they were words of hope, she held onto them. Then looking intently at Noshkins, she vowed to be helpful.

He weighed her at ninety-five pounds and asked if she'd had a hemorrhage. Again, he tapped her chest and back. Then he told her to dress and left the room.

Michalina helped Emilia, and when she was all buttoned, they went out to Noshkins' office where he waited for them behind his desk. They looked at him expectantly.

"I must tell you the truth," he said. "It is serious."

"But you said you would help me to get well!" Again, she cried and wrung her hands.

"I will, but you must follow my directions...exactly. If you want to live, you must help."

"Anything, Doctor. We do anything." It was a solemn promise Michalina made.

Emilia nodded, wild-eyed. "Tell me what to do."

"Do you attend school?"

"I'm working. I'm graduated from eighth grade...went to business college. Now, I'm a stenographer-typist."

"I think you like your work, but you must give it up...for awhile, anyway."

"It's not too hard. I sit a lot."

"From now on, you must stay in bed until I say otherwise. Your meals will be served to you in bed, you may read a little in bed, but mostly, you will sleep. You will get up only for the toilet." He shifted his gaze to Michalina. "Do you have an enclosed porch? Open to the sun and air? Protected from the winds?"

Michalina nodded and answered, "Is in back...from kitchen...is nice."

"Perfect. She must have a warm nightgown and many blankets, but that is where she must sleep...day and night."

He outlined her diet: four egg nogs daily - two eggs in each - liver for lunch and supper, bacon and eggs for breakfast, orange juice whenever she wanted it, and fresh citrus fruits with every meal.

"I'll take your address and come to see how she's progressing next Friday afternoon."

Michalina stopped him. "Is good for us...what you say. But I must know...now...how much is this all costs."

"Of course, Michalina. I know. Money is a worry for all of us. The food is rich and expensive, but my fee...it will not be too great...two dollars each visit...and you may pay me when you are able."

"Nine children we have. Five boys...all working...two, not married. It's be all right."

Noshkins smiled and nodded, patting her arm.

"Doctor...who must knows of the sickness my Emilia has?"

"You want to know if I'm going to report this to any authorities?"

"Ya."

"Michalina, I'll decide that next Friday. You must be very careful so others won't get sick...this disease is contagious...it spreads easily. You will have to keep Emilia's dishes separate from everyone else's, wash them separately with boiling water, keep the family away from her, let them talk to Emilia from the kitchen. Everyone must wash hands frequently. Can you do all this, Michalina?"

"Ya." Michalina nodded vigorously.

"It's extremely important you follow these directions. I don't want to report this to the authorities. They will insist upon taking her to the sanitorium, and I don't want her to go there. Too many die there."

Emilia became frightened again. "We'll follow the directions, Dr. Noshkins. I don't want to go to the sanitorium, please!"

"I know." The tone of his voice soothed her.

"Doctor?" Emilia's gaze dropped shyly to her lap. "I have a boyfriend, Frankie. He wants to marry me."

"There can be no closeness, no kissing, no physical contact between you and others for awhile. You will have to wait."

Tears welled in Emilia's eyes, but Michalina stared disapprovingly at her.

"You wait! Only hour ago, you think you die. Now, you think you live, you want get married. No! You wait!"

## CHAPTER 5

The next week, Michalina and Frankie sat in the cheery kitchen at the big table which seemed extra large now with only the two of them there. Tata was at the park district tending the rainbow of flowers in which he took such personal pride. Walter and Harry were downtown at the dental laboratory which they owned in partnership with their brother, John. The other children who had been coming almost every day to visit Mil, were either home with their own families or out working for them. The girls...Stasha, Ludmilla, and Helcha...were respectively, twenty, seventeen, and fifteen years older than Emilia. They all had children of their own now, nevertheless, they had made time to visit Mil, especially since she was looking no better. Her eyes were more intense, sickly bright, and more sunken. They were following Noshkins' prescriptions, exactly, but despite all the fattening egg nogs, Mil gained no weight.

Though all the healthy foods prescribed were expensive, Michalina, nevertheless, managed to pay all the bills. This surprised her, for Michalina still lived in the past, remembering how hard it was in the beginning, when all the children were young and at home. Oh, how tight was the money then. Now, in addition to the fact that so many were married, both Walter and Harry had voluntarily increased the amount of money they paid to her weekly for room and board. Michalina felt grateful for that, and for all her family's help.

But about Mil's health, Michalina began to feel hopeless, though she said nothing. She supposed the sisters and brothers and Tata were also feeling the hopelessness of the situation. And about Frankie's feelings...she didn't know. He just came every evening...happy, smiling, making jokes, telling Mil they would soon be married...just as he did now. Ya, always, he was happy and smiling, even with the redness of his bashful face. He was good, she thought, even if he lived in the *old* neighborhood. Then she saw Mil smile at him through the kitchen window that opened onto the porch.

"Oh, Frankie, will you still love me if I'm fat?"

He laughed. "Silly angel. You fat? Uh-uh."

Though he worried about losing the time, Frankie felt he was right to take the time off from his work at the mustard factory to be with Mil today. He was tense and it showed in the muscles of his powerful arms. He could see Mil was worried about Dr. Noshkins' visit to their house today, about this second examination, and probably, she worried about his taking the day off for her, but Mr. Schmelling, who owned the factory, understood. He had known Frankie since his tow-headed toddler days, before his father died.

Frankie didn't really remember his father, being only three when he died, but his mother and his brothers and sisters talked a lot about his Pa. Frankie owed his mother a great deal, they all did. She worked in their tailor shop and kept the family together all these years. Frankie was always glad he had dropped out of school after sixth grade and helped out by working at the mustard shop. Mr. Schmelling often laughed and reminded Frankie of how he looked when he first came to ask for a job - a little boy in knickers who said he was sixteen; Mr. Schmelling hired him anyway.

The guys at the shop were very good about accepting him and teaching him. Then, there was Vera Olchinski, who worked at the factory too, and used to tease him and say she believed he was sixteen. He knew she didn't, but she sure must believe it now, because she paid him a lot of attention...*real* attention...but he didn't want to think of

Vera now, it made him feel disloyal to Mil, and anyway, Vera couldn't compare to Mil, not even with her actress build.

Yeah, Mr. Schmelling was swell. He paid a guy well, nevertheless, Frankie knew he'd have to find other work soon, something that paid better since he was a man now, and he and Mil would soon be married. He had been going to night school all this time. He didn't bother much with English or spelling, those he could learn on his own by reading, which he did. But it was the mechanics, and the machine work, and the mathematics to go with it, those were the things he took and studied. Soon, he felt he would be ready.

The doorbell rang. Michalina jumped to answer it. Frankie opened and closed his fists as he looked at Mil who stared at him wild-eyed, like a frightened doe stalked by a hunter. If only he could ease her fear.

The dwarfish, bustling figure of Dr. Noshkins swept in, hat in one hand, black bag in the other. He stopped abruptly in the doorway. His face clouded.

"You have followed my directions?" he asked, slipping out of his coat.

Together, they answered yes.

"Well, we must listen to your chest."

As the doctor approached her, Mil looked imploringly at Frankie, so he left the window. It was so quiet, Frankie thought he could hear the beat of Mil's heart without a stethoscope, but it was probably his own heart he heard.

Mil lay still, watching the doctor's face very closely. He frowned in concentration, but that was all she could see. He returned the stethoscope to his bag.

"Dr. Noshkins...please...?"

His eyes met hers. "It's been only a week...too soon to tell anything. You keep following my directions...and hope..."

Michalina said, "Oh, Doctor, we pray...all of us...we pray. Every day to church I go...there I pray. God, He is good. He must listen...ya?"

"Michalina, you keep praying. That is always good. Every good doctor prays with every movement, with everything he does."

"Oh, you are Catholic, Doctor?"

"No, Michalina. I'm a Russian Jew, but God hears us both...I think."

"Ach..." Surprise flew across Michalina's face, but she continued smoothly. "Ya, you are good man, Doctor. Tata and I...all of us...we are proud to know you."

Noshkins understood Michalina's surprise. His own mother would have reacted similarly - had the situation been reversed. How long, he wondered, would it take ethnic groups to accept one another's differences? But enough philosophy, he told himself as he prepared to leave.

Smiling at Emilia, Noshkins said, "You continue with the treatment. I'll come by again in the middle of the week."

"Doctor?" Michalina felt hesitant, but she had to ask her question. "Will you report about my Emilia's sickness?"

"No, not yet...but soon all the family will have to see me for periodic check-ups. We wouldn't want anyone else to get sick, would we?"

"Ach, no, Doctor. You tell us. We come.

Noshkins smiled once again as he swept to the door.

Frankie grabbed the doctor's hat from the table and followed him.

"Doctor...uh...your hat..."

"Thanks, my boy." Noshkins scrutinized his face. "I think you want to say something more, what is it?"

Frankie yanked his coat from a hook by the door. "Let's go outside."

A sharp wind hit them, as they moved to a sheltered corner of the porch.

"Now, my boy, what is it?"

"I watched you...your face...when you saw Mil. It's bad, huh?"

"Yes."

"She can't die, Doc. She can't!"

"You're the boy she would like to marry?"

"Yeah. She's an Angel, Doc. You know...my job...it's good. Soon, I'll have a better one. I could take care of her."

"I'm sure, my boy, but I don't think you understand how weak she is...how very contagious this disease is."

"My buddy...he's had it...and I've asked around. I know how it is, Doc."

Noshkins admired this boy...his lean body...the strength of his workman's arms...his soulful brown eyes, different somehow from most workmen... thoughtful...now blazing almost red with love and idealism. But he had to be honest.

"Then you know it's impossible. You couldn't have any physical relations with that girl now. It would probably kill her and destroy you also."

Frankie blushed. "I can wait, Doc. I wouldn't touch her...not yet. I don't want to hurt her. I love her, and she loves me. She needs me. She'd fight...more, I mean...if we were married."

"You would marry her...to give her your name...to give her a reason to live?"

"Yeah. It would work...I know. And anyway...if there's a war...well, she needs to have that...to know we belong to each other no matter what, even if I have to go away...maybe..."

Again, Noshkins searched the wide set brown eyes, and found them reflecting a feeling so deep it seemed nearer pain than love, but he thought, love and pain were often one. He was so young...this boy...his body, taut, like a rope stretched for a heavy pull, perhaps he could carry it off, perhaps he was what she needed, and if she died...well, the boy's heart was with her anyway...he couldn't be hurt anymore.

"Well, Doc? Please...I need to tell Mil's Mama and Tata it's all right...that we can be married."

"Do what you must...but remember what I told you."

Determination shot its way through the shining red of Frankie's face as he grasped the doctor's hand and shook it firmly.

# CHAPTER 6

When Frankie returned to the kitchen and reported his conversation with Noshkins to Mil and Mama, it pleased him to see how they reacted...surprised... protesting...acquiescing. It made Frankie feel he was in charge...gave him a real feeling of power. Now, he had more reason to be strong, and he could be...he would be. They would marry soon, tomorrow - if Mil's parish priest would let them. Frankie even had a plan. They would go to the rectory together - he and Mil and the two mothers - in the morning they would go, and if the Father said yes, the mothers would be their two witnesses and then they would get married right away, right then and there. Then they'd come back and Frankie would move in and take care of Mil and they'd wait till Mil was better before they'd really live like husband and wife. And she *would* get better.

Mil argued at first that it was crazy because there was no sense marrying someone who couldn't be a wife. Mama walked back and forth, saying, "no, no, no, no..." but Frankie convinced them it would be all right, that he could move in and set a cot for himself at the far end of the porch, and that it would really be healthy for him because he would get to sleep out in the fresh air. The more he thought about that, the better it seemed. It would be good for him after being cooped up in the factory all day, every day. Then he left them, to go and tell his own mother.

Once outside, the wind bit at him again, but he didn't care. He whistled happily and swaggered across the street to the trolley stop, hands deep in his pockets. He knew now, that everything would be fine. He and Mil would be married tomorrow and she would get well and strong again. Yeah.

When the trolley came to his corner, he jumped off before it was completely stopped and ran across the street to his house. It wasn't a bad looking house, tall, narrow and neat, with a great garden in summer, but it was a left-over, fighting for space between two factories. He opened the iron gate, crossed the narrow wooden walk and took the front steps two at a time. It was near one o'clock. His mother might just be there - having lunch.

The hallway was full of the sweet smell of baking bread and laughing kids' voices. The bread smell meant his sister, Lily was home baking for supper...for his mother, and sister, Kate, and his brother Ed, and for Lily's husband Joe, and their son, Elmer. Kids' voices came from the Lehart's flat upstairs. It meant they were skipping school. He wished they wouldn't, after all, they weren't working or anything, so they should be happy to get educated. He'd talk to them again sometime, but not today. He had something more important on his mind right now. He opened the door.

"Lil?"

"Sh! Don't slam that door. I just got the bread into the oven."

She came through the dining room to meet him, wiping her floured hands on her apron. Ma named her after Lillian Russell and it was right. She had jet black hair, an hour-glass figure, and a heart of pure gold. Of course, he didn't know if Lillian Russell had a good heart, but it didn't matter, because he didn't think anyone, not even Miss Russell could be as good as his sister, Lil.

"Well, Frankie, how's your Milia?"

Frankie watched her stop by the roll-away bed under the dining room windows and put her hand on Busha's wrinkled forehead. He didn't remember his father, but he'd never forget Busha, his father's mother, though he wished he could. Once, he'd thought she was beautiful, but that was a long time ago. Now, he just wished that Mil and her family would never have to meet Busha. He was ashamed, like he was ashamed of this old house, and this old neighborhood, and all these people living here in this one flat. He knew Mil's ma wouldn't think much of it. He hated it that he was ashamed of them. Again, he looked at Lil... she was great, they were all great...except Busha...but he was ashamed.

"Lil, I gotta go."

"But, you just came..."

"Yeah, I know..but Ma's not here. Is she at the shop? Is she coming for lunch?"

"I don't know. She must be at the shop..."

Lil wondered what was wrong with Frankie. He didn't even answer her question about Milia. Oh, God, was she worse, poor girl? She was going to ask, but Frankie didn't wait, he ran out even as she said his name. She watched him from the front window, running down the street...a kid...worried...in love...what else...she didn't know. She was twenty-seven years old, with an eight year old boy of her own, and what would he be like in a few more years...probably running down the street himself, running to her about his girl. She turned and looked at Busha again...how fast time went.

As Frankie raced down the steps toward the sidewalk, he heard a "yoo-hoo" from across the street. He saw the red hair and neat figure of Vera Olchinski. She was smiling and waving in that way she had. She wore her dresses shorter than most, and he could see well-turned ankles almost dancing from under her work apron. Things must have been a little slow at the mustard factory, so she was getting her "breath" as she would say. Mr. Schmelling was good about things like that. Frankie tossed a small wave in her direction as he continued to run on. He felt a blush creeping down his neck. Vera always made him blush. Vera was older...liked to tease, and she did have a reputation with the guys.

Frankie put Vera out of his mind. He had to hurry. The tailor shop was three blocks away, though it seemed farther right then. His breath was coming short...funny, since he'd never gotten out of breath running to the shop in all his life, and he'd been running there as long as he could remember.

Finally, he saw them...the big store front windows. They were steamy; Ma liked it warm. He pushed the door open, hearing the bell tinkle like it had hundreds of times before. It was clean inside...also just as Ma liked it. She must have swept the floors a dozen times each day. Yeah, it was clean all right, but old.

Funny how everything looked old today, even Ma, and she wasn't really...only forty-seven. It was her white hair that made him think old, though it had been white for as long as he could remember...but her face was young. Her cheekbones were high and they seemed to pull her skin tight and smooth and they made her mouth pull up at the corners so she always seemed to smile a little. She took her foot off the machine treadle and looked up at him.

He remembered when he was a kid at school, he'd heard about Catherine the Great. He thought of that now because Ma always reminded him of the Queen - both Catherines.

"Frankie?" Her eyes peered at him over the rims of her glasses. They were interesting eyes which looked like two large almonds set behind glass. Always, she seemed to look deep inside him, as though she were looking deep into the lining of a coat.

"You're out of breath...sit here," she said.

Pushing a pile of clothes aside, she made room for him on the chair next to the sewing machine. He sat, feeling the red rise in his face like mercury in a thermometer, and maybe the red did measure a fever, the fever of his need. He waited. He wished she'd make it easy for him...that she'd try to guess why he came, but she wouldn't. Ma never guessed. She always waited in solemn patience for people to tell things in their own time. It seemed so long that he sat there...wanting to marry Mil...wanting to feel free to do that...wanting to help Ma out with his wages a little longer, but still wanting to be his own man, wanting them all to live a better life...in a better place... wanting...wanting...he always seemed to be wanting.

"Ma," he said, "when are Lil and Joe going to get a place of their own?"

"When they can. They're saving. They want a house when they get a place of their own, not just a little flat."

"But, that's all we got, Ma...just a little flat!"

She stopped sewing and looked at him again.

"Ma, you're doing pretty good in the tailor shop now, and we're all grown up, we could all move to a bigger place...maybe..."

Feeling warmer, he pulled his coat off and threw it on the pile of clothes behind him. A button came loose and dropped to the floor. She began sewing again; she didn't answer.

"Ma?"

"You ran all the way down here to tell me we need a bigger house...well...I suppose that must be important right now."

"No, Ma, no...it's not the house...not really...it's Ma, I wanta marry Mil... tomorrow...and she's never seen our house...she don't know how we live...and..."

Ma waited, but he couldn't finish. He wished she'd say, "No, you can't marry her," or "I'm glad," but she only raised her eyebrows the smallest bit.

"God, Ma, did ya hear me?"

Again, the machine clicked as she looked back at her work.

"I heard." She kept sewing. "I have never met this girl. None of us have, not in all the months you've known her. I only know she's been sick, and now you say you'll marry her...tomorrow yet. What is happening, Frankie?"

Frankie's head felt heavy. With his hands, he covered his face. His shoulders began to shake.

Her boy...was he crying? She wanted to go to him as though he were small again, to put her arms around him and draw him close, but she couldn't. Before her sat the youngest of her five children, a man now, a man who needed comfort, a man weighed down by many early responsibilities, but she couldn't do it, no, she couldn't make herself go to him...coddle him. Soon, he would look up at her and she would comfort him with her eyes...surely, he would know she cared.

"Frankie, look at me."

"Ma, she can't die. I want to marry Mil...so she'll live."

"Die! Frankie, it's that bad? What does the doctor say? And her family?"

Looking at Ma, Frankie felt like a kid again, wanting to feel the comfort of her touch, but he knew better. Love spilled out of her eyes, those eyes that saw everything, and so he told her all about Mil's illness, and all about their "arrangement".

Ma walked to the window and looked out thoughtfully, then she walked to the little glass covered case on the wall and took her thread and thimble, as she seemed to be sorting and sifting all her thoughts, putting them in order before she spoke. Then she started sewing the button back on his coat.

"Frankie, I don't think she's good for you. Besides being very sick, she's made you feel ashamed of us."

He went to Ma...reached toward her...then let his arms fall to his sides again.

"God, Ma, she never made me feel ashamed. She's been wanting to come. It's me, Ma. I wouldn't let her. I'm ashamed...me...we could do better...live better."

Ma examined the other buttons, then put the coat back on the chair.

"Frankie, you were three and Lily was twelve when your Pa died. Everybody else was in between. And we had Busha to care for. It was hard, Frankie. You know that. You helped. Everybody helped. But the money...there was none...for a long while. And now, Frankie, we're never going to be without money again...not for a better house, or a newer neighborhood, or more room, or anything else. That's the way it's going to be, Frankie."

"But, Ma..."

"That's the way it's going to be, Frankie. She's your girl, and if you want to marry her, I'll love her, but she'll have to love me...us...the way we are. That's the way it's got to be, Frankie."

Frankie looked at her standing there, small, determined, and different. Even her hair was different from everybody else's...white and short...he didn't know any other woman with short hair...but Ma's was short and fluffy because that was best for her. Yeah, he knew that was how it had to be. He felt ashamed again...ashamed of being ashamed.

## CHAPTER 7

"Hey, Ma, hurry, huh? We gotta leave. I told Father Prybyl we'd be at the rectory by ten o'clock."

Frankie stood before the mirror in the dining room adjusting his tie. Carefully, he brushed his hair back and pushed a little wave in at the front. He sighed as he caught the reflection of the room in the mirror..pink wallpaper with blue stripes and flower bouquets running all over it...not bad looking really, it was just that nobody else he knew had to use the dining room for a dressing room, and on top of it all, he had to be watched by Busha, who lay quietly on the cot staring glassy-eyed at his every move. Well, at least she wasn't yelling senseless things at him, like some he'd heard of; she was quiet.

Damn flat,...it sure was too small...dark too, with those factories on either side. If only Ma would get rid of the renters upstairs, the Leharts...then, Lily and Joe and Elmer could move up there...maybe even take Busha with them. No, that wouldn't be fair. Lily was stuck with Busha most of the time now...she deserved some peace some time...of course then it would probably fall to his sister, Kate, to care for her, but Busha couldn't live forever.

He hated thinking like that. If only he could remember something good about Busha, but she'd been that way as long as he could remember, right after Pa's death, that's when they said she'd gone crazy, but Lily remembered a time when she was different.

Well one thing was sure. He wouldn't bring Mil and her Mama here today. If the Father would marry them today, everything would be in a rush anyhow, and meanwhile, he'd think of some way to introduce everybody slowly...maybe at Mil's house, and then later, much later, they could come here. Maybe the Leharts would take Busha upstairs for a couple of hours. That would be good. That way, they'd get used to the neighborhood and the house first, and then they could get used to Busha some other time. Yeah, there was a way to do everything...if you thought about it long enough. Hell, it must be getting late.

"Ma!"

"Sh! I'm here. I'm here. Lily is resting. She has a bad headache."

"Ma...you look different...swell, I mean. Really classy, Ma. I never seen those clothes on you."

Frankie blushed. He felt foolish paying compliments to his mother like she was just any other woman.

Catherine smiled, and for a minute her almond eyes sparkled.

"Just in case my son gets married today, I dressed like this. I stayed at the shop late last night so I could work on it."

He felt proud of her right now. She looked like one of those models in the fashion magazines that his sister Kate and his Mil always read. She was wearing a fur-trimmed coat, a little black velvet hat, and even a fur muff to match the coat, and finally those new high buttoned boots that looked like Kate's. Yeah, she looked classy. He smiled to himself, thinking it was swell of Kate to lend Ma the boots.

Then Frankie surprised himself by extending his arm to Ma as he bowed deeply. Like a queen, she nodded her head solemnly and slipped her small arm through his.

Outside, it was bright...no sign of snow, which made him glad because he'd borrowed Harry's Tin Lizzie, and although he was anxious to drive it again, he sure didn't want to take any chances with someone else's car on snowy streets. Besides, Harry had sunk a lot of dough into the car, thinking it would be good advertising for the dental lab if they looked prosperous.

He helped Ma into the front seat and they started out. One day, he'd own a car like this and he and Mil would ride everywhere.

"Nice," Ma said, "better than the streetcar." She felt the upholstery as she settled herself on the front seat.

They didn't talk much. Frankie was thinking about what he would say to Father Prybyl, while Catherine was thinking her own thoughts..wondering what kind of girl she was about to meet...how she would look, if she was so sick...thinking she must not show surprise on her face, no matter what. Then the car stopped in front of Mil's house.

Catherine looked out the window. Nice...even in March, when things looked dull in Chicago. Nice neighborhood...nice red brick two-story...only brick house on the block as far as she could see. Big house, it seemed. Frankie said only three of the nine children were still at home, but the house had at least three bedrooms, she thought, and it had a front porch...open...and she knew there had to be a closed back porch...for Mil and Frankie. Oh, and the vines...all over the sides and front..must be beautiful in summer.

Well, no matter to her. They had a very good house of their own...older... maybe smaller, but Frankie would soon be gone, then Lily and her family...and Kate would be getting married...hum...the house would soon be too big. Yes, she was satisfied...and besides, it was close to the tailor shop.

"This is it, Ma. You wait in the car; it's getting late. I'll bring them out."

Frankie took the stairs two at a time and reached for the bell, but the door opened before he rang. He couldn't believe the way Mil looked. She was so sick...yet the sickness seemed to make her more beautiful. Mil was almost as tall as he was, so he didn't look down at her the way he did at Ma. Mil's eyes were almost level with his...blue eyes...and big...looking bigger because they were deep now, with delicate blue shadows brushing out from the upper lids. Her hair was so soft and light... cheeks and lips, fever bright...nature's own paint.

He couldn't say anything...so he just picked her up easily...too easily...and carried her down the stairs. Mama closed the front door and followed them. At the bottom of the stairs, Mil broke the silence.

"Frankie, please put me down."

"No, you have to get in the car fast. This isn't good weather for you, the wind is too bad when it comes."

"Please Frankie, I want to walk over and meet your mother."

"Frankie," Mama said, "do like Milia say. She walk to meet your mama."

Frankie set her down and arm in arm they walked to the car.

Introductions were made and Frankie hurried Mil into the front seat. Catherine and Michalina sat in the back.

"Let's hurry, Frankie," Mil said, "Father Prybyl doesn't like it when people are late."

It was a quick ride to the rectory - two blocks - during which silence was punctuated by strained conversational comments. Catherine understood that Frankie thought Mil was a beautiful girl, but she felt he was fooling himself about marriage. It would only be a short *arrangement,* by the look of her. He'd never know the joy of sharing a warm bed with his Milia.

For her part, Michalina didn't wish to stare at Catherine, but she couldn't imagine such a one...a widow lady with five children...and she wore such nice clothes, and had bobbed hair under her capelush. Michalina's roughened hand went up to touch her own hair, to make sure the bun was properly pinned at the nape of her neck. Then she smoothed her plain black coat, sweeping a quick look over it, checking for blond threads of Emilia's hair.

A small cough began to push its way through Emilia's lips, and Frankie prayed that she wouldn't have a hemorrhage, not now when they were going to approach Father Prybyl; he didn't think he'd know how to cope with that. Quickly, he reached for his clean white handkerchief and handed it to Mil. It'll be all right, her too-bright eyes seemed to say to him. But he wondered.

How relieved he was to see the rectory loom before them; carefully, he parked the Tin Lizzie.

As they stood waiting on the rectory porch, Emilia began to shake with panic, but she was determined to calm down and to hide her fears. How could she have agreed to all of this! Father Prybyl would think she was a selfish woman of the street, wanting to marry Frankie only for her own benefit, so she could call herself Mrs. Frankie Jagienczak and feel important, just so she could claim Frankie all to herself and have him care for her, yet she wouldn't be a real wife to him. It was crazy! She was crazy to ever have considered doing this. When could she be a real wife to him? Would she ever be well enough for that? Maybe Frankie would only have the trouble of her sickness and the expense of her funeral...oh, God, please...what was she thinking? No, she wouldn't die! Didn't Dr. Noshkins say she could get well if they followed directions? Well, they were following directions, and besides, he gave Frankie permission to marry her. It would be all right...they would soon...but her thoughts were interrupted by a business-like voice.

"Come this way, Father is waiting for you."

The housekeeper was leading them into the priest's office and Mil hadn't even noticed they'd rung the bell.

Seated behind a smooth walnut desk, which matched the paneled walls, sat Father Prybyl, bent over his paper work. They entered the room, and at the sound of the housekeeper's voice, the priest rose. Emilia hesitated a moment, then Frankie urged her forward. Father bowed his head slightly toward Emilia in recognition. Everything was quiet...awkward...Mil stirred, feeling the warmth of Frankie's eyes upon her as though he expected her to speak. She supposed she should, since it was her parish...her Father Prybyl...but words wouldn't come.

Father came around the desk and offered his hand to Frankie.

"My boy?"

It was a question, Mil knew, but she didn't know how to give an answer.

"Emilia...Michalina...how are you?"

Again, she couldn't give an answer, and again Frankie looked at her. She began to cry; then the coughing started, and in panic, she pressed handkerchiefs to her mouth.

"Father, I'm Frankie Jagienczak from St. Mary's Parish, and I came...that is...we came..."

Mil coughed again, and Frankie led her to a chair.

"Excuse me, Father, Mil hasn't felt too well. Oh, and Father, this is my mother, Catherine Jagienczak."

"Father..." Catherine extended her small hand.

"Father, Mil and I, that is...I wanna marry Mil."

"Yes, well, my children, it's good you came early. We'll have time to make all the arrangements, and after Easter..."

Mil began to cry again; the crying caused more coughing. Desperation engulfed Frankie as he tried to comfort her and to organize his words for Father Prybyl. Realizing he couldn't speak freely of Mil's illness in front of her, he asked Michalina and Catherine to calm her and then he asked Father Prybyl to step out of the office with him for a few private words.

As quickly and as clearly as he knew how, Frankie explained the situation, ending with his request that they be married now, that very morning.

Father Prybyl's eyes enlarged considerably as he cleared his throat and assured Frankie he understood exactly why he was in a great hurry to marry Mill, and that he had much experience with the "con", but he also had to know if there was any *other* reason why the marriage must be hurried.

Father continued, "Surely, my boy, you can see that this marriage is not in the best interest of your young lady. I can't believe you will not sleep with her...unless of course, you already have, and there is a special need to rush the wedding."

Frankie clenched his fists, wanting for the first time in his life to hit a priest. Quickly, he prayed for forgiveness.

"Father, Mil is a good girl. We don't *have* to get married."

His face felt hot and he knew his voice was growing loud.

"Anyway," he continued, "she can't have children, not for awhile; she's too sick...but we have Dr. Noshkins permission to marry."

"You have the doctor's permission, so you come here to demand...and I suppose the good doctor is Catholic...I suppose he told you to live in abstinence until such time as Emilia is well enough to risk bearing children?"

"The good doctor is Jewish, and he doesn't care what we are, he only cares I'm willing to marry Mil and wait. He only cares she'll have a reason to fight harder to live."

Frankie couldn't believe he was hearing himself talk this way to Father Prybyl.

"No, that is too much strain on both of you, and it is the Lenten Season besides. There will be no wedding today."

Sternly, he returned Frankie's challenging glare, but before he turned away abruptly to go to Mil and the Mothers, Frankie thought he caught something else come into the old man's eyes...perhaps...compassion...understanding...Frankie wasn't sure.

"Michalina," Father Prybyl said, "why have you come here with Emilia, you know the rules of the church."

"Ya. But Father, you see her now...you see my Emilia...sick...so sick...but she loves Frankie...and I am her mama." Michalina turned to Catherine. "Mrs. Jagienczak, you are understanding this, no?"

Catherine put her small hand on Michalina's arm and nodded.

"Father Prybyl," Catherine said, "Frankie's a man. My husband died when Frankie was only a small boy. Frankie has helped support the family since he was eleven years old. He can take care of Emilia and this is what he wants."

Father Prybyl turned to Emilia. "My Child, you want a little happiness, I know, but your greatest happiness awaits you in heaven."

Emilia cried out to him. "I'm not in heaven now, Father Prybyl! There's war everywhere. What will happen to us if Frankie has to go? Father, I love him so, and what if there isn't much time?"

"My child, if you love him, you'll wait."

Frankie went to Emilia's side. "Father," he began, but a knock at the office door interrupted him.

The Priest's housekeeper came in and announced a visitor from the diocesan office.

"Michalina, Mrs. Jagienczak, my Children, pray for God's help. I must go now."

"But, Father..." Frankie began.

"There will be no wedding...it's impossible." Father Prybyl left the room, as much if not more, for his sake than for theirs. He knew how they ached, but he felt there was nothing he could do.

Emilia was crying very hard, and Frankie tried to soothe her, while Michalina made certain she was ready for the outdoors. Catherine walked ahead and opened the door. Out on the porch, Emilia was seized by the wracking coughs once again. Then the hemorrhage came...bright and heavy. Handkerchiefs couldn't contain the flow of blood, Again, Frankie rang the bell, and they were ushered into the vestibule, to a leather sofa, where Frankie settled Mil, holding her head, while Michalina wiped her face with the handkerchiefs, then with cold cloths which the housekeeper provided. Father came in and watched the scene with eyes that seemed to hold some deep hidden sorrow. Could he ever have been in love? The thought flew through Frankie's mind quickly as a winged dove. He couldn't dwell on that.

"Father," Frankie yelled, "We will..."

But the good priest interrupted him gently. "My boy, not today. We can't have the wedding today. Perhaps, next week."

Gradually, Mil's body began to feel a sense of peace; she reached for Frankie's hand.

And so it was decided that they would be married the following Friday morning at ten o'clock Mass, in a very private ceremony, including only the immediate families since it was Lent, a time for Penance, rather than a time for celebration. Banns would be announced at morning Mass on Monday, Wednesday, and Thursday of the next week, and the mothers were asked to swear on the holy missal that neither of the children had been married before.

When Mil seemed better, Father addressed her with a few instructions, making sure she understood there could be no white dress or veil during the Lenten season. Emilia agreed, but wished Florchak could sing "Ave Maria", however, Father said there could be no music during the penitential season.

Catherine stepped back, watching silently, thanking God that none of her children had to fight the "con"...not yet.

Leaving the office, walking down the stairs, these were difficult for Emilia, so Frankie carried her to the car. The ride back to the red brick house was even more silent than the ride to the rectory, for each was absorbed in many private thoughts.

When Frankie pulled up to the house, everyone seemed surprised, as though the suddenness were a terrible intrusion upon their reveries. Michalina was first to recover, so she quickly invited everyone for coffee and cake. Catherine felt it would be too much for Emilia, but the bride-to-be begged everyone to come in and share the happiness of making plans. Catherine relented and they went into the house.

It was comfortable, Catherine thought, not elegant, but comfortable...mohair furniture and rose wallpaper...light oak woodwork...cheerful...especially the kitchen with table big enough to seat twelve. Yes, it was a nice family Frankie was marrying into, now if only he could have a wife. She didn't want to think gloomy thoughts, but the evidence was clear.

Michalina interrupted those thoughts. "Here, Mrs. Jagienczak, sit here...in the sun."

"Thank you. Please, call me Catherine. And you, Emilia, what would you like to call me?"

Frankie made sure she was comfortably settled in her bed on the porch, then he pulled a chair up close to her.

"No, Frankie," Emilia whispered, "don't sit here, you know it isn't safe. Go in the kitchen, with our mamas."

"Mil..."

"Please, otherwise, I'll know the *arrangement* will never work."

Frankie went back to the kitchen and sat at the table where he could easily see Emilia from the window.

"Emilia," Michalina called sternly, "Catherine, your...how you say...mother-in-law...she asked you question."

"Oh, Mrs. Jagienczak, I'm sorry, maybe I could call you Mother J."

Catherine smiled. "What's best for you, that's what you call me."

Silence reigned for an uncomfortable moment.

"Well," Frankie said, "at least the wedding's only a week away. Maybe some of the family will be able to come."

"Only the married sisters," Emilia said, "everyone else has to work."

Michalina cut the coffee cake and filled the cups as she spoke.

"Ya, but Tata, he will take the day from work. You are youngest daughter... youngest child. He will come to church."

Slowly, they groped their way through the conversational abyss, filling it gradually with words from family reservoirs, feeling more comfortable with every exchange, until they were interrupted by a knock on the back door.

"Ludmilla! Elinora! Ach, come in...come in."

Elinora's jolly laughter rang through the house as she bowed her head this way and that greeting everyone in the room.

"Mama!" Ludmilla hugged her mama closely and kissed her cheek while her eyes fastened their curious gaze upon Catherine. Ludmilla was the seamstress in the family who made many of Mil's clothes, plus her own and Mama's. Now she looked genuinely impressed by her sister's soon-to-be-mother-in-law.

"Ludmilla, you come together with Elinora?

"No, Mama, we met on the stairs."

It was fun, the general commotion that followed. It broke the strained atmosphere. There were introductions, greetings, and explanations, with Elinora managing somehow to take over.

"Emilia, you see...what did I say to you? I say Dr. Noshkins is worth a try, no. And now you are getting married...next Friday yet. That man...oi...he is better than I thought."

Oh, she had a way, even Emilia laughed with her, forgetting for a moment that no miracle was involved, just a foolish plan to say a few words before God to make them man and wife. How could they? Then she said, "Mrs. Steech, I think *you* are the miracle worker."

"Oh, I would show you miracles...you just leave me alone with your young man..."

Elinora's raucous laughter rang like the slap she gave her thigh, but Emilia turned her head away, remembering the words of her girlfriends about one man not satisfying Elinora Steech. She began now to understand what they meant, and to know why she never liked this woman. She couldn't help it. Perhaps it was a harsh judgment, but she wasn't used to such talk.

When she saw Emilia's face turned to the wall and Frankie's face turned crimson, Michalina knew she had to change the subject.

"Elinora, come. Sit here...by Ludmilla. We have coffee and cake...you too, have some."

"Ya," she roared. "What's a little more fat? Huh?"

"Emilia, Mama," Ludmilla said, "what about a dress? What will we do by next week?"

"Ludi, I don't know. I'm so tired, I don't think I can shop." Emilia started to cry again.

"Tears, she has again," Michalina thought, "is too much."

Catherine spoke. "Emilia, perhaps I could make your dress."

"Oh, Mrs. Jagienczak...Mother...that's so good of you, but Ludi makes most of my dresses...maybe...if you could work together...it's such a big job...a wedding dress."

"Say, that's a good idea," Ludmilla said, if you don't mind, Mrs. Jagienczak. I know you have a tailor shop."

Smiling, Catherine answered, "It would be nice for both of us...to have help."

"Now, Mil, what should we get? Satin? White? Ivory?" Ludi seemed eager and ready to start.

"Ludi, Father says I can't wear white...it's Lent...so I don't know."

"I know, Mil. We'll get a light color...so light it's almost white. Right, Mrs. Jagienczak?"

"Right, Ludi. Perhaps lace over satin?"

"My, that sounds beautiful! When can we shop?" Ludi was more excited now than Mil.

"Emilia," Catherine said, "would you like Ludi and me to shop for material Monday morning?"

"That would be swell, but will there be enough time to make a dress? Monday to Friday...that's not very long."

"Mil," Ludi said, "with two of us working? There'll be time to spare. But, Mama, when will the families meet? We don't know one other."

"Now it comes," Frankie thought. "We'll have to invite them all over. They'll have to see our place."

"Ach," Michalina said, "I think is too much for Emilia. You understand, Mrs. Jagienczak, no? We meet here after wedding and then everybody comes for supper."

"Of course it's too much. Only a week for all this. We'll meet next Friday. It won't matter. Nothing matters now except Emilia's wedding dress."

"Huh? Nobody's going to make a suit for me? I'm in the wedding too, you know."

"Frankie, I have your brother's suit in the shop. I'm almost finished remaking it for you."

At the other end of the table, Elinora chuckled and clucked with earthy approval. "Haha! With such a young, strong body, you don't need a suit! Right Emilia? When he takes off those pants, then you see a miracle...Noshkins or no. Ya, Girl," she leered, "then you'll be well."

The red in Frankie's face embarrassed him so much, he left the room, but Mil was trapped. Where could she go? She had to stay and listen to that cherry-faced woman who seemed ready to invite herself to the wedding. Mil didn't want her. She didn't want her near Frankie...ever again. Then, swinging her legs down with an energy and urgency she hadn't felt in a long time, she prepared to join Frankie in the other room. That would show Elinora, if she had any feelings at all, that would show her what they thought of her.

With one hand on the wall to steady herself, Emilia glared toward Elinora. "Mrs. Steech," she began, but the words slithered right out of her mind, as the room went dark and engulfed her.

When Mil's eyes opened again, they were all around her, even Elinora; it was more than she could bear. She only wished to be left alone now. If only they would all go away and leave her. She was lying on the bed, and Frankie was holding her hand, that's all she cared about. That Elinora, that dirty woman, she didn't understand. She made their love sound bad, like it was bad what they would do together, but it wasn't, it wasn't at all. It would be beautiful, their love, the most beautiful thing in the world, and no one like Elinora Steech could ever understand.

"Emilia," Elinora said, "rest now, Child. I go home. Elinora Steech talks too much. Jan, my husband, he tells me all the time to watch my tongue. It's just I can't watch what I can't see...no?" She laughed...less heartily...and grabbed Mil's arm, gently.

Unexpectedly, Mil felt sorry for Elinora, but nevertheless, she flinched under her touch.

## CHAPTER 8

It was a busy week with everyone preparing for the wedding as though there were no question everything would work out, despite Mil's occasional delirium and her additional weight loss. At eighty-five pounds, she was now almost translucent. Beautiful in a mysteriously expectant way...spiritual. And so, everyone expected with her, expected that she would live long enough to become a married woman.

Friday, March thirtieth, roared into being like the newspaper headlines currently menacing the streets. Everyone was fearful of war except Emilia who struggled daily in her own private war with death. She'd been waking at night sometimes, gasping for breath, unintentionally waking Mama and Tata who slept lightly, leaving them exhausted from watching and praying. In spite of her consuming illness, Mil never doubted for a moment that she would see her wedding day; Mama and Tata marveled that she woke at all that Friday morning.

How strange and sadly wonderful to have Tata show his concern the way he did. In all her memory, Mil had no recollection of Tata touching her. Despite his reserve, she knew he loved her, knew he cared by the way he referred to her, gave her everything, but he never touched her, seldom spoke directly to her, except when gruffly disguising his gentleness, but now, he came to her bed, helped her to sit, and gently supported her with one strong arm while he arranged the pillows with which to prop her.

Silent tears crept from the corners of her eyes. Gently, Tata brushed them away.

"Humph, Mama!" he called. "Breakfast is ready now?"

"Ya, Ya, Tata, come. I fix tray for Emilia."

Mil watched them, passing one another silently, wondering if they loved one another...physically. Of course they did! They had nine children. But that was long ago...they were old now...and at sixteen...she was the youngest. How sinful, she thought. What was she doing thinking about her parents that way. Still, they understood her need for Frankie. She loved them, they loved her...she guessed they loved one another. Strange, she'd never thought about that before. Would she have children someday who would wonder about her this way? Would she live long enough for that? Could this maybe be her last day? She was happy enough to die. Foolish...she was happy enough to live forever. She pushed her food away.

"Momchu, I can't."

"Ach, Dziecko, tomorrow Frankie makes you eat everything."

"Yes, Momchu, tomorrow."

Ludmilla came and helped her dress. It was a marvelous dress of pale beige lace over light brown taffeta, setting off her light curls and translucent skin to perfection.

In her present excitement, talking came easily to Ludi, as she described for Mil how she planned the coordinating colors for the wedding. Michalina and Catherine were wearing dark green dresses with brown accessories, which they already had, while the girls...Ludi, Stasha, Helcha...were wearing the gold dresses they had worn three years ago for cousin Magdalena's wedding. Frankie's sisters...Lily and Kate...both had pale green party dresses which they had agreed to wear. None of the brothers, except Harry and Frankie's brother, Ed, would be able to come to the church. Anyway, nobody looked at men's clothes - but Frankie, Tata and Ed would be wearing their best. They would be handsome. Ludi settled Mil in one of the dining room chairs and buttoned her high brown shoes. Standing back, she looked at her slight, saucer-eyed sister, then hugging her, she thought how beautiful Mil looked, but she was unable to say anything for fear they would both cry.

In regal solemnity their procession progressed from the house and moved down the front steps toward Harry's Tin Lizzie. The others were all settled when Harry came, carrying Mil.

Never before had two blocks seemed so long, but today it was long enough for Mil to notice everything about her world.

It was Friday morning, March 30, 1917 and there was a bright blue sky quilted with cotton cloud puffs through which the sun played hide and seek. On the naked Poplar branches tight, tiny plump buds waved as though in excited welcome to spring. It was spring, and Mil felt it in every breath she took, though the roaring wind tried to frighten her into thinking winter was still chasing her. She knew better. After today, winter would always be far behind.

At the top of the church stairs, the great oak doors swung open as soon as Harry navigated the Tin Lizzie to the curb. Mil knew it was Frankie up there opening those doors, getting everything ready to welcome her. Then she saw him in his neat blue serge suit, his broad shoulders looking strong enough to hold the world for her... maybe they would have to...for awhile.

As soon as she saw Frankie, Michalina worried. Frankie would see Emilia before they were married...bad luck it would bring...he should be in sacristy...waiting for her...like always the grooms did. Ach, so...soon they would be married. Michalina was tired from the week's preparations and worry. Let it come, whatever would come...too much it was already...she couldn't worry anymore.

Harry swept Mil out of the car and up the church steps, trying this best to shield her from the unruly wind, as Tata made sure the car doors were all tightly shut.

"Good Christ," Harry thought, "there's nothing to her anymore...no weight at all."

Disregarding all superstition, Frankie took Mil from Harry's arms and held her. She was shaking. He pressed her close and kissed her.

"We made it, Mil...we made it."

"Ach, Frankie, you go now, Ya? Is bad luck...go."

Stepping up quickly, Catherine came to Michalina's aid.

"Go Frankie," she said. "Your time is coming."

He walked to the front of the church, turning back every few steps to be sure Mil was still there, still watching him, still seeming able to make it through the ceremony.

"Please, God...please..." he whispered to himself, while walking to the sacristy door, where the best man, his oldest brother, Ed, waited for him. Soon, he would be a married man...married to Mil.

It was good the church was empty, he liked it with just the family...with Lily and Kate smiling at him from the front pew, their white teeth set off like pearls by their dark, curly hair and dark complexions. They looked classy in their pale green silk dresses and little matching hats. Yeah, it was no wonder the Jagienczak girls always had a lot of boyfriends. Their beauty was much different from Mil's, but it was there. And Frankie noticed too, how older guys always turned around to look at his Ma a second time. Maybe Ma'd get married again, when they were all gone.

Then, thoughts of all others stopped, as he saw Mil start down the aisle holding her father's arm on the one side and Harry's on the other. Poor, beautiful, sweet angel. She needed them both for support, but she was walking straight and tall. She never looked more beautiful.

No wedding march rang through the church rafters, but the strains flowed through Mil's brain like a rising tide and she walked slowly to its tempo forcing Tata and Harry to follow her step. Mil's eyes swept around the church, touching everyone, everything lightly, much like a quickly moving feather duster. She saw the exotic, dark-eyed beauty of the Jagienczak girls, and the wide, blue-eyed animation of the Kaszmierski sisters. She saw Momchu's soft plumpness offset by the classic golden-brown bun pinned at the nape of her neck, and the regal appearance of Mother Jagienczak. Then she fixed her gaze on Frankie. Her vision was filled with his big dark eyes and black smooth hair...his broad shoulders. Then she was there, at the front of the church, conscious of Harry and Tata kissing each cheek lightly, of Frankie's arm, firmly encircling her waist, giving her support...of someone beside Frankie, looking so much like him, but older, with a few silver threads webbing his black hair. Somehow they'd walked up the two little steps and Frankie settled her on a dainty chair just beyond the communion rail, the place where she'd watched so many brides, over the years, kneel for their blessings. Though it was bright outside, the sanctuary was church-dark, illumined only by the glow of candles, and the soft light of the side altar lamps. The sparkle of the golden altar vessels hypnotized her into wondering if it was really happening. Was she truly a bride, soon to say the words which would commit her to a lifetime as Mrs. Frankie Jagienczak? A lifetime...how long would that be...

Because of Emilia's condition, the ceremony was short. Mil and Frankie repeated their vows, Frankie promising to cherish...Mil to obey. Her fuzzy brain told her that was a foolish word "obey", for a wedding ceremony, because she was certainly now a woman, not a child. However, she took that word also to her heart. Then Father Prybyl smiled at them, pressed their hands firmly together, and pronounced them man and wife. During the low mass that followed, Frankie knelt beside Mil's chair. Somehow, she'd expected to feel different, but she didn't, though she was excited...and feeling very light-headed. It seemed to her that the mass was over too quickly...that there was little time to keep her eyes fastened on Frankie's kneeling form, little time to realize the magnificence of the truth that he belonged to her...forever.

How warm she felt. The church was becoming too warm for her swimming head...but then Frankie lifted her in his arms and she put her head against his chest, and Father Prybyl's smile faded away...so did Frankie and everything else.

When her eyes opened next, they fastened on Frankie's shoes, empty and pointing at her from under his roll away bed at the far end of the porch. She felt as though the liquid warmth of the sun were basting everything around her. Voices - many of them - floated through the kitchen window, hovering over her, blanketing her confined world with security. Then she saw Frankie, leaning on the kitchen window sill smiling at her, a new smile, a smile of possession.

"Hello, Mrs. Jagienczak."

Then Frankie swung himself right over the window sill and stood next to Mil's bed.

"Hey, everybody, my wife's awake. I toldja she'd be fine!" He kissed Mil's forehead. "This is our wedding day," he whispered.

There was no way to describe how Frankie said it..."Their wedding day". Mil knew how he felt. Apparently, everyone had come from the church to their house. It seemed some of the other family members had arrived too. How good it was to know that everyone was celebrating her wedding day...hers and Frankie's. And all the family members were meeting one another. They were talking and smiling, and Mama said something about more of the family coming a little later, but nothing seemed too clear to her. Frankie's sisters and his brother Ed were talking to Mil and joking with Frankie, but somehow, her mind kept leaving them behind, though her eyes were aware of them part of the time. It was like they were talking to her so they could call her back, but she didn't know where they were calling her from...where she kept drifting to...but it was far...so far away. And then she stopped smiling...fighting to stay with them...she didn't let them call her back; she knew they left, probably went back to the kitchen. She knew it, just as she knew Frankie stayed, even if she couldn't see him. Their voices, like ghosts, kept drifting around her. It was comforting...very comforting.

*****************

Several hours passed as Mil lay in her semi-conscious state. All the brothers and sisters, and their husbands, wives, and children had come to the house, meeting and greeting, becoming acquainted rapidly as though there were little time left. They saw Mil and wondered just how long they would be related. Frankie sat at Mil's side, keeping his lonely vigil, wondering for the first time, if he'd made a mistake. Oh, he loved Mil, he knew that, but maybe he shouldn't have insisted upon marriage, maybe it was too much for her, maybe the reaction would be opposite of what he thought. What if Mil never woke again...if she died during the night? Oh God! What would he do then? Would they all hate him...her parents, brothers and sisters? And his own Ma...what about her? She told him not to marry Mil.

Eventually, the background voices fell to hushed whispers and the wedding quieted...saddened...became funereal. And then the family left, but first, they filed past the window, just like they were going past a casket. They didn't mean it, he knew, but he wanted to punch them all. Then Ma came out to him.

Swiftly, she knelt and hugged him, as though she had to do it before she changed her mind.

"Frankie, Mil did it. She lived through her wedding day...and yours. Do you understand? I didn't think she could. Now you pray, Frankie. No one knows what God will do. You helped her to live a week longer...now you pray."

Tears rolled down Frankie's cheeks and he buried his head in Catherine's coat.

"Oh, Ma...what'll I do?"

"Frankie, take good care of her tonight. I told Father Prybyl you were a man."

Catherine left...wondering if she would get a call during the night.

When the company left and Mama and Tata finally went to bed, Frankie sat alone on the porch and watched Mil's fever-flushed face and shallow erratic breathing. He was afraid to turn the lamp off, afraid that when the light disappeared, it would take Mil with it. Her arms thrashed occasionally, and her eyes opened, but she never saw Frankie, never realized he was there...her husband. Sometimes, she cried out, even called his name. He was so frightened. He didn't know what to do for her. He wished Mama and Tata would come out to see how she was; then he wondered how Mama and Tata had managed all this time to take care of her.

Eventually, everything grew quiet, and Frankie fell asleep in the chair. His dreams were restless; first, he was trying to carry Mil up the church steps, but she kept slipping out of his arms; then the Priest stood before them as Frankie said over and over, "I do...I do..." and they waited for Mil, but she never said the words...her mouth moved, but she never said the words. In one dream, Tata stood scowling, telling Frankie to go home. Sometimes, Frankie would waken and see Mil still lying quietly, breathing quickly. He would get a drink of water and then doze fitfully again.

Suddenly, it happened...a pitiful wail that brought Frankie to his feet, and Mama and Tata racing from the dark of their room. Mil sat up straight, blood spurting from her mouth. It ran down the front of her nightgown and over the covers, like paint spilling over a canvas, like paint picturing the final moments of a story. Mama tried to clean her... make her more comfortable, while Frankie held her until he couldn't stand it any longer.

"Oh, God...God! We have to do something!"

Never did he imagine it would be like this. He was so helpless. Then he saw Wladek and Harry watching from the doorway, crying.

"Harry," he begged, "let me take the car to Noshkins' house. He's got to come...he's gotta do something. Oh, God she's gonna die..it was too much...all this...she's gonna die..."

Frankie wept. It couldn't be. All of this couldn't be happening on their wedding night.

The brothers came nearer. Wladek spoke first.

"Hell, Frankie. What can Noshkins do? What can anyone do?"

Harry said, "I'd take you, Frankie, if I thought it would help, but damn it to hell, what can Noshkins do...what can he ever do about all of this..."

Harry's voice trailed to nothingness...his arms spread out in an encompassing gesture of futility. In despair he turned away from Mil's bed.

"For God's sake, Harry, let me get him. Maybe there's something..."

Harry looked at the sagging shoulders and the tear-stained face of his brother-in-law and he knew they'd have to go...to try something...anything...even if it was just to get Noshkins out for a cause he couldn't help.

******************

It was about an hour before they returned with the doctor, and all that time Frankie worried...and prayed...that Mil would be alive. Noshkins lived near his office, a long ride from the Kaszmierski's house. The Doctor had been sleeping soundly after a busy day with his practice, but he roused himself, dressed hurriedly and accompanied the boys back to Mil. They told him everything as they rode back to the house.

Silently, Noshkins wondered if it was an unnecessary trip they were making. Such a sweet girl, with so much to live for, but more and more he doubted she would still be alive when they arrived at her bedside.

Before Harry had come to a complete stop, Frankie dragged Noshkins from the car. The lights were still on. For some reason, Frankie felt encouraged. He raced up the front steps, Noshkins close behind, but as he pushed the door open, he heard Mama and his heart began pounding in a quick warning rhythm, like some ancient tribal drum.

"Oh, Jesu...Jesu, Kochanji..."

She was wailing and holding Mil - rocking back and forth. Frankie stopped. Mil was dead. He knew it. He had taken too long...

Suddenly, Frankie felt Noshkins thrust him aside. The doctor threw his bag on the bed, dropped his coat on the floor, and pushed Mama aside. He listened to Mil's heart with his stethoscope, felt her pulse, placed his finger under her nose. "Oh my God..." he moaned, clenching his fists and covering his eyes, and then, the look of excruciating pain which had momentarily frozen on his face, transformed to something akin to divine inspiration. He looked at his palm, then pressed it to Mil's chest. With a light pounding action, he repeated this...fist upon palm...punching at her heart in staccato fashion.

Frankie didn't understand his action, but Noshkins persisted...for a moment...an eternity...he didn't know. Suddenly, the doctor stopped, and perspiration mingled with tears as they all watched what seemed to be a mirage...the slight rise and fall of Mil's chest. Cautiously, Frankie moved closer, as did the others. She was breathing. Mil was alive...brought back from the dead.

Frankie cried. They all cried and hugged one another, and thanked God for the miracle He allowed Dr. Noshkins to perform.

Noshkins stayed the night, and the family stayed awake, as they talked together, drank coffee, and told jokes and stories, but mostly, the boys wanted to know about the doctor's treatment. Noshkins couldn't explain fully; he'd acted on instinct, feeling suddenly that he must help Mil's heart by simulating its action. He'd never done such a thing before, but...thank God...it worked. Mama reached a thankful hand to Noshkins often during that night. Tata smoked his pipe and rocked in his rocker, head back, eyes closed, and no one interrupted his communion with the Lord.

As dawn drifted into the room, and the birds began to chirp, Mil's eyes opened and she smiled. At Dr. Noshkins' command, Michalina forced a little egg nog down her throat. They hoped the worst was over. Though Mil must continue to lie on the porch, in God's own weather, her face now seemed less flushed, her eyes calmer and not so abnormally bright. She'd faced death, succumbed, and come back stronger...it seemed. Perhaps they could truly dare to hope for her future.

## CHAPTER 9

It was early Saturday morning when Dr. Noshkins left the house. Long hours after he'd helped Mil's heart to beat again, he gave her the smallest dose of morphine, then waited to be sure it wouldn't cause her heart to stop once more. He felt the drug would help her to rest completely, and possibly would prevent any further excitement which might bring on hemorrhage. Mil was very weak, and another major hemorrhage might put her beyond his help. He gave strict orders before leaving, that no company should be allowed for at least three days. During this period, Mil was to have complete quiet, good food and fresh air...sunshine too...if the weather would cooperate.

Frankie knew he should go to work, but he was exhausted, and Mil needed him. Watching Tata, Harry, and Wladek struggle off to their jobs, he felt guilty, but decided he couldn't leave. He would call Mr. Schmelling and explain. Being a good man, Schmelling would understand. Hadn't he always understood the Jagienczak problems? Why six years ago he gave Frankie the job, and in all that time Frankie hadn't missed more than three or four days of work. Yeah, Frankie hated to call, but Schmelling would understand.

Frankie drank a cup of coffee, thinking how lucky it was Mama and Tata had a phone - not many people did. Funny, though, how he never thought of the phone last night...to call Noshkins. In the horror of the moment, no one did. But driving out to get him turned out for the best. Noshkins said he'd had trouble with his own car that day, so there might have been more delay if they'd called first. God had been with them. How close a call it was! And if Noshkins hadn't had that inspiration! Yes...if God hadn't given him that idea...Frankie shuddered, realizing he would be a widower this morning had things been a little different, if the timing had been off just a little bit. Again, he whispered his thanks.

Frankie made sure the blankets were tucked well around Mil. She hadn't stirred, but her breathing was very regular now. Then, he walked softly back to the kitchen and phoned Mr. Schmelling at the mustard factory. Schmelling was really a good man. He told Frankie not to worry, to stay home another day if he must, but Frankie hoped it wouldn't be necessary. He had more responsibility now, as the head of his family, even if that included only Mil and himself right now. He hoped with all his heart that when Mil was well, they would have children...maybe one or two...a boy and a girl. Yes, that would be nice...and yes, now he was in charge of Mil and himself. He had to work hard if they were to manage. Once more, Frankie checked to see if Mil was all right, then he crossed the porch and fell on his cot. He pulled the covers over his eyes to shut the light out and fell asleep.

Mama worked quietly around the house so she wouldn't disturb them. Mil would sleep...so weak she was. But Frankie, she didn't know. So tired he must be after yesterday...wedding...company...death... Noshkins...life...miracle...beautiful miracle. Ach, such a wonderful man that Noshkins...Jewish, too. Enough she couldn't do for him. Her thoughts continued to translate back and forth from Polish to English as she worked around an already clean house. At nine o'clock, she decided it was time to call the families...to tell them of last night's miracle, and the wonderful Dr. Noshkins, and the sleeping bride and groom.

Stasha was eldest, so it was fitting she should hear first. Stasha, twenty years older then Mil, was not too preoccupied with her own five children - the oldest being one year older than Mil - to worry and exclaim over her youngest sister's health and miraculous return from death. Over and over, she questioned Michalina about Noshkins' actions, finding the story so wonderful and hard to believe. Finally, she broke into tears exclaiming over the wonder of God's mercy, then urged Mama to rest now that the situation was under control.

Michalina looked at the clock. She'd spent more than half an hour talking to Stasha alone. She couldn't call them all. Stasha would have to call Helcha, and Helcha would call Ludmilla, and they would divide the calls to the sisters-in-laws. So it was settled, and Michalina put the receiver onto the hook.

She glanced out the window. Both children were asleep on the porch. Frankie was very tired, perhaps he would sleep all day. His family should know what happened. Michalina decided she must call Catherine and tell her how good Frankie was last night, how he brought Dr. Noshkins and now everything turned out right. She found the number and called.

Lily answered the phone. Catherine was at the tailor shop, since Saturday was a good business day. Michalina knew that must be true. Didn't she go to the tailor shop herself on Saturday...ya...but not to Jagienczak's. It was too far away.

Lily repeated over and over, "Oh my...oh my...such a wonderful doctor. And she's still alive, Mrs. Kaszmierski! How wonderful! Oh, my...oh, my..."

Telling the story seemed to take longer the second time. Lily promised to contact the others. She would go to the shop and tell Catherine herself. There was no phone at the shop. Catherine would allow only one phone bill, so it was decided the phone should be at home, and if there were business messages, someone would walk to the shop to deliver them personally. Frankie's sister, Kate, was at the shop with her mother. Most days she worked there, unless she was needed at home to help with Busha, or needed at some relative's house to help with necessary chores.

Once again, Michalina replaced the telephone receiver, feeling certain Frankie's family would have the news soon. Lily was very conscientious...had to be...with so many responsibilities. They were good people, even if they lived in the *old* neighborhood.

The rest of the weekend passed slowly. The Kaszmierski's weren't accustomed to such quiet. The phone rang intermittently as one of the sisters, or brothers,or in-laws called to check on Mil's progress. The report was always much the same. Mil slept most of the time, except when Frankie or Mama forced a little food down her throat. Wladek and Harry stayed home - unusual for them on Saturday and Sunday - but they wanted Frankie to have company, since he wasn't having any honeymoon.

They tried to talk about light, happy things, to keep everyone's mind off Mil's and Frankie's predicament, but somehow, the discussion always came back to the war. Would the United States be dragged into it? Things looked bad. President Wilson was a smart man, knew how to keep things peaceful, a real diplomat, but the boys, reflecting the general feelings of the nation, began to feel the time had come; things had gone too far. If the Heinies were to be stopped, Uncle Sam would have to get into the battle.

"What difference does it make?" Frankie said. "A lot of our guys are already there. Why don't we make it official and wind the whole thing up?"

"You're right, Frankie," Wladek said. "Mama doesn't know this, but I think I'm going to enlist."

Harry said, "Oh, good Christ, Walter, what are you saying? Mama would die!"

"I know she won't like it, but...she's strong. She remembers what it was like when

Tata was in the army in Poland...before they came here. They were always battling for their lives. It was the Prussians, the Russians, or the Austrians...always some battle...some revolution. There's been a lot of army in Mama's and Tata's lives."

"Yeah...sure...but they hated every minute of it." Harry figured he wouldn't convince Walter, but it was worth a try.

"So, nobody likes it, but sometimes you have to go and fight."

Frankie watched the faces of his new brothers-in-law. He listened to them and understood them both. He hated fighting and killing, but if he were old enough, he would want to go. It was said this would be a war to end all wars, and he wanted to be part of that. He would like to feel he'd done his share to make the world a better place. But it was no use for him to think about it. He was too young, and there was Mil. She needed him.

All weekend they talked about the war. Frankie knew Wladek was looking for the right time to tell Mama and Tata how he felt, but with Mil being so sick, there was no right time.

Frankie told them all about his cousin, Stash, who was already in France, fighting. Frankie and Stash had been very close as young boys. They looked more alike than Frankie and his own brothers. Stash had a real talent. He was a violinist, and he was so good that he had a job on the Lusitania entertaining all those rich people that traveled to Europe.

It was almost two years now, since that Heinie sub attacked and sank the Lusitania. Stash was one of the few survivors. They'd heard through the Red Cross. They hadn't heard much of anything else because everyone was afraid of the German spies who infiltrated everywhere, so Stash's story would remain pretty much a secret until he got back. Frankie hoped he would. Secretly, Frankie wished he could go overseas to help, to do his share, maybe to fight alongside Stash. But he probably never would.

******************

Early Monday morning, Michalina packed Frankie's lunch, then tried to hurry him out the door as he lingered for another look at Mil's face.

Mama, do you think she'll be all right when I go?"

"Ya. You know Dr. Noshkins say she need much rest. So she sleep now, ya? She sleep if you stay home or if you go to work. You must go, Frankie. Mr. Schmelling is nice man...you must not...how you say...take advantage of him. So you, go."

"All right, Mama, but if she wakes up, you tell her I'll be home just as soon as I can."

"Ya, ya... now you go."

Mama had tied Frankie's lunch neatly in a newspaper parcel, just as she did the others, put it in his hand, and pushed him out the door. She looked at Mil and sighed. How long would it be before Mil could pack Frankie's lunch? It would be a happy day for all of them when she made that much progress.

The days continued to follow one another as always. Frankie went to work each morning, and the guys, with real concern, asked about Mil, then with friendly taunts, they made remarks about his non-existent honeymoon, or they took turns leering at Vera Olchinski, or making passes at her. She knew how to take it and how to give it all right back to them. Frankie always knew whom she favored for the week, because that was the guy who stood on the sidelines and pretended to ignore her. She was older, but a good looking broad - in a cheap way. She had always teased Frankie, ever since he started working there as a kid, but it was different the way she did it now, still, he thought she knew he was Mil's guy.

At home, Noshkins dropped in daily and briefly examined Mil. Frankie felt restless. He paced and worried, phoned and prodded the doctor for information. Noshkins had none to give. Mil was alive, she was breathing, her heart was pumping, she'd had no more hemorrhages. He couldn't tell them anymore than that. She had been extremely weak...she had been dead for a few moments when her heart had stopped beating...now they must wait. He couldn't tell them anymore.

On Friday morning, Frankie woke unusually early. He washed and dressed quietly, then pulled his chair close to Mil's bed. It was their anniversary - one weak of marriage, and he'd hardly seen her eyes open. Well, this was what he'd wanted... what he'd thought would be best...now he wondered but it probably wouldn't be any better for Mil, even if they hadn't married. He glanced at the calendar on the kitchen wall. It was April 6, 1917...Good Friday...the day Christ died for their sins. Oh, good Christ, last Friday Mil died, and she couldn't have many sins - she was an angel. Make her well...let her live...let her live a long time. He sighed. His eyes closed, and for a short time he dozed. He woke with a start, worried that he'd overslept. He jumped to his feet, looking through the window at the kitchen clock. What a relief! It was still early. Even Mama wouldn't be up yet. When he turned back to settle in the chair a while longer, he saw Mil smiling at him. Oh God! She was smiling like she knew him, knew where she was, what it was all about! Her lips said, “Frankie”, but he didn't hear any sound.

Frankie dropped to his knees beside Mil's bed, and took her hand. A few tears ran down his cheeks; he didn't care.

“Oh, Mil...Mil...I've been so worried, so scared. Oh, God, Mil, I love you so much.”

Frankie lay his head beside her, but she pushed his head down further, so she wouldn't breath on him. She held his hand, and they stayed that way a long time.

Soon they heard sounds coming from Mama's and Tata's room. Frankie looked at Mil and smiled, then tucked the covers around her. Suddenly, in the intimacy of the moment he felt shy. He was conscious of his hands, of his movements, of how he touched her. Mil was weak, everything was forbidden to them, he didn't know how to act. He couldn't look at Mil's face. Then he felt her hand on his. She drew his hand to her breast. It was soft, and small, and warm. He was overcome by a feeling he'd never had before. He was shaken by a thrilling warmth that pervaded his being and made him tingle. He wanted to throw himself down beside her on the bed.

“Ach.” It was Mama's soft voice. “You are awake.”

Frankie pulled his hand away self-consciously.

"Yeah, Mama, Mil's awake! She even knows who we are!"

"Milia! Dziecko!"

Mama ran out to the porch, hugged her baby, and crooned things to her, like she thought Mil was still a kid. Frankie watched and smiled. He knew Mil was no kid, she was his beautiful, warm, soft, wife.

Whistling "Sweethearts", Frankie swaggered into the kitchen to make his own lunch. He wanted to leave as soon as possible, so he could come home as soon as possible. He looked at his hand. He could still feel the softness and the warmth of his wife on that hand. It was a beautiful morning, and he was going to make some delicious rye bread sandwiches, and then he would catch the streetcar, and do the best day's work for Mr. Schmelling, and then he would come home...and well...he didn't know what wonderful things would happen then.

## CHAPTER 10

Frankie was still whistling when he swung through the factory doors. He took his apron from its hook, and whistled his way partially down the stairs to check the mixing vats. About half way down, he met Vera Olchinski. Her bright red hair hung down her back in curls. When she talked to him this morning, Frankie's face flushed. Somehow, he was more aware of her and how she was built. The guys always talked about her big bust, and for the first time, unintentionally, Frankie's eyes lingered.

"Hey, Frankie," she crooned at him in her low voice as she put her hand lightly on his arm. He noticed it was delicate and cool. "How's your wife?"

She was covered by the same old white shop apron, but Frankie noticed her deep breathing. His face felt warm.

"She's...she's a lot better this morning," he stammered.

"Oh?" Vera said. "The guys say you're getting a tough break. I'm sorry.

Frankie didn't know how to answer. It made him mad they were talking behind his back.

"The doctor says she'll be well soon." He wondered why he lied; it was foolish.

"Swell, Frankie." She squeezed his arm a little. "Well, if ya wanna talk about it some time, I'm a good listener." She winked and smiled at him like she meant a lot more than she was saying.

Frankie said, "I gotta hurry downstairs."

Quickly, as he went, Frankie rubbed the cool from his arm where she'd touched him. He wished he hadn't even seen Vera today, much less talked to her, and then been touched by her. It was very hard to take right now. He was still feeling warm all over from touching Mil this morning. Was it like this for everyone...the first time? The world suddenly seemed blue with rosy color spreading all over, and...and it felt like red lightning streaks were flashing through everywhere. When he left the house, he felt happy, thinking there was so much more to look forward to, but now, Vera made him remember Noshkins' warning, that Mil was too sick, there could be no physical contact for a long time. Hell! What had he been thinking? They shouldn't have gotten married. How long could he take it? How long could he keep away from Mil? And she shouldn't have done that this morning. Didn't she know what it would do to him? He checked the vats and stomped back upstairs.

******************

Emilia slept on and off all day. It was the most beautiful delirium she'd ever known. In all her dreams, Frankie held her, and whispered to her, and petted her. Whenever she woke, she'd look at the clock and think of how many hours it would be before he came home...to her. Noshkins said they couldn't have any close physical contact, but surely he didn't mean touching. She'd never been touched before. It was beautiful...and the happy look on Frankie's face, oh, she'd remember that all her life, even if she lived to be ninety. She passed her hands lightly over her bosom, wishing she were bigger, had more to offer him, but maybe when the sickness was gone, and she gained a little weight.

******************

As the damp, dark walls of the factory closed in around Frankie, he began to feel the day would never end. Every time his eyes wandered over to Vera, she was standing sideways, and even her apron couldn't hide how far her bust came out. It was crazy, how all of a sudden he couldn't get his eyes and mind off Vera's bust. He'd never before felt like this in his whole life, but he could have run over to her and thrown her down on the floor right there, and...what was he thinking! Oh, God...his poor, beautiful delicate, angelic Emilia was lying in bed at home, fighting the bravest, hardest battle in the world, a battle for her very life, while he was lusting after Vera who'd probably known every guy in the factory, except him, at some time or other. It was all crazy, and he'd gotten himself into the whole mess, but somehow, he'd never thought about how long it might take before Mil got well...if she ever did.

******************

When Mil looked at the clock again, it was four-thirty. Frankie would be home about six-thirty. That gave her two hours. She would make herself as pretty as possible for when he came home. She wouldn't breath at him and they couldn't sit close very long, but it would be so wonderful. Besides, it would feel so good to clean up. She'd slept for a solid week...on and off...all day, everyday, but it was worth it, if now she felt well enough to get out of bed for awhile.

"Mama? Could you bring me a pan of warm water, and a face cloth and a towel?"

"Ach, Dziecko, it be better if I help you to toilet. Is too cold on porch for washing."

"Oh good, Mama! I would like to get up for awhile."

"You get up for few minutes only. I wash you quick, and you go back to the bed."

"No, Mama, I'll wash myself. And maybe you could bring me my bottle of toilet water."

"Dziecko, what you do?"

"I'm only going to wash up before Frankie gets home."

Michalina looked at Emilia as though she tried to pierce beneath the surface of her skin. Emilia lowered her gaze, self-consciously.

Emilia washed, but slowly. Frequently, she had to sit on the edge of the tub, holding on to steady herself. It would be good to lie down again, though for the first time in a long time she was without the cold-hot, sweaty feeling. Nevertheless, she guessed it would be a long time before she felt completely well.

Meanwhile, Michalina busied herself around the stove, thinking how unwise it was for Mil to pretty up and make herself smell so good. It was bad for Frankie now, but she didn't know how to tell her daughter this. How could she say such a thing to someone, especially to her own daughter? Maybe she should call one of the other married daughters. Maybe they could say something to Milia. But what would she say on the telephone? How could she put this into words? Ach...she didn't know.

"Mama?" Mil called. "Please can you come help me back to bed? I'm a little tired from all this."

"Ach, Dziecko, tsk, tsk, tsk..."

"Mama, what's the matter?"

"Milia, you look too pretty for laying in the bed."

"Well, Mama, maybe later I could sit up in the chair for awhile."

"No, Doctor say you must lay in the bed. I help you. We go."

Mil put her arms around Michalina's neck and kissed her on the cheek.

"Oh, Mama, sometimes, you say such funny things."

Michalina shook her head, frowning in disagreement.

"But it's all right, Mama. I'm so tired now, I'll probably just lay down and sleep till Frankie gets home."

*****************

At last it was five o'clock. Frankie could hang up his apron and get out of the factory. Now that April was here, at least it wasn't completely black out when he opened the great wooden doors to the outside world.

It was crowded on the street tonight. People seemed to be rushing everywhere. There was a little crowd standing around the news stand on the corner where he was headed to wait for the streetcar. The little Niemczyk kid was walking up and down with a stack of newspapers under his arm yelling, "Extra! Extra! Read all about it!"

Frankie's heart seemed to somersault. He was afraid to see the headlines, nevertheless, he ran to the news stand.

Black words waved across the top of the DAILY NEWS like a black crepe announcing death.

"WILSON SIGNS: WAR IS ON"

Frankie, forgetting about his need to save money, pulled a penny from his pocket, set it on the shelf with all the others, and took his paper.

"Oh, God," he said aloud, "it's really happened."

Then he was conscious of someone standing very close beside him.

"Will ya hafta go, Frankie?" Vera said it softly, her green eyes looking deep into his own.

She linked her arm through his; he left it, feeling that hand resting ever so lightly on his arm as he continued to stand there, so conscious of her warmth, of the fact she was a woman. Then, she tugged gently.

"C'mon, Frankie. I live right around the corner. Like I said, I'm a good listener."

In spite of himself, he wanted to go, and then he pulled his arm away, so he could maybe think straight. It was a little better when he did that, and he became aware again of the Niemczyk kid yelling, "Extra!"

"Look, Vera," he said, "I gotta go."

"You sure do, Frankie Jagienczak. Ma hasn't seen you for days!"

It was his sister, Kate, looking cute as a fashion model with her black curls peeping out from under her little brown hat. He was so glad to see her...his "big" sister Kate...really very tiny and petite...the one who had always come to her kid brother's rescue. Now, here she was, doing it again.

"Frankie, you're not getting on the trolley until you've come across the street and talked to all of us for a couple of minutes. Everybody wants to know all about Mil...she's such a beautiful girl, and nice too." Kate looked at Vera like she was sending ice darts right into her heart.

Mockingly, Vera smiled and bowed her head slightly in Kate's direction as she moved away from Frankie.

"See ya tomorra, Frankie," Vera said, "and good luck."

Frankie's face burned in his confusion of greatfulness and resentment. It was a relief to have Kate come along just then, yet as a man, he resented her interference. He probably wouldn't have gone with Vera...or would he? No, he wouldn't. He loved Mil too much.

"I meant it, Frankie, we haven't seen you for days. Come on across the street for a few minutes."

"Kate, it's getting late. I've gotta see if Mil's all right."

"Oh, sure, but it wasn't too late to go with that hussy, Vera!"

"Damn it, Kate! Shut up! What do you know about it? What ya know about any of it?"

He turned away from her and walked out on the street; the trolley was coming.

"Frankie, you come back here!" she ran after him and pulled his arm. "Please,

Frankie."

Kate's eyes brimmed with tears. Well, there was no use hurting her, even if he was a man and she was just a foolish girl who had no business butting in. She was trying to help, he guessed.

"Please, Frankie..."

"All right. Come on, let's go, but only for a couple of minutes."

Light filtered through the lace curtains, telling Frankie Ma was in the dining room. Kate broke ahead and ran toward the stairs.

"Last one in's an alley rat!" she yelled.

Shoving one another, playfully, they scrambled through the front door.

"And this is our married man?" Ed said. "Racing with his sister?"

Frankie looked at them gathered around the dining room table. He didn't know they'd all be there, but it was good to see them.

Ma was at the head of the table, her white hair glistening. Lily and Ed flanked her sides. Next to Lily sat her thoughtful husband Joe, sucking his pipe, sparse brown hair neatly combed. Their son, Elmer, knelt on a chair, hind end in the air, as he rolled a marble across the table. Willy, the short brother, not even as tall as Mil, sat with an arm around his Italian wife, Jenny. Busha lay still following all movements with her eyes. Joe's tall, handsome brother Hank was there too. He walked over, shook Frankie's hand, then put his arm around Kate's shoulders. It wouldn't be long, Frankie thought, before they got married.

"Hey," Frankie yelled, "we got a reunion!"

"Stepping out on the wife already," Willy said.

Ed poked his elbow into Willy's ribs.

"Frankie, how's Milia?" Ma asked, a frown creasing her forehead.

"She's better, isn't she?" Lily asked.

"You won't believe it!"

"So, tell."

"This morning, Mil smiled at me. She knew who I was!"

Everyone surrounded him, talking at once, slapping his back, congratulating. Even little Elmer, hind end still in the air, yelled, "bout time."

They talked for awhile about Mil and went over the events of the past week, and then they talked about the day, Good Friday, April 6, and the headlines, and the war. They were all gathered because Ed had enlisted. Recruits were badly needed, so he would be leaving for camp very soon.

"Ed," Frankie said, "I wish I could go. Now it'll be you and Stash, and Mil's brother, Walter, maybe."

Ed shrugged. "You got your own war here, Frankie."

"Sure...sure...I couldn't leave Mil."

Ma said, "Frankie, one soldier in the family is more than enough."

As she searched his face for some sign of agreement, a feeling of discomfort enveloped her, a small nagging fear.

Joe set his pipe on the table thoughtfully. "You know, Frankie, this would be a good time to change jobs."

Lily looked at her husband in surprise. "What are you saying that for, Joe? Mr. Schmelling has been so good to us, especially to Frankie. We owe him."

"Sure, Schmelling's been a God-send, but Frankie's done a good job to repay him. He'll never make good money there. He's been going to night school, and there are plenty of war jobs opening up in the machine shops."

Willy began nodding his head furiously. "Ma, Joe's right." Turning back to Frankie he said, "You're a family man now. You better think about what Joe is saying."

It was true. All this time he'd been preparing for a better job, but never really considered leaving Schmelling's. He began asking many questions, and for the next few hours, they were all absorbed.

******************

Dinner was over, the boys left, and Tata pushed his chair back, giving himself more room to open the evening paper, as Michalina cleared the table. Emilia lay on the porch in the dark. She hadn't eaten her dinner and she wasn't speaking. Humming softly to herself, Michalina pretended not to notice Emilia's silence, but she too worried about Frankie. This morning, he'd been so happy, so anxious to go to work so he could return to Milia.

"Mama, what time is it now?"

"Ach, Dziecko, take nap, then Frankie be home when you get up."

"Mama, I want to know the time."

"Is eight o'clock."

"Oh, Mama...what could have happened to him?"

Mil began crying.

"Ach!" Tata crushed his paper and left the room.

"Is all right, Milia. You hear Wladek and Harry say is war."

"But what does that have to do with Frankie? He should be here. He doesn't love me. I knew we shouldn't have gotten married."

Stroking Mil's head gently, Michalina continued to soothe her...try to reason with her...hoping to avoid any possibility of further anguish...or hemorrhage.

Mil cried herself to sleep. Michalina continued to sit at her side, afraid of any movement lest it disturb her sleeping daughter, so she simply sat...absorbed in thought. What could be keeping Frankie so long when all he wanted in the morning was to come back to his Milia who knew him for the first time since their wedding day. Maybe Milia was right, but no, Frankie was a good boy, devoted to Emilia. It had to be the war. Maybe someone came and took him away to fight. But no, they were in Chicago, America, 1917. Only in Europe did people come without warning and take others away. Michalina reached into her apron pocket and withdrew her rosary. With closed eyes, she began to pray. Soon, in the quiet, she heard sounds on the steps...someone running, maybe...two stairs at a time. She sighed with relief. It must be Frankie. The door opened and spring rushed in with him.

"Mama? Anybody?" he called softly.

Michalina came to meet him, finger on her lips.

"Shh...you wake Milia."

"Oh, it's good that she's sleeping."

"Not easy, she falls asleep. Where you were, Frankie? Is so late...Milia worries."

"Doesn't she know? Didn't anyone tell her there's a war?"

"Frankie?"

As Frankie turned he saw Mil steady herself on the door frame, her golden curls tousled like his mother's silken crochet yarn after the kittens had gotten into the sewing box. Her eyes were glazed and swollen red. Her pretty white flannel gown was rumpled. Worry filled his soul...what was wrong...what had happened to her since she smiled at him in the morning? He ran to her side.

"Mil! What are you doing up? You look funny. What's wrong?"

"I hate you, Frankie Jagienczak! I hate you!"

He tried to help her as she stamped back to her bed, but she pushed his hands away.

Michalina, rosary in hand, started after them to explain to Frankie, decided she mustn't, then went to the parlor to join Tata.

Mil felt Frankie's arm wrap around her waist...strong...angry. But why should he be angry? He'd kept her waiting for hours and didn't even care if she worried. Where had he been? Wherever it was, knowing she was home waiting for him wasn't enough to bring him to her.

"Mil, please, Honey, stop it. Tell me what's wrong."

"What's wrong? I thought you'd want to hurry and come home to me. I waited. I waited since six o'clock!"

"I'm sorry. It's just that..."

"Yes, what is it, that it's just that...?"

"It's war, Mil."

"Oh, and were you going to go to the army tonight?"

"No, Honey...I ran into Kate...and...and...she asked me to stop at the house."

"Tonight? Tonight of all nights, you stopped for hours? You could just forget about me?"

"Hell, Mil! How could I forget about anything? There's a war. Ed's going. Stash is gone. I gotta wife, but I haven't got a wife. Damn it...what d'ya want me to do?"

"I wanted you to come home and hold me...when I was looking pretty...and now..."

"Gee, Mil...you still look pretty...and I do want to hold you...only..."

"Only what?"

"You know what Noshkins said."

"Oh, Frankie, he didn't say you couldn't touch me."

She sat on the bed looking so thin and helpless, as if the simple act of sitting were too much effort. Her eyes seemed to be churning, restless pools of water...blue and bottomless...and Frankie lost himself in the depth of their feeling.

They lay side by side on her little bed for awhile. They caressed. They talked. Frankie explained about going to Ma's, but he didn't mention Vera. Happiness, warmth and contentment spread over Mil like a comfortable blanket, while Frankie was wrapped in a state of confusion - a kind of happiness, but also discontent. Everything was happening so fast. Mil didn't know anything or anyone for a whole week. Now suddenly he was lying with her in the bed. It felt like he had waited so long; now it was hard to settle for half a marriage. Thinking Mil was asleep, he quietly moved out of the bed.

"Frankie? Where are you going?"

"To keep my part of the bargain."

"You're going to your cot?"

"Yeah, and that's where I'm staying from now on, until Noshkins says it can be different."

Mil turned the light on and looked into his face. It was stern and tense...jaw set...he looked so much like a man now. She began to understand what she'd done...how frustrated her husband must feel.

"Frankie, I'm sorry."

"Go to sleep, Mil."

He left the room. She heard water running in the bathtub.

## CHAPTER 11

Frankie lounged down the street. It was a two block walk to the streetcar stop and he was in no hurry, having left the house earlier than usual. He'd always enjoyed mornings, they were his time to relax and think things out. It was Holy Saturday...their war would soon be a day old...he needed a new job. It would be hard leaving Schmelling's; he was used to it, the only place he'd ever worked. The guys were a good bunch..all older than he, but a good bunch. Vera had always been good too...like an older sister, until lately, that is. Coping with Vera today, wouldn't be easy, but easier than yesterday, for he felt more settled...felt he'd learned a lot about the world and people in just one day. Anyhow, everything that happened, well it belonged to yesterday. After the incident with Kate, Vera probably thought he was still a kid. Well, he'd tell Kate next time he saw her that he was man enough to take care of himself. What he really had to think about was a new job. Joe was right last night. At Schmelling's, he'd never make much money, and after all, he was seventeen, nearly eighteen, and had a wife. There was no use being sentimental about it, he had to have a new job.

Once around the corner, he stopped at Pops' news stand. The old man sat dozing in the haze of the early morning light. Another fifteen minutes and business would be pretty steady, not that it mattered. Everyone left his penny on the shelf and took his own paper whether Pops was asleep or awake. Without disturbing the old man, Frankie set his penny down and slid a Tribune from the top of the pile. He would read the want ads on his way to work.

Frankie hopped the trolley without his usual crowd this morning. What a difference fifteen minutes made, he thought. Not only was it empty, he didn't even recognize the conductor. He paid his fare, then lurched to the front of the car. Sitting in the front, he propped his feet on the long seat that ran under the windows. He opened the paper and marked the ads that were of interest to him. There were five...one far south, and four much closer to home. Then he sat back and watched the scenery change with every passing block. He transferred cars twice and thought about how much more crowded it became as he neared his own neighborhood...the *old* neighborhood. The first part of his ride took him past more homes, and small family businesses. Now he passed the big stores like Wieboldt's and Woolworth's. Factory buildings were older...windows grimier. And always the streetcar whistled a monotonous tune as it skimmed arrow-straight over the tracks, appearing to race with the deep red street bricks. He felt like sleeping now, but it was nearly time to get off. He folded the paper so the want ads were still visible and jammed it in his pocket. Then he swayed out to the platform, and jumped from the streetcar as it began to screech in warning of an approaching stop. He managed to get off right in front of the mustard factory. That was the little game he played every morning since his marriage, and this morning he did it. Some Gypsy would probably tell him that was a good sign.

Yeah...it would be a good day. He had new job possibilities, Mil seemed to be not only better, but understanding his feelings a little, and if they were careful and Mil kept making progress, Noshkins would probably tell them soon it was all right to be husband and wife...really.

Smiling and putting the want ads in his pocket, Frankie entered the factory. The pungent odor of mustard hit him; he liked the smell. He pulled his time card and rounded the corner. Vera was there, tying her apron, laughing heartily as Big Jash, plant foreman, walked away from her. Still laughing and tossing her red curls, she winked at Frankie.

"Hi, Frankie, boy." Bouncing up the stairs, she tossed the greeting at him over her shoulder.

Not wanting to join Vera and the guys upstairs while his face flushed flaming red, Frankie stalled. As he reached the upper landing, he saw Big Jash, Turtle, and Rubber Belly talking to Vera. Then raucous laughter burst from them and Rubber Belly nudged Big Jash as he noticed Frankie coming toward the group.

"Hey, Kid." That's the way the fellas greeted him.

Suddenly, Frankie knew why they called one of them Rubber Belly. His protruding stomach actually bounced with every step. Frankie was sure they were plotting to trick him, otherwise they wouldn't have scattered so quickly.

******************

When Noshkins came, Milia looked fresh...rested...and a telling glow shown from her face. He examined her more quickly than usual. There was improvement, but he couldn't approve of what he thought he saw in her face. She was not that much improved.

Emilia, you are looking extremely pretty this morning...like a bride."

The glow intensified like a smoldering ash bursting into flame.

"I see I'm correct in my assumption."

"No, Dr. Noshkins...I don't think so...not exactly."

"Emilia, you're better, but you're not well. You're weak. You're still contagious. Don't play with Frankie's health. Don't chance a relapse for yourself."

"Doctor...we only touched...a little...Frankie slept on the cot."

"Touching...that's not good for Frankie, Emilia. Let him stay on the cot."

A.look of surprise jumped into her eyes. She'd begun to think, last night, that maybe touching wasn't good for Frankie right now, but she didn't really think that Dr. Noshkins would say this to her. She hoped she was wrong in her thinking.

"Emilia, we talked about this before the wedding. I had my doubts then about the "arrangement", though I'm not completely sorry I gave my permission. It was good for you, but it's much too hard for Frankie. Perhaps...he should move back to his house for awhile."

"Dr. Noshkins...no, please...I need him..."

"I thought you also loved him."

"Yes, but..."

"Think about it, Emilia." Brisk as usual, he swept into his coat and prepared to leave.

"Goodbye, Michalina," Noshkins called. "Oh, yes...Happy Easter."

Noshkins didn't wait for Michalina to respond or to see him out. Watching the door swing shut, Emilia began to wonder if the scene between them had really taken place. Even after Frankie's words last night, Emilia secretly expected Noshkins to say it was all right, that a little bit of loving was better for Frankie than none at all, but Noshkins said something exactly opposite. Emilia turned her face to the wall, hiding her tears from Michalina who bustled into the room a few minutes too late to see the doctor or to hear his words.

Emilia felt so ashamed and guilty...so selfish...and heaven knew she didn't want that feeling, nor the responsibility for having hurt Frankie. It was his fault too, she thought, for insisting they marry, in fact, maybe it was more his fault. If they were single and he lived at home, none of this would have happened. If he lived at home..huh...wasn't that just what Noshkins had suggested? Oh, how could she let him go now. A small cry caught in her throat.

Michalina dropped the duster and ran to her daughter's bedside.

"Oi, Dziecko, what is?"

"Nothing, Mama."

"Is something. What Noshkins say to you?"

Emilia threw her arms around Michalina's neck and buried her face in her mother's bosom.

"Momchu...oh, Momchu. He said Frankie should go back to his mother's house for awhile."

"Ach...so...ya..."

Emilia pushed back. "Mama, what do you mean? It sounds like you think he's right."

"Milia, I not know how to tell. Frankie suffers. Is not good for young man to have pretty girl so close...to have...how you say...wife he no can take."

"Oh, Mama..you say that too? Mama...does Tata even say this?"

"Ach, Dziecko...Tata, he know everything, but he say not much. He think...he walk up and down and he think...and he look at newspaper when he not read. Ya, he know."

"But I love Frankie too much. I don't want him to go!"

"Ya, Milia. You love him...ya...but you must think how much do you love him."

"Mama, you're all wrong. Even if I tell Frankie to go, he won't. He won't leave me, Mama. No. I'll just stay under my covers, and he'll stay on his cot."

Michalina rose. "Is much to love, Milia. Is much to understand about...to love."

Michalina reached for the latest fashion magazine and dropped it gently next to her daughter's outstretched hand.

******************

Frankie thanked God silently for the lunch whistle at noon. Now the Lenten fast was officially ended, and he could celebrate by eating his big lunch. He'd packed it himself to insure getting just what he wanted - two big bologna sandwiches on paper thin rye bread, a link of Mama's pre-cooked fresh homemade Polish sausage, which would be the best part of his lunch and every guy there would want a taste. Once, even before they married, Mama gave him a piece of sausage to put in his lunch, and the guys told him if he had sense, he'd marry a girl with a Mama who could make such sausage. He'd enjoy making them suffer a little. They deserved it for talking so much about him and Mil behind his back.

He went outside, sat on the plank loading dock, and unpacked his lunch, lovingly, setting aside his two pieces of pound cake for dessert, to go with his milk. Again, he spread out the TRIBUNE want ads, wondering when it would be best to talk to Mr. Schmelling about his plans.

The door opened and Vera came out.

"Hey, Frankie. It's such a beautiful day. Mind if I sit out here with you and have lunch?"

"Plenty a room here, Vera."

"Sure."

She pulled an empty wooden crate over and sat near him.

"Whatcha doin' with the want ads."

Vera spread the wax paper from her sandwich over her lap and took a healthy bite.

"I need a new job. Time I used what I learned in night school."

Vera looked surprised. She left the crate and sat on the dock next to Frankie.

"Hey, you're gonna leave us?"

"Have to."

She looked into his eyes a few seconds...seriously.

"It won't be the same here without ya."

Then she looked away, putting all her effort into eating the sandwich. It looked like liver sausage on homemade white bread. Frankie wondered suddenly if Vera made her own bread in the evenings. She smelled good, even amidst the smell of mustard and burning coal. He watched her, noticing how much she enjoyed eating, thinking that's how she enjoyed everything she did. Suddenly, she started coughing and gagging...turned all red. She threw her arms up, but still looked as if she were choking. She reached back as though trying to slap her own back. Frankie tried to help. It seemed to take a long while, but finally she stopped coughing.

"Thought I was a goner at an early age." She laughed. "Honest, Frankie, I ain't real old."

She grabbed has hand and squeezed. "Thanks fer helpin'."

"Yeah. Sure."

"Frankie, I think I twisted somethin'...right back here..." She pointed to a place in the small of her back. "Wouldja mind rubbin'...just a little?"

"Yeah...sure..."

Frankie rubbed. She felt soft and fleshy. Vera closed her eyes and dropped her head back. The skin on her neck looked rosy white in the sunlight. She straightened up and opened her eyes, laughing softly, then grabbed his gently moving hand and pulled it around her waist. Frankie quickly pulled away.

Vera laughed and stood up, raising her skirt ever so slightly to shake the bread crumbs away.

"Oh it would be fun...breaking you in for your Milia..."

Her green eyes glinted and she went inside just before the twelve-thirty whistle blew.

Quickly, Frankie scrambled up the remains of his lunch, cussing quietly. He hadn't even gotten to the Polish sausage...or the pound cake. For sure he would look for a new job, and he'd tell Schmelling today.

He wondered if Jash, Turtle and Rubber Belly had planned all of this for him this morning. Haha! Lunch with Vera. Frankie stomped back into the building...two minutes late.

# CHAPTER 12

At Kaszmierski's, the Holy Saturday evening meal was a preview of Easter Sunday with its steaming hot Polish sausage, boiled potatoes, sauerkraut with caraway seeds, cucumbers in sweet-sour sauce, and ice-box cake, the family's special treat made with a batter of butter, hot coffee and cherries spread luxuriously between four layers of tea cookies. Because of the war, there was no Polish ham. Michalina had worked diligently for several days preparing her yearly feast. It seemed strange that this Easter, Emilia had no part in the preparations, but she did feel strong enough to eat with the family at the dinner table, and even though they hadn't checked with Noshkins, Michalina felt it would be all right. Seated there, were the usual home group: Tata, Mama, Harry, Wladek, Frankie and Emilia. The group was small when compared to the numbers the kitchen would host next afternoon.

Everyone tried to draw Emilia into conversation, but she was contemplative and silent.

Giving up on his sister, Wladek turned to Michalina.

"Momchu, I know this is a celebration, but I can't wait any longer to tell you. I've enlisted. Soon, I'll be going to war."

"Oi, Wladek...no, no...no, no...why you do this!"

"Momchu, it's a big war...almost all the world's involved...I have to be a part of it."

"No! I think we finish with fighting when we come to Chicago, America. You should not do this. Und you should not tell now...on Holy Saturday."

"Mama, please. You love it here in this country, but don't you see? I do too. I have to do what I can for this country. For all of us. I have to fight the Heinies."

"No, I no can see! You must go away. You run somewhere...out of city."

"No, Mama." Tata spoke without looking at Michalina. "Wladek signs...Wladek goes. Here, he sign because he want. In Europe, he go because they take. Is good he fight for what he want."

Walter jumped up and hugged Tata, planting a kiss on both cheeks. "Thanks, Pa. I knew you'd understand. You were a soldier once. You know how it is."

"Ya, Chopiec. Ya, I know." Tata took the linen napkin from his lap, rubbed it hard across his lips, then with reddened eyes, he left the table.

"Wladek," Michalina said, "you make mistake to tell now."

"No, Mama, no! We should celebrate. I'll be a man with an adventure. Mama, it's what I want...just like you and Tata wanted to take a chance and come here."

"Walter, I told you how Ma'd take it," Harry said.

"Mama," Frankie said, trying to help Walter's cause, "my brother Ed might be in the same outfit with Walter."

Mil said, "Walter you can't expect Mama to want her boy to go to war."

"Momchu?" Walter pleaded.

He looked to his Mama for her words of blessing as Tata returned to the table.

Michalina looked at her husband...tried to read his face...his mind. She thought about Frankie's family in the old neighborhood and his brother, Ed's enlistment, then directed her attention once more to Wladek.

"Ya. We take chance. We come here. Now...you must take chance like Frankie's Ed. But if you go, is because Tata say. I not like...never. I no can help."

They finished the meal in silence.

After ice box cake and coffee, Frankie helped Mil out to the porch and sat next to her on the bed. The others pulled kitchen chairs up to the windows so they could converse easily.

"Frankie, you'd better sit in the rocker now, away from me. Maybe we're getting careless to be so close."

"What d'ya mean?"

"Dr. Noshkins says I'm still contagious. I'm getting better, but if you got sick too, well that wouldn't help either one of us. Somebody's got to work."

Frankie smiled. Mil was talking like her old self again, like someone who had a real grasp of the situation, and understood the problems facing them. For awhile there, he had begun to wonder.

But as she watched Frankie's reaction, a feeling of utter disappointment overwhelmed Mil. He seemed so pleased, like he wanted to get away from her. Oh, God, why had he really married her? Why didn't he say something that would refute her words?, Maybe he didn't love her at all. She turned her head to the wall, thinking about Noshkins' visit that morning, and his suggestion. She pushed it out of her mind, and turned back to them.

"What are you doing with the want ads?" Harry was asking.

Mil saw Frankie spreading the newspaper on his lap.

"I thought maybe I'd look for a new job," Frankie said, "You know, one that pays more."

Tata nodded his head in approval.

"I've heard some factories are paying ten...twelve dollars a week," Harry said, "Might as well look, you're a family man now."

"Frankie," Michalina said, "you maybe find something closer here?"

"Two places are closer, but not much...more west...and one way south."

"So, what will you do?" Walter asked.

"Well, I'm not sure. First thing is to tell Schmelling, I guess."

"He'll probably be angry," Mil said.

"I don't know. Naw. He's been pretty understanding."

"Umph. He be understanding when you work for him, but not when you say you go."

"I don't know, Mama, I wanted to talk to him today, but he left early. I didn't get a chance. What d'ya think, Tata?"

Tata removed the pipe from his mouth, sat pillar-straight, and scraped the bowl.

"Only one job I have since I come here...to this city...my flowers...is what I know good. But Frankie, you go to school at night. You learn new things about machines. I think Schmelling knows this, ya?"

"Oh, sure. He encouraged me. Schmelling really thought it was a good idea when I told him I would go."

"Hmmmmmmm....then I think he tells you congratulations...or maybe he gives you better job at his factory...no?"

"I never thought about another job, Tata...but...naw, I don't think so. He's got juicy Jack repairing machinery."

Mil's eyes opened wide. "Juicy Jack? Why do they call him that?"

"He spits a lot of tobacco juice...he's never without chewing tobacco."

"That's goofy. You have nicknames for everybody in that place."

"Yeah...but I guess it's just everybody's way of saying, hey...I notice ya...I see what you do."

"Well, what about you, Frankie. What do they call you?"

"Kid, mostly. Or Frankie, Boy."

"So, what are you going to do, Frankie Boy," Harry grinned, "talk to Schmelling on Monday?"

"Yeah, I guess so. Hafta ask for a day off to go and apply."

"I think sure he get mad, Frankie, if you ask for day to find other job."

"Naw, Mama. Hafta try. Don't know how else to do it."

"If you don't try, you'll never know," Walter said, winking.

Mil turned her head to the wall. "I'm getting very tired," she mumbled, "I think I'll just go to sleep, if you don't mind."

"That be best. Tomorrow we have much company. Everybody comes."

The lights were switched off and everyone but Mil went to the parlor. In the quiet darkness, Mil thought about everything that had happened in the past few weeks. To her, none of it seemed good. Even now, Frankie didn't offer to sit with her until she fell asleep. Instead, he seemed anxious to leave her alone and join the family's conversation. They didn't even leave the kitchen light on, and Frankie knew how she hated to be alone in the dark. Even if they weren't married long, he knew that about her. It was one of the first things he'd learned. She remembered it well. It was at the picnic. She'd walked to the out-house just as dusk was settling in. Florchak had offered to go along, but Mil told her to stay with Frankie and roast a few marshmallows, since the out-house was just up the hill within their line of vision. It was a ramshackle little building, with a squeaking door barely movable on its hinges, and an opening for air and light that consisted of screening and a hinged wooden panel usually pushed up during the day and pulled down when the building was not in use. Emilia had leaned on the door to keep it from swinging open, bouncing lightly to make sure it was secured, then the vibration made the wood panel fall, covering the only source of light in the tiny building. It was pitch black and Emilia could think of nothing except getting out, but when she pulled the door handle it wouldn't budge. She tugged, pulled, pounded and screamed for them, but the crowd noises and the breeze blowing away from the bonfire kept her cries from reaching them. However, it couldn't have been more than five minutes before they heard sounds and came to investigate. Frankie pulled the door open, but by this time, Emilia was completely hysterical. She'd sobbed on Frankie's shoulder and told him how she hated the dark. He'd been so wonderful with his comforting ways, telling her she'd never be alone in the dark again...if he could help it. Now, they'd been married little more than a week, and here she was - alone in the dark. She got out of bed and turned on the night light.

The next morning, everyone rose early for sunrise Mass. Emilia was tired. She slept through Mass time while they were all at church, and she slept for hours more after they returned. The boys went back to bed...so did Frankie, and Mama and Tata busied themselves...Mama with dinner preparations, and Tata with grating horseradish near the open window, stopping occasionally to wipe his smarting eyes.

When Mil woke, the house smelled wonderful. Mama was still in the kitchen, and the murmuring sounds of voices indicated that Tata and the boys were in the parlor. Daylight was high in the sky; she guessed the family would soon be arriving. This was the first year Mil hadn't helped with the dinner preparations. She thought Mama looked unusually tired. Mil took a deep breath; it hardly hurt at all. It was as if God had cut the chains from around her chest. Strange how this sickness had hit her. She seemed to have been attacked very suddenly, then literally to have died. After that, it was a week of almost constant sleep, and now she felt some heaviness on her chest toward evening, and her temperature tended to rise then, giving Dr. Noshkins reason to say she was improved, but not well. Down deep, she realized she was still contagious, so she made a resolution not to eat at the table with the rest of the family. Perhaps they could move the table closer to the window so she could be included easily in the conversation.

Mil pulled herself up slowly, stretched, breathed deeply testing again her freedom from heaviness and pain, smiled at the realization she still felt better, then slipped into her robe and slippers.

"Mama?"

"Ach, Dziecko! How you feel? Is beautiful day for Happy Easter."

"Yes, Mama. I'm going to wash a bit before everybody comes."

"Is good." Michalina kissed her cheek.

"Oh, Mama, I'm sorry I can't help."

"Oi, Milia...you help! You get well!" Her eyes filled with tears.

Mil placed her head on Michalina's shoulder and embraced her.

"And, Mama, don't set a place for me at the table."

"Dziecko, why? You sit yesterday at the table with us."

"But maybe I shouldn't yet, Mama. There will be kids."

"You no feel good, Milia?"

"Mama, don't worry. I do feel good. It's just...I'm not exactly well yet."

"Ya...ya. Is only little while."

Feeling dizzy, Mil leaned on the wall, and when it passed, she moved down the hall to the bathroom. Uch, ugly, she thought as the wide eyed vision in the mirror stared back at her. No wonder Frankie wanted to get away, didn't love her anymore. In all the time they'd known one another, he'd never seen her like this...glassy eyes, accentuated by deep circles, hollows in her cheeks...pale skin...pale lips...but it was her hair that really looked bad...needed washing desperately. Ugly...yes, she looked ugly. She sat on the rim of the tub and cried. Even when she was deathly ill she hadn't looked this bad. Noshkins was right. Frankie would have to go back to his mother's for a while. Maybe if he didn't have to look at her like this all the time...maybe he would love her again. Then she decided to chance everyone's anger and wash her hair. As she filled the sink, the water felt merely tepid, but when it touched her scalp, it felt very cold. She shivered...tried to hurry...but cold and dizziness slowed her progress. Rubbing her hair slowly...painfully...she thought what a major undertaking a simple task had become.

Harry knocked on the door and called to her, "Mil, are you all right?"

"Yes, Harry."

"You've been in there a long time." Harry looked at Frankie who stood shyly next to him, not able to question his wife through the bathroom door in his in-law's home. It seemed...indecent to him.

"Only a few more minutes."

Her dear Harry had to ask about her. Frankie wasn't even concerned. Tears rolled down her cheeks again. She was so cold. Emilia took the towel from her head and crept unobtrusively back to the bed. Even Mama was in the parlor now...good...no one would scold her. She could rest in the golden warmth of the sunlight, before the others came. How tired she was!

When Emilia woke again, the sun was much lower, jabbering voices and laughter filled the empty spaces of the house, and the comfortable warm smell of holiday food rushed in waves to cover her. She barely saw their heads over the window sill, but Mama and Tata reigned over their kingdom at either end of the table; she knew that. Would she and Frankie ever be able to reign over a family table? She had doubts.

Tata and the boys had made long benches to use at table for the holidays when all the family gathered. That way, almost everyone could be seated at once. She could see the group, sitting in families, with children at the table too, so not everyone had been able to come, otherwise her nieces and nephews would have been eating at second table. Most of her nieces and nephews were about her age, though some were considerably younger. Stasha, the oldest sister sat next to Mama at one end of the table. She was usually quiet, and seemed to be so today. In fact, she seemed preoccupied and Mil noticed her husband, John, wasn't there. It was confusing in their family...so many doubles of names...Johns, Wills, Franks, Helens, Harrys, and her oldest niece, a bit older then herself, was Emilia. They had to speak of one another by first and last names to keep things straight. Next to Stasha, sat her line of children...oldest to youngest... Emilia, Helen, Johnny, Eugene, Harry.

Mil's brother Steve, and his son, Willie were alone. His wife, Elizabeth, may have been involved at her church. She was the only non-Catholic member of the family, though she didn't think so. She belonged to the Polish Roman Catholic Church, a small sect which had broken away from the leadership of the Pope, and celebrated Mass in Polish rather than Latin. She was a very active member of her church. Steve objected, silently, as he took to the whiskey bottle too frequently, making them both unhappy.

Will's son, Elmer sat next to them. Will was the oldest brother and he sat next to

Tata at the head of the table, with his wife, Frances on Tata's left. Will was a lot like Tata, quiet and thoughtful, but he lacked Tata's strength; he complained a lot, about things in general. All three members of Will's family were rather quiet.

But, Sister Helcha, the only heavy one in the family, and her small husband John, and son, Irving, made up for the quiet ones. They joked a lot, and laughed...enjoyed life...found something optimistic in every situation. They were a joy to everyone.

Brother John, his wife, Helen, and son, Herb, came next. They were the dignified members of the family. Helen wanted the good things of life and John was determined to get them for her. Herb was a happy-go-lucky kid, great friend of Stasha's boys and Irving. The other nephews were younger.

Ludmilla, the seamstress, and her husband Frank had been married over a year now, but they had no children. Wladek, Harry and Frankie sat together. Practically all faces at the table were happy.

The nephews were all excited over Walter's coming army induction, expressing various desires to go with him, write him, or run away after him, while Mama kept noticeably silent, and the sisters and sisters-in-law marveled that he would even consider going, expressing great relief that their own sons were too young for the army. Tata listened intently, stealing occasional glances at Mama, who sat with lips tightly compressed. Harry and John promised to keep the dental lab going while Walter was away. Then Mil heard Frankie.

"Wish I could go with you Walter."

"Good Jesus, Frankie! What a thing to say! You've got enough to do with taking care of Mil and finding a new job." Harry said.

"Yeah...it's just...war's a man's job."

Walter said, "Right, a man's job, and you're not old enough."

"I am!...Almost eighteen...working...married."

Mil looked at Frankie. His red face and angry scowl told the story. She felt nervous and began to cry. Why did they have to talk war anyway? They were like little kids fighting over games...stupid war and gun games...and on Easter Sunday, Frankie shouldn't be fighting with her brothers and sisters at Mama's dinner table.

"War talk...that's all you hear about," Will said. "Terrible things are happening to everybody because of it."

"Sure, it's terrible. That's why I'm going to fight and end it!"

"How're ya gonna end what's happening at our place?"

Helcha laughed. "Oh, you and Frances have your own war going, Will?"

"It's not funny. I'm talking about my job...the factory."

"What's happening, Pa? Shooting and stuff?" Elmer's eyes fired with excitement.

"When they make a man crawl across the floor on his belly, they might as well shoot him."

"Oh, my God, Will. Did they make you do that? You never said." Frances looked as though she would cry.

"Not me...but Karl Kaiser."

"Oh, good Jesus," Harry said, "why?"

"All the spy talk. He was accused. Everybody shunned him. He begged and pleaded...nothing. Then Winiarski, he got the idea. He said if Karl was a good American, he'd prove it by crawling across the floor on his belly, to kiss the American flag. Everybody started yelling and some even went after Karl, so he did it. They brought the flag pole, and Karl pulled himself across that filthy floor. Winiarski kicked him in the behind and said there was no such thing as a German-American."

"Is not right," Tata said. "Karl lives on your street many years. Everyone knows he is no spy."

"Hah!" Steve pounded the table. "Too bad he didn't have a bottle in his coat pocket to pass around. Then he would have been a good American."

"That's a disgusting story." Sister-in-law Helen turned her platinum head away from the table.

"I guess there are no more German-Americans like there's no more sauerkraut. Remember, we're eating "liberty cabbage". The note of sarcasm in Helcha's voice was unusual accompaniment, coming from her.

Helcha's husband, John, threw one arm around her and the other around Irving.

"All of a sudden, we're supposed to stop remembering the happiness our parents brought with them from the old country. But how do we do that?"

"You remember all right, but you play the game while you're remembering." This, from Brother John, who like an Americanized Tata sat sapling straight and with precise dignity sliced another piece of sausage into even bits.

Herb looked at his dad quizzically. "What game Pop?"

"The name game." There was an expectant pause. "Maybe they're right. None of us should be hyphenated. Who's to know about loyalty? After all, even Tata was in the Prussian army once."

"But, so what, Pop?"

"So...we're changing our name to Kazmier. Easier to spell, and much harder to know how to hyphenate."

"Janush!" Michalina stared at him...surprise quickly turning to disapproval. Such an Easter she couldn't believe! Her family was becoming crazy with war. They moved from Poland to escape war, poverty, and prejudice. She couldn't understand.

From her bed, Emilia watched them all in the confusion of disagreement and agreement, but Tata's reaction was different from all. She could see he ached to the very marrow of his bones. Pain seemed to shoot through his spinal column like an electric shock, forcing his usually upright posture to exaggerate itself. His bright blue eyes narrowed, appearing to splinter like two shattered icicles. Beads of wetness glistened on his forehead. He rose partially from his seat as though preparing to strike out at someone, then sat back heavily with a grunt.

All comments were lost to Emilia's ears, but the confusion rose and fell in waves before her eyes, then finally dashed itself to silence as Tata left the room. Emilia felt she must do something to help. She tried to smooth her hair, make herself look healthy and presentable. She pinched her cheeks hoping for a rosy glow, then slipped into her robe and slippers and determined to join the family, as she stood unsteadily in the doorway.

"I have crazy brothers! All of you...bringing such unhappiness on Easter Sunday."

She saw them all turn to her at once, like carved wooden puppets. This made her laugh, seemingly without reason, as tears rushed down her cheeks. The lightness in her head forced her to grip the door jamb tightly, then Frankie was at her side, and that was all she remembered.

And then, the family forgot the war and the name change in the worry of the moment, and they hovered and spoke in quiet voices as Frankie sat in the rocker on the porch and slowly moved back and forth with Mil on his lap.

"I'm calling Noshkins," Harry said, "now!"

Frankie looked at him blankly, then nodded. Gently, he placed Mil on her bed, tucking the covers close around her. He listened as Harry called the doctor, happy that someone remembered the phone, happy that Mil's condition didn't seem nearly as serious as it did on that other night which now seemed so long ago.

Still, he was worried...nervous...and too upset to sit. He paced back and forth, wishing desperately he'd known Mil was awake. He blamed himself for becoming so wrapped up in war talk. It was true; they had a war to fight right here, and they'd all better remember that from now on.

Walter put his hand on Frankie's shoulder. "She's not hemorrhaging. It can't be as bad as last time."

Tata, still seated at table, watching, nodded his head.

When the doorbell rang, Helcha answered. Noshkins swept in, astonished by the crowd of faces. His steel-gray brows knitting together behind the gold spectacles, trembled with fury.

"Leave! All of you! Go into the parlor...anywhere...just leave this room. But, Frankie...you stay."

Like Christ chasing the money changers from the temple, this small Jewish man eyed them all with righteous fury. And without question, they left. In his usual brisk manner, Noshkins examined Emilia, snapped his black case shut and turned to Frankie.

"Exactly what happened?"

Frankie explained.

"What must I do...send this girl to a sanitorium? Is that what it will take to make you all realize the danger of this situation?"

"I won't go," Emilia said softly. "I'll die first."

Mil kept her voice steady, despite her panic at hearing the last of Noshkins' comments as she awakened.

Noshkins sat at the side of her bed again and grasped her shoulders firmly.

"Emilia, Emilia...only yesterday I told you to be careful...that you were still contagious. Obviously, you didn't hear me. What are all these people doing here?"

"It's Easter. The family always comes."

She said it matter of factly...as though there were no reason Noshkins shouldn't understand.

"This Easter is different. It's a matter of your life, their health and my profession."

"Dr. Noshkins..." Frankie began.

"No! No more explanation. Do you children realize what trouble all of this could cause? Do you know I have not reported Mil's case to the authorities? What if any or all of these people contract tuberculosis? I would be considered responsible. There can be no more of this!" Noshkins paused as if waiting for his words to sink in. His tone was firm, almost angry.

Mama and Tata stood in the doorway, listening attentively.

"Michalina...Caspar...you must understand."

Wordlessly, they looked down at the floor.

"And Frankie, I think it will be best if you move back to your mother's house for awhile."

"Doctor!...I can't!"

"No more arguments! It must be settled...once and for all."

"Dr. Noshkins," Emilia said, "it's all right. Frankie will move back home."

Emilia looked at Frankie with sad, pleading eyes.

"Mil!"

"Please, Frankie. We can't cause Dr. Noshkins trouble. It's not right."

"But...you and me, Mil..."

"It can't be you and me for awhile. Oh, Frankie...it'll be better for both of us. It's hard this way...and you have a chance for good jobs...maybe the one on the south side."

"That's too far."

"But not if you lived at your mother's. And I'll try so hard to get well Frankie."

"Mil..." Frankie dropped to his knees burying his head in her side.

Noshkins grabbed Frankie's shoulder, urging him up and back from his wife's rumpled bed.

"Then it's settled. I'm leaving and everyone must be gone in five minutes."

Leaving no opportunity for argument, he swept out the door.

After everyone left, Frankie sat in the rocker. For awhile, he and Mil were quiet. Then he spoke.

"Honey, I don't want to leave you."

"You heard him, Frankie." Mil said what she had to, but her heart jumped with joy at his words.

"Mil, it could take years! So we'll both be sick...so what!"

"No, Frankie. I'm going to work at getting well, so we can live together... soon...and you work at getting a new job and lots of money, so we can have a place of our own when I do get well."

Frankie saw resolution firmly set on Mil's face. He was too tired to fight. Accepting his loss, he kissed her forehead and went to his cot.

## CHAPTER 13

Emilia turned the newspaper page back, folding it carefully. Her eyes wandered listlessly over it. Suddenly her eyes were arrested by a small section near the top, heavily outlined in black ink. It was a poem. In hushed tones, she read it to the gently wafting lily-of-the-valley-breezes.

'IN FLANDERS FIELDS by John McRae
Take up our quarrel with the foe;
To you from falling hands we throw
The torch; be yours to hold it high.
If ye break faith with we who die
We shall not sleep, tho poppies grow
In Flanders fields.'

Sobs caught in Emilia's throat and she cried hard. Tears still came easily these days, despite her gaining strength. How could it be...this perfect end of May day in a world so filled with pain and suffering.

She lay her head back and watched the clouds scuttle across the sky like giant ships on a sapphire sea. Despite her personal battle, today she was occupied by the world around her and its great war. So much had happened since her wedding day...a month and a half of years.

She didn't actually like reading the newspapers and thinking about the war, it was all beyond her help, but Frankie chided her for blocking something so important out of her mind, and though he tried to be gentle in his criticism, it seemed they had grown so far apart that she would do anything to please him.

Three times a week he came to see her, just as he had before they were married. She lived for Sundays, Wednesdays, and Fridays when Frankie left his mother's house and came to her, but it was as though every act of world-wide violence seemed to pound itself deeper between them splitting them farther and farther apart. Though she felt and looked so much better, all the things she'd read about in recent weeks lay like a hardening mound of sand upon her chest. Both Walter and Ludmilla's husband, Frank, had already completed boot camp and awaited orders to go overseas. Frankie's cousin Stash had been over there a long time and they feared Ed was on his way. The papers were filled with new and old stories of war, with warnings of rising prices, with ads and pictures of Uncle Sam urging men to become soldiers...with pleas for people to buy liberty bonds and liberty stamps. How fast news reached them since the first transcontinental phone call was completed only a year and a half before. So many new inventions...so many tied in with the war.

Henry Ford seemed frequently to be in the news urging people toward more devout acts of patriotism, reminding people of the dreadful Lieutenant-Kapitan

Schweiger and his submarine attack on the Lusitania two years before, of his own trip a few months later on the Oscar II as Peace Ambassador, the trip which many called a "scream" when he returned with orders for tractors from Russia. Ethnic papers continued to pit one nationality against another with great fervor.

Once again stories had been resurrected about British born nurse, Edith Cavell who'd died a heroine's death at the hands of the Germans for helping allied captives escape prison camps. Time and again, people were reminded to keep silence so would-be spies, like famed dancer Mata Hari could be thwarted in their attempts to help saboteurs.

And why did Emilia persist in worry over these things? She couldn't change them...but *they* were changing her life. Frankie's visits were less and less like those of a lover. He read passages from the paper to her, worried over the fate of family members, seemed totally absorbed in his new job which involved making parts for guns and ships...and they never touched. Meekly, he would kiss her forehead at the end of a visit, and leave.

Oh, he talked about the money he was able to save for them, but he spoke with detachment, always coming back to the fighting, and the job "real" men were doing.

She didn't understand, and she worried, but Harry reassured her that Frankie was too young for the newly passed draft law. Frankie was not twenty-one, so he couldn't be included in the lottery which was to come up in July, but still, she was frightened.

Breathing very deeply, a habit she'd unconsciously developed, brought a freedom-smile to her face. Since Easter Sunday there hadn't been any real pain in her chest. She never had a fever during the daytime now, though occasionally night brought one on. But what if a total return to health were her destiny, what difference would it make? Would Frankie be with her to share it? She shuddered. Maybe Noshkins should have let her die. Maybe if they hadn't married, losing Frankie to some other girl would have been easier. It was hard to come so close to happiness only to feel it slipping silently away.

A frantic pounding on the back door pulled Emilia out of her reverie. The sound was so pressing she made an attempt to get up, but Michalina, puffing noticeably, bustled from the front of the house to the back door.

"Elinora! What is?"

"Telephone! Telephone!" Elinora's high pitched scream transformed the word into a fearful alarm.

Michalina stepped aside as Elinora pushed past her to the telephone stand.

"Operator! Operator!" She clicked the receiver up and down as though delivering a Morse Code message.

Emilia's gaze soldered itself to Elinora's bulging eyes, as she heard the number given. It was Noshkins'.

"Oh, my God," she thought, "something bad has happened to Elinora."

"Dr. Noshkins...Elinora...it's my Jan. At home he falls. I can't move him."

Michalina and Emilia waited tensely as Noshkins replied at his end of the phone.

"No, no, Doctor. He grabs his chest and falls to the floor moaning."

With frightened fascination, Emilia watched the tears running down Elinora's full round cheeks.

"Doctor, will you come right away? Yes, yes, I will do this."

As though unsure of her surroundings, Elinora lurched toward the door. Michalina grabbed her arm.

"Noshkins says it could be his heart. Oh, good Jesus! I must go."

"Oi, I come too. Emilia, you be all right?"

"Don't worry, Mama."

Emilia saw her mama's hand instinctively reach for the rosary in her apron pocket as she flew out the door after Elinora.

"Heart attack," Emilia thought. All this time I've been sick, but healthy Jan has a heart attack and could die right away. What would Elinora do if he died? She'd already had three husbands. Would she marry again? Oh, what was she thinking? A man could be dying and she worried about another marriage for Elinora. Nevertheless, it was hard to put out of her mind.

******************

A few hours later, when Michalina came home to prepare supper for Tata and the family, Emilia knew the worst had happened; it was there in Michalina's face for anyone to see.

"Momchu?"

"Jan...he dies. Ach, is nothing we can do. Noshkins comes, but we know Jan is die when we come in house. He lays white on floor...mouth is open...und eyes. Elinora runs to him...to make him sit...but she can no do it. I get mirror. Is no breath. Elinora screams and screams, and I slap her, but no tears will come. She sits dumb...like statute. Doctor is good, but he must go back to office. He say he call Elinora's brother so she can't be alone. It be good if she cry."

"Oh, Momchu."

"Dziecko. You no cry. Much, much happiness Eliñora has. Now she know...she feel...how much good she have. Is how you say...price she pay."

"But Mama, why should she pay? What for? Who wants her to pay? What's wrong with being happy!"

"She pay to God. He puts here happy und sad...like see-saw. When one side get heavy, other side fly up. For Elinora, happy is heavy. Happy comes down. Now is her time to pay God."

"Oh, Mama. You mean God watches everything? If I'm too happy, He's going to give me sadness?"

"Ya. Is God's way. You watch. Is important...always to pray und be ready."

"Mama, you and Tata are always right, but about this, Mama...I don't know. You make me afraid of God."

"Is love und hate. Is good und bad. Is happy und sad. From where we get this? From God. The priests tell to pray and sacrifice und be happy in heaven. Is the way."

Michalina peeled the potatoes and Emilia lay flat on the pillows, thinking about God and Mama's words. How could one God love us perfectly and be so strict and unbending? What had she ever done to cause her sickness...maybe even to lose Frankie? Was she destined for a great heavenly reward? Heaven was far away, a place she'd often heard about but didn't know. She wanted some happiness here and now. She'd have to think more about this - but she didn't think she could believe Mama this time.

It was a long and depressing evening. It wasn't Frankie's night to come, and everyone else was very quiet. Jan's death had a sobering effect even here in their house.

Emilia was happy, this time, to be sick and unable to attend the wake or the funeral, though she didn't ordinarily mind these things, for as Mama said, they were a part of life. Actually, she didn't understand why Jan's death affected her so much. Maybe it was all that talk about happiness and paying for it. Did she resent Elinora's carefree happiness over all these years? Yes, she did envy Elinora some. Why not? Here she was just turned seventeen...young and pretty...but sick and unable to love her husband. Elinora had loved three husbands. God was supposed to be so just, but she didn't think He was giving her justice.

Of course, if all that Mama said about Elinora was true, she was not to be envied now...most of the time staring tearless into space, often not recognizing anyone, living in the past, talking to a Jan who no longer lived. Dr. Noshkins saw her everyday in the hope of bringing her around but nothing changed for her. Mama was sure she would be better if only she could cry.

In the next two weeks, nothing changed much except the blooming flower garden. Day by day Emilia watched the changes in its life cycle...infancy to full bloom. She walked more now, no great distance, but around the house and yard. Often, if the weather was just right, she sat bathing in the warmth of the sun, or sitting under the rose trellis, resting her head against it, sometimes with bare feet fondling the soft thick carpet of grass beneath her.

Meanwhile, Michalina continued to tend Emilia's needs, and those of Tata and the boys, while making some time, at least an hour daily, to visit Elinora...to try to cheer her...to help her to bring forth tears.

However, nothing seemed to help Elinora, so once weekly she was to begin going to Noshkins' office. There was no recurrence of the old tuberculosis, but there didn't seem to be much help for her present depression. More than anything it was hoped the weekly visits to Noshkins' office and the conversations with him would bring out the expression of her grief, bringing her tears and peace.

And so, Emilia thought, they were all waiting for something, like fevered children suffering through illness, they waited for their time of carefree play to come again.

Soon it was Wednesday! And sunny. Emilia waited impatiently for time to pass. Usually, she hated the dark evenings. She compared them to death, as she did the winter when the beautiful blossoms were gone and the ground often a deathly white, but these past few months evenings had been her refuge, the time when Frankie came to her. Of course, the days were longer, inviting seven o'clock to come around earlier, but the visits still seemed few and far between. She'd decided to ask Frankie tonight if he could visit daily now that she was better, and the days were longer and travel easier. She couldn't wait to see him!

******************

The day had seemed long to Frankie. He was glad to be boarding the streetcar for home. The job was good. He was making money and saving some, putting away every penny he could, cutting every expense he could, so he and Mil would have a good start when she was well. Still, he missed Schmelling's factory...its smell...the friends he'd made there. These days, he went into the big new building, and did a hard day's work, collected his seventeen dollars every Friday, and waited for a better life.

He looked forward to seeing Mil tonight, but any excitement he felt was dampened by his worry over Ed and Stash, his concern about the war in general, his wish to be part of it. He wondered too about his brothers-in-law, Walter and Ludmilla's Frank. Frankie felt as though he were missing out on all the important things in life. He was eighteen now, but still not old enough to be called. If only he and Mil could live together. Maybe he could stop at Noshkins' office before going to her house tonight. Her house. He didn't even think of it as their's anymore. Well, Emilia did seem much better. Maybe it wouldn't be long. He would stop and find out.

The streetcar was nearing his stop. Frankie moved out to the platform. The smell of smoke filled his nostrils. As he craned about trying to see what was happening, thick black smoke curled skyward before his eyes. Sharp red flames shot through the ominous black curls.

"God Almighty! It's the mustard factory! Or the hospital!"

Frankie sprang from the platform, and ran across the street in front of the trolley. Hordes of people stood around watching; policemen pushed them back. Firemen tugged the hoses while barking frantic orders.

Schmelling's mustard factory was burning like a giant hungry bon-fire. As Frankie tried to break through the crowd to reach the old familiar work crew, he heard his name called. He turned to see Kate running toward him. He stopped and waited.

"Frankie, I heard the sirens coming and coming. Isn't it awful?"

"I can't believe it! Does Ma know?"

"No, I'll have to run to the shop and tell her. Where's Mr. Schmelling? Is he all right?"

"I just got here. Don't know anything yet."

"You try to find out. Lily's on the porch. I'll run across to her, and then I'll go tell Ma."

Frankie elbowed his way through to Big Jash who stood gaping open-mouthed. Vera hung onto his arm, tears streaming down her face.

"What happened? Where's Schmelling?"

The fire was hot on their faces. The changing wind blew smoke at them and they coughed violently and closed their eyes to stop the smarting. Some of the firemen backed away, but smoke followed them. Policemen yelled, waved their clubs and pushed the crowd farther back. Everyone seemed to be unaware of Frankie as though he hadn't spoken at all.

Frankie shook Vera. “Schmelling! Where's Schmelling?”

Her eyes never left the blaze. Like Dickens' specter, she raised her hand and pointed toward the hungry licking flames.

Frankie stared and then turned away to vomit, careful even in his misery as he tried to avoid splattering anyone. How strange it seemed to him, that even now, he should think of ordinary politeness.

He left them there, working his way across the street to his own front porch. He sat on the top stair and Lily sat next to him, putting her arm around his shoulders.

“I heard, Frankie. I heard.”

They continued to sit like mannequins, even after Ma and Kate came, after the others came from work, after daylight began to pale, and only when the crowd began to thin and the fire smoldered, did Frankie attempt to go inside to call Mil.

When he entered the dining room, Busha's wide eyes fastened on him. Despite his preoccupation, Frankie noticed there was life in them...feeling.

As he gave Mil's number to the operator, they stared at one another. He saw hate, but why? He'd never harmed Busha. They lived in the same house, though he didn't really know Busha; he didn't think she knew him.

“Mama? It's Frankie. How's Mil?”

“She is good today...walking in yard little bit.”

“That's good, Mama. D'a think she could come t'the phone?”

“Oh, ya! She waits all day for you Frankie.”

“Oh, God,” he thought, realizing for the first time how late it was, “well, she'll understand.”

“Frankie? It's so late! What's the matter?”

“Honey, I can't come tonight.”

“Can't come?”

The terrible hurt and disappointment in Mil's voice caused Frankie to hesitate before answering her question.

“There...there was a fire...at the mustard factory...almost nothin' left.”

“I'm sorry.” Her voice was clipped, like her words. “But why can't you come?”

“Maybe there's something I can do. Schmelling's dead, Honey. At least they think.”

“Well, then...what can *you* do?”

Oh, yes, she was angry...he knew.

“Honey, I don't know. But maybe there's something. I hafta be here...to see.”

“Oh, Frankie! You always have to see to everything. I've been waiting all day. I can't stand it if you won't come.”

“Honey, I'll come tomorrow, and then that'll be two days in a row.”

Mil was silent. Frankie felt Busha's eyes on him. He felt nervous. Finally Mil spoke.

"When I can get away from here, Frankie, I'm not waiting for anybody...ever again!"

She was crying. "Honey...please. Nothin' like this ever happened before."

"You promise you'll come tomorrow?"

"Yeah...sure...a course I do."

"I love you Frankie," she said softly...hesitantly.

"Me too, Honey." He hung up quickly, not wanting to cry himself...wondering why he wouldn't say the words in front of Busha. She'd never know the difference. Again he looked at those eyes, now...not blank...rather...hateful.

"Dialbo."

Frankie couldn't believe his ears! Busha had spoken, very softy, but she'd spoken. He knew it. He not only heard, he'd seen her lips, first twitching, then painfully form the word. Busha had called him devil.

Frankie walked to the rollaway bed and leaned down to her. Could he have been mistaken? Busha hadn't said anything as long as he could remember. As he watched, her lips seemed to snarl at him, then again, he heard the word.

"Dialbo."

God Almighty. She did say it, but Ma would never believe it.

Hearing the door open, he looked up.

"Ma! Busha said something."

"You're imagining, Frankie. After all these years, what would she say?"

"It sounded like...dialbo." Frankie shuddered.

"No, Frankie, no...it can't be. Why after so many years would she suddenly speak? And dialbo...of all words. Why would she be thinking about the devil?"

Frankie shrugged. "But, Ma...there was life in her eyes when she watched me...like *hate.* I couldn't believe it, Ma."

Catherine went to the cot and knelt down.

"Busha?" She whispered softly as she passed her hand across the old woman's forehead. Once more, the eyes were expressionless.

Frankie watched. It struck him how gentle and considerate Ma was with Busha. He wondered how Ma could still act that way toward Busha after so many years of painstaking care. Then Catherine rose and moved toward the kitchen.

Catherine sighed...a long, wistful sigh.

"It was a strange accident of fate," she said. "Busha's nothing now. Come, we must eat."

"I'm not hungry now, Ma. I'll sit on the porch awhile."

"Frankie, you've seen everything."

"Yeah. I've seen everything." Still, Frankie knew he had to go back out there. "I'll be in soon."

With the blaze dead and gone, the air was much cooler. Occasionally, sparks flew up from the rubble like short-lived fireflies. The last fireman mounted the back of the engine as it pulled away and North Avenue assumed the silence of a cemetery for awhile.

Frankie dug his hands deep into his pockets and crossed the street. He started toward the rubble, then backed away. Schmelling's ashes mingled with wood ash? He couldn't step there. It felt disrespectful.

Suddenly, a voice mingled with Frankie's melancholy.

"I knew you'd be here Frankie."

It was Vera's voice floating into his thoughts.

"God A'mighty...Schmelling..I can't believe it."

Vera was crying softly. Without looking at her, Frankie put his arm around her shoulder and they stood silently staring for quite awhile, sharing their grief, warmth flowing like waters from a summer stream - from one to the other.

"Frankie, walk me home, huh?"

They walked toward the corner. Vera took Frankie's arm and let her head rest on his shoulder.

## CHAPTER 14

When the trolley stopped, Elinora lumbered down the steps.

"Jan, did you see that? Sure...fire...Frankie Jagienczak's working place, I think. Bad. But what else did you see, Jan, hmmmmm? I'm sure it was Frankie with that red-head. Over by the street lamp. Older than him, I think. Humph! Poor Milia. Hard for those kids. Could you wait like that, Jan? No, no, I know you couldn't. Hmmm? No, no, nothing to Emilia. I will watch my tongue, Jan."

Elinora entered the hallway and mounted the steps to Noshkins' Office.

"Jan, should I tell Noshkins? No? All right, I will be quiet. I will say nothing."

Elinora opened the door to the waiting room and sat down...all alone...though she very carefully left the seat next to her vacant for the dead husband whom she carried in her heart with her...everywhere she went.

*****************

Vera stopped. Frankie looked up the long flight of stairs. It seemed funny he never knew exactly where Vera lived. It was like that in the neighborhood. Friends knew everything - acquaintances, little. Even now, he knew only that this was Vera's building; he didn't know which flat.

"What're ya gonna do now, Vera? 'Bout a job, I mean."

"I hafta find somethin' right away. I'll look in the paper tamarra."

"They're hiring women at my place, Vera."

"Oh, Frankie! Couldja gimma directions?"

"Yeah."

"Come on up fer a cupa coffee, huh?"

"Well..." Frankie looked up and down the street, furtively. "I could give 'em to ya right now."

"Hey, Frankie." There was hurt in Vera's eyes. She looked away from him and spoke again. "Oh, God! I feel so bad. Please come up, Frankie. I needa talk to some-buddy fer awhile."

"Sure."

Frankie understood Vera's hurt...her need to be with someone...someone from the factory...someone who understood how good Schmelling had been to all of them. Yes, Frankie understood. He was hurting too. Maybe they could help one another.

Vera led the way up the stairs, and Frankie followed.

The hallway was lit by a green-shaded bulb hanging from the ceiling. Their shad-ows, cast in grotesque caricature, preceded them up the stairs.

"We gotta climb some more. I got me a little attic flat."

With every creak of the stairs, Frankie felt a twinge of guilt. But why? Vera felt bad tonight. So did he. There was nothing wrong with him going up to tell her where to find a new job. Anyhow, he'd been sitting out a long time today, a warm cup of coffee would go good.

"I can't stay long, Vera."

"That's aw right, Frankie. I just needa be with somebuddy fer a little while."

It was one big room she had, with a bathroom in the dormer - no tub. It was nice...green skirt around the kitchen sink, green curtains, a little table with drop leaves and two chairs. A dark green mohair sofa and a screen separated her brass bed, bureau and mirror from the rest of the room. Nice...small but comfortable.

"Sit, Frankie. Naw, not by the table...on the sofa. Softer."

It was very comfortable. He was tired. Right after the coffee, he'd leave.

Vera moved around the kitchen end of the room softly...like her feet were gliding. She must like green, Frankie thought. Lots of green in the room, and she was wearing green...a skirt that showed the tops of her shoes...with a pretty white blouse...and no shop apron. The guys were right about Vera. She was built. Vera tossed her red curls back and wiped the sweat from her neck with a handkerchief. She smiled at Frankie as she balanced two coffee cups, and swayed toward him. Such a beautiful rhythmic walk.

"Here's yer coffee, Sir. I'll getcha piecea cake."

Her little bow...her mock politeness...it made them both laugh.

"Naw. Thanks, Vera. No cake."

Vera sat on the other end of the sofa. The coffee was good. He kept thinking about everything. He didn't know what to say to Vera.

"Schmelling? D'ya know for sure?"

"Yeah, Frankie. He wouldn't leave until he was sure everyone got outa th' place."

"God, Vera. How'd it start?"

"Here, gimme yer cup." She put everything on the table and sat on the sofa again.

"I guess the trouble started a couple days ago when the old guy Schmelling hired to take yer place hada quit becuz he kept gettin' sick. Then this new guy came...twenty-five...six..mebbe and Schmelling hired him cuz he needed someone right away."

"What was his name? Anybody we know?"

"Na. Name was Victor Jarro. Said he came from the west side. Well, he started causin' trouble right away."

"How? What d'ja mean?"

"Always had somethin' to say about Schmelling...the rest of us too. Finally, him and Big Jash got into it. Then Victor called Schmelling a dirty name and Jash let him have it. Schmelling called the guys inta his office, and then Victor left."

"What d'ya mean...left?"

"Canned. He hada go."

"That's not like Schmelling." Frankie was puzzled. He looked at Vera's face. She swallowed hard, like she didn't want to cry anymore. Frankie reached over to pat her hand. Breathing a sad sigh, Vera moved closer to Frankie and put her head on his shoulder.

"Yeah, I know. Schmelling always gave everybody another chance...but we don't know what happened after Jash left the office. Only thing was, Victor stayed longer, then came out, got his stuff...and...and..."

Vera's words muffled against Frankie's sleeve; he felt the wetness of her tears on his arm as he waited for her to finish.

"Frankie...then he threatened. He said he'd get even with that dirty Heinie SOB...he'd get even with all of us. He was ravin' mad when Jash chased him outa the place."

"Vera, are you sayin' maybe the fire wasn't an accident?" Frankie placed his hand under her chin raising her head, forcing Vera to look at him. A line creased her forehead and tears streamed down her cheeks. She didn't answer, but he knew from the look on her face.

"Oh, God! Oh, my God...Schmelling killed by the skunk that took my place. Oh, Jesus." Frankie rose, began pacing back and forth, rubbing his hands through his hair.

"If I wouldn'ta left, Schmelling might be alive."

Vera watched him, compassion spilling from her eyes.

"Oh, God. All those years he helped my Ma...our whole family. He gave me a job when no one else would because I was so young. Sometimes, I used to think maybe he'd marry my Ma someday. And now...oh, God...my God...it's all my fault."

Vera saw his pain; her heart ached for him. Then, rushing to Frankie, Vera pried his hands away from his face, put her arms around him...soothed him...so gently. And like a boy, he held fast to her, needing her then, so much, forgetting where he was, and whose lips he'd suddenly found to comfort him, whose warm, soft, sweet smelling body melted into his.

*****************

Frankie knew as he strained to see the wall clock, that they'd lain together a long while afterwards, but as Vera left his side and reached for her robe, he snapped his eyes shut feeling as if he must get out of there, yet lingering, though not wanting again to see any part of that lovely generous body. He mustn't compound his crime. It was done. Oh, God, it was done. But never again...never...not with anyone but his Mil. He moved his head to the side, feeling the dampness on the pillow where their tears mingled. They'd shared so much, physically he felt relieved, but now...the thought of Mil who had wanted so much to see him tonight...the thought of her...he heard a sob; he knew it came from him.

"Frankie...don't."

He pulled away from her, conscious of his nakedness, fumbling for his clothes.

"Please Frankie. I don't wantcha ta think it was like this with all them other guys."

Rushing to ready himself, he tried to shut her words out. There was no explanation for the wrong he did. All this time he'd waited for his Mil...to hold her...only her...now this. What would God do to punish him? What if He let Mil die! Mil...how could he ever touch her again...how. He'd given in to his pitifully weak, throbbing body like a dog in heat. Oh, he had to get home...to wash himself clean of this. He had to hurry.

"Frankie...Frankie...you can't go like this," Vera pressed her body against the door, her robe falling open, but Frankie pushed her aside.

"Frankie...I understand...I wouldn't take you from your Milia...it just happened...we needed...something...someone..."

Vera fell to the floor, crying...as she heard the street door below slam shut.

"Oh, God," she whispered, "take care a the kid."

******************

Frankie ran down the street...stumbling...crying...hardly noticing the big woman lumbering toward him.

"Frankie, Jan said it was you coming...he said this was your shop, huh?"

Frankie didn't stop for Elinora; he never heard her words. Somehow, he ran across the street, stumbled up the stairs, and fell into the house. Catherine called to him from her room. She was rocking slowly back and forth in her rocker as she worked a piece of knitting.

"Yeah, it's me, Ma. I'm back from a walk."

"You were gone a long time, for walking."

"Yeah. I'm tired. I'm gonna get ready for bed."

"So early?"

Frankie didn't answer. He merely closed the bathroom door, eliminating further conversation. He washed once, then twice...pulled his robe tightly around himself, as he passed through the dining room to his own bed.

Bŭsha stared at him. He remembered how she'd called him a devil. Oh, God, in her silent way had she known what terrible thing he would do tonight? What could he do now? What could he do?

Pressing his eyes tightly shut, Frankie tried to clear his head, to will sleep, instead tears streamed from beneath his lids like water from an open faucet. Mil...Mil...how could he ever touch her again? He tried to picture her, but instead he saw Vera's red head, soft round arms, rosy white throat, the beautiful mounds of her breasts...and...and...oh God, no...no...let him forget.

And Vera? What of her? What had he done to her? Nothing, his mind shouted. Nothing. Hadn't she been teasing...wanting...setting him up? But no...not tonight... tonight was different. It just happened. Still, he owed her something. What? The factory address. She needed a job. He would write down the directions, and leave them under her door. He would do it early in the morning. Then he wouldn't have to see her. He couldn't see her...he couldn't...

## CHAPTER 15

Frankie was tired. He'd worked overtime for two reasons: to earn more money and to avoid Vera. By working later, he accomplished both.

Frankie was glad Vera had landed the job at Crane's, nevertheless, seeing her so often was driving him crazy. Vera seemed to love him, but he certainly didn't love her, in spite of that night after Schmelling's fire and death, and though he didn't love her, he still wanted her. To complicate matters, Vera had a way of looking at him that said she wanted Frankie too. It was a dangerous situation, and he knew it. If only he knew, in real terms, how long it would be before he and Mil could have a normal life together. If only he had a definite time limit to hang onto for moral support.

Frankie rubbed his eyes as though trying to rub out any memory of Vera as he quickened his pace. One more corner to round and he would be home. He hadn't bothered to transfer streetcars this evening, just as he hadn't for the past three weeks. It felt good to walk the last three blocks home. Then, very abruptly, Frankie stopped.

Again, the poster stared at him, just as it had for the past three weeks. Again, Uncle Sam was accusing him...pointing at him...demanding he come. Frankie stared back at the poster, then suddenly he knew what he must do. Uncle Sam had the answer for him, so there would be no more of Vera's silent pleading eyes surreptitiously searching him out at the factory, pushing into his thoughts as he labored at his machine; no more of Mil's hurt, angry confusion as she reached for him, phoned him, begged explanations for his distance...his outright absence. Sometimes it seemed they fought an emotional duel over him...Mil and Vera...as he tried to separate them and drive them from his mind. It became harder and harder to concentrate on his job. It was Mil he loved and wanted...that hadn't changed. Mil was still the girl he wanted to hold and touch and spend the rest of his life with, but he kept remembering the night he turned to Vera. That night haunted him...ghostlike...a ghost coming to chain his soul. But Vera was the first woman he'd ever lain with, the first woman to answer his manly needs, and now he looked away from her, hoping she would realize that he could never truly love her, not the way he loved Mil.

Again, he focused on the poster. Yes, he knew what he must do. Frankie opened the wooden door with its ornate oval of glass and entered the office feeling the urgency of quick motion engulfing him as the sounds of many voices pierced the air and questionnaires appeared to be deftly processed. Irrelevantly, he thought with surprise about the large numbers of women working everywhere...at the factory - here - in the shops lining the streets. It seemed to him, as manpower went away, woman power came forward.

Hurriedly, he moved on to the nearest desk and addressed the pert young woman seated there. She seemed to anticipate his words.

"I wanna enlist."

******************

Frankie wished the ride to Mil's would last forever. He rehearsed different ways of telling her what he'd done, but none seemed right. If only he could tell her about Vera - but he couldn't - not without losing her, so any explanation he attempted, sounded empty. Mil would never know how miserable he felt...or why. Vera's very existence was unknown to her, so how could Mil understand the burden of shame he felt when even, accidentally, he glimpsed Vera's quickly moving ankles. And poor Vera...she alternated these days between avoiding him and secretly watching him, between eating outside at the other end of the building, and laughing gayly as soon as she saw him anywhere near, as though wanting him to think everything was fine and she was totally untouched by their experience. By her actions he knew that wasn't true. He knew...he felt...he remembered that night, and how she told him it was different. Funny, he hadn't really been cognizant of her words then, but now, his memory tortured him constantly. Why was God asking so much pain of him - for just one mistake? Why? If only he could be sure he was buying Mil's life with his pain, then he would suffer gladly. Please God, take his shame and his pain, and don't let Mil suffer...or die.

******************

Mil was busily engaged in making herself look healthy...pinching her cheeks, biting her lips, rearranging her curls saucily, to frame her face in the fashion of the models in recent magazines, but nothing seemed to help. The hand mirror merely confirmed the visual facts...deep bluish circles under her eyes...boney pallor...worried countenance. Listlessly, Mil dropped the hand mirror on her bed, and sobbed into her hands.

"Oh, God, please, please...don't let me lose Frankie. If he doesn't want me, let me die..."

Then a light knocking sound at the back door tapped its way into her consciousness. She pulled a handkerchief from under her pillow and dabbed her face. Maybe it was Frankie! "Mama..." she called.

Then remembering the family had gone to Ludmilla's to keep her company, Emilia rose, steadied herself on the table and answered the door.

"Elinora...Mama isn't home."

"Oh..." She sounded so disappointed.

"They went to Ludmilla's...so she wouldn't be alone on the night of her wedding anniversary."

"Alone?" Elinora sounded confused.

"Remember? Frank, her husband, is in the army now."

"Oh, sure...well, Jan and I, we come just for a short visit. Sometimes, my Jan, he needs to get out, you know?"

Oh, dear Lord, she was still talking to a Jan who wasn't there. She guessed Noshkins couldn't do anything for Elinora. When Frankie arrived, she didn't want Elinora there with them, but the woman looked so lonely and confused that Mil suddenly felt sorry for her.

"Elinora, come in for a few minutes...until Frankie comes."

"Oh, your Frankie is still visiting?" She sounded surprised.

The question angered Mil. "He's my husband! Even if he can't live here right now..." Tears welled and spilled.

Elinora didn't seem to notice, she merely followed Mil to the back porch where they settled - Mil on the bed and Elinora on a chair nearby.

"Your Frankie...I wondered if he comes anymore...Jan and I we see Frankie with...hmmmmm? What you say, Jan?"

Panic flashed from Mil's eyes. "Elinora, finish!"

"What...finish?"

"Where did you see Frankie...when...tonight?"

"No, no, Jan and I, we see Frankie with...with tears we see him..when his shop burn down."

"Tears for his shop?"

It was a dull questioning echo, then Mil's eyes flashed, looking deeper set in their blue sockets, and her voice rose. "Tears for his shop! He feels for everyone...everything...but me. Mrs. Frankie Jagienczak..huh!"

She hurled the little hand mirror across the porch watching it splinter like the fragments of her life.

"Bad luck...you will bring to yourself bad luck from breaking your mirror."

"My luck can't get any worse, do you hear, Elinora? It can't get any worse!" Again, she sobbed into her hands.

The back door opened, and Elinora turned to see Frankie standing there. He looked from Mil to Elinora and back to Mil, eyes narrowed. Vaguely, he remembered passing Elinora the night he went to Vera's. Fear stiffened him, and silenced his tongue.

Mil turned to him, wondering why he just stood there. Wasn't he concerned about her? Didn't he wonder why she was upset? He made no attempt to move toward her. Indeed, he had stopped caring. Everything between them was gone...she knew it now.

Elinora spoke first. "Come Frankie, hold your wife. She is worried."

"Worried? Why? What did you tell her?"

"We don't talk yet. Jan and I, we just come in."

Frankie hesitated.

"Come, Frankie. Sit by your Milia...she needs you much."

Slowly, he came to the porch and pulled a chair close to the bed. Mil pulled back stiffly. Elinora sighed.

"You know...Jan, he is my third man. We are good for each other, and we love much. Never do we go to bed mad. The bed is for us a beautiful playground where we can forget all of the bad things that happen to us in a day. It was long...a long time before we learned this.

"My second man, Albert, I divorced him. Many, many days sometimes, we would go to bed mad, and then in the morning, we couldn't talk to each other and the next night, we would stay far apart. It was not good.

"And my first man? Mmmmmm, he was beautiful...full of fun...always laughing...always friendly...loving...everybody loved him. One time, I passed the tavern when I was going to the store. I looked in and he was sitting there, next to a pretty girl. She smiled at him and leaned closer, rubbed his neck. He smiled. I felt fear, but I didn't go inside to say something. He didn't come home that night. The next day, I was mean to him. He asked forgiveness, and I wouldn't give it to him. Every day it was worse for us until he stopped asking forgiveness, and then he stopped coming home. I got a divorce from him. The neighbors talked, and I cried much. I remember many times, my first man. He was a good man, and I loved him very much, but I didn't make things right with him. I was too proud. Too late I found, to be proud is to be cold."

Elinora reached over, and placed Frankie's hand on Mil's.

"Come, Jan. I think we must go."

They sat in silence for awhile, Mil watching Frankie's pained face as he stared at the mirror splinters. What was he thinking, she wondered.

"Frankie, do you love me?"

"Oh, God, Mil...only you." He buried his face in her small, perfect bosom.

Gently, she pet his head.

"What's wrong, Frankie?"

"Mil, I don't know how to tell ya."

"Just start, I promise to listen."

"Mil...Mil...I...I enlisted..." Frankie's head bowed to his chest. He couldn't look at Mil.

The sound of the pendulum on the kitchen clock seemed loud as a striking hammer in the tense stillness of the room.

Mil pushed Frankie away from her and looked into his face.

"Enlisted?"

There was no anger in her face; Frankie felt some sense of relief. Then as a look of pain and hurt began pushing its way between them, covering Mil's first quizzical confusion, he winced and backed away. Mil slumped down into the pillows and blankets, turned her face to the wall and cried, softly at first, then louder.

He knelt beside her. "Mil, Honey, please don't."

She looked at him, fury firing her eyes. "Liar!" She began pounding her fists on his chest. "Liar! Liar! Liar!"

Astonished, he grabbed her arms, marveling at the strength of this girl-woman.

"Mil, please..."

"How could you? Just minutes ago you told me you loved me...no one but me...Liar!"

"Mil, please...Honey, listen to me."

Then as suddenly as it opened, the eye of Mil's storm closed, and nothing was left but a quiet resigned rain of tears. Mil's arms went limp. Her eyes were glazed and dull as Frankie cupped his big hands around her face and kissed her forehead, her nose, her cheeks, then pressed her head to his shoulder.

"Honey, please listen...try to understand. I do love ya...so much I hada enlist. I can't go it this way. I love ya so much I can't stand to live away from ya, not be able to touch ya...Holdja...love ya. It's my fault, I know, but now we're married, I can't keep the arrangement. Don't ya see, Mil? I love ya more than anything, and I can't live this way no more."

As though he used a soothing balm on her hurt, Mil turned shining eyes toward him. She couldn't speak.

"And, Mil, in some way, I hafta be a man."

"Oh, Frankie, Frankie, what am I doing to you?"

"It's not you, Honey, it's life. Everything's so hard...but we're young, and when I come back, you'll be well...I know."

"When you come back...yes...oh but, Frankie, what if..."

Her unfinished words caused pain, but the pain, like a chain bound them together. She hoped they'd be bound forever.

After a while, Mil clasped her arms around Frankie's neck, and pressed her lips to his in a way she never had before. Gently, but willfully she pulled him down on the bed next to her. She was his wife. He couldn't leave her without knowing it. As he held her close, and touched her again, she knew there was no turning back for either of them. She had never felt so warm, so alive. Oh, God, she would get well, and Frankie would come back to her. This wasn't the end for them...it had to be the beginning. Then she stopped thinking, and gave herself to feeling...feeling a rhythmic rise and fall...rise and fall. Over and over again, she felt washed and rinsed by feelings rising and falling like powerful waves covering her. Then, finally, ebbing, they lapped gently to oblivion. She was Frankie's wife. She had never known anything like these moments, and instinctively, she knew she never would again, not if God allowed them to come together for years unending. Never again could it feel like this.

They spoke little for the rest of their time together, just lay side by side covered by a kind of contentment new to both of them.

When Frankie left, he kissed her lips so tenderly, with a strange always-never-kiss filled with promise, fulfillment, sadness...with contradictions she couldn't understand.

He tucked the blankets carefully around her and walked away. She shuddered. As Frankie walked across the kitchen to the door, she saw not the swagger of a boy fulfilled, but the walk of a man, feeling something so deep, so foreign to her, she felt she would never be allowed to understand. Frankie...oh Frankie...

The door closed but she continued to lay on her bed a little longer, savoring her thoughts and feelings, the remembrance of her pleasure. Then after a while, hearing footsteps on the back stairs, she rose, went to the bathroom, closed the door, hugged herself joyfully, and smiled.

******************

Frankie closed the front door quietly. It was late and he preferred not to talk to anyone. How differently he felt this time as he readied for bed. After Vera, he tried to wash even her scent away, now he stood...wishing he never had to wash again...wishing he could keep close to him everything about his Mil. Oh, they were meant for each other. They felt and moved as one. But he had to go away from her. They were wrong to do this tonight. Noshkins wouldn't approve. Mil wasn't well enough and he knew it. Somehow, it had just happened between them, as it had with Vera. What was wrong with him suddenly? For eighteen years he'd lived like a monk...and now two women within a short time, hurting both because though he had a right to one of them, his sense of right and duty would allow him neither. His Mil, she needed him and wanted him as much as he did her, especially tonight when she knew he would go away. If only he hadn't been unfaithful. And what if a baby would come! Oh God! But no, it couldn't happen her very first time, and in her weakened condition. No, that was a foolish thought deserving only to be pushed out of his mind.

And Vera? She was smart. She wouldn't have a baby. But what of her and her hurt? In a way, she loved him too. He knew she would take him without strings, whenever he would allow. Vera, with her rosy white skin, her rounded sensual body, cat-like rhythm. How well he remembered her slow, giving desire.

But his Mil, so creamy white, so alive, amazed by the sudden bloom of a demanding passion. How he adored her! Still, he felt for Vera. Frankie pressed his hands to his eyes, as though trying to shut out the world. What had he done? What had he done! Ah yes, he had enlisted, and when he returned, everything would be better. Perhaps Vera would marry and move away while he was gone.

As he passed the dining room, Busha glared at him, again with some feeling in her usually vacant eyes. He rushed past to the bedroom he used, now Ed was gone, and wished himself to sleep. He wouldn't have many more days to avoid Vera, and he mustn't allow himself the privilege of Mil again, not until his return. Besides, they would probably not have the opportunity to be alone again.

## CHAPTER 16

Mil walked slowly up and down the red bricks, clinging to Frankie's packet of letters as tightly as a nun holding a missal, hopping a little at times the way she and her sisters had done years ago as young children when playing follow-the-leader. Suddenly, she yearned to see Florchak, so they could share secrets once more, share their feelings of happiness and sadness, but Florchak was also married, just as Mil was, and now Florchak lived far away in Indiana. Just the other day, Florchak's mother had proudly announced to Mil's family, the news of Florchak's pregnancy.

Hugging Frankie's letters closer to her bosom, Mil continued to walk up and down the brick walk, noticing the beauty of the day. Everything was still so colorful, it was hard to believe the cold gray winter would soon be upon them. Mums, marigolds, and asters bordered the green-brown October grass with deep yellows, oranges, and blues. Occasionally, bright marigold heads pushed their way between the red bricks, swaying slightly in the breezes like ballet dancers on stage. Carefully, Mil stepped over them. She had asked Tata not to pull these little dancers from their place in the sunlight, for they were her companions on her daily walks through the garden. The blue sky looked so intense, like a protective mother shielding her world of beloved living things against the feathering white cloud cover of winter storms to come. The generous poplars, so heavily covered with whispering leaves...those trees which she so dearly loved...had shed much of their crunchy golden-brown glory, stretching baring arms to heaven as though helping Mil with her prayers.

Mil walked down the bricks toward the alley, hoping to see some sign of a visitor, one of her sisters, perhaps. She looked past the gate at the cracked dry clay dirt of the deserted alley floor and sighed deeply. Somewhere in the distance, she heard the clomp, clomp of a vendor's horse. Turning back, she stepped cautiously around several loose protruding bricks.

Seven months ago she had become Mrs. Frankie Jagienczak. So many things had happened since then - new things. Even her name was new, for both families had decided to anglicize against the unbearable discrimination bedeviling all nationalities. She was now Mrs. Frankie Jagien, and Mama, Tata and the boys had become Kazmiers - much to Tata's resentment. Tata had finally agreed to the change when the boys appealed to his patriotism. With "ski" on the end of his name it was impossible to blend into the new "melting pot" concept...to become one of the new generation of Americans fighting for a great and lasting peace that would end all wars forever. Tata grumbled and resisted...finally, relented.

There were new magazines, newspapers, new discoveries and inventions, abbreviated new fashions...shorter skirts with less fullness. And the NEW YORK TIMES with its brown-tinted pictures in the rotogravure brought the war closer to home for all of them. On Sundays, she studied the pictures of the Yankee doughboys in France, hoping to see someone she knew...her Frankie, or her brother Walter, or perhaps Frankie's brother Ed, or Ludmilla's Frank. Recently, Kate's husband Hank was added to the ranks. Did Frankie know they were married? She wasn't even sure of that. Sometimes, letters to the fighting boys were delayed...even lost.

She'd always thought France must be an extraordinarily beautiful country, but the Sunday papers didn't picture it that way. American doughboys were always surrounded by clouds of dust, trains, and artillery. Occasionally there were forest trees in the background, but nothing picturesque.

Mother Jagien subscribed to the ILLUSTRATED REVIEW - for fifty cents a year. It had so many pictures of all these new things and many pictures of the war. It also had those dreadful lists of names...soldiers missing...wounded...dead. Mil hated those pages of names, but she loved seeing some of the pictures. And when Mother Jagien brought the magazine, Mil could breathe easily, because that meant Frankie's name didn't appear on any of the lists. Mother J. would come some Sunday, or some evening, smiling and carrying the magazine and then Mil knew Frankie was all right.

Her Frankie. Where was he now? What was he doing? Did he remember their wonderful togetherness, that magic time when they truly became husband and wife? Her pace slowed to a stop and she rubbed her tummy. The sickness had caused her periods to be unpredictably irregular, but in the four months that Frankie was gone, she'd only come around once, and that was very lightly...about two months ago, it was. Noshkins hadn't noticed anything, at least he hadn't made any comments about changes. Of course, he came only once every two weeks now that she was so much improved. Despite the improvement she was afraid to ask him if she could be pregnant. What if she were and he wanted to take the baby away because of her illness? She'd heard of such things. She knew she was not yet cured, though Noshkins marveled at the suddenness with which she was gaining strength. Of course, she knew in her heart why she was better, but she couldn't possibly tell him. Even though Frankie was gone, she now knew precisely what she had to live for, and she would. Yes, she would be alive and healthy for Frankie when he returned.

She sat on the bench under the rose trellis. It reminded her of Mama, past blossoming, but with a full rich foliage that came only after a full season of life. Her in-process knitting waited on the bench as always, and with a slight grudge, she picked it up and worked on it. Never did she think knitting would become an all consuming pastime. One thing was certain, after this war, she would never knit another pair of sox. But it was interesting to think about how many boys were wearing her sox, boys who didn't even know her. All those unknown boys were her main impetus, though the "knit your bit" slogans she saw and heard everywhere also played a part. Well, next time, for change of pace, it would have to be a sweater.

Sparrows flew about chirping noisily as her needles clicked. Pleasant sounds. After a while, she set the knitting aside once more and reread Frankie's letters, though she knew them all by heart. In her ribboned packet were only ten letters. Ten letters in four months, a low tally. When she allowed herself to think about it, she felt frightened, for the infrequent letters indicated to her how busy Frankie must be, and she was afraid to dwell on what sorts of things kept him so well occupied. What must it be like to fight a war...face gunfire...see death. He must have lived a lifetime in the four months he'd been a soldier. They'd kept him at Camp Grant in Rockford only six weeks before sending him to Camp Upton all the way in New York. Then, after three more weeks, they'd sent him all the way to France with Pershing and the First Division. Now it was the end of October and she hadn't heard from him for a month. She was so worried...so frightened. Descriptions of his living area overseas were frequently interrupted by the censor's scissor, though as she progressed from the first letter to the last, there were fewer holes. She didn't care much for those parts of the letters anyway, since she knew Frankie was in France. That was enough knowledge for her. She didn't want to learn things that would make her worry more. There was no point to worrying since she was too far away to be of any help. Her prayers were with Frankie always, no matter where he was, whether in France, or on North Avenue, or in his factory on the south side. Now, over and over she read the parts of the letters truly meant for her, those parts that told how much Frankie loved her. *That* was important to her. *That* was her world.

"Milia!"

"Yes, Mama."

"I go to store now...maybe stop at Elinora's house for minute. You be all right?"

"Yes, Mama."

Mil carefully made a bow in her pink ribbon, keeping her links to Frankie tightly secured, then she went inside. She was still sleeping on the back porch, covered by a pierzyna and a wool blanket these cold October nights - with windows partially open. Putting the letters back under her pillow, to keep them close all night might help bring precious dreams of dearest Frankie. Tenderly, she ran her hands over the bed, remembering. Then, rubbing her tummy, she stretched out for a few moments, and closed her eyes, hoping to sleep a little, but instead, she frowned and tossed. Giving up, she opened the kitchen door and went inside. It was quiet. She knew no one was home, but nevertheless, she listened cautiously and looked into each room. No one...good. She moved on to the bathroom, closed the door and locked it. It was a large room for the limited activity taking place in it. The mirror was wide, situated over the sink, across from the toilet. She unbuttoned her sweater, folded it, and lay it neatly over the rim of the tub. Then she proceeded to remove the rest of her clothing, folding and setting it aside. She looked down at her stomach. It did seem swollen...a little. Could she be carrying a baby? A part of herself and Frankie? Four months...she hadn't felt any life. Maybe it was still too early. She was afraid to ask her sisters for fear they would suspect something. Should she ask Noshkins when he came next? She closed the toilet seat, stepped on it, stood sideways and examined her reflection in the mirror. She did seem to have more fullness, but then she'd also gained five pounds. If she were pregnant, they'd all be mad at her. If she had a baby, Frankie would come home to two people instead of one, though they'd never had much chance to be husband and wife. Would he mind? Maybe she was wrong to love him that night. No, it was the right thing to do. Definitely. What if something happened? What if Frankie didn't come home? Oh God, don't let her think that way. Of course he would come home. But if something did happen, at least she had the memory of his love, and perhaps a part of him. She must ask Noshkins about this, even if he scolded, she must ask. He was due tomorrow.

One last look, then she stepped down and into her chemise, then the rest of her clothing, and finally the sweater. There was no resting now. She would go back outside.

Passing through the kitchen, she stopped in the pantry for an apple. The brown bag of peach and apricot pits still stood on the shelf. She must ask Mama to turn them in. They were so badly needed for making gas mask filters. Carefully, she closed the bag and tied it with string, setting it on the kitchen table where it would be seen and remembered. Then she set another bag on the shelf to collect any pits from preserves they might eat.

Once more out in the garden, she settled herself under the trellis, dropped her apple core, and making a wry face, took up her knitting. Lost in worrisome thoughts, she hadn't noticed Mother Jagien until she'd been standing in quiet observation for some minutes. Mil looked up, but her smile of greeting froze into place like something a young child might have scratched into the face of a snow lady.

Mother Jagien's face was serious...no sparkle in her almond eyes as they fastened their steady gaze to Mil's questioning eyes. Thoughts darted through Mil's head like blind, frightened bats. It wasn't Sunday. There was no magazine in Mother's hands. She gasped: Oh, God, something happened to Ed. Was it Ed? Maybe Hank. Please God, let it be anyone but Frankie. Why didn't she move? Why was she standing there like some frightening apparition in a nightmare? Why was she here on a weekday afternoon? She never left her work at the tailor shop without grave reason. Grave reason...grave reason...grave reason...the words turned round and round in her head like a phonograph record stuck in one place. Oh, Dear Jesus Christ, God Almighty, make her move, make her talk, make her smile. Smile! Smile! Damn her! Smile!

There was no smile. Mil stood, knitting tumbling to the browning grass. Without a word, they came together...clasped tightly. She felt Mother Jagien's shoulders begin to quiver, and then Mil screamed, and screamed, and screamed. Back porch windows opened and neighbor's heads appeared, then silently withdrew when they saw Frankie's women standing together that way.

Together, they sat under the rose trellis. It was some time before Mother Jagien was able to calm Mil enough to speak to her of what she knew. Two weeks ago, they found Frankie's name listed with those missing in the ILLUSTRATED REVIEW. They prayed and didn't tell Mil, hoping there would be no need. They wouldn't chance a relapse without positive proof. They contacted the Red Cross to see if they would get further information. However, this morning, the special letter came, signed by Col. James. It told them Frankie was dead. The Army was sorry. Frankie'd been brave. His identification and pay book were found next to his body. Frankie was dead. Killed in his first battle.

They were crazy words that took only a few breaths to tell. Mil tried to push them from her mind. Of course, it really didn't matter. Mil knew they weren't true. Oh, but Mother J. waited so long to tell her. If she'd known about the list, she could have prayed harder. Why did Mother wait so long? She knew. Mother told her why. But what now? And why did the army notify Mother rather than Mil? She was Frankie's wife. She should have been the first to know. It was her right! She should have been first! First? Crazy. Why should she want to be first to hear such news? She passed her hand over her eyes. What did it matter. What did any of it matter now. Oh Frankie...Frankie...Frankie...

Strange sounds echoed round in her head. Could they be coming from her?

Somehow, they'd moved back into the house, and Momchu was there, holding Mil and petting her, crooning softly to her as Mil clung with all her might. Dusk was beginning to cover the world and Catherine went home, but Michalina continued to hold Mil, making no move to begin supper for Tata and Harry.

"Momchu, why? Why now, when I'm better?"

"Ach, Dziecko. Who can say?"

"God. He can say! What kind of "thing" is He?"

"Milia! No! Is sin to talk so."

"Sin, Mama? No. It's a sin what He's done to me! What did I ever do to Him? What did Frankie ever do?"

"Maybe He take Frankie's life for yours. Maybe Frankie asks Him this."

"That's a crazy bargain, Mama!" Her words came between gulping sobs. "A crazy bargain..."

Mil's arms wrapped so tightly about Michalina she could hardly breathe. The steady ticking of the clock pendulum filtered to them through the glass with hypnotic regularity.

"Mama...I think I'm going to have our baby."

Michalina's arms tightened, but she said nothing.

"Mama? Did you hear me?"

Michalina drew in her breath sharply. "Ya, Dziecko. Ya, I hear."

"Say something, Mama. Say something!"

Michalina grasped at her flying thoughts. How could this be? When could this happen? Never were they alone together. Ach...sometime...yes...but she couldn't remember. So, what difference it makes. Is Milia, her baby, now with baby of her own. Is Frankie now dead. What to say? What is to say? Ah, yes, Tadeiusz Konarowski. Milia doesn't know about him. So far in Wisconsin they live. Milia doesn't know of his story. Not always do children want to hear old country stories. Michalina decided to try.

"Milia, I tell you story about Uncle Tadeiusz. You must listen, ya? Is important."

"I don't care, Mama. Tell me if you want, but first, Mama, do you hate me? Do you think I'm bad?"

"Bad to haf your Frankie's baby? No, Milia. But you must eat good. You must take care. Get well."

"Yes, Mama." There was a small silence between them. "But Mama, if God makes bargains, I'll tell Him now. He can have this baby back, if He'll give Frankie back to me."

"Ach, Milia, don't talk such. Listen now to me."

"Tell the story, Mama. I'll try to listen. But you have to know. God has to know. I'll do anything. Anything at all!"

Mil knew Mama had some point to make with her story, and she needed something else to think about, so she might as well listen. She concentrated hard on this uncle of whom she'd never heard, hoping to hear some magic that would help her.

"In Poland, we are peasants, living in country outside Cracow. We haf only small cottage - one big room, with dirt floor, thatched roof, und furniture hand made by mine step-father. He was good to mine half-brother Tadeiusz and me after our Mother dies, but he was no longer healthy. We peasants were released from slavery, and able to own small plot of land and little cottage. Tadeiusz, Father and I, we worked land together, raised most of food we eat, sold some little...what we could...in city now and again.

"It wasn't bad life, and not educated like great men in Cracow, we not worry much about world around us once we have freedom. Always was political troubles in Poland, and often soldiers come to take young men to army.

"Tadeiusz and I, we had job of taking vegetables to market for selling. We had small wood cart and old horse to take down little dirt road to Cracow. It was good flat road, and we can see for long way. Sometimes, there are trees and we rest and talk in shade. We are young...I - eighteen, Tadeiusz - seventeen, and we do this for many years already, so we are not afraid, even when many times soldiers march by to drill. But every year, there are more soldiers, and when Tadeiusz grows older, they watch more carefully.

"One day, when we are sitting under big shady oak tree, soldiers come by and they stop. Sergeant talks to Taddy, to ask where he lives, how old he is. He smiles, and they go on. We sell vegetables, but Taddy tells me he is afraid. He doesn't want to be soldier, to fight and kill for Austria. He can't do this...too much he loves life. He worries because sergeant talks to him, asks questions, and because other peasants...the boys...go to army without warning. On way home, he is quiet. Next day, when we are working in garden, we hear sounds, like horses coming, not old horses like peasant horses. Taddy looks to me, and then he goes to house.

"In minutes, the soldiers come, on big beautiful horses. They call to me and ask for Taddy. I say he is gone to little lake few miles from us to fish for supper. They smile and go.

"Taddy knows they come for him. He tells goodbye, takes small kerchief of food, and goes toward woods. Papa and I, we understand Taddy. We know he can't kill. We know he can't fight for Austria.

"When soldiers come back, they say Taddy is not at lake and they search house. We know they will be back, and we know they will search for Taddy all over countryside. Papa and I, we work the garden and we pray for Taddy. It is long time before we hear from Taddy again. We cry because we think he die, but then he tells what happens.

"He has good start because soldiers don't look for him until next day. They think he is gone maybe to have good time. But Taddy knows they will look because in Poland is serious crime to run away from army. Three days he runs through woods and sleeps in trees. When he comes out, he finds small cottage...like ours, with only a Mama and a girl living there. Girl is beautiful, very dark like gypsy, but very big with child. Taddy thinks their men are gone to city. He asks for water. He goes inside and they give to him water and some bread. They talk with care and Taddy learns the Papa is dead, killed by soldiers who say he steals. The girl is dark of skin, but even darker with anger for she carries a soldier's child. She doesn't want such a baby, but she knows it is great sin to take life. Taddy listens, and he thinks he can tell that he runs away. The Mama tells him to stay because it is hard for two women alone. Taddy says he will stay for awhile, but he thinks the soldiers will come to look and he will have to go before long. But the Mama says together, they will make plan. So Taddy stays.

"It is not long before horses' hooves echo through woods, and sounds of swords clinking in scabbards are heard outside door. But when soldiers enter, a dark girl big with child lays on mattress moaning, like she will have child, and her mama is busy helping her, and no one else is there. The soldiers leave and girl screams like she is bearing child. Mama hears shed door creak open outside, and swords clink more, and boots crunch on dirt, and then the horses go back to echo. The Mama looks through window, then out door, even in shed. Is no one. When she comes back, Taddy is brushing himself from soot. Soldiers not look in chimney.

"Dark girl has baby few days later, beautiful like herself, and Taddy loves both. He wishes them to run with him, but the Mama begs they should stay. For while they do, and Taddy grows beard. The Mama gets papers for him from boy who dies from diphtheria and is much like Taddy. Then one day, neighbor takes them in cart to Cracow, to hide and work with friends. With so many people around it is easier. It is more than year before Papa and I hear of Taddy and his family. And then Taddy sends for us to come. He says we go to America. Papa is old and bent. He say no, he will die on his own land. It is hard for me to leave him and our home, but I should go, and so we save money for passage, and I come to America."

Emilia continued to sit on Mama's lap, resting her head on Mama's shoulder, eyes dry. It was an interesting story, but she couldn't decide if Uncle Taddy was brave or cowardly. Some of both, she guessed. Anyhow, she didn't like the story. She envied all of them for having everything turn out right. For her, nothing ever seemed to turn out right. Uncle Taddy lived. He came to America. He had a life.

Frankie went to France...and Frankie died.

"Emilia? You are sleeping?" Mama continued to stroke her head.

"No, Mama. But right now, I don't care about Uncle Taddy, or his struggles, or his living."

"Milia, no Dziecko, you don't hear right."

"I heard it all, Mama."

"My Step-Papa and me, we think sure Taddy is die, because we don't hear, but inside, is always small fire of hope, like match flame."

Mil's head jerked to attention. She searched Mama's face.

"Are you telling me to hope, Mama? Do you think Frankie could possibly be alive?"

"Without hope, people die inside, Milia."

"Oh, God, Mama. I don't know if I can stand to hope."

"Hope, Milia, hope..und time takes care of everything."

Mil wondered if she dare risk such a hope. If she kept that match flame alive and it was later blown out, she felt it would kill her. But maybe Mama was right. She'd always known Mama was love, but she began also to think Mama was very wise in her simple peasant way. She didn't know things from book learning, she seemed to know them from her heart, like all the things of nature that seemed to know God instinctively.

After Mil fell into a deep troubled sleep, Michalina called Frankie's family. Together, they shed more tears as they discussed the terrible letter from Col. James. The information was all there. They had to believe. Then, Michalina told Catherine of the baby...Emilia's and Frankie's baby. Even though it was not yet confirmed by Noshkins, Michalina felt it was right they should know. Somewhere, in all the misery, there should be a ray of hope. Catherine accepted the news gratefully, even in her sadness.

## CHAPTER 17

Mil woke, forcing her eyes open despite the crust that, like a light coating of wax, sealed them shut. Lying back on her two pillows, motionless except for her roving eyes, she felt a great sense of relief. Sun spots jumped like carefree spirits between the shadows cast by bare poplar branches bobbing on the porch wall across from her cot. Beyond the windows she saw the blue sky. All of this made her certain she must have had a terrible nightmare from which she was now waking. She must think. Perhaps she had eaten sauerkraut before bed. That always gave her nightmares. Her gaze drifted cautiously toward the table top at her side. No, she hadn't eaten sauerkraut, and she didn't have a nightmare. The white envelope was there, where she'd left it the night before. It was the letter from Col. James. The letter Mother Jagien had given Mama. The letter Mama showed her much later. The letter that said Frankie was brave, but Frankie was dead. Frankie...dead? No, those were dark words, not the kind of words for sunny days like this...like yesterday...today. She closed her eyes tight.

"Please, God...please...let it be a letter from Florchak. Let the letter from Col. James be part of the nightmare. Please God...please..."

Hesitantly, she reached for the envelope, withdraw its contents, and read.

"Jesus, God Almighty...Jesus, God Almighty...Jesus, God Almighty!"

The words burst from her like a religious intonation, each utterance louder, higher in pitch. She crushed the letter, throwing it from her, then flailed her arms wildly for a few moments before clenching her hands into fists. With gasping fury, she punched her pillows repeatedly, threw the covers from her cot, rose and stared down at her bed of love for only a moment before smashing her fists desperately against it. Finally, exhausted, she crumpled to the floor sobbing.

"Oh God, God, it's so unfair."

Michalina hurried out to her side.

"Dziecko, Dziecko...no, no! You must not."

"Oh, no, Mama. God must not! I hate Him, Mama!"

"Milia!"

But before Michalina could say anything more, Mil ran from her to the other end of the porch and began punching her stomach.

"I told God last night that he could have this baby! All I want now is Frankie!"

Without warning, Michalina slapped Mil's face, then grabbed her arms. Emilia was stunned.

"You stop, Milia! You no tell to God what is to do. Baby is not only yours, is Frankie's too. *You* make this baby with Frankie. You must have baby. You no hurt baby."

Mil cringed, then allowed Michalina to lead her back to the cot. They sat together, rocking back and forth, Michalina still holding Mil's hands.

"Mama..I wanted this baby so much. But now...now Frankie's dead, I don't think I can love it."

Before Michalina could answer, the back door buzzer sounded. She went to answer.

Lily and her son Elmer stood hand in hand on the stoop, Elmer's hair waving in the breeze as if in merry greeting. The picture evoked by the small boy was a sharp contrast to the dark hollow look around Lily's eyes.

"Mrs. Kazmier." Lily nodded a solemn greeting.

"Ach, Lily...und Elmer."

The women embraced, gently patting one another's backs.

"Come in. Come."

Michalina took their coats, hanging them neatly on hooks beside the kitchen door. Then she led the way to the porch. Lily sat beside Emilia on the cot and hugged her. In response, Mil lay her head on Lily's shoulder. Shyly, Elmer came to her other side and kissed her cheek. Mil encircled his waist with her free arm. They sat like this a few moments, and then Lily spoke.

"Mil, I'm so sorry. He was my baby brother, you know. Many times he took care of Elmer for me."

Lily wiped her eyes. Mil stared at her. Of course, they all loved Frankie, like she loved Walter, but they'd had him a long time, like she'd had Walter. She'd had Frankie only a few months, and most of that time at a distance. Only once, once did he really belong to her. And now he was gone, and she wondered how long she would remember the color of his eyes, his hair, the broad shoulders, the way his face turned red from embarrassment. How long would she remember this? Long enough to tell the baby when he was old enough? Baby. Humph. He? No, she didn't want a baby who would go to war. She'd rather have a girl. What was she thinking? She didn't want a baby at all, not if Frankie couldn't be with her.

She watched Lily take something from her handbag. It looked like a prayer book, with a ribbon marking a place which she was now opening. She withdraw something. A photograph. Lily extended it toward her. Mil did not reach for it.

"Here, Milia," Elmer said, taking the picture and handing it proudly to his aunt.

Mil looked at the picture blankly, registering no feeling.

"It's Frankie, with his soldier suit. Ain't it a nice picture ta have?"

"We just got it, Mil. It's the only one we have. Taken just before Frankie left. It's not much, but we thought you might like to have it."

Still, Mil did not reach for the picture. Elmer held it out proudly, a child in worship of his uncle, the hero. Worshipping this madness? Why it didn't even look like Frankie, that solemn face, that head covered by a jaunty overseas cap. And they were going to let him worship death and killing? Oh no, she would show them. She would show them what to do with such a memory!

She snatched the picture from Elmer's grasp and tore it in half before their startled eyes. Then, quickly, she took the two pieces and tore them again in half, throwing the pieces toward the open window. Missing the window, the pieces drifted slowly to the floor. Lily gasped and Elmer's chin trembled.

No one spoke, as Mil glared in defiance at the picture pieces. Then, she crossed the floor and ground her heel into the torn fragments, grunting and moaning strange animal-like sounds as she did this. At the same time, she hit her stomach with her fist...softly...rhythmically. Neither woman tried to stop her. The violence of her actions was much subdued now. It was as if Mil's emotions strained to play themselves out completely. After awhile, Mil stood still, feet planted on the picture scraps, arms hanging limply at her sides. Lily went to her and brought her back to the cot. Elmer took the scraps from the floor and tenderly wrapped them in his clean white handkerchief.

Lily spoke without looking at Mil.

"Joe and I are so glad to have Elmer. He's our second baby, the one Doctor Krushna said we couldn't have. That was after our first boy was still-born. People make mistakes, you know. Always, as long as there are people, there will be mistakes. Like the doctor saying we couldn't have any more babies. But we had Elmer. And he was so healthy. Crabby, but healthy. I guess we were more happy than most people because we had lost one."

Lily paused, lost in thought. The others sat quietly. The scene presented such contrast - subdued people, quiet in mourning, while the day itself flaunted is vibrancy mockingly in the energy of its playful sunbeams which seemed to flash to every corner of the porch and kitchen beyond spotlighting only brightness and gaiety. The bright yellow of the upper kitchen walls, and the spotless white below were unsuitable setting for grief. The warm light oak ones of the woodwork, the furniture, the icebox seemed to be trying hard to push sadness away. Even the painted gray of the back porch brightened as the sparkling windows invited more and more sunlight to penetrate the scene.

"I think, Milia, that you're going to have your baby. Frankie would want it. He would love it very much. I know by the way he took care of Elmer. Frankie was just a little boy himself, but he would go to the bassinette when Elmer cried and pick him up and walk with him. He was very careful. He would sing to him. Frankie had a beautiful voice then, high like a little girl. Now he sings very low like a man." Lily smiled in remembrance. No one interrupted her.

"Even when Elmer had scarlet fever a few years ago, and the doctor told Frankie to stay away, even then he went to Elmer when I was busy. And he never got scarlet fever. You see, that was two mistakes that smart people made. The doctor told us that we wouldn't have Elmer, and the doctor told Frankie he would get scarlet fever if he came close to Elmer. People make mistakes, Emilia. They do."

"Sometimes. But there was no mistake about my sickness."

"But you're alive and the first doctor said you would die."

"Humph. Yes, that was *some* mistake. And now, there's all this."

"Ach, Milia. Ya, you too were fine mistake. I was old lady, and you were come. You were born miracle...you live...that is miracle. Every day is miracle, Milia. Always, you must have faith."

Mil's face was wan...drained...her shoulders slumped. There was an air of quiet acceptance about her. She pulled her robe tightly around herself, pausing to rub her tummy gently.

"Miracle. So many miracles. Baby, are you a miracle?"

"Love is miracle, Emilia."

"Yes, I know." Mil sighed. "And the baby is part of our love - mine and Frankie's. And I always wanted a baby. But now - I don't know. There's no Frankie.

"Ach, Milia. You must believe."

"And Mil," Lily said, "I still have the bassinette. Ma made it. It's really beautiful. All net and lace, and pink ribbon. We thought it would be a girl."

"I want a boy, *if* I have this baby. We'll call him Frankie like his daddy. But he'll never go to war! Not even if I have to run away."

"Hey, Yeah. Let's have a boy so I can be an uncle!"

"Elmer if it's Frankie's and Milia's baby, you'll have to be a cousin, whether it's a boy or a girl."

"Rats. But I'd rather take care of a boy anyhow."

"It'll be a boy," Milia said. "I only hope I can love him." She looked at Elmer. "You'll have to help me."

Lily and Elmer prepared to leave when Mil spoke again.

"Please put the picture together again, Elmer. And you keep it for me awhile. Someday, I'd like to have it."

"Sure!" Elmer's smile showed his happiness and relief over the change in Mil's attitude.

After they left, Mil wandered to the backyard where she waited for Noshkins. Like the previous day, it was beautiful. Mil wondered why as nature was flaunting its regal glory, God was striking her with unbearable tragedy. Under a brilliant blue sky, surrounded by russet colors, and the peaceful sounds of a late autumn day, she'd been told her husband...the father of her baby...had been killed by some enemy in a far away country. By an enemy? How could they be enemies? How could she hate someone she didn't know? How could people so far away, across the ocean, cause her such great pain and suffering? Pain greater than she felt from her physical illness. Somehow, it had been easier to hope, to believe she would get well than to believe that Frankie was still alive. Oh, why should that be? Why should she feel so hopeless and empty now. She sighed and smoothed her face with her hands, as though she were trying to smooth away the events of the past few days. She felt a need just to sit outdoors. It would be a while before Noshkins came, but that was good, and it wasn't cold, just pleasantly cool. She strolled up and down the walk as she had the previous afternoon, again noticing her faithful marigold dancers gracefully and proudly standing on the brick runway, the beauty of the colorful expanse marred only by two protruding bricks. Tata said he would fix the bricks on Sunday before they were pushed completely out by the quickly approaching winter freeze. Suddenly, she felt weary.

"Momchu," she called up the back steps, "what time is it?"

"Only it is twelve o'clock. You haf time before Noshkins comes."

It was early; she had time for a walk.

"I'm going to Belmont, Mama."

Michalina bustled to the back window. She called out to her baby. "No, Dziecko. Too far."

"It's not far, Mama. What's the difference if I walk up and down the backyard, or walk to Belmont. It's still walking."

"Noshkins no say for you to do that."

"Mama, I have to get out of here. I have to see something besides this backyard. All these backyards, and fences, the alley. Please Mama. I'll be all right."

"Wait, Dziecko. I come too." Michalina began to undo her apron.

"No, Mama, please."

Michalina sighed and shrugged her shoulders.

"Dziecko, careful."

Mil released the catch on the white picket gate. How many times she and Frankie had done that. Walking through the narrow gangway, darkened by the two flat next door, she felt so alone. Her vision of Frankie, walking here, holding her hand, made her shudder. Mil put her hands to her temples, rubbing with a circular motion. If only she could clear her thinking, if she could establish her own, real, reality. What was real? Was it real that Frankie was dead? Dead...killed...no, no, she must push that from her mind. She shook her head sharply from side to side. She wouldn't...she wouldn't think about *that* now.

Mil looked up and down the street, wondering how it could be that everything looked so bright in the spotty sunshine. How could Nature play games in the wake of her heartbreak? It was as if even the sun played hide-and-seek with the world as it peeked in and out from behind the cloud screens which rolled across the endless blue dome above her. The little Swiniarski kids next door darted in and out among the evergreens, not even trying to be quiet for her. What difference did it make. They didn't know...understand...didn't even see her. Besides, their fun would be short lived when their Grandmother caught them.

Oh, Frankie...did he do things like that when he was a boy? Would their baby play such games? No, she must stop thinking of Frankie or she would lose her mind. She looked up, trying to think of something else. Ah...the sprawling poplars. Though they stood naked and silent all up and down the block, they seemed to acknowledge her presence with an occasional bare-branched wave. Today, their very bareness pleased her, for it was somehow fitting. But the mums...they were a contrast - everywhere burgeoning forth in colorful sprays before basement windows as far as she could see, as though inviting her to lie down somewhere on the tawny grass and pillow her head. Pillows...to dream of Frankie. But it would do no good. There was no Frankie. She *must* find some way to push him from her mind, at least for a little while.

Frantically, she looked for something to capture her attention. There. The bouncing curve of a squirrel's tail caught her eye. She would talk to it the way Frankie always did. She stooped, clucking and snapping her fingers at the squirrel. It sat on its haunches, eyeing her speculatively, wriggling its nose and puffy cheeks at her, then apparently deciding she had no nuts in her hand, it turned and scampered up the only catalpa tree on the entire block, peeking occasionally around the few drying brown leaves still clinging to it. She sighed. Even the squirrel left her. Mil continued toward Belmont Avenue.

The metal on metal screech of braking trolley wheels pushing against the tracks broke into her consciousness. It seemed so long since she'd heard that familiar sound. Even the small band of old drunks weaving around on the corner outside the tavern were a welcome diversion, though Frankie always hated it that she ever had to be near them. But they'd never bothered her. In fact, she and the drunks had always ignored one another. But it had been a long time since she'd been to the corner, and now they stopped and looked after her as she passed. Did they know about Frankie? Maybe...but not likely.

She was tiring from the walk, but she didn't want to return to the backyard. She couldn't sit there. Digging deep in the pocket of her sweater jacket, she felt for coins. Nothing. Nevertheless, she would walk to the fruit store for an apple. Mr. Poulis would let her take one and pay tomorrow, though Mama wouldn't like her doing that. Mama was very strict about staying out of stores unless you had money to pay, but surely one apple would be forgiven.

As she waited on the curb to cross, Mil saw cement sidewalks as far as her eye could see. They were better than the old plank walks, she thought, and wondered when they had been completed. Frankie would be surprised. Again she did it. But why not? Mama said she must believe.

She crossed the street, avoiding a manure pile from Mr. Krawicz's horse. His cart and wares were parked down the street where he and one of the neighborhood ladies were arguing. Must be over the price of the lace curtains he was holding up. Mil wanted to run, to pull the curtains from his hands, and throw them into the manure. People had no right to go on as though nothing had changed. Her world had changed! Frankie was dead!

The effort of crossing the street and of controlling her anger left Mil breathless.

The heaving of her chest as she gasped for air, caused her to feel dizzy. She sat on the black pipe fence outside the fruit store. It was silly to have such a fence, for it didn't do a very good job of protecting the patchy green grass inside its boundary.

Oh, why had she walked here? She felt no better. She must close her eyes, shut out the world and the warm sun. But the world would not go away. Its sounds interfered with her sadness. The sun, as though trying to bestow its own strength upon her, penetrated her sweater and settled on her chest. She sat so, with her eyes shut, and after a few moments, Emilia heard the familiar voice of Elinora Steech.

"Milia. You look fine. Doesn't she, Jan?"

Mil opened her eyes, half expecting to see Jan standing beside Elinora. The woman was beginning to convince her that Jan was actually alive. Well, maybe Emilia could learn from Elinora. Perhaps, if she tried hard, she could learn to keep Frankie alive, as Elinora kept Jan alive.

Elinora took Emilia's hands and pulled her to her feet. Then Elinora embraced her, patting her back - swaying and crooning - squeezing the breath from her. Emilia gasped for air.

"Ach, poor Milia...poor Milia. I'm so sorry your Frankie went away to the army...to be killed. Never to come back to you again."

Emilia stiffened as though she'd heard the words for the first time. She pulled away and stared at Elinora. This crazy woman! This crazy neighborhood! News spread like cold dirty water running down the streets after a terrible rain. How dare she say this! How dare she remind Emilia of her horror! What was wrong with this insane woman clinging to her own irrationality while she forced reality upon Emilia. How selfish! How totally, unbearably selfish! In her hurt, Emilia struck back.

"Yes, Elinora. Yes, Frankie is dead...dead, just like your own husband, Jan. Jan is dead, Elinora! Jan is dead too!"

Trembling, Emilia turned away from Elinora and ran into the fruit store. Once inside, she looked back through the big window. She saw Elinora slowly crossing the street, looking so alone. Mil took a few steps toward the door, then stopped. Elinora seemed to be heading toward her home. It was no use for Emilia to go to Elinora. There was no helping her.

From the front of the store, Mr. Poulis called to Emilia. She turned to see him sitting with his ledger spread open on the long smooth counter, leaning on his elbow, head resting thoughtfully on his palm.

"How good to see that you're getting out again, lovely Emilia."

She had nothing to say.

"What can I do for you, lovely Child? Anything. You name it."

He'd called her lovely Child. His voice was warm. Emilia felt as if she were seeing him for the first time. He wasn't as old as she'd always thought...younger than Mama...maybe under forty...despite his graying dark hair. His eyes were kind...dark. As he stood up behind the counter, she saw he wasn't very tall, maybe as tall as Frankie. In some ways, he reminded her of an older Frankie...mostly his ways, she guessed. He was much slighter...didn't have the broad shoulders. And his skin was much darker.

And his face thinner. A nice man.

Emilia turned away from him. Why hadn't he married, she wondered. His brother, Peter, was married...had several children...but Marcus Poulis was not.

Again, he spoke. “Would you like something, Emilia?”

“Mr. Poulis, I didn't bring money, but if I could have an apple, I'd pay you tomorrow. Maybe even later today.”

“Emilia! How many years do I know your family? Of course. You take an apple, as many apples as you want. I know you'll pay. I don't even have your family's name listed in my books. Much less have they ever owed me anything.”

Swiftly he came around the counter, put his arm around her shoulders and led her to the apple bin in the center of the window. He chose the biggest, reddest apple, polished it on his apron, and handed it to her.

“My get well present to you.”

“Thank you, Mr. Poulis, but Mama wouldn't like that. I'll pay you tomorrow.”

Marcus Poulis heaved an exaggerated sigh, spread his arms wide in a helpless gesture and nodded his head.

“Whatever you say.”

Emilia clutched the apple, nodded in appreciation, then hurried home, afraid Mama would begin to worry.

The walk back seemed long. She was relieved to be opening the back door again, calling up the stairs to tell Mama she was home.

“Ya, Milia. I see you come. Noshkins be here soon. You come inside now?”

“No, Mama, the sun feels good on my chest. I'll wait here.”

She settled on the bench under the rose trellis, brought her feet up, making a head rest of her knees. She set the shiny apple next to her, then dozed in the comforting heat of the sun.

Before long, she felt rather than saw, a presence at her side. As she opened her eyes, Noshkins placed his hand on her shoulder. Seeming to know her need for quiet understanding, he said nothing, simply looked at her solemnly, with sympathy. Emilia grasped his hand, pulled it to her cheek and cried softly. After a while, she dried her eyes and Noshkins sat next to her.

“Emilia, you are destined to be a survivor.”

She turned questioning eyes to him.

“Frankie helped you to survive. He did everything he knew how to do to cover you with strength...no to fill you with strength.”

“And then he left me.”

“Emilia, Frankie had needs too. You would have paid a very high price if you'd made him stay here.”

“Not higher than the price I paid letting him go.”

“The death of a loved one is sad. But to live many years with a bitter dying love...that's tragic. It's destructive to the human spirit.”

“But inside of me...I'm dead now.”

“No, you're numb, unfeeling, anesthetized by shock. That's good. It's nature's way of healing."

She pondered this. He interrupted her thoughts.

"Emilia, your Mama tells me you think you're pregnant."

She nodded.

"Come inside. We need to examine you."

She sighed. Together they rose. She rubbed her tummy gently, thoughtfully, then looked around the garden at the few dying greens and out into the alley beyond. Noshkins took her hand, urging her toward the door. Suddenly, her eyes opened wide. Her face flushed with confusion...recognition...joy! She broke away from Noshkins, running with her arms outstretched toward the alley gate. Noshkins called to her. She didn't turn. A uniformed soldier walked briskly down the alley toward them. The soldier drew nearer and Emilia ran faster. It was Frankie. She knew it was Frankie. It had to be Frankie! Then, suddenly, she felt herself flying forward...frantically, she grasped at the empty air. Nothing broke her fall. The sound of the thud as her body struck the bricks, rolled through her head. She couldn't breathe. Stabbing pains began to shoot out from some deep recess within her body. A strange flowing warmth spread between her legs. Oh God, she thought. Again, she reached a hand toward the alley, but no one took it. The soldier was gone. He hadn't even seen her fall. Oh my God, she thought, as her toes felt the rise of the protruding bricks. Through her fog she heard Noshkins' voice talking to someone. Mil's eyes wouldn't open. Maybe it was Frankie...going to surprise her. Maybe he was here. And then, Emilia heard nothing more.

Several hours later, Noshkins left the house. He'd told them the male fetus was about four months along. Michalina had sprinkled it with water, said the words of baptism, and called it Frankie.

## CHAPTER 18

Listlessly, Mil traced her index finger over the gilt edge of the small oval frame standing on the chest beside her bed. Little Elmer had done a swell job of gluing the torn fragments of Frankie's picture together again. He'd forgiven her too for tearing it up; that was very important to Mil. Elmer was just a little boy of eight; there was no reason to bind him with the same rusty chain of hurt and guilt that seemed always to pull tight around her whenever she looked at Frankie's picture. Elmer worshiped his uncle...so be it. Frankie was a hero; she knew it. Now, she could even admit that to herself...despite the terrible resentment she felt over such heroism, the heroism that caused Frankie to leave her side to join the ranks of soldiers. He'd fought for liberty, now it was as good as accomplished, worldwide, but she was alone. Young...everyone said. You're so young. There'll be others. But they didn't understand. Never would there be another Frankie.

Mil looked toward the window where November's morning sunlight beckoned to her freely, for the nearly bare poplars now lacked the power to stifle the sun's warming rays. She felt like a November poplar branch herself...denuded and barren. Only four weeks had passed since she'd lost both Frankie and baby Frankie. Nevertheless, the hurt within her seemed to grow and ripen, causing the death and miscarriage to loom fresh in her memory even now, while on the other hand, in the world at large, so much was happening so fast that her personal tragedy seemed in some ways to have happened long, long ago.

Germany had a new Chancellor, Prince Max of Baden. The newspapers were filled with him, with rumors of his supposed peace overtures. The Swiss Embassy was said to be involved. They were the neutral power through which contact was being made with President Wilson. Peace. How ironic. Now it seemed the war games would end, but that was no help to Frankie. Frankie was dead. All those foolish young men who thought it glamorous to be soldiers might soon be marching home, but Frankie, who felt it his duty to fight for his family's freedom, he would stay there, on that foreign soil, on that land their parents once fled. The incongruity of it all caused her to reach a decision in the past few months. She decided that if there were a God, He was neither loving nor just. He was not a "thing" either as she'd once thought. No, He was merely a cruel game player. A powerful Being who enjoyed always taking the power away from His little creatures. She'd turn to Him no more. He had no need of her...no need for any of them.

The doorbell rang.

"I'll get it Mama."

Mil threw her dust cloth on the lawson sofa as she passed through the parlor. It was all right she threw the cloth there. She hadn't used it yet, so it was clean. She smoothed her housedress, fluffed her hair, and pinched her cheeks. That was a habit now well ingrained by her overwhelming desire to look healthy. Funny, not so long ago, she wanted to die. Sometimes, she still thought death would be a peaceful alternative to fighting for a healthy life when her men were dead, but somehow, something deep within her soul urged her on.

Mil raised the green linen door shade. Sunlight rushed in, flooding the hallway with warmth, and casting dancing rainbows upon the walls as light rays filtered through the prismic bevels of glass around the edges of the long rectangular window in the door.

Mil opened the door. Before her, stood a young man in uniform, overseas cap barely covering a tousle of red curls. He looked rather solemn, but mischief danced in his eyes, as though eager to spill from those confines. Mil looked at him quizzically.

"Hello. My name is Billy Stark."

Mil waited for further explanation, since she didn't recognize the young soldier. She guessed him to be about twenty-two.

"You don't know me, but if your mother is home, she'll vouch for me."

How would Mama know him, Mil wondered. He wasn't anyone she recognized from the neighborhood. She didn't think he was Polish with a name like Stark, but then you couldn't tell anymore. Everyone was Anglicizing. However, he didn't look Polish either...too impish.

"Mama..." Emilia called.

"You're Emilia, I think. Of course, you look much different today."

Mil's eyebrows shot up in surprise. Her sickness had truly done strange things to her. She had no recollection of ever having seen this young man before.

Mama bustled to the door.

"Ach, Billy, yes? That is how you are called?"

He nodded, removing his cap.

"Ach, excuse, please. Come inside."

Mama motioned to the parlor, then led the way. Emilia and Billy followed.

"Milia, you know who is this?"

She shook her head, feeling even more confused, since Mama seemed quite pleased by this visit.

"Is soldier who comes in alley when you fall."

Billy caught the look of resentment that came unbidden to Mil's eyes, and he immediately delivered an apology for coming and disturbing them. Then he went on to explain his reason for coming.

"I...well, I just wondered how you were doing."

Mil couldn't answer.

"Well, I mean, I guess I sort of felt...well...responsible."

"Ach, Billy...no," Mama said.

Emilia thought, "Mama, speak for yourself."

Billy continued to watch Mil's face, then he said, "I'm just so sorry for what happened to you. If I could change it..." Billy looked down at the floor helplessly, not knowing what else to say.

His penitent look softened Mil's feelings of resentment.

No, Emilia thought, I guess it's not really his fault. I'd like it to be, but it's not.

"Thank you for caring," Emilia said. "It was my own fault, I guess...maybe the fault of my sickness...maybe of my grief and bitterness."

The room was quiet, giving needed time for Emilia's own words to sink into her head...her consciousness. Mentally, she pressed down on the words, as though sealing an envelope shut. Then she sighed. She felt lighter, somehow. Maybe by admitting such a thought, saying such words aloud, she'd suddenly had a great weight lifted from her soul.

Thoughtfully, she rose from the chair...paced about...ignoring the presence of Mama and Billy. Thoughts tumbled through her brain. She'd already begun to realize that God didn't need her and she didn't need Him, but now she felt a furthering of truth filling her mind just as lamplight might flood a room. Yes, she'd been grief-stricken and bitter, but that was God's fault. He had taken her man. He was the Supreme game player. Suddenly, Emilia knew she would no longer play His games. She would forget God...turn her back on Him...and then her life would change. She would concentrate only on living a life of peace and happiness. She would begin her future.

Unconsciously she squared her shoulders...raised her chin...as though in preparation for the task ahead. Then she sat down again on the edge of her chair.

Mama eyed Milia suspiciously, knowing some change had taken place, wondering if she had something to worry about, for Milia was very unpredictable these days.

Billy, on the other hand, watched too, knowing he'd witnessed something...some change...and he wondered if he'd ever know just what, at that moment, had happened.

Emilia pulled herself together, and looked at Billy. She questioned him.

"You saw me fall, then?"

"No, I heard your cry. I've heard many such cries of pain in the past months. I came back instinctively."

She studied his face for a moment. The mischief was gone from his eyes. There was a world of pain in them. Yes, she could see he'd suffered too, very much. No wonder he understood her pain so well. No wonder he had to return to check on her. Maybe it was the only opportunity he'd had in many months to witness survival. His need to know she survived must have been very great. What could she say to make him feel better? Perhaps this was her chance, too. Maybe someone, somewhere, had said the right words to Frankie at a time when he needed them. In any case, she knew her Frankie would want her to help this young man in any way that she could.

"How terrible it must have been for you." She paused a moment, but Billy didn't respond. "Anyway, now you're home."

Billy nodded solemnly. The quiet of the room was heavy, full of unspoken thoughts. Then Billy cut the silence.

"Well, I'll go now. I just wondered...hoped you were all right. I see you are. You sure look a lot better." He smiled.

Mil returned the smile. Then Billy rose from his chair, and Mama and Mil did likewise. Billy started for the door and Mil followed.

"Thank you for coming, Mil said.

"You haf here Mama un Papa, Billy?"

"No, they died when I was just a kid. In France, I met John Muziel. He lives a couple blocks down the street here. I promised to visit his family. That's why I'm here."

Billy searched their faces for a sign of recognition, but they didn't seem to know John. He knew how that was...city life. A couple blocks from home, and you didn't know a soul.

"You come again, Billy," Mama said. "Our Wladek, he not be home still. We need 'nother young man at dinner table on Sunday. So you come, yah?"

Billy looked at Emilia, wanting to sense her approval before committing himself. She smiled, kind of small and sad, he thought, but she seemed to approve.

"Sure!" Billy said. "Thanks a lot. What time would you like me to come?"

"One 'clock be fine."

"I'll be here," Billy said as they closed the door behind him.

Michalina turned to her daughter, seeking her approval for issuing the invitation.

"You no mind, Milia? I ask Billy?"

"He seems nice, Mama. No," she sighed, "I no mind."

Then she took Mama's hand and squeezed it. They both smiled at her perfect imitation of Mama.

## CHAPTER 19

November, 1918...the next year.

It was Sunday morning. Mama and Tata had just returned from church. Emilia grasped her magazine tightly and hurried into her own room. She didn't wish to see their accusing glances. If only they'd simply say...go to church...then she could argue...say it was no use. She'd reached a conclusion...that she didn't need God, and He certainly had no need of her. However, as it was, the silent battle Mama and Tata waged stood like a threatening monster between them.

Soon, Mama called to her. Emilia dropped the magazine, trembling a little as she left her room to answer the call, figuring that maybe the time had come, and they had finally decided to bring their objections into the open. Good. She was determined to be strong, in spite of her fear.

"Emilia, come Dziecko, help mit peeling potatoes."

Emilia sighed with relief. She really wanted to talk about her feelings, but better not today. The sun was shining. Why spoil it?

"How many, Mama? Who's coming today?"

"Is only Tata, und you...und I am here."

"You mean Billy isn't coming?"

"He's not calling...und he no stops here for some days. Maybe he's not here this week."

"Hmmmm, seems funny. He's almost like one of the family now. He's been here so much, 'bout every Sunday, and any other day you're able to get him to come."

"Yah. Und how many times he jus stop und say hello. How you are."

Emilia couldn't help laughing. It struck her so funny that even when imitating Billy, Mama couldn't put the phrase together quite right. Still, she said, 'How you are.'

"What you laugh, Emilia?"

"Oh, Mama. It seems to me Billy always says, 'How are you?'"

"Yah. So I say it...'how you are...?'"

Emilia laughed again and hugged her Mama.

Mama shrugged, but her eyes shone. Is gut, she thought. Emilia is better. Billy is gut company. Maybe he comes again.

Time seemed to be dragging by...only 11:30. Emilia was hungry. She hustled the potatoes into a pot, salted the water and put them on to boil.

The table did seem empty with only the three of them. Harry was out today with friends. They hadn't heard from Walter in several weeks, but that could be a good sign. Perhaps he was on his way home. Of course, the war was still on, and it might not be likely...although Billy was home...yes, she would hope.

Billy had been lucky, in a way. A leg wound had sent him back, but at least the leg healed perfectly...left no permanent damage...and now, he was home. But how well she knew that things like that didn't happen to everyone.

Emilia thought about the soldiers on Frankie's side of the family. It was thought that Ed might be returning soon. He had been in a Red Cross Hospital for some time recuperating from an injury. Kate's Hank was unscarred as far as they knew. Kate. Yes, she was so positive the war would end soon and Hank would return to her. Well, maybe she was right. She was hoping to celebrate her first wedding anniversary with her husband.

So, enough of that, Emilia thought. If Mama needed no more help, she'd go outdoors for awhile.

"Mama, how long before we eat?" Emilia untied her apron.

"Only minutes. Maybe 10."

"Good. I'm so hungry!"

Mama smiled appreciatively at that, thinking how long she'd waited to hear those words.

Emilia grabbed a warm coat from the hall closet and called back to Mama that she'd be out on the front porch for awhile. She wanted to take advantage of the sunny day. It was warm for the ninth of November. But November in Chicago could be like that...unpredictable. And why not? It really wasn't winter yet...only autumn. And this autumn of 1918 had been pleasantly warm anyway. Emilia wondered if it had been as warm in Europe where all the boys were fighting. They'd surely have many stories to tell when they returned. When they returned...bitter-sweet words. If Frankie could return, he too would have stories to tell. Resolutely, she shook her head. No, no more of that. No more dwelling on Frankie...or his son. That was past, and she was now looking to the future.

But what would the future bring her? Could she find another good office job? It made her nervous to think about it. Her working life seemed so long ago...so far away from her now. What would a prospective employer say? Of course, with all the boys away fighting, "Help Wanted" signs were still prevalent in many places, so her chances could be pretty good. Time would tell. In fact, she would ask Noshkins about returning to work the next time she saw him.

Mil savored the feeling of warmth against her back. The house bricks, having stored sunny heat within themselves all morning, were now wonderful conductors of that soothing heat. She settled comfortably. Then Mama called her. Mil hated to go inside, for at this moment, she wanted to choose the sunshine over hot pork and kluski, even though the aroma now wafting past her nostrils, tempted her greatly. She started toward the front door when an eager call stopped her. It was Billy.

"Emilia! Emilia, wait!"

Mil turned to see him rushing toward her, face flushed with excitement. What on earth could have happened, she wondered, but knowing Billy, even for this short time, she knew it wouldn't take long to find out. He wasn't the secretive type.

Emilia smiled. "What is it Billy? What's happened?"

"It's over, Emilia! The war has ended!"

"Ended?" Her question was more an astonished echo. How incredulous, she thought. The news had been full of such promises, but somehow she wasn't able to really believe that this awful catastrophe would finally end. All the boys would really be coming home. Tears came again. She wished they wouldn't, but they were tears of joy...mostly.

"Come in, Billy. Tell us all about it."

As Billy reached her side, Emilia noticed the rolled newspaper tightly clutched in his hand.

"It's right here, Emilia. Right here in the paper."

"What, Billy. Hurry. What does it say?"

"It says that Wilhelm II gave up his throne. He's fled to Holland. So, Germany has surrendered. The war is over!"

Billy grabbed Emilia, hugging her closely. "Oh, Emilia...Emilia...it's over."

For a moment, Emilia rested against him, letting the words wash over her. Then she raised her hands to his face, and gently pulled Billy's lips down to hers. Without brushing the salty tears from her mouth, she kissed Billy. It was a very warm kiss...a warmth stemming from the joy of the feelings they were sharing...a warmth that, like a blanket, covered their brief moment of intimacy. Then they broke away, suddenly self-conscious. Billy took Emilia's hand, and they laughed.

"Come," he said. "Let's tell your folks."

Together they rushed into the house. Billy unfolded the newspaper and spread it out on the end table in the parlor.

Tata crossed himself, and bowed his head whispering a silent prayer of thanks.

"Ach, Jesu kochanji," Mama said, reaching into her apron pocket to fondle her rosary beads.

Then Mama crossed the room and embraced Mil, ready to comfort her should she react badly...but no sound and no more tears came from her young daughter. Michalina pushed Emilia back a little and studied her face. She had been crying, but not now. For some reason, Michalina remembered Mil's reaction the day she met Billy...here in their own parlor. Something had happened to her baby that day. Something both good and bad. Emilia laughed more now, ate better, smiled more, and though her eyes were mostly free of tears, those eyes seemed to Michalina often to look unnaturally bright. Just as they looked now. And Emilia's face. It, too, was different...determined, maybe. Michalina wondered. Should she encourage Emilia to believe, just a little, in one corner of her heart that Frankie might return? Would that be bad? Maybe such belief would die naturally...a gradual death...if Frankie didn't come home.

Ach, such foolishness she was thinking. What would be, would be. Maybe she herself, Michalina, still clung to a strong thread of faith. Maybe she thought...if Taddy could live...so could Frankie. But...better not to tell Emilia of this hoping. Maybe it was too much, to think such blessings would happen two times in one family. No, she wouldn't encourage Emilia. She touched her rosary again.

In a while, they ate dinner...thinking about what life would be like now the war was over. It was a day special to them...November 9, 1918.

******************

After Billy left, Mil kissed Mama and Tata good-night, picked up her latest issue of HARPERS, and settled in her room to read and to think. Soon, however, she closed the magazine. Her mind wasn't on reading, or fashion, instead her thoughts wandered toward peace, and what the world would be like. She had trouble keeping Frankie from her thoughts. His face floated before her mind's eye, causing her to dream of the impossible...of flats, and decorating, and jobs Frankie might find, the kind of jobs that would bring enough money so they could live comfortably on their own. Again and again, she chided herself. She had come into her room so she could think about possible jobs for herself, but it was no use. She might as well ready herself for sleep and try again in the morning when she was fresh.

She slipped into her flannel nightie, letting it fall in soft warm folds over her body. How warm and comfortable it felt...how relaxing. She turned out the light and climbed under the covers. No more back porch. No more Frankie, either. "No, no, Emilia," she told herself audibly, "none of that." This is a new life. Still, Frankie's face swam before her closed eyes. Then, finally, she fell asleep.

At first, her sleep was quiet, her breathing rhythmic. Then, as sleep closed in more soundly, Mil began to thrash about the bed. Her head burrowed into the pillows. A muffled scream stirred the darkness. Mil woke...sat bolt upright...listening... eyes searching the darkness. Nothing. Still, she was frightened. She trembled.

There was no reason, Mil thought. She was still in her own room. The muffled scream...her own. Mil closed her eyes in relief and fell back against the pillows, hoping for sleep to overtake her once again...quickly. She tossed uncomfortably. Sleep wouldn't come. Instead, the memory of a strange dream swirled into her consciousness, flooding it like the waters of an overflowing river.

In the dream, it had been dark...a night without stars...Frankie came from nowhere, taking her hand. She tried to throw her arms around his neck, but he stopped her...led her into a small dark, shed-like building. She tried to pull him out, but he wouldn't or couldn't move. His face...white...strained...frightened. The oppressive dark surrounded them, as though they were captives in some deep dark hole. Mil tried to speak to Frankie, but no sound came from her open lips. As she pulled frantically at the door of the shed, wanting desperately to escape, a terrible exploding sound shattered the night air and a blinding blue-white light filled the sky. Mil feared the world had come to an end. She screamed and screamed. That's how she'd wakened...by her own voice...her own muffled screams.

She felt damp...her body...her nightie...wet with perspiration. Shuddering, she swung her feet to the floor, intending to rush to Mama's and Tata's room for comfort.

They would know the meaning of such a dream. She rushed to the door, hand on the knob, then paused. No, she wouldn't do it...wouldn't disturb their sleep. She'd done enough of that in her lifetime. Now, she was a woman of eighteen, a widow for more than a year. She was simply a woman who had experienced a strange, bad dream...a nightmare. She must grow up...draw on her new-found courage. She wouldn't go to Mama and Tata.

## CHAPTER 20

Silver streaks of sunlight ushered the morning in, as Mil lay under her covers... eyes wide open...sleepless. She'd been dwelling again on her dream of the other night...what it meant. She had tried very hard to analyze it, the meaning of its stark, mysterious happenings. The dream seemed to have no connection to her life, still she couldn't dismiss it as simply another dream...a cold, dark nightmare. Something, some deep feeling growing within her, told her to call Mother Jagien...to visit Frankie's family. She hadn't seen them for quite awhile. And she'd never seen their home. It was strange how Frankie had managed to keep her away from that house. He'd later told her he was ashamed of it, and though she insisted that was silly, it was then too late for her to go there, because of her illness, because of Noshkins' orders requiring her to stay home, on the porch, away from people. So, she'd never been there. Now, however, she was well...almost, anyway...and she was sure Noshkins wouldn't object to a streetcar ride and a visit to Frankie's family. Somehow, she knew it would help her to go there. Probably no one could tell her the meaning of the dream, but she felt that the dream was really a signal telling her to visit Frankie's Ma and the rest of the family. Maybe they needed to see her. Maybe they needed to know how much she still missed Frankie...loved him...and that in spite of that love, or because of it, she was starting over, beginning a new life. Maybe a visit like that would help her to actually begin that new life.

She threw the covers back...shivering in the damp, November morning chill. Perhaps today the papers would tell more of the peace. Perhaps. She went to the closet, choosing carefully. Her black hobble skirt and white blouse with the high neck would be just right for her planned outing. Carefully, she dressed. Mil positioned the hair *rat* neatly on top of her head, then brushed her hair back over it. "There" she thought, "a nice high, off the face hairdo...makes me look healthy." She dusted a puff of powder over her nose as a final gesture to her toilette, made the bed, and left her room, to join Mama and Tata, whom she heard out in the kitchen. She was hungry and eager for breakfast.

Mama and Tata were seated at the table, Farina filled cereal bowls in front of them. They talked together very softly.

"Good morning, Mama." Mil passed behind her Mama's chair, squeezed Mama's shoulders, and planted a kiss on her cheek. She looked across the table, smiled at Tata and blew him a kiss.

"Ach, Milia, telephone ringing did wake you?"

"Telephone, Mama? No, I didn't even hear it. I'm hungry that's all."

"Humph." Tata grunted.

"Oh, I'll bet you're wondering why I'm all dressed up this morning."

"Ya, Dziecko."

"Well, I'll tell you in a minute. But first, who called? Stella? Helcha? Ludmilla? Not one of the boys, I guess. It would probably break their arms to raise the telephone receiver."

"No, Dziecko. Is not girls. Not boys either."

"So...who?"

"Is Frankie's Mama."

"Mother Jagien?" Emilia rooted to the spot, holding her coffee cup in mid-air. Her face went pale.

Mama said quickly, "Is all right."

"Of course," Mil said, trying to bluff even herself. "Why shouldn't she call. But so early? Something happened. Didn't it?"

"Ya. But is nothing you should worry."

"So then tell me!" Mil knew there was impatience in her voice. She hated it that sometimes she was short tempered. But why didn't Mama get to the point! Emilia knew why. Mama was only trying to protect her. Still, sometimes it became very annoying.

Mama sat down again. "Is Frankie's Busha. She is die."

Mil sighed with relief, happy to hear it was nothing more serious. Of course, she chided herself, Busha's death would be serious to those who knew her, but Mil didn't. She pulled herself together to answer Mama.

"Oh, that's too bad. Frankie never talked too much about her, but I guess she had to be pretty old."

"Ya. Is eighty years. She is living with Frankie's family for long time."

"Hmmmm...yes. I guess her husband was dead a long time."

Mil poured her coffee and set two pieces of bread on the rack to toast. She saw Mama's questioning eyes, and answered the unspoken words.

"Mama, you know I have never liked cereal...especially Farina. I'll just have toast.

"You should want I make you eggs?"

"Mama," Mil said, trying to keep exasperation out of her voice, "if I see another egg, I'll die. I've had enough eggs in the past year to turn me into a chicken."

Seeing Mama's hurt expression, Mil reached over to hug her.

"I love you, Mama...Tata...it's just, I'm trying to start over...to grow up. I *need* to start doing things for myself. Well, it's even more than that. I *want* to start doing things for myself. Do you understand, Mama? Do you?"

Mil searched her face...Tata's too. Of course, Tata's face was impassive, but Mama's seemed to relax. She guessed they did understand. And why not? She had to keep reminding herself, but the fact was, they too were young once. She sat down between Mama and Tata at the table, eating her meager breakfast with gusto.

"So, why you are dressed up, Emilia? You go to church?"

"No, Mama," Emilia answered, forcefully, "I'm not going to church. The fact is...I was going to visit Frankie's family today. That's why I was so shocked to hear Mother Jagien called. Such a coincidence."

"Ya. Is funny you are going there and she is calling. But, Milia, Noshkins says it is alright?"

"Well, I don't know, Mama, but I thought either I'd call him and ask, or I'd stop there on my way to Frankie's house. After all, Frankie's house is not far from Noshkins'."

"You wait, Dziecko. I get coat and we go."

Mil stood up quickly, busying herself with clearing the table. She hadn't thought about the possibility of Mama wanting to come along. She searched her mind for the right words, then irritation overcame her again, as she wondered why she should feel guilty for wanting to go somewhere alone. Particularly for wanting to visit her mother-in-law, alone. However, she waited a moment before answering, trying to calm her thoughts and maybe her voice. Then she spoke...her tone casual.

"Oh, Mama, it's a long ride, and I know you've got lots of things to do on Monday mornings. I really don't want to keep you from your work. You've given so much time for me already. And also, Mama, I just want a chance to visit with Frankie's family, without thinking about what time I have to get home."

Mil wondered if Mama would understand. Probably, since Mama's face, which usually read like headlines on a newspaper, was looking passive, rather than saying 'I'm disappointed...hurt'. Yes, Mil guessed it would be all right.

"Ya, Milia," Mama said thoughtfully. "Is gut you should go alone to Frankie's Mama."

Mil turned away, trying to hide her face. She didn't want Mama to know how surprised she was at such complete understanding.

"By the way, Mama, when did Frankie's Busha die?"

"Is yesterday...in morning."

A look of disappointment covered Mil's face. The family might be too busy for a visit. Mama didn't notice her disappointment. She had other news for Emilia.

"Dziecko, Frankie's mama tells the war is not over...but maybe soon."

"What do you mean, Mama?"

"Is how you say...rumor. So, is nothing special..Nov. 9."

If Frankie were still alive, Emilia would have cried, as it was, she felt only fleeting pangs of disappointment. Walter and the others would be gone even longer.

"Oh, Milia," Mama said, "today is how you say...when the Busha lays in casket...?"

"Wake, Mama? Is that what you mean?"

"Ya."

"Where, Mama?"

"At home they are having her."

"Oh," Mil looked hesitant. "Well, maybe there won't be a crowd of people there so early in the day."

She'd hoped to see Mother Jagien pretty much alone. Well she could see the family and also pay her respects, though Mama would probably want to go to the wake sometime, too. Maybe, tomorrow.

Mil cleared the table and helped with general straightening of the house, then she slipped into her sweater coat, took a few coins from her "personal" savings and left the house.

It was 9:30. The morning rush was over, so the streetcar was quite empty and Mil had her choice of seats. She figured it wouldn't take more than half an hour at this time of day to reach Noshkins' office; that would place her in the waiting room at just about the right time. Noshkins had hours from 10 - 11 in the morning. Then he was off to the hospital...if he had patients there, but usually there weren't many. She knew how much people hated hospital confinement. Patients seldom went to the hospital unless they needed surgery, or were seriously ill, perhaps near death. Actually, Noshkins probably had more home visits to make, the kind of visits he'd made to her house when she needed him. She wondered, did his wife and children ever see him? Not often, she guessed. She decided Mrs. Noshkins must be a very strong woman.

Mil stifled a yawn, wishing she'd brought a magazine along. Having forgotten to do that, she lay her head back, resting it against the cane seat, and began to study the ads lining the topmost sides of the car.

The string of ads parading around the car sides just below the roof, reminded her of the wall-paper borders pasted around the top of Mama's walls at home. Some of the ads were funny, some serious...especially those regarding the war...some were glamorous, others - silly - but reading them kept her busy...passed the time, so before she knew it, the conductor was calling Ashland. Quickly, she rose from the seat and hurried to the door, as though the motorman wouldn't wait for her. And maybe he wouldn't, she thought. He couldn't read her mind, after all, and there was no crowd waiting to leave the car, so he might not see her.

"Ashland, please." As she said the words, Mil felt the diminishing speed of the car, soon followed by the screech of metal upon metal as the brakes were applied.

The familiar corner brought a flood of memories to her mind...especially of her first visit to Noshkins' office...with Mama. How shocked and depressed they had felt...almost hopeless. Now, here she was, one year later, having lived a lifetime, arriving upon the same scene, but this time...starting over.

Starting over. Was that the way to think of it? Perhaps...yes. In a little over one year, she'd lived one whole lifetime, and though the interval had been comparatively short, that period of her "lifetime" had literally ended. She'd left behind her a job, a husband, a baby, and most of all, a sickness, one which had dictated her way of life... and Frankie's. Maybe someday, she'd marry again, but it was hard to think about that, feeling the way she still did about Frankie. Time would tell. And maybe this visit to Noshkins' office would tell things too.

## CHAPTER 21

"Emilia, my dear!"

Noshkins grabbed both her hands with his, holding them firmly. "How good to see you."

Then he surprised her completely by kissing her lightly on the cheek. She blushed. Noshkins laughed.

"Child, you must remember, I feel like a special person in your life. I feel like your second Tata."

Then Emilia threw her arms around Noshkins' neck and hugged him, thinking as she did so, of her new beginning...of how she must now behave like a *woman.*

"Come in. Let's see how you are coming along."

Noshkins led the way into the office. "Have you come alone?" Noshkins sounded surprised.

"Yes, I'm alone. Isn't it all right? Shouldn't I come alone?"

"Of course," he laughed. "But I didn't think Mama would allow you to be out of her sight for several hours."

Now Mil laughed. "Well, you're right. She doesn't like the idea, and she did want to come along, but I asked her not to."

"Good. You need to become your own person again."

Emilia's eyebrows arched. Again, she was surprised. She hadn't expected Noshkins to say what she'd been thinking.

"You think I behave like a child, Dr. Noshkins?"

There was hurt in her voice. It was all right for her to think such thoughts, but not for others to think and say them.

"No, Emilia," Noshkins said, taking firm hold of her shoulders. "But I do know it's only natural that your parents will now want to overprotect you, to try to keep any and every harm from coming to you. After all, they almost lost you once. For awhile, they will fear it might happen again. Do you understand what I mean?"

"I think so."

"Good. You will understand better, with time. Now, what brings you here today?"

Mil told him of her need to see Mother Jagien and the rest of Frankie's family. She told him about Busha's death, even about her nightmare. Finally, the best of her news, which she saved for last...her resolution to grow up...start over...to remember her love for Frankie, but not to live in false hope. The pride she felt as she told him shone in her face. Her decisions were hard won, for the realization of these truths hadn't come to her easily. So many major events had taken place in her young life so quickly, and in such a brief span of time, that, in trying to cope, she could have retreated into herself completely, never to go on with living. However, she'd now picked up the pieces of her life and found she could glue them all together again. The hurtful cracks still showed...maybe they always would...but the cracks would merely serve as helpers...reminders...not as rules of her life. She told him too about Billy...that his visits had somehow helped her to straighten out her thoughts.

As she and Noshkins spoke, other realizations came to her. She knew that she'd begun to change after Lily and Elmer visited, when she tore Frankie's picture into little pieces. The direction of change grew more pronounced when she was able to accept Elmer's efforts at gluing Frankie's picture together, to look at the picture, to admit and accept the fact that Frankie would always be a part of her life, even if she married again, and that it would be all right to think of Frankie sometimes...even if ever she did marry again. Of course, in her mind, that was a very big "if". She would have to meet someone very much like Frankie. A man who was gentle, kind, and understanding. She didn't feel at all sure that it was possible.

Emilia thought it was a good visit they experienced...both Doctor and patient...those two who had become close as blood relatives. The examination went well, too. Once again, Emilia felt confident...confident that she would not only live, but that she would pick up the fragments of her life and begin anew.

"So, it's all right, Dr. Noshkins? I mean, all right that I visit Frankie's family today?"

"I think it's good, Emilia."

"I won't bring any harm to them?"

"No, not tuberculosis, Emilia, if that's what you mean."

At that, Emilia's eyes opened wide. "How else could I harm them?" Her tone was incredulous.

"Oh, my child, of course they will want to see you, to know what's happening in your life. But you must remember, they have lost someone very dear to them too. Others will soon be coming home, but not theirs. And there was the baby as well."

"Don't say such things to me, Doctor. Please! I lost them, too. And I didn't have the time to know them well."

"I only ask you to remember, Emilia...you are hurt...they are hurt. If you remember that, all will go well."

Emilia considered that; then she answered, "I'll remember."

Again, Emilia slipped into her sweater coat, slowly clasping it shut. She picked up her purse, hesitated, then turned back to Noshkins, instead of moving toward the door.

"Doctor, there's something else I know now."

"Yes, Emilia?"

"I don't worry about God anymore. Not about hurting Him, or praying to Him, or worshipping Him. I know now that He doesn't need me, and I don't need Him."

Noshkins looked at Emilia closely. She thought he suddenly looked tired. Then he spoke to her again.

"I need Him, Emilia. I pray to Him very often."

Defiantly, Emilia raised her chin, then turned and left.

Noshkins watched her from the window. She crossed the tracks to wait for the streetcar. She was a delicate girl...her movements, graceful...still, he noticed a new determination in her step, the swing of her arms, the tilt of her head. How long would it take before she understood that he, Noshkins didn't cure her alone. That without God's help, she would never have lived to experience a miscarriage. He didn't know how long it would take, or what would cause it to happen, but happen, it would. He knew her well enough now to know that.

"Leonard," he called out to his brother in the next office. "Come here. I want you to see a walking miracle!"

## CHAPTER 22

Mil raised her hobble skirt enough to permit an easy step-down from the streetcar to the pavement. She'd ridden only a few blocks after boarding the North Ave. car, and now she was here at Frankie's house...no, not anymore...not *his* house. She'd arrived at the Jagien house...Frankie's family home.

His description of the house came flashing back to her mind..."it's like a thin piece of sausage squashed between two fat slices of bread.".

That was true, she guessed, in one way, because it was a fairly narrow frame home situated between two large brick factories. But Mil felt there was more. She stood quietly after the streetcar left, head cocked first to one side, then the other, simply examining Frankie's old home. It was different, she decided. The only words coming to her mind were unusual...quaint. Yes, that was it...quaint...almost like a page from a history book. The house was narrow and tall, painted a clean white, with charcoal gray trim around the windows and double front door. The doors were large and solid looking, one leading to Frankie's flat and the other to the flat upstairs, she guessed. The doors must have been oak, covered with clear varnish, making them look warm and inviting. The sidewalk surrounding the house was still made of wide wooden boards. To the right of the house, she saw the tops of bushes and hedges, some bare, some turned dull green with autumn sleepiness. The oranges and yellows of mums, like spices, added variety. That garden touch was also unusual looking, for not only was the garden large and sprawling, but it lay five or six feet below sidewalk level. Mil had never seen a sunken city garden before...not anywhere else, either. It was striking, she thought...and very colorful. Then she felt deep sorrow, sorrow that Frankie had felt ashamed. She wished she'd seen the house before, so she could have told him how charming she thought it was.

As she crossed the street, Mil noticed something more coming into view...a little rock castle, perched atop its own small mountain of earth, standing majestically below the plank sidewalk, in the center of the garden. How fascinating! She couldn't wait to see the inside of the house. Upon reaching the stairs, she saw someone walk around the back corner of the house. A man. She stopped...caught her breath...stood staring after him as he disappeared behind a back door. The man looked so like Frankie. It was befuddling...but no...it shouldn't be...Frankie's house, she thought...the house of his family. She mustn't allow herself strange thoughts or she would become another Elinora Steech. The man must be one of Frankie's relatives...probably his brother, Willie. After all, they looked so much alike. Having settled that in her own mind, she continued up the stairs.

The door opened before she could ring the bell. A small pair of arms tangled themselves around her waist. At the same time, Elmer's muffled voice tones filtered up to her from the folds of her sweater coat.

"Emilia! It's 'bout time you're here. I didn't think you'd ever come to see us."

Emilia hugged him back. "I'm sorry it took me so long."

"Are you well now?"

"That's what the doctor said today!"

"I knew it! I told Frankie!"

Emilia froze. Her eyes searched Elmer's.

"I'm sorry, Emilia." He gave her an extra squeeze. "I wuz meanin' ta say Willie. C'mon." He pulled her by the hand. "Busha's inside. She's in the casket, you know. Come see."

Emilia pulled herself together, trying to shake off Elmer's mistaken reference to Frankie. She knew it was a natural mistake...nevertheless, hard for her. She followed Elmer into the parlor. How spooky it looked in the dim light. She felt surprised that Elmer didn't seem to mind this parlor wake. But then, why should he? He never knew Busha as a person...as someone to talk to or play with, she was only the silent body on the bed. Someone who'd required constant care, especially from his mother, for many years. For the first time, Emilia wondered exactly how long she'd lain there. In fact, she began to wonder many things about this...Busha..this person she'd never even met.

Elmer ushered her all the way in. The parlor was dim, shades drawn. The casket biered in front of the windows, flanked on either side by tall burning tapers standing watch in mournful black holders. Emilia caught her breath. The odor of flowers was overwhelming. The atmosphere at this early hour was silent and eerie, for there were no mumbling voices...no people...only she and Elmer approached the coffin.

Emilia gasped...surprised..."Why she's beautiful..."

In death, Busha's face was serene, clear, unlined...framed by white, white hair that appeared to be loosely bunned at the back of her neck. She appeared to be smallish, but not tiny. She couldn't have been easy to care for, Emilia thought, the Jagien women were not large themselves. She continued to stare...spell-bound. Mil thought that Busha's tight-skinned face, illumined only by the glowing candles, resembled that of a sleeping silent screen movie star. Out of habit, Mil knelt down upon the kneeler provid-ed in front of the coffin. She prayed for the soul of this woman who certainly couldn't have done any wrong in these last many years, for all she did was lie on her bed, sick, weak and unknowing. Suddenly Mil wanted to know more about this woman. Her reverie was interrupted by a man's voice.

"It's good to see ya, Mil."

Again, that frightening tug at her heart, but the voice, so like Frankie's only rougher, she knew, belonged to Willie. Nevertheless, the unexpected shock of hearing Willie speak without seeing him at the same time, nearly caused her to collapse. She steadied herself on the coffin. Perhaps she'd made a mistake in coming here...alone... without Mama. No, she assured herself...no, she hadn't. Starting over was not easy...not ever...Mama had told her that long ago. Then she was forced to discover that for herself, when she became ill. That terrible illness forced her into a new way of life. Clinging to that restricted way of life hadn't been easy either, but she did it. She'd manage again...now. Emilia turned to Willie.

"I'm sorry about this...about Busha," she stammered. "But, I...I was coming anyway. I needed to see the family...all of you." Waving a hand toward the coffin, she added, "She's so beautiful."

"Yeah. I'm glad you could see her, Emilia. Glad you said that, too. She was sick so long, and well, sometimes, we felt like she was in the way, so it made us kinda forget that she was a beautiful woman."

Emilia took Willie's hand and covered it with both of her own.

Elmer had gone to find Mother Jagien, and soon she came, followed by Lily and Kate. The women greeted one another, embracing and kissing. Happy though subdued voices drifted through the still parlor air, for everyone seemed genuinely happy to see Emilia. She felt pleased.

Again, to the women, Emilia expressed her surprise over Busha's extraordinary beauty. She never thought of dead people as being beautiful, especially very old dead people. She still felt in awe each time her eyes drifted toward the vision in the casket.

Like Willie, the women were very grateful to Emilia for this observation. They too, felt a need to be reminded of this fact. It had been difficult for them to keep Busha's beauty in focus, especially lately, since her mental and physical condition had deteriorated so rapidly. As a result of that condition, they were required to give her so much extra time and attention, and to expend so much hard physical labor, that they all tended to think of her only as she had been in recent times. They felt it was good that someone who hadn't even known Busha in the past could now stand beside her final satin-lined bed and appreciate Busha as the woman she once was.

Emilia finished with, "I'm so curious about her now. Frankie didn't speak much about her."

Kate said, "Frankie never really knew her when there was anything good to remember, did he, Ma?"

"No," Ma answered as she looked again at the serene face cradled in the soft satin folds of pillow. "Isn't it sad that she must leave the earth without a trail of good memories following her. But if nothing else, I would like us all to remember this. Busha was your Grandmother, the mother of your father. Without her, none of the rest of us would be here now."

"Yes, that is the Lord's truth," Lily agreed.

"Ma, you know something?"

"What is it, Kate?"

"Busha has that trunk in your room...the one you told us never to touch. Maybe we'll find out something in there. Something to help us remember her."

"Yes. Perhaps. Now that Busha is dead, we must go through her things."

"You mean you never looked in her trunk before?" Mil asked. "But it stood there so long! Didn't you want to know what was in it?"

"The trunk was all that was left of Busha's life...all that was left of her privacy. We had no right."

Mil thought about that. She decided it was very true, and she admired her mother-in-law for thinking that way. She also decided, more than ever, that she had to tell Mother Jagien about her nightmare.

"Mother, later, when we have a few minutes, I'd like to tell you about a dream I had last night. It frightened me so. I wonder what you'll make of it."

"This dream, what was it about?"

"Frankie...mostly."

Mother tried not to show it, but she looked uncomfortable. That was the only word Mil could think of to describe Catherine's reaction. In fact, they all looked uncomfortable. Why? Were they afraid she'd have a relapse? Probably. But she really wasn't *that* delicate anymore. She was a woman now. She'd have to remind them of that. In fact, she'd show them...right now. She could talk about Frankie without collapsing, and then she could change the subject and talk of something else too. She'd show them...right now.

"Mother, have you heard anything more about Ed? When he's coming home...how he is?"

"He is still at the Red Cross Hospital, recuperating well. They feel he'll be home in a short time...maybe weeks...maybe a month or two."

"If the Armistice comes as quickly as everyone thinks, maybe he'll be home sooner."

"Perhaps."

Mother looked as though she wished to change the subject. Well, Emilia wouldn't let them do that for her. She turned to Kate.

"What about Hank? Will he be home for your first wedding anniversary?"

"That's only a month away, Emilia. It doesn't seem likely. But we'll just wait till he comes home. Then we'll celebrate! Then we'll have a baby."

Suddenly everyone became uneasy...self-conscious. Mil figured they were thinking of baby Frankie.

Kate looked down at her folded hands, then spoke again to Emilia.

"I'm sorry."

"It's all right, Kate. I've got to start over. I've got to."

"Look, let's change the subject...in spite of yesterday's headlines, and all the peace talk." Kate wrinkled her pretty brow. She looked so pert...so determined. She took Mil's hand and led her toward the kitchen.

"Really," Mil said, "I am all right. Why just a few minutes ago, I lived through the shock of thinking Willie was Frankie."

Kate released Mil's hand, and turned to look at her face. Kate's eyes were big as brown marble shooters. “What do you mean?” she whispered.

“Just what I said. I thought Willie was Frankie. He was walking around the back of the house. They look so much alike, I thought it *was* Frankie. I'll admit, I nearly collapsed, but I didn't. So, you see? I'm changing...getting stronger...braver.”

“Yes, Mil, you are. That's good. You'll need strength. We all do in this life. Come. Let's look in Busha's trunk.”

## CHAPTER 23

The trunk was in Mother J's room, had been for years, according to Kate. There was no space in the dining room for its storage, since the dining room had been crowded enough with the big table surrounded by its ten chairs, then off to the side, under the windows that overlooked one of the factories, but also the lovely garden, stood Busha's bed. Mil thought it was a strange place for the bed. She wondered why they had never built a small room for Busha by partitioning off a section of their large front hall. She could see that would have been a definite possibility. She asked Kate about it.

“Well, when the boys were young, there wasn't enough money for anything like that. And now, Ma figured it was best to keep Busha in the dining room - near the family.”

“Hmmmm. But she never talked or anything, did she?”

“No. But Ma always said you couldn't tell for sure that she didn't know what was going on. Sometimes, she'd make laughing sounds in the right places when people told jokes. And Ma said that she was a person. If God was letting her live...then we had to do the best we could for her.”

More information...not only about Busha...but especially about Mother J. These things made Emilia think she was a very strong and brave woman...just as Frankie had said. Still, she wondered how others in the family felt about Busha. With Mother J. at the tailor shop so much of the day, she wondered who cared for Busha. She asked Kate.

“Well, it fell to Lily more than to anyone else. The rest of us took turns when we could...even the boys.”

“Even Frankie?” Mil had to know.

“Well, Frankie not as much as the rest of us.”

“Because he was youngest?”

“Partly. But more because Busha always got upset when Frankie took care of her. Especially when Frankie was older.”

“What do you mean...older?”

“Oh, from about fifteen on, I guess.” Kate shrugged. “It seems so long ago, but it's really only a couple of years that she acted that way, I guess.”

“Isn't that odd,” Mil mused. “Do you know why?”

"Uh-uh." Kate took a brass key from Mother's dresser drawer. It was rather small for such a big trunk, but it was pretty...unusual. On the head of the key, flowers were carved...roses, Mil thought. She'd never seen anything like it before.

"Oh, Kate. Isn't that pretty! Let me see, please."

Kate handed the key to Mil. She examined it carefully as she turned it over and over in her hands. The key was sturdy and it felt heavy, yet the appearance was delicate. Reluctantly, Mil handed the key back to Kate. Mil had a strong desire to insert the key into the trunk lock herself...to inspect the contents of the trunk... immediately, however, she knew that privilege belonged to Kate, who'd cared for Busha. Putting her inquisitive desires behind her, Mil pressed Kate for more information.

"Did this trunk come from Europe with Busha?"

"I'm not sure, but I think so."

Finally, Kate unlocked the trunk and lifted the squeaky lid. "Maybe we'll find out."

"Oh, I hope so."

Both girls peered into the trunk. It was large, but not very full. Mil expected to detect a musty odor when the trunk was opened, but to her surprise, the trunk smelled like her very own cedar chest.

"Why, this is made of cedar!" Mil exclaimed.

"I was thinking the same thing."

"Of course, I don't know why we should be surprised."

"Me either, except that I don't remember ever seeing anyone's European trunk made of cedar. They always seem to be, well, just any kind of wood."

"Yes." Mil was so eager to see the contents, she'd lost interest in conversation. "Kate, please, let's have a look."

First, Kate removed a quilt that lay on the very top, exposing a pitifully small number of possessions beneath it. The quilt appeared to be all blue until the girls opened it and spread it out on the floor. They found the cotton backing was a lovely sky-blue, but the front of the quilt was made of white muslin squares...20 of them...each with a beautiful scene stitched on it, and the whole front was bordered with the same sky-blue cotton that backed the quilt.

"Oh, what beautiful work! Who made this, do you think? Busha?"

"I've no idea," Kate said. "But squeeze this...feel it."

"Feels like feathers, doesn't it?"

"Um-hm. But it's not heavy and thick like a pierzyna. It's light weight, seems to have only a small amount of filling."

"I've never seen anything like it."

"Me either," Kate said. She studied the pictures. "I think it tells a story."

"Maybe you're right. Look at the row of squares...almost like chapters. I'll bet that's what they are!"

"Do you think so?"

"Well, look at the first row. It begins with a group of faces, then a horse drawn carriage, a big house, finally a garden."

"Somebody must have been rich...I wonder who."

Kate shrugged.

"What's this...in the next row...this third picture?"

"I'm not sure."

"The first picture is easy...a bed...white, it seems...with a black figure bending over it..."

"Oh that's eerie."

"Then a cradle...a broken heart...and the last, this beautiful young woman, weeping."

"Busha, do you think?"

"Ummm."

Together the girls studied the pictures in the third row: the sun, shining behind a forest of trees...a scorched plain...a boat in harbor...the Statute of Liberty."

"That's her trip to America!"

"It has to be...Poland to America."

"But now, look at the fourth row. Isn't it strange?"

"It starts with some sort of bottle...like from whiskey, a cradle, a needle and thread, and then again, the weeping woman."

"And the whole last row seems to have nothing on it but flames."

Mil touched the quilt again, very lightly, afraid it would fall apart in their hands. She was hesitant, too, to dig any further into the old trunk, for though her curiosity continued to grow stronger, so did her nagging little fears about what secrets they might uncover. There was some sort of mystery here, she knew, so she knew also that it wouldn't be possible for her to leave without examining all of Busha's possessions...all that remained of her life.

Again, Emilia turned her attention to the quilt. The handwork was beautiful. Busha...if she created this quilt...was an artist. Too bad, Mil thought, that such artistry seemed to be telling a sad story.

## CHAPTER 24

Busha's quilt stirred Mil's imagination more thoroughly than it had ever been stirred before.

What a small legacy to leave the family, she thought. Of course, the quilt was probably an antique, as well as a rare work of art, and maybe worth considerable money, but who would ever want to sell it? For that matter, who would ever want to buy it? She wished some of them would someday become wealthy...maybe even leave a great and lasting monument to the family...maybe even to the world.. Oh, to accomplish something great! If not great, at least something worth remembering. She'd never thought about such things before, but now she was thinking of it. Yes, and she'd spend more time thinking about it. After all, others knew fame and fortune, why shouldn't they?

Kate brought Mil back to reality, and together, they removed each article from the trunk, examining each one carefully. There weren't many items...a lovely lace shawl, a long rosary strung of wooden beads which appeared to be hand-carved, a sugar spoon blackened by time and lack of use. Mil tried to polish the spoon by rubbing it gently along her skirt. It was so delicate...the handle being almost completely covered by blackened silver roses. Finally, they uncovered several old leather bound books. That was all.

As the girls pored through the books, they found three to be printed in Polish; one was hand-written in Polish. The hand-written book appeared to be a kind of diary. Neither of the girls read Polish very well, especially not the magnificent scroll-like handwriting of the older generations, so deciphering what it said was impossible for them.

"How I wish we could read this!" Mil said. "Don't you think it's Busha's diary?"

"Ummmm."

"You don't sound like you think so."

"Well, I just can't picture Busha writing a diary. I mean, knowing her the way we did, well it just didn't seem like she'd ever had an interesting life."

"But this trunk..." Mil opened her arms as if to embrace the treasures.

"Yes, I know. It's like this belonged to someone I never knew."

For a few quiet moments, the girls continued to finger the newly uncovered remnants of a life. Then Kate broke the silence.

"I think Ma will be able to read this book. Maybe not very fast...all this fancy writing...but she'll probably be able to figure it out, or maybe she'll know someone who can."

"C'mon. Let's show it to her."

Kate clutched the book with both hands, and started slowly toward the parlor. In her black mourning dress, she looked much like a nun marching to Matins, where, with all the other nuns, she would pray away the cares of the world.

Mil followed and thought...if only it were that easy, but with a God who didn't care much about His creatures, well..it just wasn't that easy. Prayer didn't solve life's problems. It didn't bring people back from the dead. It didn't keep them safe. It didn't keep them from getting deathly sick. No, prayer was no automatic solution to life's problems. She'd found that out from personal experience.

When they reached the parlor, they found several neighbor ladies there talking to Ma, so the girls settled themselves in the chairs lined along the wall and waited.

It was then that Emilia noticed a woman standing somewhat apart from the others. She was striking in appearance -had the most beautiful head of hair...heavy... silky, shining...a brilliant auburn color. Emilia guessed her age to be about twenty-eight. Yes, she was striking, but in a sort of tough and obvious way. There was nothing subtle about her. She wore green, in several shades, which complimented her fragile, light skin. She had lovely large eyes which Mil guessed were probably green, but it was too dim in the room to see. And even with her coat on, Mil could tell the woman had quite a figure. She was the only one in the room without a hat. Daring, Mil thought...and boldly unconventional...not at all polite...though she could understand why the woman wouldn't want to hide a bit of her gorgeous hair.

Mil nudged Kate. "Who is the red-head?" she asked.

"That's Vera."

"But who is Vera?"

"Oh, she lives in the neighborhood. Used to work at the mustard factory."

"Oh."

Mil couldn't explain why, not even to herself, but suddenly, she felt a pang of jealousy. But she knew there was no reason. Even if Frankie had known Vera when he worked at the mustard factory, he didn't choose to marry her. He had married Mil.

After what seemed a long while, the parlor emptied, leaving only Kate, Ma and Emilia. The girls took quick advantage of their opportunity, and handed the book to Ma. She looked quickly through it, and agreed that it was probably a diary.

"Can you read it, Ma?"

"Not very well, especially in this light."

Ma scanned the pages again.

"But I do think that later, when we have more time and are able to sit down with this book, well, I think we'll be able to figure out most of what it says."

"I'm so glad," Mil said, "because I really wish I had known Busha. I just can't get over it. She's so beautiful. And the quilt! She must have been very talented."

"Yes, she was."

Emilia studied Ma's face. Ma had said those simple words with some surprise and awe...like she couldn't get over it that she hadn't thought about Busha's great beauty and talent recently. But, Mil guessed, that was natural. Busha had been a burden so long that there wasn't time to think of her as anything other than a burden. But how strong and brave a woman Mother J. had been to take care of her family and Busha too, all alone, for such a long time. Emilia decided, very definitely, that Mother J. was no ordinary person.

"Come, Emilia." Mother J. took her daughter-in-law's hand and led her toward the kitchen. "We will go to the garden and sit awhile. You must tell me of your dream. Kate," she said, "please keep the watch here, in case anyone else comes."

Together, Catherine and Emilia walked through the house to the back door, down the steps and out into the garden. Catherine led the way to an old stone bench standing near the little castle Emilia had seen as she first climbed the front stairs. What a comfortable place, Emilia thought.

Then she told Mother J. all about the nightmare. She described the darkness, and how Frankie suddenly appeared from nowhere, how he pulled her into the terrible dark shed, and wouldn't allow her to pull him out again, how he wouldn't allow her to touch him, much less to hug him. Then, most frightening of all, the terrible explosion...the blue-white light...her terror...and now...now it was all so real once more that she thought she heard Frankie moan...soft...low...a painful, guttural sound, like a wounded animal.

Mil held tight to Mother's hand and squeezed, until the older woman winced.

"Mother, I'm so sorry...it's just...I'm frightened. The dream was so real, that I... that I thought I heard Frankie moan just now."

Mil threw her arms around Mother's neck and clung to her. She wiped her sweaty forehead dry on Mother's shoulder...tried to moisten her lips...all the while, clinging desperately to her mother-in-law, as though trying to establish an unbreakable bond.

Mother J. clasped her arms around her daughter-in-law in a return gesture, locking her arms in place...rocking...rocking...patting her back.

"Oh, Mother, what does it mean?" Mil whispered. "What *could* it mean?"

"Emilia, let's not think about meaning. Let us think of your dream as a painful nightmare...the workings of your anger and frustration coming out in a dream."

"But it feels like something more. I can't help it, Mother, I've got to say it. It feels like something much more...that darkness...the way I've always feared darkness...as though it were some terrible foreboding."

"Oh, my child...I don't know. Maybe it is. Maybe it is."

Catherine tightened her grip; Emilia felt it, but, she felt no more secure.

"Mother, do you think I'll ever know what the dream was all about?"

Mil looked into her mother-in-law's eyes, searching them for some answer.

"Emilia, I wish I could answer that for you, but I can't. Maybe someday. Who knows."

They sat together, silently, for a few minutes until Kate called. Then the two women returned to the parlor...to the wake, and the people who came to pay their respects in deference to Catherine Jagien, for none of them had ever known the woman, Jadwiga, whom they all called Busha...the lifeless figure in the coffin.

## CHAPTER 25

It was nearing supper time when Emilia began the walk home from the streetcar stop. For the eleventh of November, it was fairly warm, though the chill Emilia had felt in the morning, had become a cold nip now that evening had arrived. Mil walked briskly, turning one corner then another. She was hungry, but hadn't dared accept Mother J.'s invitation to stay for dinner, knowing that Mama would have worried too much about her coming home alone in the dark and cold. Actually, her sweater coat was beginning to feel insufficient. She walked faster, almost running. As she neared Pop's newsstand, she saw a group of people gathered there. She heard shouting...cheers...saw the group...men, mostly...probably coming home from work... slapping one another's backs, as they shouted. Mil broke into a run, anxious to know what had happened.

Pop saw her approaching.

"It's peace! The war she's over. The generals have signed for peace."

Pop hugged her. Others hugged her. She hugged back. Emilia was happy...for all of these people, and for those boys still alive, who would be coming home.

Emilia looked around at the group of faces surrounding her. They were about a dozen in number, mostly men in their thirties and forties. Did they have brothers, sons, other relatives to hope for, to think about welcoming back? She had a brother and brothers-in-law, but she had no husband. Damn those tears coming to her eyes! Emilia brushed them away, opened her purse, found her pennies and placed two of them on the stand, taking a paper in return. Mama and Tata would be happy to read of this...the peace that had been falsely announced just two days ago. Somehow, this time, she knew it was no mistake, even though she had not yet read the newspaper account.

Emilia folded the paper and clasped it to herself as she hurried toward the end of the block where she would turn the next corner and be able to see her own house down at the end of the block.

Someone grabbed her arm. She turned.

"What is happened?" A little old lady stood before her, clutching at her sweater, trying to keep the chill wind from hitting her chest.

"It's peace...the end of the War. No more guns, no more shooting and killing. The world will be quiet once again."

"Ach!" The woman's eyes lit up. "I must hurry."

The old woman pushed on to the newsstand and Emilia pushed on toward home.

Mama and Tata were waiting for her, and Billy was with them. The newspaper was spread out before them and their faces were happy. Emilia knew she wouldn't be the first to bring them the news. They already knew the war was over.

Mama left the table and hurried to her baby's side.

"Ach," Mama thought, "Emilia is tired. Too much is it she should go alone to Frankie's family, to see the dead Busha. Now she is come home und hear of peace, but she is no have Frankie to look for. Ach, Jesu."

Mama hugged her baby and helped her out of her sweater.

"Come Dziecko. Is soup."

Mil sat down to the clear beef broth, savoring the sight and odor of the homemade dumplings dancing in the bowl. Billy sat with her. Mama handed him another bowl of soup so he could keep Mil company while satisfying his own hunger.

Afterward, the four of them sat talking for awhile. As always when Billy was there, they talked of the future, of what they would do with their lives. Tonight, however, Mil couldn't think about her future, or anyone else's either. She was too involved with thoughts of the past...her own...and others. Frankie, his family, Busha...they were all entangled in her brain. She deliberately stirred thoughts of beautiful Busha, of her trunk...of her diary. She concentrated on the clues to Busha's life. Perhaps Mama would go with her to the Wake tomorrow and then they could question Mother Jagien about Busha's diary.

She told them, as briefly as she could, of what had happened at Mother J.'s, and then excused herself. They understood. Billy said good night, and Mama promised they would go together to the Wake the next day, early.

November twelfth dawned grayish...a typical November morning. Mil hurried into her clothes, then helped Mama with preparing breakfast and tidying up. Shortly after Mama prepared and wrapped Tata's lunch, he was off to the park, and Mama and Mil were free to set out for Jagien's and Busha's wake.

Excitement was in the air all around them. People they met as they walked, and people they ran into on the streetcar...strangers all...spoke to them about the Armistice. Everyone was friendly. Like Christmas, Mil thought. If only people were always so eager to greet one another, to be friends maybe there'd never be another war in the world. Wouldn't it be wonderful? No more war...no more unnecessary killings of young men...of young girl's husbands. Young men could stay home to be husbands and fathers. Wouldn't it be wonderful, Emilia thought.

Once again the streetcar stopped in front of Frankie's house, and once again (twice in two days, Emilia thought) she stepped down from the car, only this time, not alone. This time Mama stepped down with her. Emilia felt worried. What would Mama think of the house. The "old neighborhood" was never a favored place as far as Michalina was concerned.

Before the streetcar pulled away, an insistent gust of wind grabbed their attention. Michalina placed her free hand over the little black capelush which covered her head, thus managing to keep it in place despite the November wind that threatened to blow it off. Then, she gave her full attention to the frame house sandwiched between the factories.

"Hmm," she thought, "ya, is old neighborhood, but is nice house. Clean."

They crossed the street and Michalina continued to look.

"Ach," she thought again, "such a garden down under. Is pretty. Is not like other places we see. Ya, is nice, even if in old neighborhood. Ach so, is nice like Mrs. Jagien."

Then Michalina caught Emilia's face, studying her. Knowing her daughter would be wondering about her thoughts, Michalina spoke to the silent question.

"Is nice house, Milia. Frankie is born in nice house. Ya, und he haf nice Mama too."

Emilia smiled...satisfied...and squeezed Mama's hand.

This time, Emilia didn't ring the bell. She simply led her Mama through the hallway, into the parlor where they saw Mother J. She rose to greet them. Mama extended her sympathies, and together the three approached the casket to pay their respects and to pray for the soul of the one lying there. For her part, Emilia merely went through the motions this time, feeling it was no use to pray to a God that didn't care. They rose from the kneeler and Michalina commented on Busha's unusual beauty.

Afterward, the three sat, talking softly. Other members of the family came in, and they visited...pleasantly. However, Mil was restless - anxious to finish with visiting. She wanted so much to ask Mother J. about the diary. Then Kate joined them, and at the first opportunity, she brought up the subject of Busha's diary.

"Ma, did you tell Emilia yet?"

"About the diary? Not yet, Kate. We've only just had an opportunity to finish our visiting, to catch up on family news."

"Well, I hope you're all caught up, Ma, cause I know Mil is dying of curiosity." Kate turned to her sister-in-law, "Right, Mil?"

Emilia nodded. "Were you able to read any of it, Mother J.?"

"All of it. Late last night. It was a surprising story...so fascinating...so terrible... I couldn't put it down."

Emilia's heart began to beat faster. What terrible things could have been written in the diary. Whatever they were, there was no turning back now, for any of them. They knew. Now, she must know.

"Please, Mother...tell us."

Mother J. was about to begin, when another woman entered the parlor. Mother J. spoke to her, then returned to Mil and Mama.

"Mrs. Kazmier...Emilia...if you would like to hear the story, perhaps we should go to another part of the house. The others will stay here so we can have a little time for this. The story is interesting, but so sad, and I don't feel right now that I want strangers to hear."

Mama nodded her head in agreement. She knew what it was like...that feeling to keep family things in some secret. They were sacred to family members...these little stories of private lives. Strangers had no business to share these things.

The three women retired to Mother J.'s bedroom where the cedar trunk belonging to Busha still stood in its customary place against the wall. It really was a beautiful piece of furniture. Mil knew Mama thought so too, because she ran her hands over it very gently, as though handling a fine piece of jewelry.

Mother J. opened the trunk. Michalina handled its few treasures very carefully, and like the girls, felt she'd seen something rare. Then Catherine took the diary. She opened it to the first page, scanning it, trying to remember exactly what was written... exactly how she ought to tell this story to do it justice. She didn't wish to misrepresent anything Busha had written. It was after all, her story. An unusual story. A very sad and private story. Also, the story explained much about Busha, the woman she was, the woman she became. Yes, and it was a story they'd waited a long time to come to know.

Catherine began:

"Busha seems to have been a natural story teller. Her diary is beautifully written. I wish I could translate directly as I read from her pages, but that's a very difficult thing to do, sometimes impossible, as your Mama knows, Emilia. However, if you'll bear with me, I'll try my best to tell her story."

Mil and Michalina sat quietly...waiting...anticipating.

"Busha wrote this fifty-eight years ago. The year was 1860...the Civil War was brewing in our country, and Busha was a twenty-two year old widow with a son named Frankie. Busha and Frankie lived here - in Chicago. That son of Busha's, that Frankie, was my husband...your Frankie's father...your father-in-law, Emilia.

"Busha was born in Poland, as you know. She lived with her parents, five brothers and two sisters on the estate of a great nobleman...a descendant of King Jagiello. So his lineage went far back into Polish history.

"Busha's parents were servants...more like slaves, actually...to this man and his wife. The wife was sickly and the couple, childless. Busha describes them as a very handsome pair.

"The nobleman, whom Busha refers to only as the 'Dark One' was a frequent visitor to their home. He was very kind to them, frequently bringing them extra food...offering gifts. This cedar trunk was apparently one such gift.

"But the Dark One and his wife, did even more for the family. They often treated the children to vacations. One by one, the children were brought to the palace to stay for short periods of time. Finally, as Busha, who was the youngest of the children, grew old enough to leave her parents periodically without crying and complaining, she too, was taken to the Palace on the hill for her vacations. Busha described these visits as wonderful. She felt like a fairy princess in a story...sleeping in a soft bed, eating rich foods, served by others. She felt like someone else...like an actress playing the part of a rich and pampered princess. As she grew older, the Dark One and his wife bought her beautiful clothes. She spent more and more time at the Palace. She literally became a pampered princess - fussed over and adored by the noble couple.

"The Dark One's wife spent hours choosing just the right outfits for her, while the Dark One, himself, spent more and more time with Busha. He seemed to be genuinely fond of her, taking her everywhere with himself, teaching her everything he could so that she became quite knowledgeable in the ways of gentry life, but not necessarily in the ways of the world.

"The two were so good to her, that Busha began to think of them as substitute parents. She loved them and trusted them implicitly. She must have been a charming and beautiful child.

"Then one night her world was shattered. The *unthinkable* happened. Busha was ten years old at the time...very young...so sheltered...naive, but by her own description, already looking womanly. These looks were accentuated because of the beautiful clothes the couple provided for her.

"It was April...spring...warm. She was again spending more time at the Palace, enjoying her fantasy life there.

"One night, as she lay dozing amid the soft comforts of the royal bed they'd provided for her, the door opened and the Dark One entered. She was frightened, but he soothed her. After all, he'd always been her kind, fatherly friend. Though she didn't really understand what was happening to her, it was something she knew she couldn't tell her parents. So, she remained fearful and silent. Many such encounters followed, and the couple insisted that she spend more and more time with them.

"A few months later, during the heat of the summer, the Dark One announced to Busha's parents that he and his wife were going to their mountain retreat, to escape the discomforts of the summer. The Dark One told them that Busha would accompany them. Busha's parents didn't want her to go. The Dark One insisted, reminding them of how good the mountain air would be for the child. Then Busha's parents began pleading, saying they would miss her so badly. Finally, the Dark One told them to let Busha decide...to ask her if she would like to go to the mountains. To the surprise of her parents, Busha quickly said she would like very much to go. Of course, Busha's parents had no way of knowing that the Dark One had threatened the lives of the entire family if she didn't go with them to the mountains.

"Though the Dark One returned periodically to check on things around the Palace, Busha never came with him. But the Dark One always brought news of her to the family...glowing accounts of her health, of her maturation, of how much comfort and company Busha provided for the Dark One's wife. Busha was being tutored he said. She would be prepared for a great place in the world. He said Busha's family should be proud, that he had chosen one of their family to treat as one of his own...as a member of royalty.

"Busha's parents were not learned people, and so the Dark One was finally able to convince them that they should feel honored to have such royal attention given to their child. He convinced them that he was doing the best possible for their child.

"When Busha returned to her parents a year and a half later, she was not yet twelve, but she returned with a husband. Her family was shocked to see, not only a husband, but a beautiful young woman whom they hardly recognized, for Busha looked very mature, particularly when in the company of the dashing rogue whom she introduced as her husband, the man who was taking her to America.

"Busha's parents pleaded with the Dark One to interfere. They wanted their daughter to stay with them, at least for a while, but the nobleman told them they were selfish. That they must think of their daughter's own good...of the opportunities she'd been given. Busha's parents were uneasy about all of this...they were unhappy about losing their daughter, but once again, the Dark One convinced them. He told them about the trouble he'd gone to, to arrange such a good marriage for Busha. He said he'd given the young couple more than enough money to begin a new life in America.

"So, the couple (she not yet 12; he almost 30) stayed with Busha's parents for several days before leaving for Hamburg where they would board ship. There were tearful farewells while Busha assured her parents she was well, and she was happy and that she was doing exactly what she wanted to do. However, she had grave doubts about her parents believing this, for she feared her eyes spoke beyond her words, and all her life, she wondered...feared...that she wasn't able to completely hide from them her unhappiness.

"And she never knew whether or not they ever learned the true identify of the baby boy the Dark One and his wife brought home to the Palace with them, shortly after Busha's marriage and departure for America. She wondered if the baby grew to look anything like her, or any of her family members, but she never knew, for her letters to the family were never answered...never returned. For the rest of her life, she worried and feared that harm had come to them."

Mil had to speak. Her heart was full to overflowing for this child-woman.

"Mother, that's the most awful story I've ever heard."

Catherine nodded, sadly.

Mil continued, "But I'm surprised the Dark One didn't keep Busha with him...somewhere...in hiding...maybe to bear another child for him."

"Well, Busha writes a little about that. She says that after the birth of the child, the Dark One's wife felt threatened. She feared the genuine attachment the Dark One had for Busha. No doubt the wife was the real cause for Busha's deportation...and for the husband she was *given.*

"And Busha's name, Mother...her first name, I mean. What was it?"

"Funny, we never thought of her as anything but Busha."

"Don't you know her name? Isn't it down anywhere?"

"Oh yes, I know her name. It was quite pretty, actually. Her name was Jadwiga."

"Jadwiga Jagien." Mil turned that over softly a few times. "That's pretty. It rings...like chimes. It suits her."

"Yes. It's too bad we never used it."

"Mother, does Busha...Jadwiga say what happened to her after she came to this country with her husband?"

"From what I've read in the diary, it seems like only sadness befell her.

"Jadwiga was given to Frankie along with a handsome sum of money, a kind of dowry. However, it didn't take long before he gambled and drank it all away. They lived in New York for awhile where Jadwiga learned to sew, and eventually became a very good seamstress. By age fifteen she'd not only learned to support herself and the man she was forced to marry, but she'd also given birth to three dead babies. At that point, in her bitterness, she wanted no more babies. The one living child that she'd born had been taken away from her, never to know her. The only comfort she felt was a certain instinctive feeling within herself. Somehow, she knew the boy...whose name she wasn't even permitted to know, was living a good and happy life. She only hoped and prayed he would be a man of goodness, one who possessed a strong character, but, under the circumstances, that wasn't hers to know."

Mil wiped away her tears. "And she never heard anything about the child? Not even in the newspapers?"

"No. The Dark One was apparently a minor nobleman...no one of interest outside of his own country. However, somehow, she did manage to hear some news...I don't know how...she doesn't say, but here in the diary she mentions of hearing... sometime after coming to this country...well she mentions hearing of a fire that destroyed her parents' home in Poland. The fire was supposed to have taken place sometime after Busha and her husband sailed for America."

"Why that's just like the quilt...the first row."

"Yes. The sun in the forest...maybe that signified her childhood happiness. The scorched plain...her family's house destroyed by fire."

"And maybe, her dreams turned to ashes."

"Perhaps...it could have a double meaning."

"Then, they came to America by boat...the Statute of Liberty... the rest is obvious, I think...except this last...the fire again."

"I think you'll understand that too, before we finish."

"But Mother J. Jadwiga must have had another child. Didn't she?"

"Yes. A short time later. It seems Jadwiga and Frank decided to move to Chicago. Probably, it was pretty much Jadwiga's decision, because by this time, Frank drank so heavily, and he relied so much on Jadwiga for money, that he went along with many of her decisions.

"But, to move along here, Jadwiga writes that she was again pregnant when they began to move west. It was an unwanted pregnancy. She had never loved the man who was forced upon her as a husband, and by that time, she truly hated him. He was always drunk, demanding in every way, and he was hot tempered. Sometimes he would hit her. At those times, she often thought of killing him, however, she also thought, even hoped, that one of those times she might lose the baby...as she had the others.

"That didn't happen, however, and several months after the couple moved to Chicago, Jadwiga gave birth to a live baby boy."

"And she named him Frank?" Mil asked incredulously.

"Yes."

"Buy why? She hated her husband, didn't want his child, still she named the baby after him."

"Jadwiga's husband entered the name on the certificate of birth. He was a proud man, claiming the noble lineage, and he made certain the mid-wife knew this.

"Though Jadwiga does note here, that the boy was named not after his father, not in her own mind anyway, but rather after St. Francis of Assisi...a man known for his peaceful and loving ways."

"But was he a peaceful man, Mother?"

"Yes, certainly more peaceful than his father had been, though he did, at times, have a tendency to drink too much. We quarreled about that. It was the only reason we ever quarreled."

"You loved him, didn't you, Mother?"

"I loved him. In spite of the drinking, he was a good, kind man. Never, would he ever consider mistreating his wife or his children."

"Maybe he remembered being mistreated by his own father."

"Well, maybe, though he was quite young when his father died, and Busha doesn't mention much about what happened between the father and his son."

"I'm sorry. I'm making you get ahead of the story."

Michalina looked at Mil. "Ya. You must let Frankie's Mama finish with story telling."

"One day, when Jadwiga and little Frank were in their tiny parlor, and she was putting the finishing stitches into a dress for one of her customers, she heard her husband come into the kitchen. He'd been out all night. She'd been glad he didn't come home. She often prayed he'd stay away all night so she and the boy could have peace. When she heard big Frank stumble in, she hoped he would fall into a state of dead stupor, without even discovering where she and the boy were.

"It was a dark day, so Jadwiga had several oil lamps lit in the parlor, lighting her work place. She had patterns and other sewing supplies strewn around her.

"Big Frank stumbled into the room flailing his arms like a wild man. He shouted terrible things at her, screaming dirty names at her. Then he hit little Frank, slapped him hard across the face. Jadwiga's long pent-up rage broke loose; she jumped up from her chair, knocking over the oil lamp. In her fury, she wasn't even aware of what she'd done as she charged at big Frank like a wounded animal after its tormentor. She knocked him down. Behind her, the sewing supplies had become a raging bon-fire. Jadwiga screamed in panic. She ran to snatch little Frank from the outer edge of the flames. Pulling open the door, she threw the boy out in the street. Cool winds blew in through the open door, fanning the flames. Jadwiga rushed to big Frank's side. She tugged at him. His dead weight wouldn't budge. She shook him, screaming at him, hating him, but wanting to revive him. She didn't want responsibility for his death. He roused only enough to push her away. The flames, licking closer, began to singe his hair. She watched in horror and fascination. Then she ran from the room, shouting, 'Dialbo! Dialbo!' as she ran to her boy, and left the father to die in the burning house.

"Busha writes that though she hated her husband, Frank, and often wished him dead, she never wanted to be or feel responsible for his death. The memory of what happened, of what she'd done - even though the fire was an accident - that memory never stopped haunting her."

Emilia and Michalina clutched one another's hands, unable to speak. Each was filled with private and sorrowful thoughts. Each, in her own way, pitied this poor woman whose overwhelming beauty brought her such savage pain.

Then Catherine broke the silence. She held the diary out to Emilia and Michalina, spreading open one of the last pages, exposing a small pencil sketch.

Emilia couldn't believe her eyes. "Why, it looks just like my Frankie!"

Mother J. nodded. "Apparently, Busha's husband, my father-in-law, Frankie's grandfather...apparently, he and Frankie looked so much alike, they could have been twins."

"Jesu, kochanji," Michalina whispered.

Mil continued to study the picture; then she spoke again.

"Kate said yesterday that Busha didn't like to have Frankie take care of her. That must be why."

"Yes, I think so. You know, when the mustard factory burned, she called Frankie 'Dialbo.' We couldn't understand it then, but I think we do now."

"Oh, how sad. What a sad, sad life."

"Yes. And you know, she had periods of strangeness throughout her life after that. As she grew older, they came more and more often, until about ten years ago. She took to her bed, and never got up again, never spoke, just lay there, watching us."

Mil thought about that, about how tired Jadwiga must have been from all those unnatural struggles. Maybe that was why she just decided to lay down and let the world pass by. She must have needed to ignore life. So she did.

Emilia sat there, wondering if it would have been better if they'd never come to know Busha's story. But it was too late now. They'd read it. They knew it. And now, they knew why she was the way she was. Mil vowed such things would never happen to her. She would never record such a sad life. She would never leave such a sad quilt behind as a legacy, a quilt that ended with pictures of painful, consuming flames.

## CHAPTER 26

Mil and her Mama hurried home from the streetcar stop. The weather was still comfortable, for November twelfth, but they knew it would cool down soon...as soon as the sun set. Darkness came early these fall days. Mil wished it wouldn't. She hated the dark so much. Again, she warned herself against becoming like Busha or Elinora. Indeed, she must forget about all the things she feared and hated. She had to be strong, and that meant strong about the dark too. Then Mama interrupted her thoughts.

"Milia, is enough time. We stop at fruit store. Maybe some cabbage we get."

"All right, Mama. But let's hurry. It'll be dark soon, and you know Tata will be waiting."

"Ya, Dziecko. We must hurry."

As they passed the display windows of the fruit store, the produce, reflecting the store lights, sparkled at them as if in welcome. They stopped to study the contents of the window, and to make a careful choice. They then saw Marcus waving in greeting...motioning them inside, as he sorted and rearranged the bright balls of color.

"Michalina! Emilia! Have you come to buy, or to smile?"

"Ach, Marcus, cabbage we come in for."

"And you, Emilia? Are you buying cabbage too?"

"I'm here with Mama, Mr. Poulis."

Marcus laughed in his usual throat-husky manner; it was a gentle warm sound.

"You girls mustn't be so serious. But...come, come, Michalina. Over here. Look. The cabbage is beautiful today."

He's right, Emilia thought, and not only about the cabbage. Look how good he makes us feel with his laughing, silly talk. Yes, he's right. We need to joke more. She filed that away in her mind, along with all her other resolutions.

Marcus teased and joked some more; they laughed and looked, until finally, Marcus showed them the "perfect" head of cabbage he thought they should buy. Michalina exclaimed and opened her pocketbook as Marcus hurried to the counter to complete the sale, telling them as he hustled, that he feared they'd change their minds. Taking him seriously again, Michalina flushed as she assured him they would really buy the cabbage and he needn't worry. She even showed him the contents of her pocketbook, so he would understand that the money was really there. Then Marcus flushed, still shocked after all these years, that they would believe his silly little jokes...that they would think he didn't trust them. Didn't they know? They weren't merely customers, not even mere acquaintances, they were friends, not house-to-house friends, but friends, nevertheless. Marcus reached for an apple, rubbed it to a bright shine on his apron and held it out toward Emilia.

"Ya, Marcus. We buy. How much is, for one apple?"

Marcus flinched a little, his face becoming quite serious. Was there no way he could win, he wondered. All he wanted was to present Emilia with one very small gift, a bright, shiny apple. Would he always say or do the wrong thing with these people whom he wanted so badly to befriend. Then he thought of something.

"Michalina, Emilia, please...take the apple. I have a problem, and I must ask a favor."

Michalina's eyes opened wide. She looked with genuine concern, as well as surprise, at the fruit man. She couldn't imagine how they could possibly help him, but surely they would, if it was in their power to do so.

"Ya, ya, Marcus. What is we can do?"

"Well, Peter hasn't been feeling well lately..."

"Ach, mine goodness. What is matter?"

"Nothing to really worry about, Michalina, he's just getting over a bout with colds, but Doc says he must rest, so he hasn't been able to come to the store much lately. That leaves me with everything to do, so I wondered...well...if Emilia is up to it...well, maybe she would help me out here for a couple of weeks."

"Ach, Marcus...Milia, she never works in store like this."

Michalina looked questioningly at her daughter. She didn't know what to say. Emilia was very young, she'd been sick a long time, she hadn't worked since her illness, and that had been office work, so what in the world would she do in the fruit store? How would she knows the prices...what to do with the cash register... Michalina didn't feel it would work. That was a great responsibility for her baby.

For her part, Emilia turned the idea over carefully in her mind. Hmmm...a fruit store. This wasn't an office. No desk. No typewriter. Nothing but fruits and vegetables, a counter, and a cash register. And what about the customers? She didn't know how to joke with them the way Marcus did.

Marcus tried to read their faces. Hesitation? Consternation? Whatever it was, he decided he'd better interfere with their thoughts.

"It isn't a hard job. Why Emilia, you know almost everyone that comes in here, all women from the neighborhood. And I'd help you, especially at first."

He continued to study their faces...saw expressions changing...becoming more receptive...so he continued.

"All the fruits and vegetables have prices marked above them; you'd have no trouble with that. And well, I know you've been sick too, like Peter, so you need to start slowly back to work. This is a good job for starting slowly. And, well...I *need* your help."

He really did need their help. He had to admit that to himself, and why not? He was human. But he must convince these ladies of his need. He knew it was important to their pride. They needed his need as much as he needed their help. Marcus opened his mouth to say more, then decided he'd said enough. Now, it was up to them.

Michalina looked at her daughter. “Maybe we should go to home and see what is Tata says?”

Emilia thought about it. This was her new life...her new beginning. She was an eighteen year old woman. She'd been a wife and a mother...neither for long, but she'd been those things. She was afraid of this new kind of job, of these things she'd never done, but maybe she should try. Yes, she would try. After all, Marcus had asked her. He was the one who needed her help. She would do it. She looked at him and said yes. They decided she would come in the next afternoon...after Busha's funeral...to begin work.

Marcus shook both their hands warmly and told them how grateful he was. Michalina felt proud. They would be helping Mr. Poulis, and Emilia would be involved in a neighborhood business. Michalina was impressed. She couldn't wait to tell Tata. She hoped he wouldn't mind.

Emilia was thrilled. Her own womanly decision! “May it be the first of many,” she thought.

Suddenly, she thought of Billy, and wondered why. She hoped he would stop by soon. He would like to hear about her new job. After all, he'd been nice enough to worry about her health after the miscarriage...to visit...to take Walter's place at the table on many Sundays. But maybe Billy wouldn't need to take Walter's place much longer. Maybe Walter would soon be home, now that peace had come. Maybe, instead, Billy and Walter would both be at the table having Sunday dinner with the family. She hoped so.

Arm in arm, Michalina and Emilia left the fruit store, stopping next door, at the Sugar Bowl candy store only long enough to buy an evening paper. It would be good to read more news of the Armistice.

Tata was already home, working in the basement. Mother and Daughter decided to wait for him to finish his work before breaking the news of Emilia's job. As Michalina prepared dinner, Emilia read the newspaper to her. Several times, she read the paragraphs describing the signing of the Armistice.

‘At five o'clock in the morning, on Monday, November 11, German and Allied Officers met in a railway car on a spur line in the Forest of Campiegne, and there they signed the paper calling for an end of hostilities at eleven a.m. on that same day.’

Emilia looked at the clock. It was Tuesday, November 12...4:30 p.m.

“Mama,” she said, “the peace is only 29 1/2 hours old. It's just a baby.”

“Ya, Dziecko. Is baby...after four years that we are waiting for this baby.”

“Yes, Mama...a long time we waited, but it's a big baby worth waiting for, isn't it?”

They laughed, rejoicing together.

Then Emilia read of other things...tragic stories of death, brave stories of survival, courageous stories of battle. Soldiers on both sides were relieved...praying for speedy trips home, though not all soldiers were even aware of the Armistice at that moment. The front was long...1,000 miles...and news traveled slowly. It was estimated that those in remote areas might not hear the wonderful news for several days.

Some nations wanted vengeance. England, France, and Italy had suffered greatly during the War. Their representatives, Lloyd George, George Clemenceau, and Vittorio Orlando wanted vengeance, not mercy. President Wilson, on the other hand, urged U.S. delegates to press for formation of a League of Nations to promote and oversee future peace keeping forces. Turmoil seemed to reign midst victorious celebration.

Michalina and Emilia simply hoped for continued peace and the chance for their family members to return. Not Frankie, but all the others. Time would tell.

Hearing Tata's heavy footsteps on the stairs, the women began to prepare themselves, each thinking her own thoughts about how to break the news of Emilia's job at the fruit store.

"How silly," Emilia thought. "Why should we be so anxious, so worried about telling Tata. Mama really makes all the big decisions, we all know that, even Tata, yet we play this silly game. We continue always to pretend that Tata will over-rule what Mama says and we'll have to change everything around. It's not so. Tata never does. Is it because he believes in Mama's abilities to decide? Or is it that they've lived together so long, that each knows what the other will do, that they think so much alike there's no need to over-rule? I wonder," Emilia thought.

As Michalina stirred the tapioca pudding on the stove, she too thought.

Ach, so, Noshkins he say Emilia should live again. He say she be good in her health. So, what is. To Belmont she can go by herself for a few hours each day. Today, und yesterday, she goes to Doctor and to Frankie's family. That is long ways. Still, she goes, und Doctor say is all right. Yesterday, she even goes by self. Ya, she is feel gut again. First, I must tell these things to Tata. Then, I must tell him about job in fruit store. He will say is mine job to say. Sure. Ya. Is mine job. Tata works, and I take care Emilia. Still, I think Tata will wonder should Emilia work everyday with this man who is not married. Ach, so we are knowing him long time. He is good man. And Emilia is good girl. She be lonely without Frankie. In fruit store, she laugh with Marcus, and with customers. Ya,is gut. I tell to Tata that.

The door opened. Tata entered. He seemed to study their faces. His eyes narrowed. Emilia thought he know something was coming, but even more than these things, Emilia noticed how Tata's eyes had softened when he opened the door and saw his women there. Though his voice said nothing, his eyes seemed to say, "Ah, at last you're home. Now my world is complete."

Why, he really loves us deeply, Emilia thought. All of his gruffness, it's just an act. He really loves us, he really loves Mama, and that's why he knows she'll decide right. He loves her and she loves him. It *is* just like me and Frankie. It really is.

Then Tata's voice interrupted her thoughts.

"Nu," he grunted. "Co cie tam?"

And they told him. Mama mostly. She told all about Emilia's new job with Marcus and why it would be good. Here and there, Emilia added a word.

Tata waved his hand at them, dismissing the whole subject, saying, "All right. All right. If that's what you want. But no late nights in the store. It is not safe."

And so Emilia began to hum. Again, she wished Billy were there. It would be nice to have someone her own age to share this news with. After all, she was excited. It would be a new and different experience she would have.

However, Billy did not come. She hadn't really expected him. It wasn't Sunday. Or even Saturday. And he didn't know it was a special occasion. And so it was that Emilia spent the evening on the telephone, calling her sisters one by one to tell them about all the news of the past few days. Together, they exulted over the end of the war, they discussed Busha and her sad life, and they blessed Marcus and his need for help. Together, they all decided it was very good to be alive on Tuesday, November the 12th, 1918.

Only Ludmilla felt a bit despondent. She hadn't heard from her husband, Frank in nearly three weeks. However, the sisters decided that no news was good news.

## CHAPTER 27

The funeral was over, leaving Emilia with a great feeling of relief. Everyone said it was very nice. She guessed it was, for a funeral...if funerals could ever be nice. It wasn't very crowded because most worked on Thursdays, but those who were able, came...for Mother J.'s sake.

Emilia sensed that Mama was glad to go to the funeral. Oh, not because Busha was dead, but glad because for the first time in a long time, Mama saw Emilia in church. Mama didn't say that, but she didn't have to; Emilia knew how much it bothered Mama that her baby didn't attend church anymore. Well, it was a fact, and Mama would have to accept it. Emilia didn't need God and God didn't need her. So it was, and so it would be.

Besides, after hearing the story of Busha's diary, Emilia was even more certain that God didn't care about His people. She began now to wonder if there were a God. Did Mama ever wonder that? Probably not. Mama had believed for such a long time, that belief was automatic with her. She probably never thought to question the existence of God, just went on always believing in Him. Maybe it was good not to wonder about such things...easier. But that wasn't for Emilia. She was beyond that. Belief couldn't be automatic with her, not now...not ever again. God...if He existed, had shown her in many ways that He didn't care.

Well, enough of that, she thought. The funeral was over, Mama was on her way down the street to their house, and she, Emilia, was on her way to the fruit store, to a new job, and to furthering a new course in her life.

Emilia paused a bit longer, watching Mama as she hurried on her way...her pretty black coat swaying softly from side to side. Emilia sighed. She was such a good Mama. Then Emilia crossed the street and began running to the store. After all, she didn't want Marcus thinking she'd quit her new job before she'd ever begun.

Emilia was out of breath as she pushed the door open. She hadn't run like that in a long time. She felt stimulated, not only by the running, but also by the sound of the tinkling bell as she pushed the door open. It was to her as if the bell were making announcements...her arrival, and her new adventure.

The store was so crowded and Marcus so busy, that he didn't even look her way. From the look of things, she guessed that Thursday was shopping day for most of the neighborhood ladies. Of course, it was Mama's shopping day, so why not everyone else's? Emilia looked about, wondering where to begin. She started toward Marcus, but he was so busy she didn't wish to bother him with questions.

Without speaking to anyone, she slipped behind the counter and into the back room. Several white canvas aprons hung from hooks near the doorway. Emilia removed her coat and hat, took an apron from the nearest hook, and replaced it with her coat, hat, and purse. She stood near the wall at the back of the store, studying the people in front of her as she tied the apron strings behind herself.

There were seven women and one child in the store. Of these, she recognized four...all from the neighborhood. She wondered if they would expect her to know where everything was, and all the prices, simply because she was from the neighborhood and had shopped at the store for so many years. They might, she thought.

Nervously, Emilia rubbed her palms along the sides of the apron, as she tried to recall everything Marcus said and did whenever she and Mama came into the store. After recalling as much as she possibly could for the time being, Emilia took a deep breath, and walked toward the woman with the little boy beside her. That woman, Emilia didn't know. She felt more comfortable starting with a stranger.

"Good afternoon. May I help you, Lady?"

The woman turned in surprise at the sound of her voice. She looked Emilia up and down carefully...all ninety-seven pounds of her. Then she snorted and turned back to the apple bin.

"Humph. Whatsa matter?" she asked without looking up again. "You don't think I can pick out my own apples?"

Emilia was flustered. "Oh, certainly, Lady. Oh, yes, yes, I do. I just thought maybe there was something I could do."

"I don't know what. From the looks of you, you don't eat much of *anything*. If you don't eat, how do you know what's any good?"

Emilia stammered, not knowing how to respond. She felt her face turning crimson. She wanted to walk away from the woman, but didn't know if that would be the right thing to do. So, knowing that she'd made another mistake, feeling very awkward, she continued to stand there. She began to think Mama was right again. She'd never done such work before. Obviously, she wasn't up to it. Perhaps she should take her coat and hat and leave before she made a mess of Marcus's business, and he asked her to leave.

The woman's voice stopped her.

"Hey, Marcus," the woman called. "Where did you find this one? She doesn't know how to eat by the looks of her, and she doesn't know how to talk." Emilia felt all eyes on her. She heard laughter. The women were laughing at her! Hot tears began welling in her eyes.

Out of habit, she automatically muttered to herself, "Oh please, God, don't let these tears spill over. If they do, I'll die."

Then she realized she'd called on God again and she became angry. She had no business calling on God again, just as she'd always done! After all, she'd made up her mind about that. Nevertheless, she felt the tears go back to wherever tears go when they don't spill. So, she thought, it's good I'm angry. Now I won't cry. And God? He had nothing to do with it at all. So there! Meanwhile, Marcus, seeing what was happening, and Emilia's reaction to it all, hurried to her side, put his arm around her shoulders and smiled warmly.

The woman who had shouted stood looking at them. Then she pointed at them, and again spoke in a loud voice.

"Aha! Got yourself a young one. Well, I guess she don't need to know nothing in *here*!"

Marcus laughed in his good natured way and then introduced Emilia to the group.

"Ladies, my new helper. Peter is sick, I'm getting old, and Emilia needs a job." Marcus looked at Emilia affectionately. Then, he turned back to the ladies. "You mamas be good to this little one. She has much to learn. So, come, Emilia. I'll show you how to work the cash register. The ladies will find everything they need all by themselves." As an afterthought, he added, "And no cheating at the scales, Ladies. I can hold the bags in my hands and tell you to the ounce how much you have."

All of them laughed.

My, how they joke, Emilia thought in astonishment. Then she wondered if Marcus really could tell the weights without using the scales. How amazing! She didn't think she'd ever be able to do that.

The rest of the afternoon passed smoothly. Marcus patiently taught Emilia how to operate the cash register, and where and how to file the credit cards. She simply had to file the little pieces of paper in a metal box, according to the alphabet.

By the end of the first day, she'd rung up at least a dozen sales, collected the money for them, and counted out the change. She was pleased and felt much more confident, especially after Marcus complimented her, saying she'd mastered this new art very quickly.

Emilia's afternoons in the store passed quickly and pleasantly as she worked with Marcus, both through observation of what he did and through his direct teaching. She thought she liked best what she learned about humor and dealing with people. Of course, only Marcus could joke the way he did, so Emilia never tried to copy his style. Instead, she worked on developing her own sense of humor. However, more often than not, she felt frustrated about that because the ladies didn't seem to understand her way, but with Marcus' help, she came to understand that it didn't matter anyway. Marcus merely required her to be polite and courteous to the customers, which, he assured her, she always was. After a few weeks, Emilia began to relax, enjoying the work more and more.

Her afternoons in the store passed so quickly, that Emilia couldn't believe a month had gone by, but the calendar said December, and she and Mama, along with her sisters and sisters-in-law, were beginning preparations for Christmas, so there was no doubting the passage of time.

They all looked forward to Christmas, especially now that the war was over, but they wanted more than anything to have their beloved boys home again. The waiting was particularly hard for the family, because several of the neighborhood boys had already been discharged and had returned home. Of their own, however, knowledge was very limited.

Ludmilla had finally heard from her Frank. The news relieved, yet saddened her, for she was certain that he was still somewhere in France and wouldn't return for awhile.

The family hadn't heard from Walter in about a month and a half, though his girl, Lydia, had received one letter, a very cheerful letter from somewhere in France, and since she read most of it to them, everyone felt better...less worried. Of course, it was an old letter, because in it, Walter had said he was anticipating the end of the war and his discharge afterward. They all wondered if he knew now that the war had ended.

On Frankie's side of the family the news was also good, for everyone that is, except Frankie. Kate was overjoyed at the prospect of having Hank home soon. He was at Fort Lee awaiting discharge.

Ed was still hospitalized in France, but now able to write his own letters. He did not yet discuss his injury.

As for Frankie...no miracle message came to Emilia...not directly...not indirectly through the family. No one encouraged her to keep the flame of hope burning any longer, not even Mama. Mother J., Kate, Lily, Willie...none of them encouraged Mil to hope either. In fact, Frankie's family never even discussed him unless forced to by Mil's prodding. That bothered her, but she guessed she knew why. They simply didn't want to upset her.

Christmas without Frankie would be very hard...harder, Emilia knew, if she allowed herself to think too much about it, and so she was more and more grateful to be going to the store every afternoon. The work kept her mind occupied and her body tired.

Most afternoons the store was so busy, that even Marcus, with all his experience, became weary. He was really surprised by the heavy sales, since food rationing hadn't yet been completely lifted. He claimed the ladies were all celebrating Armistice by spending extra hours at their stoves preparing holiday gifts and treats to save for their returning young men. With so much business at the store, Marcus needed more and more help. Frequently, he asked Emilia to return in the evening after dinner. She was delighted.

The Thursday before Christmas was one such evening. Mil was anxious to go; there was so much excitement in the air, and the excitement always carried over into the store. It was fun to be there.

On that Thursday, Billy stopped to visit shortly before dinner, and though Mama,

Tata, Harry and she, herself, had teased him about his timing they did convince Billy that he ought to stay for dinner. Billy joked a lot, like Marcus did, and they all enjoyed his company. He always livened conversation at the dinner table.

Emilia thought it was funny, how much Billy and Marcus were alike. Of course, there were differences, the big one being age. Marcus had celebrated forty birthdays to Billy's twenty-five. They differed greatly in physical stature and coloring too. Marcus was short and dark, with mischievous, squinty eyes, while Billy was tall and fair-skinned, sporting the look of a red-headed, over-sized elf. Different, yet the same, Emilia thought. Both good men.

When dinner was over, Mama cleared the table and Emilia poured steaming cups of coffee all around. Then, after checking the time, she decided against a second cup, excused herself, and grabbed her coat. Billy joined her, offering to walk along to the store.

They left together, teasing and bantering their way down the front stairs, like two very old friends.

As they walked along, Emilia thought how nice it was to have Billy there with her.

The evening air was damp; the sky full of clouds. It felt like snow...a quiet kind of evening. Neither of them spoke for awhile. Then Billy took Emilia's hand in a friendly grip and broke the comfortable silence between them.

"Emilia, do you know why I really came over tonight?"

"You mean it wasn't just to see me?"

Emilia couldn't believe she'd said that. She was glad they were walking outdoors along the darkening street. That way, Billy couldn't see her red face.

Yes, she thought. Billy and Marcus were exerting quite an influence over her. A few months ago, she could never have said such a thing. She smiled to herself, thinking it was good, even though she still felt the hot flush of her cheeks.

Billy continued, "Oh, your Mama's cooking has a little something to do with my visits, I guess."

She looked at him, wanting to see and appreciate the impish grin she knew would be accompanying his teasing remark.

"All right, Billy. I'm asking. Why did you really come over tonight?"

"I don't know if you're ready for this, but...I have a job prospect. In fact, I think it's a pretty sure thing."

Emilia squeezed his hand. "Wonderful! Where?"

"Just a few blocks from here, at the showhouse. The Grand."

"At the showhouse!" That was about the last thing Emilia ever expected anyone to tell her. She couldn't hide her astonishment. "Whatever would you be doing there?"

"They need a piano player for some of the vaudeville acts...movies too."

"I didn't know you played the piano, Billy. But, the showhouse...you must be awfully good."

"Well, good enough that they're considering hiring me."

"That's really something, Billy. I feel so honored...walking with a star!"

"Hardly. Just a piano player. But, who knows what that might lead to."

Emilia looked at Billy in surprise.

"What do you mean by that?"

"Oh, I'm not really sure." There was a moment's silence as Billy seemed to be sorting out his thoughts before answering further. "I guess...I've always thought, secretly, that show business would be a nice way to make a living."

"Really? That's funny, because I always said I'd like to be an actress. We used to put on some fancy shows...all of us neighborhood kids. You know...just down in the basement. We'd charge a penny sometimes. For special shows."

"Yeah, I know. We used to do that in our neighborhood, too. That's when I was pretty young, though, before Mom and Dad died. It was harder after that, when I lived with Aunt Mattie."

"Oh, Billy, I'm sorry."

"Why? I'm not. That's the breaks. That's life...as they say."

Emilia was astonished that he could talk so matter-of-factly about the death of his parents. Didn't he love them? She thought she'd die, if anything ever happened to Mama or Tata. She had to ask more about Billy's ideas.

"Billy, didn't you love them?"

"Who?"

"Your parents, silly."

"Of course."

"You don't sound like it."

"Because I'm not breaking up in tears?" Now astonishment showed in Billy's face as he turned to Emilia. "Em, what good would that do? They died a long time ago, and there was nothing I could do about it. It was in the cards. Their time was up. That's that."

Mil was distracted for a moment. No one had ever called her 'Em' before. It sounded nice, coming from Billy. But she had to continue. She had more questions.

"Don't you sometimes miss them?"

"It's been a very long time. Sure, I cried a lot when I was a kid, but Aunt Mattie helped...even though she had to work hard to keep us in food." Billy paused, as though he were remembering it all right then. She used to say, 'Life goes on, Billy. Your mother and daddy are dead, but you and I? Well, for some reason, God wants us to live.' And you know what, Em? I found out she was right."

There it was again. Someone else thinking that God really cared. That God really had a plan of some sort for them. And this from Billy! She thought he was too sensible for such ideas. She wanted to talk more about that, but it would have to wait until another time. They had reached the store.

"Oh, dear." Emilia couldn't hide her aggravation. "Elinora Steech is in there. I don't want to see her. Let's go."

"Hey, wait a minute."

"I don't want to go in. She'll leave soon. Let's walk around the block."

Billy didn't know what the problem was, but he didn't think it could be bad enough to keep them out of the store, whatever it was. Particularly, since she was expected to be there for work. Maybe Emilia needed a little help with this. Sometimes, she seemed too reluctant to do things...too timid to face situations. Maybe that's what happened when you had a big family around, people always around to protect you. Maybe he could help her a little with this.

"Come along, Em. I'll go in with you."

Before Emilia could turn away, he had her by the hand and was holding the door open for her. Reluctantly, she followed him inside.

At the tinkle of the bell, Marcus turned from his conversation with Elinora. His eyes narrowed at the sight of Emilia and Billy. That young man was no relative leading Emilia into the store, Marcus thought. Who was he? What was he doing there?

Then Marcus chided himself. What concern was that of his? He wasn't Emilia's father, and certainly as her employer, he had no right to approve or disapprove of her friendships. Besides Emilia was young. She needed companionship. She needed male companionship...young male companionship. Yes, he must keep in mind that Emilia was his employee not his personal charge. Marcus moved a few steps toward them.

"Well, Emilia. Who is your tall young friend?"

Emilia introduced them. They shook hands. Marcus spoke again.

"I'm sure you know Elinora, Emilia. Billy, this is one of the charming ladies from our neighborhood."

Elinora's chubby cheeks rounded in a big smile.

"Oh," she said, "and my Jan. Marcus, you forgot my Jan."

Marcus ignored her statement. Billy seemed confused. Emilia sighed in disgust. Marcus then ignored them all, and changed the subject.

"I was just telling Elinora, that if Herbert Hoover doesn't remedy his ways, I'll be out of business."

"You're referring to the food rationing, Mr. Poulis?"

"Marcus, please. Yes, the food rationing. I want it lifted completely so there will be more meat and sugar to go with my fruits and vegetables."

At that moment, as if on cue, several people entered the store...one man and three women. They entered one after the other, as though trying to make a mockery of the statement Marcus made. The four of them turned to see who entered, and Billy began to laugh good naturedly.

"Mr. Poulis...I mean...Marcus, I don't think you have to worry. The butcher might have some concerns, but from what Emilia tells me, you don't."

Marcus slapped Billy's back lightly and laughed along with him. Then Marcus handed Billy a brightly polished apple. "Go along, now," Marcus said. "We have work to do."

"Yes, I see. And aren't you lucky to be able to hire Emilia? Why if it hadn't been for the war, I might be working here instead, and I'm not nearly so pretty."

"No, and you wouldn't work so cheap, either."

"Why, Marcus," Emilia said, "you pay me well. Mama was so surprised. Tata too. They never heard of a woman earning $7 a week."

"You're right, Marcus, I'd ask at least ten dollars," Billy said.

At that, Elinora's eyes opened wide. "Ten dollars? Jan, are you hearing that? Ten dollars he would ask. I wonder. Did that lady in California earn so much for painting the flagpole?"

There was a little silence as Elinora seemed to be listening. Emilia knew she was listening...to the voice in her head...the voice of her dead Jan. Then Elinora continued, as though to her Jan.

"You know the lady I mean. The one who took her husband's place when he went in the army. That's who, and now she paints flagpoles, maybe signs too. I don't know."

Billy wasn't sure about what was going on, but he knew nobody was standing next to Elinora, so she must have some sort of problem. He thought it a shame. There was something child-like about the woman. She seemed very nice. He made a mental note to ask Emilia more about the woman when he saw Emilia next.

"Well," Billy said. "Thanks for the apple. I'd better get home before it gets too late. My landlady won't let me use her piano after 9:30."

"Bye, bye, Billy. Let me know how the playing goes."

"I will, Em...*if* the playing goes, but it does look real good for the job. I might even be able to get you in to see the next movie."

"Oh, what is it?"

"A return of Tarzan of the Apes.".

Emilia laughed. "I like that one. I like Elmo Lincoln."

"You can have him. I'll take his leading lady...that gorgeous Enid Markey."

With that, Billy left the store. He walked down the dark street, thinking things over as he munched the crisp apple. Marcus Poulis, he decided seemed like a good guy. He decided also that Marcus Poulis loved Emilia Kazmier. It was obvious in the way Marcus looked at Emilia. Billy wondered, though, if the man knew it himself...or if he'd even admit that to himself. Maybe Marcus was kidding himself into thinking he'd be an *uncle* to Emilia. Billy shrugged. He liked Marcus anyway...and he'd probably be very good to Emilia. Billy's thoughts lingered on that for a bit. He wasn't sure he really liked the idea of Marcus and Emilia. Could he be falling in love himself? Hmmmm. No. He wasn't quite ready to do that.

## CHAPTER 28

Emilia watched Billy from the window until he turned the corner. She was about to ask Marcus if he had anything special for her to do, when she felt his hand on her shoulder. Then he spoke to her.

"Nice boy, your Billy."

"Yes, he is nice," Emilia agreed, "but he's not *my* Billy."

Marcus studied her face carefully for a few seconds. He saw no special sparkle in her eyes. Maybe she meant that. He felt strangely relieved. Foolish, he thought. Why should he care? Enough, he thought. They must tend the customers.

"Come, Emilia. You handle the cash register tonight. I'll go over the ledger books and credit cards."

Emilia walked eagerly to her post. Already there were two people waiting to be rung up.

During the next hour, customers came and went so quickly, that neither Emilia nor Marcus noticed the misty rain which had begun to fall, but as it turned to sleet, tapping soundly at the big windows like hungry little birds at a feeder, both of them took notice.

"Oh, Marcus, winter is here." Emilia shivered.

"Not quite...but fast approaching." Marcus studied the sparkling ice droplets, frozen to the windows. "You don't like winter, Emilia?"

"Not once the holidays are over. Then I wish spring would come right away...right on the stroke of midnight...oh...say...January 7."

Marcus laughed. Then he thought how much she probably wished she were at home.

"It's quiet in here now. I don't think many more people will come out in this weather. Why don't you go home. Would you like that?"

"Oh, yes, Marcus! Then I could help Mama with the sugar cookies."

"So, go ahead. But only if you bring a cookie tomorrow afternoon."

Emilia began untying her apron. "Fine! One cookie tomorrow afternoon."

Marcus turned once more to his bookwork. Emilia donned her hat and coat.

"Good night, Marcus," she called, heading toward the door.

Suddenly, the lights dimmed, became bright, then dimmed again. Seconds later, they went out completely, everywhere...even the street light on the far corner. The sudden blackness blinded Emilia. Such awful darkness! Fear gripped her like a vise closing tight.

"Marcus. Marcus!" Emilia's usually quiet voice grew shrill as the squeak of a badly played violin.

Frantically, she reached out, trying to touch something familiar...the fruit bins, the counter, anything. Only the stilled air touched her fingertips. Panic wrapped itself around her like a tightly pinned shroud. It was hard to breathe. She screamed.

Then, she felt Marcus pulling her close, folding his arms around her, trying to comfort her.

"There, there, Emilia. It's all right. The lights went out. That's all. Probably because of the sleet. Made our lines too heavy."

Emilia was shaking. She tried to pull herself together. She heard Marcus speaking to her. What was he saying? She must listen. But oh, it was so dark...so, so dark.

Then, lightning! Oh God! Like in her dream. Lightning...one flash after another...illuminating the sky, like fireworks.

She called out to the stilled black air in the store.

"Frankie...Frankie! Where are you? Somewhere out there, you need me. I know it. I know."

Emilia began to sob.

Marcus gently led her to a chair.

"Come, come, Emilia, child. What's wrong?"

"Oh, Marcus." She clung to him. "Marcus, I don't know."

"There must be something, dear Child." He paused, but she said nothing more. "All of us are a little frightened of the dark. Darkness is uncertainty...like knowing something's about to happen, but not knowing what." Still, she said nothing. He continued. "But, Emilia, most of us are not so frightened as this."

He held her cold hands in his own, trying to warm them.

"Tell me, Emilia. Tell me why you call out to Frankie."

Her sobbing began to subside. Again, Marcus urged Emilia, in his gentle way, to talk about her fears. Finally, Emilia spoke, telling him of her dream...her terrible dream of Frankie...of Frankie pulling her into a smothering darkness with him...even though he knew how frightened she was...of how Frankie wouldn't speak to her. She heard only his anguished moaning. It was terrible...oh, so terrible.

"There, there," Marcus said, putting his arms around her once more. "Such a bad nightmare, Emilia. Yes, Emilia...terrible."

They sat quietly, Marcus holding tightly to her hands.

She broke the silence. "Marcus, when will the lights go on again?"

"I don't know, dear Child."

He began to rummage around under the counter.

This frightened her again. "What? What is it, Marcus?"

"It's all right, Emilia. It's nothing...nothing. I'm only trying to find a light. I thought there was a lantern under here, but I can't seem to find it."

"Oh, Marcus...please find it...please."

"All right, Emilia. Sit quietly. I will look...not far from you. Only at the end of the counter...here...I believe it might be right over here."

Emilia waited nervously as he searched.

"There. I've found it," he said, striking a match to light the wick.

"Oh, Marcus. Thank God!"

Marcus wondered what would be best. Should he walk the child to her home? Foolish. It was probably just as dark there, and walking on the slippery sidewalks would be too difficult, especially in Emilia's agitated state. No, he decided, better to stay where they were and wait. But, wait for what? Only the lights? No, that wouldn't be enough. Marcus decided they must try to find the reason for Emilia's terrible fear. It was unnatural. He felt it was more than one dream that caused it.

Again, he gently prodded Emilia. She insisted her fear was due to the terrible nightmare. Again they fell silent.

Emilia broke the silence once more, wishing to hear something, even the sound of her own voice.

"Marcus..truly, I don't know why I'm so frightened...except for the dream."

"It's all right, Emilia. I understand." He hesitated, searching for the right words, then continued. "You know, sometimes, we bury things we can't stand to remember. Do you understand?"

"I think so, Marcus."

"Let's try again to remember. Maybe it will help. Think hard. Were there other times you were frightened in the dark?"

Without hesitation she answered him. "Many times, I think."

"Then tell me what you remember."

First, Emilia told him of the picnic, the one she and Florchak went to, where she met Frankie, because Florchak insisted Mil should meet her cousin. That was why they went to the picnic.

They were having so much fun...until she went to the outhouse. It was a little building...off by itself. She went in. It was very dark in there. She tried to leave, but the door wouldn't open! It stuck. It was stuck...shut! She began to shout and scream. It felt like hours before Frankie came and forced the door open, but they said it was only a few minutes. She was so grateful to Frankie for forcing the door open. Maybe that's when she began to love him. Oh, she was so happy to be out of the dark, smelly place.

Marcus understood her fear, but still, he felt there must be even more reason for her great agitation.

He listened patiently as Emilia told him of the other times when lights went out, or doors closed unexpectedly, or the little kitchen night lantern had blown out, but never had anything really terrible happened to her during those times. At least nothing that she told him about. Still, he thought, there must be more.

Again, he urged her on. "Think, Emilia. When was the very first time you remember being caught alone in the dark? And very frightened?"

Emilia concentrated very hard. Then she began to remember something...bits and pieces...darkness pressing in all around her. It was so long ago. Slowly, she began to recount the memory...hoping to bring it all back.

"I was maybe three or four years old. It was winter, late afternoon...just turning dark. I had fallen asleep in the parlor...on the sofa. I'd been sick a little...maybe had a fever. I remember waking up...in the gathering dark. I called Mama. I thought I heard her answer. It sounded like she was down in the basement. I threw the cover off, got up and went to the stairs. It was dark down there, but I wanted Mama. I kept calling for her...looking. The floor felt cold; my feet were bare. I moved along the basement wall, slowly, feeling my way. I fell into something - like a hole it seemed. It was the coal bin. The door was open. In my half sleep, in the dark, I couldn't see that. I had stumbled into the bin. I heard the door swinging behind. It slammed shut! It was so dark black."

Emilia shuddered.

"I began to cry. I started screaming. No one came. I pulled and pulled on the door. It wouldn't open. Mama, I called, again and again. Then..."

She stopped, trembling...clutched Marcus' arm so tightly, he felt her nails digging deep. Marcus said nothing; Emilia stammered..continued.

"Something ran across my feet. It felt cold...clammy, but I felt it was furry. I knew...I knew..it was a rat."

Emilia shuddered...reliving the memory again. Tears ran down her cheeks.

"It's like I can feel it even now. I was terrified...so sure the thing would come back...nibble my toes...chew them off...I grabbed the door handle, tried to pull my feet up off the floor...sobbing...crying...Mama...Mama...where's Mama..."

Emilia crumbled. She sobbed...clung to Marcus.

"It's all right, Emilia. I'm here. Go on."

"I thought she would never come. I thought Mama was gone."

"But she came, Child. She came."

"Oh, yes, Marcus. I remember. She opened the door, and scooped me into her arms, and cried with me...she felt so bad. She had only run for a few minutes to the grocery store next door. She needed cream for me. She was sure I would sleep that long. Then she heard me screaming. She left the cream on the counter and ran home to me."

"Poor little Emilia. No wonder you were so frightened."

Marcus wiped the cold sweat from her forehead. It was hard for him, seeing her relive that experience, but he hoped it was best that she did.

"Oh, Marcus, I had forgotten that until just now, when you made me think of it."

"Emilia, sometimes, when we bury things deep inside, so deep we can't even remember them, they bother us, eat away at our souls like termites nibbling away at the heart of good wood. But when you pull that terrible thing out and let the sun shine on it, and look at it carefully, the termites run away. They can't face the sunshine. They leave the wood alone, maybe with scars, but all in one piece...solid."

Emilia studied Marcus intently. Then she rose from the chair he'd led her to, and planted a grateful kiss upon his cheek.

"You are a wonderful man, Mr. Marcus Poulis."

"Thank you, Emilia." Marcus was feeling something he hadn't felt in a long time. Blood seemed to be coursing his veins in a most unusual way...fast flowing...hard pumping. He heard his own heart beating. Hmmm, they must change the mood, he thought, or he might behave foolishly.

"Come. We'll play tic-tac-toe awhile. The lights must come on soon."

Emilia felt exhausted, yet relieved. She wished the lights would come on again soon, but now, she wasn't alone; she didn't feel alone.

To her surprise, and that of Marcus, a customer came in shortly after they'd begun their game. He came across the street, attracted by the lantern light. He said he had nothing else to do anyway, so he came for a little asparagus and conversation.

The three of them talked first about the peace, then about Mary Pickford's movie called "Little Princess". Then the lights came on and Emilia thought she would go right home, so Mama wouldn't worry too much. Marcus wanted her to wait for him because he didn't think she should walk alone after her emotional fright, and her emotional remembrance, but she thought it better not to wait. Emilia was sure she could manage alone now, however, the customer assured them both he wouldn't mind walking Emilia home. It would give him something to do, he said.

When she arrived home she went straight to bed, without telling Mama and Tata about the talk she had with Marcus, about how he helped her to remember. She was too tired. Crying always made her feel very tired.

## CHAPTER 29

Emilia woke next morning to the sound of happy voices. After the previous evening and the emotional experience she'd endured, Emilia felt disoriented, wondered where she was. The sight of her own familiar wall paper and furniture reassured her. Emilia was home...in bed. The morning sun was surprisingly bright; she didn't expect that after last night's freezing rain. Her clock said nine. She'd slept long.

Again, happy voices filtered through her closed door. Who was visiting already? Who could feel so exceedingly bright and cheery when she felt hardly awake? Emilia decided to slip into her robe and find out.

Before she could swing her feet to the floor, a brief, resolute knock sounded on her door.

"Mama? Come on in." she called.

The door burst open, and there stood a handsome young man in uniform... stocky...muscular. Surprised by this unusual intrusion upon her morning privacy, Emilia wasn't able to focus her mind clearly. Then, the ehthusiastic young man swooped into the room and threw his arms around her, still not speaking.

It was then that she knew him. She reached her own arms up and hugged the now-less-than-familiar form close to her. Tears of happiness coursed down her cheeks.

"Walter..oh, Walter..how good to have you home again!"

She pushed away from him, looking more closely at his face. A little pale, she thought, but looking good otherwise.

"You've become so...so...manly," she said, finally finding the right word to describe her brother.

"And you've gained about ten pounds, and put some roses in your cheeks, Emilia."

He pulled her close again and squeezed until nearly every ounce of breath left her body. She hadn't remembered just how much she'd missed Walter's wonderful bear hugs.

"Such a wonderful Christmas present!"

"For me, too," Walter said. "I didn't know if our ship would make it on time for the holidays. And then, all the red tape. Unbelievable!"

"Then you're home to stay? Completely discharged and everything?"

"Home to stay!"

Emilia wrapped herself in robe and slippers and together they marched into the kitchen, laughing and hugging. That was one thing about Walter. Each time he returned from anywhere, it always felt as though he'd never left. Of course, this time, they all feared it might be different. Never before had he been gone for such a long time. Emilia couldn't even remember exactly how long, but it was somewhere around two years. And his experiences. He'd been in France...fighting. He must have seen terrible things...destruction..suffering...death...who knows what all. She and Mama both feared he wouldn't be the same Walter when he returned. And Tata, he wouldn't even discuss

Walter, or what he thought Walter would be like, what sort of changes they might see. It was as if he didn't dare speak of his son until return was certain. Yet, here he was, their own Walter, the same big brother who'd left home to experience an adventure. She guessed he had. Then she wondered if Walter had already seen his girl.

"What about Lydia? Does she know you're home?"

"Not yet. I tried to call as soon as they allowed me to use the phone, but there was no answer. Not last night, not today."

"You probably couldn't get through last night. We had a terrible ice storm. Lights were out and everything."

"That must be it. And today, she's gone to work."

"You're anxious, aren't you? Are you going to marry Lydia?"

"You bet...on both counts." Then he added, "I'm sorry...about Frankie."

Mil swallowed hard and squeezed his hand in reply.

Mama was waiting for them in the kitchen. The smell of steaming coffee and hot buttered cinnamon toast filled their nostrils. The table was set, and breakfast was waiting.

Walter hugged Mama. "Oh, Mama," he said. "It's good to know that some things don't change."

Tears filled Mama's eyes. She couldn't speak. They had breakfast and caught up on family news. Walter told them about accidentally meeting Ludmilla's Frank on the streets of Paris. He was all in one piece which was about all he could say for anyone at that time, including himself. Frank said he'd heard rumors that his Company would have to stay longer as part of the Occupation Force, in Germany. It probably wouldn't be long, a matter of months, but he hated to think even of that short time. After what they'd been through, a few more months would feel like an eternity. Of course, a rumor wasn't certainty, but the men had learned that most of the rumors they heard were more truth than fiction. At least, Walter would be able to tell Ludmilla that the worst was over for her husband, and that he was sound and to all appearances, in good health.

Other than that, Walter was not eager to speak of the war nor of any experiences connected with it. He said, maybe in time, but not yet, even though he had considered himself luckier than many. Being in the tank corps, he felt less exposed...in every way, to personal danger than those who fought in the trenches. However, he found war to be more terrible than he could ever have imagined. He'd experienced many adventures and he was glad he went, but for the time being, he didn't want to recount any of it.

A short while later, they began the phone calls to the rest of the family. Mil knew the house would be filled that night.

Then the three of them walked to the park, to see Tata. Mil would never forget it.

The sun was so bright for December, that Mil was not surprised to find Tata outdoors, walking in the sunlight, looking at everything around him, but at nothing in particular. Tata loved sunshine and though he never complained about its lack on those long dreary winter days, Mil knew how much he missed the sun. On days like this, he looked for every opportunity to work outdoors.

Tata stopped; stood with his back to them; surveyed a covered flower bed. Walter walked up quietly behind him. Mama and Mil waited down the path. Walter said something. Tata's head jerked a little, but for a moment there was no other movement. Then Tata turned, facing Walter...facing them. His face beamed.

"Wladek."

That was all he said, but the way he said it. Mil couldn't describe in words the feeling...the emotion...contained in that one word...her brother's name. To Mil, the name never ever sounded the same again.

Tata embraced Walter and held him close. Then he reached into his pocket while gently pushing Walter away. With one swift movement, he wiped his eyes, ran the kerchief under his nose, tucked it back in his pocket, and smiled the broadest, easiest smile that Mil ever saw come across Tata's face in all her life. Mil marveled at Tata's expression, wondering if she would ever see him looking exactly that way ever again.

Such a wonderful day they had! Mama had packed a lunch; they ate together from the newspaper parcel as they relaxed on a bench on the bank of the lagoon. Tata seemed to know, to understand, probably from his own army experience in the "old country" that Walter needed time before he could discuss what happened "over there". Instead of war talk, they spoke of flowers, and trees, even of Frankie's Busha and her life. When they weren't talking, they watched an occasional gold fish dart about the water. Mil wondered that the poor fish didn't feel the cold of the water. No amount of explaining on Walter's part could convince her that the fish, being cold blooded, didn't feel the changing temperature of the water.

After lunch, Walter was able to contact Lydia. She left work and hurried to their house, where another kind of loving greeting took place. It was interesting to see so many sides of her "new" brother on that day. The lovebirds didn't stay long. Mama and Mil understood their need to be alone.

Mil was happy for them, in spite of the touch of envy she felt trying to take over her mind. She could imagine herself greeting her Frankie that way. She pushed the image from her mind.

Just before supper, Harry came home from the dental lab, which he'd been manning alone since Walter left for basic army training. The family was eager to witness this reunion, for they hadn't phoned Harry, wanting him to be completely surprised at his brother's return. He was. The brothers wrapped arms around one another, shouting, slapping one another on the back, tussling as though they were young boys once again. They laughed and cried...hugged again. Harry said it was about time Walter showed up to do an honest day's work again, but Harry was proud of his brother, and it showed...each time his eyes came to rest on Walter's uniform.

In the evening, after supper, family members came trickling along, until the house was filled with happy, laughing voices. Stasha and Helcha came with their husbands and children. The nephews had trouble understanding that Walter wasn't ready to tell them about his war experiences. Ludmilla came alone, pumping Walter over and over again about her Frank...how he looked...exactly what he said...how much he missed her...when he thought he might return.

The other brothers, Will, Steve, and John also came with their wives and sons.

Again, there were more nephews to greet and to convince that someday...maybe... Walter would be ready to tell of his many war experiences. However, when all the nephews gathered down in the basement to play games and tussle, the adults were left in peace to the happiest reunion they'd had since Mil's deathly illness took a turn toward health.

Finally, when Mama served her homemade cream filled yeast cakes, and apple strudel, they rushed to the table. Harry said her efforts were well worth the price of war.

Walter joined the kidding with the rest of them, but Mil thought she noticed a look of sadness mask his face briefly when Harry joked about Mama's cakes being worth the price of war. But the sadness passed quickly.

Yes, Mil thought. For the Kazmiers, the war was truly over.

## CHAPTER 30

December 24, 1918 brought with it an especially festive mood, not only for the Kazmiers, but according to the newspapers, for most people around the world. Despite the fact that many families were bereaved, there was an over all feeling of joy pervading the atmosphere. Government leaders, people in general were certain that this terrible disaster called World War I, and the ensuing recent Armistice has ushered in a lasting peace. "The War to end all wars", that was the phrase eagerly uttered by newsmen.

For Emilia, there were mixed feelings...happy and joyful...sad and longing, at times, but all in all, she felt that Marcus had had a decidedly calming effect upon her. So often he could sense that she was feeling worried...distraught...or that her mind was dwelling on Frankie...that she was again becoming consumed by the conviction that somewhere out there he needed her. Marcus never tried to convince her that it wasn't true, he merely listened, asked questions which led her to reason out why she might, at a given moment, begin to feel concerned. With the help of Marcus, Emilia realized that these worries became more pronounced when she was tired...overworked. At such times, they would talk together, and then Marcus would send Emilia home for a few hours to rest. Always, she came back in better spirits.

On Christmas Eve, Marcus told Emilia not to come into the store at all, however, she knew how busy the fruit market would be, and that as a result, Marcus would need her, so she planned to join him anyway.

In every household, women were preparing Christmas feasts. They would shop early in the morning, then begin cooking, then discover things they'd forgotten. The store would be busy all day as a result.

So, that morning, Emilia arrived early, a half hour before the store opened. She helped Marcus to prepare for business. Within five minutes after the store opened, it was crowded with customers. Marcus and Emilia worked steadily all morning. At noon, Emilia took time for lunch. Twenty minutes later, she emerged from the back room to relieve Marcus. By one-thirty, the pace slowed somewhat, and Marcus insisted that Emilia leave the store in order to help her Mama with Christmas preparations. He was finally able to convince her to leave, after Peter paid a surprise visit - his first since he'd been sick. Peter laughed heartily at their surprise, assured them he was feeling much better, and that he came to work because he couldn't stand being in the way at home for one minute more. Peter's wife, a sweet woman under most circumstances, was nevertheless a lioness around her kitchen, wanting no help whatsoever, particularly not from Peter.

Besides, he declared, his unexpected arrival was the best Christmas present he could think of to give either of them. Though they tried to convince Peter that his "extra" pair of hands wasn't needed, he knew better.

With Peter's arrival, and the brothers falling into their old ways, each anticipating what help the other needed, Emilia felt she really could go home. Just as Marcus and Peter worked well together, so did she and Mama. Emilia wished Peter and Marcus a Merry Christmas, kissed each one on the cheek and hurried out the door, and down the street toward home.

What a wonderful season, Emilia thought! Though the wind blew about her, washing her face with cold powdery snow, she didn't mind. After all, this was the Holiday Season...Christmas...the New Year...times of excitement and joy. The same sentiments seemed to be reflected from other faces as they hurried past her smiling, or wishing a hearty Merry Christmas. Carolers stood in a small cluster on the corner singing "Hark the Herald Angels Sing". On the opposite corner, "Santa" rang his big brass bell, a rhythmic call to give alms for the needy. Tinsel flashed from every shop window along with garlands and wreaths of holly. Emilia loved this season. Always it filled her with anticipation, then satisfaction. She felt it now. First they'd anticipated Walter's homecoming, now he was there. Others would be coming home, but there her mind stalled...others...others...she repeated the word mentally. Others...yes...not Frankie. Facing the reality again, at this season, brought sudden tears...a strangled sob...finally, renewed determination not to think about it. It was done. This was Christmas, 1918, and she determined to live anew. She would.

As she approached the back door, the aroma of Mama's spice cake pervaded her nostrils. Oh, she was hungry.

Emilia blew into the house, along with a gust of wind. Mama fixed two cups of hot tea with sugar and milk, and they rested...warming themselves for the next task.

By five o'clock, Emilia and Mama had cleaned the house, and completed their baking. As if on cue, the back door opened and Tata arrived. Soon after, Harry...then Walter with his Lydia. No one else was expected then, except Billy. He was playing at the theater until about midnight that night. Though Billy wasn't Catholic, he had planned to join the family for Midnight Mass.

After a delicious dinner of roast pork and gravy, mashed potatoes and creamed peas, Harry and Walter snuck away to the parlor, as was their custom, and began decorating the Christmas tree. Mil wanted to join them this year, but they forbade it, declaring she was still their baby sister, and the only one left to be surprised when the parlor door was ceremoniously opened.

Emilia argued, that since this year, the whole family decided to meet at their house after Mass, to exchange and open gifts, and all the younger nephews would be present, that she ought to have a hand in surprising them. However, she lost the battle. Together, Walter and Harry locked the parlor doors, and together they alone set about decorating the Christmas tree. Oh well, Emilia thought, it's tradition. She returned to helping Mama with last minute details, and with a few remaining decorations, then retired to her own room to decide what she would wear to Mass. Lydia joined her for a few minutes, then left, making excuses, but Emilia knew she was going to the parlor to join the boys. Humph, she thought, love birds.

At eleven o'clock, they all set out for church. It was a beautiful night...crisp and cold. Three and four foot snow banks were piled along the sidewalks, protecting them from the wind as though they passed through long tunnels. Candles graced the front windows of many homes, announcing in which places the families were present, for candles were never left unattended.

As they neared the church, they heard carols ringing through the air. The choir always began to sing the praises of the Christ Child at eleven. It was like magic, Emilia thought, the way the great stained glass windows reflected rainbows of light all over the clean white snow. She caught her breath, overwhelmed by the sight. Such beauty.

She felt Mama's eyes on her. She turned. Teardrops made little dancing pools of light in Mama's eyes. Emilia knew they were tears of delight, because it was Christmas and her baby was going to church.

Well, Emilia thought, it was good that Mama was happy, so there was no need to say anything about her own feelings, but she knew that after Christmas, she wouldn't be going to church again. Christmas was special. It was tradition to attend church. Though she loved the spirit of Christmas, and the preparations, and the traditions, she still didn't need God, and He didn't need her.

It was a solemn High Mass they attended, with three priests celebrating, perfuming the air with incense. The ornate altar was covered with poinsettias. Despite the turmoil and fear Emilia had often felt since Frankie's death and the baby's miscarriage, particularly in church, during that Midnight Mass, she was feeling at peace. For that, she was thankful, not necessarily thankful to God, for she didn't think He was responsible for her peaceful feeling, but for whatever the reason, she felt thankful.

After Mass, neighbors gathered in the vestibule, calling a hearty welcome and "Merry Christmas" to everyone. The priests formed a receiving line and greeted those who came through. Emilia could tell they'd missed her presence at church, because they greeted her with special warmth...except for one of the younger priests. She had the feeling he was ignoring her, as though he was thinking she had no right to be there, if she couldn't attend church...mass...faithfully every Sunday. Emilia turned away from him.

Soon, they were again tromping through the valley of snow covered sidewalks, laughing and singing their favorite carols as they walked. Twenty minutes later, they were home, greeting and being greeted by Billy who waited on the front steps. His impish grin told them how happy he was to be there, even at this very late hour.

Once inside the house, they took turns warming their hands before the stove, or trying to restrain Mil who declared she'd waiting long enough to view the tree. She didn't wish to wait until everyone had arrived. In the end, she'd won, for Billy had interceded, by telling the boys he didn't know how much longer he could stay awake. Since the boys were also eager to open the parlor doors and officially begin the Christmas celebration, they decided to go along with Mil and Billy.

So, while Mama, Tata, Mil and Lydia waited, Harry, Walter and Billy (at the boys' invitation) went into the parlor to make ready the tree and the packages.

Soon, the doors were slowly and dramatically opened, revealing the tallest, widest, most perfectly formed tree that Mil ever remembered seeing in their house. It was covered with lighted candles, which glittered brightly and reflected many times on the dancing tinsel strands, and on the walls and the windows. It was as if many trees graced the room.

The fireplace didn't really burn wood, but on Christmas Eve, it always seemed to be more than decorative, standing majestically between glass enclosed bookcases, candles flanking its mantle. Stockings hung from it, everywhere, one for every member of the family, since all were planning to come for the gift exchange this special year.

The family groups trickled in, each exclaiming over the beautiful tree. There was much hugging and kissing, even amongst the men and boys. Gradually, the young nephews worked their way to the fireplace, searching for their own particular stockings, peering at them closely, feeling the little wrapped packages within. Even Stasha's boys who were nearly Mil's age, wandered over to the fireplace, trying to look causal and somewhat unconcerned. Stasha's two girls, one of whom was older than Mil by one year, and the other one year younger, sat on the floor near the tree. They had decided to take first turns watching the candles on the tree, making sure none burned so low as to cause a fire in the beautiful tree.

Finally, Tata moved his rocker nearer the tree, and motioned the girls toward the stockings. Then Walter gave the signal and everyone grabbed for the stocking bearing his or her name. There was a gentle surge, a little pushing and tugging, but mostly there was laughter.

Suddenly, the parlor floor was filled with bodies...with tufts and wads of wrapping paper and ribbon and string.

"Like picnic," Mama thought, as she wended her way toward Tata with his stocking. She seated herself on the footstool next to him, and together, they opened their gifts.

Mama fingered hers. "Little box," she thought. "Und, pretty wrapped." She wondered who had done this for her Tata. She looked up at him, the unspoken question in her eyes.

In reply, he merely smiled down at her, dismissing the question as he motioned her to open the pretty little package. Eagerly, she did.

"Ach, mine goodness," she gasped.

In the palm of Mama's hand, lay a tiny pair of sapphire stones set in gold...the most beautiful earrings she'd ever seen. She reached for Tata's hand...pulled it to her cheek. Then Mama urged him to open his gift.

Tata's gift was contained in a larger box...a four inch square that bulged the sides of his stocking. Carefully, and methodically, he unwrapped it. With his pocket knife, he opened the lid, exposing to his view a beautiful white porcelain moustache mug.

Tenderly, he slid one hand over Mama's smooth head, letting it come to rest on the back of her neck. Then he leaned over to kiss her forehead.

Mil, who was sitting directly across from Mama and Tata stopped unwrapping her own gift to watch them. She had never seen them express their love so romantically ever before.

Mama was fifty-eight years old...Tata close to sixty-five; they'd been married a long time, and still they loved one another very much. It was beautiful, Emilia thought, and she felt privileged to have witnessed those special moments. She wondered if such love would ever be hers. Without Frankie, she didn't really think it would be possible.

She turned her attention, once again, to the gift on her own lap. It too, was contained in a small box. With trembling fingers, she opened it, revealing a round broach, no bigger than a large coat button. The edges were gold filagree, and in the center a white cameo stood out. Mil could see that the cameo opened. It was closed tight, a very tight fit. She wedged her fingernail into the crack, opening it to expose a tiny picture of her Frankie...his face as a little boy. Mother J. must have come across it somewhere. Tenderly, she touched the picture with her fingertip. What a beautiful gift. She would treasure it forever.

Emilia felt eyes upon her. She looked up to see Billy standing beside her, looking over her shoulder at the broach...at Frankie's picture. There was a look in his eyes that she couldn't read. Emilia said nothing.

Billy put his hand lightly on her shoulder and said, "That's a lovely gift, Emilia."

Together, they turned to the scene around them.

All gifts received that night were from Mama and Tata. Most were small...inexpensive...for the family was very large. However, Emilia and Walter received special gifts...Walter, because he was the returning soldier, and to his family, a hero, and Emilia, because she too was returning...returning to health and a new way of life.

Then it was time for coffee and cake. After seating themselves around the big table, each family member in turn showed his or her gift to the others. There were cars and trucks and lead soldiers for the younger nephews. The older nephews and nieces received cuff links, or tie pins, earrings, or bracelets. Finally, Emilia's brothers and sisters left their gifts for Mama and Tata in little stacks around the Christmas tree, where the packages would lay unopened until morning.

Then the families bundled up, hurriedly, and started for their own homes, for though most were going only a walking distance, the younger nephews were showing signs of crankiness, which was no surprise to anyone. The time was three o'clock. Morning was upon them, and they hadn't gone to bed yet.

After everyone left, Harry snuffed the tree candles, then closed the parlor doors on all the remaining evidence of a happy Christmas Eve.

Mil's bed felt warm and comfortable. In no time at all, she knew sleep would come. The day had been a very busy one. She was glad. It was good to be tired. Good to know she would fall asleep quickly. She tucked the broach with Frankie's picture in it under her pillow, then lay back hoping for happy dreams.

Morning did not begin until ten o'clock, when Mil heard vague sounds from the kitchen. She rolled off the bed, legs first, rather slowly, wondering how Mama managed always to bustle about so vigorously in the morning. Mil entered the kitchen to find Mama at the stove, preparing a light breakfast.

Mama hoped the aroma of hot coffee and baking powder biscuits would bring her family members out of their beds, so they could finish with one meal before it was time to prepare for the big Christmas dinner. Of course, not everyone would be coming this year, but Mama didn't mind. They had had a wonderful Christmas Eve together. Will's and John's families would be going to the in-laws, and Walter to the future in-laws. Stasha and her family would also be going to the in-laws. Billy would be playing at the showhouse. That left only Helcha, her husband John, and their son, Irving, along with Ludmilla, Mil, Harry, Tata and herself. There would be only eight people at table. She thought it was good they would have only a small group. Christmas Eve had been a very long day, and she was feeling tired.

Four o'clock had come quickly, and everyone was prompt. Mama and Emilia began serving as soon as everyone was seated and the toasting with Mama's homemade dandelion wine was completed. Then, each one of the family members reached eagerly for a steaming bowl of czarnina. The duck blood soup with homemade dumplings was a family favorite, even with the younger family members, for none of the children knew how the delicious soup was made. The soup was followed by roast duck and gravy, candied sweet potatoes, sauerkraut, creamed peas, and homemade white bread with butter.

Over coffee, they discussed whether or not women would ever be able to vote, since the Senate had rejected President Wilson's original bill proposing women's suffrage.

Harry grunted at that. "And who would you girls vote for? Probably the most handsome fellow running."

Helcha laughed at that, claiming that if that were the case, they'd have to vote for no one, because there were no handsome men seeking to become President.

"See that?" Helcha's John nodded his head vigorously, "On that basis Wilson wouldn't have made it, and he's such a smart man."

Tata grunted in agreement.

Mama joined in. "Ach mine goodness. You boys are talking silly talk. Ladies, we know what is good to vote. We know who is good to vote so we haf no more wars. Ya, we know."

Mil tried to keep from smiling. Mama seldom joined in political discussions, but she was speaking so forcefully and sincerely now, that it somehow struck Mil funny. It was so uncharacteristic. But then, Mama seemed to surprise her more and more lately. Was it Mama who was changing, or was it she, herself? Or perhaps she was just beginning to notice how much Mama really did know. Maybe Mil was just beginning to notice how deeply Mama felt about world happenings.

Mil's thoughts were interrupted by the sound of the doorbell.

"I'll get it," she said rising quickly before Mama had a chance to leave the table.

As Mil hurried to the door, she noticed snow falling again, crusting over the windows, like white sugar frosting on cake...so pretty...so cold. A gust of wind whirled icy flakes around her feet when Mil opened the door. To her surprise, she saw Marcus Poulis standing before her, carrying a covered basket over his arm.

"Come in, Marcus, quickly." She pulled him inside. "It's too cold to keep the door open."

"I hope I'm not bothering you," he apologized politely, as he removed his snow-covered hat.

"It's no bother, Marcus, I'm just surprised to see you...but it's very good to see you. Merry Christmas."

Marcus held the basket out to her. "Be careful. It's heavy."

"What on earth..."

"Only fruit. I know how much company you have on holidays like this."

Mil peeked under the cloth. "Oh, Marcus...apples, bananas, oranges...they're beautiful! Why did you?"

"You've been a big help to me, Emilia. I wanted you and the family to know how much I appreciate the help you've given me."

"Marcus, dear, it's helped me too...so much." Emilia reached over and kissed him on the cheek.

Marcus smiled broadly, his eyes shining. "You look beautiful, Emilia, such a soft, flowing dress...like a dancer...like a beautiful Mata Hari."

"My goodness, I hope not!" Emilia laughed. "She's dead now, isn't she?"

"They say. The Allies couldn't tolerate a spy...not even one so beautiful as she."

Emilia took his hand. "Come on inside. Everyone will wonder who it is I'm keeping out here to myself."

Marcus entered the room to a chorus of surprise. They urged him to stay for coffee and cake...dinner if he hadn't eaten, but he had. Marcus always had holiday and Sunday dinners with Peter and his wife. Tonight, however, he decided it was a perfect time to show his appreciation.

Then their conversation began to wander to other topics. Together, they talked of women bobbing hair, of Charlie Chaplin movies, and his enormous salary of about a million dollars a year...more than any of them could imagine ever earning...even Marcus, who said there wasn't enough fruit in the world to sell in order to make that amount of money. And they talked more of President Wilson and his dreams for a League of Nations.

About nine o'clock Marcus thought he should leave, before Peter needed the car.

Emilia walked him to the door...helped him with coat and hat. Marcus was ready to leave, but still he hesitated. Then he cleared his throat and turned to Emilia.

"Emilia, would you like to go to the movies...maybe Wednesday night?"

Emilia had never seen Marcus looking nervous, but at that moment she thought he did. Several times, he ran his tongue over his lips, as if to moisten them. "Why he's asking me out on a date," she thought. "That must be very hard for him, even though we are friends." She wondered if he'd ever done that before.

"That would be nice," she said. "Perhaps we could ask Billy what's playing at his theater."

Marcus took a deep breath. That wasn't so bad after all, and she said yes. Of course, the Grand wouldn't have been his choice, nevertheless, he nodded to her in agreement. then he told Emilia to stay home in the morning and rest.

"And leave you all alone at the store? Ridiculous!"

"I mean it. Stay. Tomorrow will be a quiet day."

"All right. On condition you'll call if you need me."

Marcus squeezed her hand and left.

Such a good man, Emilia thought. And she owed him so much. And how kind of him to invite her to the movies.

Emilia returned to the dining table, but decided not to mention "the date". Little Irving, and the others, they would tease her. She didn't wish to be teased at that moment. A movie was only a movie and Marcus was merely a good friend who felt she needed companionship.

## CHAPTER 31

The morning after Christmas, Emilia slipped out of bed quietly. She didn't wish to disturb Ludmilla. It was fun having her spend the night - just like old times, before either of them had been married.

They stayed up very late, long after Helcha and her family left, and talked of many things. Emilia even told Ludmilla about her coming movie date with Marcus. Ludmilla was happy that Mil was going to go out with such a nice man, however, thinking of such things made her cry. Thinking and talking of men and dates made her feel exceptionally lonely. She wanted so much for her Frank to return from France. She'd begun to feel that the long separation was more than she could endure.

Emilia listened to her for awhile, then pretended to be very tired, and suggested they try to sleep, so time would pass more quickly.

Ludmilla seemed to fall asleep as soon as they stopped talking, at least her breathing became even and relaxed. It was then that Emilia allowed her own tears to fall. She knew it was foolish to let herself think of Frankie, of how much she missed him; she knew how important it was that she begin her new life...but it was Christmas, she told herself. She should be allowed, no she should allow herself, the privilege of mourning.

Then, tears dried, she congratulated herself, thinking how much she had changed in the fourteen months since Mother J. had brought her news of Frankie's death. After the news, she'd cared about nothing...no one else...only her own pain...her own feeling of loss. Maybe there was something to be said for suffering. Maybe it did teach her something about life and living, even surviving, for that's what she was doing, in spite of her lost men. Yes, she was surviving.

Emilia brushed her short blond hair vigorously as she remembered these things from the night before. Again, she looked at Ludmilla. Her face wore a peaceful expression. Emilia was grateful for that.

No sounds yet anywhere in the house. Good. At least Tata had the day off for a change. He and Mama had seemed truly worn out after all the Christmas celebrating. She determined to move about quietly so as not to distrub any of the sleeping members of her family.

Softly, she opened and closed the bedroom door, snuck into the kitchen, and warmed a glass of milk. The quiet was wonderful for her thinking mood, and she allowed her mind to wander again to last night, and her late night girlish whisperings with Ludmilla. Only, she decided, they weren't "girlish" whisperings at all; they were the confidences of young married women...one waiting...one, surviving.

"Surviving"...the word fascinated her. Why, she wondered, did she survive? And Ludmilla's Frank...what about him? He bore the same name as her man, yet he survived and Frankie didn't. Who determined such things? And why?

Then she remembered again her thoughts about suffering and maturity. Had she ever matured through happiness? No, she thought, not on her own. Happiness generally caused her to feel carefree and it gave her the feeling that she needed nothing...no one, but in suffering, she turned to others. Suffering made her understand the pain of others, as well as their joy. Pain used to force her to turn to God. But, if there were a God, why did He devise this plan of suffering? No, no more turning to God. She'd turn to Marcus.

Ludmilla's soft call interrupted her morning meditation. Again, they whispered quietly for a few minutes, then Ludmilla decided she must return to her own flat. Emilia offered to walk with her. The walk would clear her head. She was overtired from all the holiday merry-making and the late hours.

It was almost ten o'clock. The sisters slipped down the back stairs and out onto the deserted sidewalks. Arm in arm they began to run toward Ludmilla's.

"Oh, wait...stop..." Emilia puffed. "Let's walk awhile. I'm not as healthy as all this!"

They laughed, enjoying the sounds of their own voices echoing down the snow-covered streets.

"Look, there's Marcus." Ludmilla waved at him through the window. "See? He's standing over the apple bin."

Emilia saw him. She needed to talk with him...about death, survival, and God, so she kissed Ludmilla on the cheek and told her she thought maybe Marcus might need her after all. She would check.

Ludmilla gave her a knowing smile.

"It's not like that. He's my good friend."

"Go, go. I have work to do at home. But stop later, if you can."

"I will."

"Good. I'm sewing a beautiful robe. It's for Frank...when he comes home. I'll show you."

They waved good-bye, and Emilia went into the store.

Not even five minutes after she entered, customers began coming and going, one by one, no crowds, but the disturbance kept her from talking much with Marcus.

She turned her mind to the ledgers that he gave her and began to work steadily. Then she worried...maybe Mama was wondering where she was. Probably not, she told herself, because Ludi was gone too, so she would call Ludi's house, and find out where Mil was. Still, she thought, maybe she should return home. Marcus agreed.

Mil cleared the books from the counter and grabbed her coat. Again, the bell tinkled announcing another arrival. She heard Marcus shout a friendly "Good morning."

It was Billy she saw when she turned toward the door.

Billy was glad to find her there, just as Mama had said she would be. He was excited and could hardly wait to tell his big news.

"It's about my job at the GRAND," he said. "They're going to let me try a little skit of my own! I'm gong to be in vaudeville!"

Marcus smiled and clapped him on the back.

Emilia was too astonished to speak for a moment, then questions tumbled from her lips.

"You mean vaudeville at the GRAND? A real theater? The acts between shows? But what will you do? Dance? Sing? Tell jokes? Do you have a routine in mind? What sort of clothes will you need, Billy?" She finished breathlessly. "What does it all mean? Where will it lead?"

"Hey, not so many questions! I can't answer any of them. But I hope it'll lead to real performing."

"Oh my, what a Christmas present for you!"

"Now, will you come? You, Emilia...and Marcus, Mama, Tata...all the family. I want an audience. And I want to know what you think."

Marcus watched her face. Was she merely delighted for a friend? Or was it something more? And what about Billy? He was glowing with excitement over the opportunity, but was there a special warmth emanating from his eyes? Marcus wished him well, but Marcus also wondered just what this would lead to for all of them. It was important, Marcus decided, to find out as quickly as possible, for he had to admit to himself that his feelings for Emilia were not only friendly, but that they held another dimension.

"You have the latest Tarzan movie playing at the Grand now, don't you?" Marcus asked.

Billy nodded, hardly moving his eyes away from Mil's face, as she smiled up at him.

Mmmm, what was Billy thinking now, Marcus wondered. Then, aloud, he said, "Emilia and I talked of going to the movies on Wednesday night."

Billy shot a searching look his way.

"We thought the GRAND might be a good place to go, didn't we, Emilia?"

Both men turned their attention to her.

Mil's face showed only excitement as she quickly agreed that the Grand was indeed the place to go. So it was settled. Emilia left and Billy followed.

Marcus watched them walk down the street together toward Emilia's house. Billy offered his arm and Emilia slipped her's through it.

A handsome couple, Marcus thought...he's young, tall and vital. He wants her...I think. She needs someone. But are they good for one another? Marcus frowned as he questioned his own concern. Was he thinking of Emilia or himself? He'd watched the girl grow up. He was always fond of her; now that he knew her so much better, he loved her, and he wasn't sure about what kind of love he felt. Was it fatherly...protective...spurred on by her illness and loss? Certainly, he'd come to rely upon her now that she'd been helping him in the store. She was a good worker. But no, it was more than that. She was the bright spot in his lonely days.

Marcus watched them turn the corner. He felt a predicament coming his way. Well, if nothing else, it would be interesting to see how it all worked out. Then he laughed softly to himself. If only he could really feel so objective. No, he had to be honest with himself. He loved Emilia as a man loves a woman. Yes, and he feared Billy did too. And if he were totally honest with himself, he'd have to admit that he wanted this predicament to work out his way. Yes, he would have to give this matter a great deal of thought.

******************

At his rooming house the next day, Billy received word that his schedule had been changed. He would be playing the piano as usual, but not performing until the following week. He was disappointed, though professional enough by this time to realize the delay was fortunate for him. It gave him more time to prepare, to sharpen his routine.

As Billy sat at the table in his room, feet carelessly propped upon a small pile of old newspapers, pipe firmly clenched between his teeth, he studied the notes spread on the table before him. These were notes he'd scribbled down in the last few days, and along with them, the jokes he'd carefully thought out and written.

His mind wandered. The GRAND THEATER presents...Billy Stark! It was hard to believe...a dream come true. He had to be good. He'd rehearse and rehearse till every word felt right. This was a small beginning, but it was something to build upon. No one would ever know how much he wanted this...how he needed it. He was making life go on, in spite of everything that had ever happened to him. Aunt Mattie would be proud.

Why, if he made the "big time" he would never have to be alone again...not in any way. Throngs of people would admire him. All those years of accepting life on its own terms would have paid off. He'd rolled with every piece of luck...good or bad...and somehow managed to turn every happening to his advantage, not ruthlessly, not in ways that would harm others, he was just plain prudent. He watched for every possible opportunity, thought about it, and used it in the best possible way. Never did he complain about tough luck. He didn't believe in it. Whatever happened was in the cards, all he did was pick up the deck, reshuffle, and play the hand to the best of his ability.

Now, he'd been dealt the best hand yet. If he played it wisely, he'd win.

He laughed softly, remembering Em's face when he broke the news to her...and to Marcus. She was so excited...so unbelieving. He couldn't wait to hear her reaction to his routine, but he'd offer her no previews...no performance until curtain time. Then she'd see him, in all of his practiced splendor. Then her reaction would be genuine. That's what he wanted...a genuine reaction...not the adoration of a friend.

What was it she'd said a while back? Yes, she said she too, had wanted to go into the theater. Hmmm. Maybe this would lead to a chance for her. Perhaps they could do a routine together. Every act he ever saw seemed to employ a pretty face. That was an advantage...drew interest...audience acceptance. And certainly, Em would provide a pretty face. Yes, maybe they could work it out...if she thought for herself. Marcus had quite a hold on her, he thought, whether she knew it or not. Sure, Marcus was a darn good man, steady, but a lot older than Em, and leading a very routine life. But above all, he was a man...lonely...and more than likely very much in love with Em...kind to her, too...a dangerous combination. Too bad she didn't have a background like his own. She'd been so protected by a large loving family that she didn't think much for herself.

Well, time would tell, but if they could work it out, Em would experience a whole new kind of life...traveling with him, working with him...and who knows what else...what sort of relationship might develop between them? Yes, time would tell. She was a very nice girl. Billy thought he'd like to see her benefit...flower...under his tutelage, so she might realize a few dreams of her own.

Enough of that, Billy told himself. He picked up the pencil and turned his attention once again to the routine he had already partially worked out. For the time being, it would have to be a "single".

*****************

On Wednesday, Marcus drove up to the Kazmier's at exactly six p.m. Mama, Tata, and Emilia were all in the window...waiting...watching. He saw Emilia clap her hands joyfully when she saw him pull up in the Ford that he and Peter owned in partnership. Yes, he was thinking, they did everything in partnership, everything, except to marry. And why not a double wedding? Because Marcus had never found a girl as sweet as Peter's. Anna had sisters, but they weren't at all like her...no, they were sharp tongued. He didn't need a sharp tongued woman in his life.

Again, he looked at the window. But did he need a girl young enough to be his daughter? Mil was so sweet, she brightened his life, but would she be a contented wife? May-December...that's what they called such marriages. He'd always been so sensible.

Maybe now he was going into a new phase...the old fool phase. But he did so enjoy taking care of her. So, what was wrong with that?

"Poof", he muttered. Enough thinking. If he didn't start moving...get out of the car...and go to the door which he'd seen open several times, the Kazmiers would begin to think he was strange. They already suspicioned that, questioning as often as they did, his sense of humor, which he despaired they'd ever completely understand.

His short, squat figure took the steps eagerly. Emilia opened the door, greeting him with her warm smile, and again his day seemed brighter. Hang the rest, he thought. Let's enjoy. That's what I'm always telling her.

"Oh, Marcus," Emilia said, "it'll be such fun driving to the movie in such grand style."

He smiled a broad, easy smile at her, exchanged a few words with Mama and Tata and off they went, down the stairs to the carriage. Cinderella was on her way, Marcus thought. He opened the door and bowed to her. She smiled and accepted, gravely. On the way to the movies, they talked...easily...of the store, and of Peter and his wife, Anna...they had no children...much to their regret, of Walter and his Lydia, of Ludmilla and how she wished Frank would also come home, and of how much the family enjoyed the fruit basket...inconsequential talk, but pleasant.

The movie was also pleasant, and they enjoyed it. After the movie, they felt the disappointment of not seeing Billy perform, though they knew they wouldn't, but several acts came on stage which were funny enough to bring tears to their eyes. After the last act, Emilia turned to Marcus and whispered to him.

"Can't you just imagine Billy up there?"

Marcus nodded, then watched as she craned her neck to see Billy better. He was seated at the piano, just below the stage, playing an intermission number, "Sweethearts" from Sigmund Romberg's MAYTIME. He played it well. Marcus thought Billy was a talented, though untrained musician. Maybe that was the best kind, he thought...a true inborn talent. He turned his attention to listening again... thinking he might revise his opinion and raise Billy to the status of "genius", for his arrangement was not only pleasing, but unique. On the other hand, "genius" was perhaps too strong a word. In any case, the theater had found a bargain treasure in Billy.

The music stopped and Marcus looked again at Emilia. Her eyes were sparkling as she waved furtively at Billy who was looking their way...eagerly...pleased. Why not?

The show ended and in the intermission that followed, Billy came over to them. They weren't able to speak long for Billy had to stretch and prepare for the next entire show. It was obvious he loved the piano playing...very much Marcus thought...probably more than he would ever to able to love a person...more even than he would be able to love a woman. Yes, it was in his blood.

Marcus and Emilia drove back to the Kazmier's. Only a small light burned in the parlor. Nevertheless, Emilia asked Marcus to come inside for coffee and cake. He declined, not wishing to disturb Mama and Tata, but Emilia insisted. She really wished to talk with him. Something was bothering her, and they hadn't had a chance for real talk in many days. Mama and Tata would not be disturbed for the dining table was far removed from their bedroom which was located at the far end of the hall. Marcus followed her in.

He watched her move about the kitchen, making coffee, cutting cake - dignity and grace, he thought. Then he helped her carry their snack to the big dining table in the far corner of the kitchen, placing more distance between their conversation and the bedrooms.

"So, Emilia, what is it you have to say?"

"It's about God, Marcus."

"Oh my, that's a big subject, Emilia. I don't know if old Marcus is up to that."

Her eyes opened wide. "Oh, Marcus, I know you are."

"Well, then, tell me, why should God be bothering you? Surely, He must love you just as the rest of us do?"

"Please, Marcus, don't joke. I really need to know."

"I'm not joking."

Emilia noticed that his face and voice sobered. She studied him seriously. Again, he spoke.

"But you see, you haven't yet told me why God bothers you." Then he smiled, looking like the old Marcus...sweet, kind, gentle, compassionate, and very serious.

"No, no. I haven't." She paused, composing her thoughts, trying to formulate them into words.

"I've decided there must be a God."

"Hmm...that's a good start. But why?"

"This world. It's so beautiful. Everything in it. People."

"So what bothers you?"

"I'm...let me find the words."

He waited for her to continue.

"They say God is like a father who loves us very much. But if that's true, why does Ludmilla's Frank still live, but my Frankie is dead? If He loves us, why does He make us suffer?"

Emilia stopped, but Marcus said nothing. He knew, from her face, there was more.

"I think of my baby, Frankie. If I had him now, I would never let him suffer, because I would love him so much. Do you see? I would do everything in my power to make him happy...always."

There was a pleading look in her eyes as she searched his face, but Marcus sat quietly...weighing his words. He saw this meant very much to Emilia. Finally, he moved his hands up to the table, and folded them together, as though preparing to hold onto his thoughts. Then he spoke.

"Emilia, does this mean you would live your baby's life for him?"

"No, no," she replied very quickly.

"Then how would you protect him from making the mistakes that children and young people must make before they learn to be grown people?"

"But, if I loved him enough..."

"Can love make people always be right?"

Emilia's mind flashed back to the day she and Frankie shared their marital bed, to the day she thought she was pregnant, to the day she punched her stomach and vowed she didn't want baby Frankie, to the day she fell on the bricks. All mistakes of a kind. And then, she thought of Frankie's enlistment - why, she wondered had he enlisted? Why had he joined the war at all. That was the biggest mistake of all the mistakes.

"No," she said, "people make many mistakes, even when they love."

"And would you want God always to come down on a cloud and say to you, 'Don't do that. It will hurt you. It will make you suffer.' Would you listen to God if He did?"

Emilia thought of the story of Adam and Eve, how they took the apple when God said no...forbade it. Then she looked at Marcus and shook her head solemnly from side to side. She began to fear Marcus might lead her to trusting God again.

"Thank you, Marcus, but let's not talk about it anymore. It's getting late."

He knew she needed time to think all of these things over. He knew also that in her mind, she was still married to Frankie. He didn't know if that would ever change. He wondered how much difficulty such loyalty would cause her in a lifetime. Oh, how sweet and vulnerable she was...how inexperienced. He feared there was much more hurt and suffering coming her way, for she hadn't really experienced much of life outside the walls of this home. That was good, he thought, and that was also bad.

They left the table, and Marcus took his coat and hat from the sofa. Emilia held his sleeve so he could find it. Then she squeezed his hand and thanked him, kissed his cheek lightly.

At that moment, he wanted to take her in his arms and offer her a home, a life, more protection, but he didn't. It wasn't the time. He didn't know if it would ever be the time. She loved another man still - her Frankie.

They smiled and bade one another good night.

## CHAPTER 32

As the days passed, Mil continued to join Marcus and Peter at the fruit store. Always, there was ledger work for her to do. The afternoons were always pleasant, with much laughter and joking interspersed between customers coming in and accounts figured. The hours flew.

One such afternoon, the door opened and Billy ambled in to visit again. He tried to look nonchalant, but there was excitement in his eyes, his step, his posture. Try as he might, he couldn't hide that excitement from Emilia and Marcus. Even Peter, who hadn't met Billy before sensed the excitement he was trying to disguise.

Billy sat on the edge of the counter, next to Mil. Since there were no customers, Marcus and Peter joined them. Billy had very good news to tell...he'd received a raise in salary...$45 a week.

Why, it was unbelievable, Mil said. He was now a wealthy man...a star. Soon, she joked, he would stop speaking to them. He would probably live downtown in a skyscraper. There'd be no telling what would happen next.

Then Billy followed that bulletin with the best news of all. He would perform on this next Sunday as the main vaudeville attraction! He could actually be the star...at the GRAND anyway. Mil could hardly imagine such good fortune.

Marcus commented that Billy's salary alone indicated he was an important property to the people who ran the Grand Theater. Then Billy invited them all to come and see his premier "Star" performance.

Marcus observed Emilia closely during this conversation. He could see she was impressed and delighted. He could see she was eager to go. He saw also a most unusual animation in her face, so he listened extra closely to her words.

"Oh, Billy, of course I'm going! And Mama and maybe Tata too." Then she turned to Marcus and Peter. "What about you two?" she asked. "Will you be able to go?"

Marcus felt disappointed. He and Mil had developed a special bond while working together at the store. They'd enjoyed several nights out together, even a few of Billy's performances. He hoped the "I" in her conversation might become "we", that she might perhaps say, "May we go, Marcus?" But she didn't. Marcus used Mil's reaction as a guide for his own words.

"I would like to go, Billy, but maybe the next time. There is something I'm committed to do on Sunday."

Marcus noticed Emilia's look of disappointment. Had she planned they would go together? Maybe. He felt a spark of hope. Quickly, Marcus added, "Emilia, you shouldn't go alone. Maybe your Mama...or Ludmilla could go with you."

"Yes, I suppose so."

That was all she said, but he thought he detected a note of dejection in her expression. He felt encouraged.

Billy spoke again, and Marcus turned his attention once more to the good looking young man who towered over him.

"Em, I'm glad you're coming. After the show, I've something to ask you."

"Oh, what?"

"Not now. After you've seen the show."

"That's mean, Billy Stark. I want to know now! You know I can't wait." She pretended to stamp her feet and pout.

They all laughed. Shortly after, Billy left the store.

Marcus and Peter busied themselves around the store. After a while, Peter left, and Marcus walked over to Emilia. He appeared to be casually straightening up the counter as he spoke.

"So, your friend is now a Star."

"Ummm..." she said without lifting her head, intent on what she was writing.

"And he has something to ask you after the show."

"Ummmm that terrible fella."

"Maybe he wants to marry you."

"Marry me?" Mil looked at him incredulously. "Billy? Whatever makes you think that? Why we've never even had a date. He's never even kissed me. Besides," she added sadly, "he knows I love Frankie."

Marcus withdrew a little. "Of course. I was joking, Emilia."

"Well, you didn't sound like it."

Marcus laughed. "You'll never understand my sense of humor, will you?"

Still, he thought, I think she's beginning to understand me quite well.

Soon after that, Mil closed the ledger book and hurried home to tell Mama and Tata Billy's wonderful news and to ask them if they would go with her to the GRAND. Mama was excited. Tata said it was good for Billy, but he chose not to go. So, Emilia and Mama made plans of their own for Sunday evening. They even decided to go out to the little restaurant on Milwaukee Avenue. The restaurant was very near the streetcar stop, and after eating, it would provide shelter from the cold as they waited for the streetcar. In the warm weather, walking part way to the GRAND would have been pleasant exercise, but now in the sharp cold, it would seem a long distance away.

******************

Sunday dawned bright and very cold. The day seemed to drag by. Since it was Sunday, Emilia couldn't work at the store, so after Mama returned from church, they fussed around the house and pressed the clothes they would wear. By 3:30, they decided to wrap warmly and leave the house.

They walked to the restaurant, hardly speaking, for the cold took their breath away. When they reached their destination and opened the heavy door, a wave of warm air washed over them. How good it felt! Eating out, anticipating the show, these things made them feel as though they were on holiday. They studied the menu, then chose cabbage roll-ups and mashed potatoes with buttered carrots. Emilia and Mama ate the good home cooking with gusto, leaving not one speck behind on their plates. Afterward they waited inside the restaurant, peering through the big window, watching for the streetcar. When it came close, they ran out and waved the car to a stop. Having been thoroughly warm before boarding, they hardly noticed the extreme cold of the early evening. However, they were happy to be attending the first show. They would be back home long before midnight, by which time the weather would be unbearable.

When they arrived at the Grand, they saw a line waiting for tickets. Good, Emilia thought. Billy must surely be making a name for himself, but waiting in the cold, that wouldn't be easy. Though it took only five or ten minutes for them to reach the ticket booth, it felt much longer.

The show hadn't yet started when they entered the theater. With the bright lights beaming down on them, Mil spotted two seats together in the third row from the front. Though neither of them liked to sit so close to the screen ordinarily, it would be good to do so on this night. They would be able to see Billy very well.

They arranged their coats and sat back on them. Then Mil saw the big sign to the left of the stage. It read:

SOFT SHOE POLKA starring Billy Stark

"Mama, look. Look at the sign! Isn't that exciting!"

Mama mouthed the words letter by letter, slowly, until she managed to make out everything the sign said. She'd just managed to read in English, and it was all about Billy. Michalina was glowing.

The lights dimmed and the movie began. Neither Mama nor Mil were able to keep their minds on the story. It was not a picture they would have chosen to see anyway. It was a poorly made western starring someone they'd never heard of. When the picture ended and the lights came on again, the audience moved about, talking, passing time for the ten minutes between the movie and the live performance.

Soon the lights dimmed once more, and the bright spots shone on the center of the stage. Plush red velvet curtains parted and Billy's scenery rolled down...simple but effective. On the backdrop was painted a colorful garden-like scene...flowers, trees, grass. Set in front of this was a park bench. A huge dog sat right up on the bench like a person. Mil thought it was a St. Bernard. He looked real, but he sat so quietly. Then, she heard someone whistling "Over There" off stage. That had to be Billy. Mil nudged Mama and as if by plan, they both sat straight up and leaned forward, straining, like maybe that effort would give Billy the confidence to feel less nervous.

As soon as she saw him, Mil laughed. The rest of the audience did too, for Billy made quite a picture dressed in a Khaki colored uniform, several sizes too small for his handsome big frame. It made him look the part of a gangly clown. Of course, it wasn't only his costume, it was also what he did that made everyone laugh. Billy danced onto the stage to the tune of his whistling, doing a fast Polka two-step. That combination was just the funniest sight. Billy danced around the stage, back to front, side to side, then huffing and puffing, he stopped directly in front of the dog, who actually looked like he was smiling.

Billy didn't begin with jokes until the audience quieted down.

Good timing, Mil thought. She watched as Billy spoke for the dog and for himself...as though he were answering questions the dog asked. Mil was dying to know where he found that dog. It was so well trained, didn't move a muscle, except on command. Billy's jokes, she thought, were side-splitting funny, and Mil couldn't wait to ask if he'd written them all himself. She also wondered if Billy's routine seemed so funny because she wanted it to be...because Billy was her friend. She guessed not, because the rest of the audience laughed hard too.

Billy's entire performance lasted only about twenty minutes, and it certainly didn't drag at all, but to Mil it seemed to last an eternity. She was so anxious that it should all go well, that he wouldn't forget any of his lines, that he would experience a very healthy sound of applause, also that the dog wouldn't have any accidents. At the end, when Billy did his soft shoe Polka and danced right back into the wings, Emilia felt so weak she didn't know if she'd be able to walk back stage or not. Mama seemed to have been just as nervous, so they linked arms for support, and went to the stage door.

They found the room by number, then knocked timidly. Billy, flinging the door wide open, revealed a closet-sized dressing room with plenty of light around the make-up mirror. Other than dressing table and mirror, furnishings were sparse and crowded.

Billy hugged them both. His face was flushed with excitement, but Mil didn't notice even a slight quiver of his muscles as he hugged them. Observing that, she decided that Billy couldn't have been nearly as nervous as they were.

"Well, what did you think of it?"

"Oh, Billy, you were wonderful!"

"Oh, ya."

"I sure hoped you'd say that."

Then he examined Mil's face closely. "Yes," he said, "I think you mean it."

"The dog, Billy. Wherever did you find him? He's magnificent...and so well trained."

"Good ol' Sanctus. He belongs to the theater manager. Sanctus and I have become very good friends in the time I've been playing here. He's followed me around since the beginning. I've taken him for walks, kept him once or twice when Max had to take a short business trip. He's such a show-off, I decided he'd be good on stage. Max thought so too."

"Where is Sanctus now. I'd like to meet him."

"A little later. He needed to go outdoors, run and take care of necessities before the next performance."

"And your material, Billy, where did you get it?"

"All original. All mine."

He grinned at Mama.

"What did you think of my Polka?"

"Is funny, Billy. To such music. Why you do this?"

"You inspired me, Mama...so did Mil. And I thought everyone in this neighborhood would get a big kick out of a routine that starred an Irish name, stepping poorly to a Polka...particularly to that music."

"Billy Stark, I think you're a real showman." Mil gave his cheek a friendly pat and a friendly kiss.

"I'm happy for you, Billy, and I'm happy we were here to see your very first 'starring' performance."

Billy responded with a pleased, proud smile.

"Were you nervous? You don't look it now."

"You've got to be kidding. When you want everything to be absolutely perfect, to please everyone, to make them laugh...well...there's no word to describe how I felt."

Mil grabbed his hand and squeezed.

"But now, what were you going to ask me?"

"Was I going to ask you something?" he teased.

"Billy, you stop that. You know you were. Please, Billy. Come on, tell me."

Dramatically, he drew them to a small settee, from which he swept his clothing, making room for them to sit down. Then he strode around peacock fashion. Finally, he spun around on his heel and pointed at Emilia as he asked his question.

"Em, how would you like to make your dream come true?"

"What dream, Billy? What do you mean?"

"I mean your dream of becoming an actress! How would you like to be my partner in the act?"

Mil was dumfounded. She said nothing, then sputtered a little at him, making Billy laugh. Mama looked from Billy to Emilia and they all laughed.

"Well, Em...what do you say?"

"Why, I don't know, Billy. I just don't know...you've taken me completely by surprise."

"I guess I have, Em. But you did tell me that as a child, you'd dreamed of becoming an actress. Now's your chance."

"Mama, do you hear what Billy is asking me?"

"Ya, Dziecko." Mama reached over to Emilia and took her hand. Though she looked very thoughtful, she said nothing more.

Emilia looked back at Billy like a frightened rabbit about to jump back into its hole.

"Em," Billy said quickly, "you don't have to answer me tonight. Think about it on the way home. But, remember, you'd not only be fulfilling your own dream, you'd be helping me to realize mine. A pretty face is always a welcome sight in show business. And, Em, yours is a pretty face."

Mil and Mama buttoned coats and prepared to leave so Billy could rest before his next performance. Also, Emilia and Mama wanted to start for home before the temperature dropped too low. The colder the weather, the slower the streetcars ran.

However, before leaving, Emilia made Billy take them out back to meet Sanctus. He dashed over to Billy, then greeted Emilia and Mama by leaving streaks of saliva on their coats. With that, they took hurried leave.

Half running, they hustled toward the streetcar stop, where they saw a couple waiting. Even from a distance, Emilia noticed the woman's beautiful red hair, hair that she remembered seeing before. The man stood with his back to them. From a distance, he appeared to be slightly shorter than the woman, and of broad, muscular build. He looked so familiar...so dearly familiar. Emilia caught her breath...pulled Mama to a stop.

"What is Dziecko? This walk...is it too much in cold?"

"No, Mama. It's not the walk, it's the man. Look at him."

Emilia pointed.

Mama looked, then she knew why Emilia had stopped so suddenly. From the back, the man looked like Mil's Frankie...even his coat.

"My God, Mama. I'm getting just like Elinora Steech. I think sometimes that I hear Frankie, or that I see him...like right now."

As they stood watching, the couple began to move on down the street...the red-headed woman apparently leading the man as he clung to her arm. They moved slowly, but steadily along until they turned the next corner.

"Is funny, Dziecko, how sometimes, people look like others."

"Yes, Mama." They walked silently on to the stop, then Mil spoke again. "Mama, I think that man was blind."

"Why you think this?"

"He was holding onto the red-head..like she was leading him."

"Ya, maybe is so."

"It gives me the creeps, Mama."

"He no can help if he is blind. Maybe something happens to him in war."

"I suppose you're right, Mama. Many things happened in the war, didn't they? It's just that it makes me feel funny that he looks so much like Frankie."

"Ya, ya, Dziecko."

Mil's mind drifted back to her dream, of the darkness and the blinding light, but she didn't tell Mama about that. She shuddered, tried to push those things from her mind. She wouldn't become another Elinora Steech, always seeing Frankie in men around her who happened to have a build similar to his, or thinking she heard his voice when she was talking about him. She had to pull herself together, continue her life. That was what this whole new year was all about. It was 1919. She pushed thoughts of Frankie from her mind, and concentrated on thoughts of becoming Billy's partner, of joining him in show business.

At last, the streetcar came. They settled back in one of the many empty cane seats, and Emilia allowed her mind to wander, to imagine what it might be like becoming a star...starting out at the Grand, maybe living in a ritzy apartment downtown, or maybe in a big hotel...becoming really famous, moving to New York or Hollywood...leaving her Mama and Tata...all of her brothers and sisters...Frankie's family. Frankie's family..her mind detoured. Perhaps she would call Mother J. tomorrow. Maybe there was news of Ed...or someone...something...

Having made that decision, Mil turned to Mama; she wanted to discuss Billy's offer. However, Mama's eyes were closed. She must be resting, Mil thought. But Mama's face looked so grim. Mil thought it might be good to disturb her, perhaps rouse her from an unpleasant dream. But she didn't.

Instead, Mil turned again to her own thoughts, continuing to weave a glamorous web around visions of stardom. Mama didn't open her eyes, nor did she speak before the streetcar reached their stop. Even then, she was strangely silent. Mil thought she must be tired.

When they entered the house, Mil suggested they talk more about Billy's offer. It was quiet; Tata had apparently gone to bed, however, Mama cut her short, excusing herself with talk of being very tired.

Though Mil was disappointed, she didn't press her wish. Instead, she kissed Mama good night and after watching as Mama retreated down the hall and into the bedroom, Mil lingered a bit longer, then prepared for bed herself.

## CHAPTER 33

Mil tossed and turned most of the night as her thoughts alternated between the "big chance" Billy was offering her, which then led to wild imaginings about stardom and fame, and her disturbing visions of the red-head leading the man who looked so much like Frankie. The latter, Mil kept pushing from her mind.

As for stardom and fame, it sounded wonderful, but it could also cost a pretty penny. Mil didn't want to leave the family, Mama and Tata, especially, but that would probably be the price of fame and fortune. On the other hand, what if there were no fame and fortune? What if they became starving actors? There were many of those. Did she want to leave her comfortable room? And even if she took the opportunity, what would she actually be doing in the act? She was no joke teller. She'd be little more than a prop, like the St. Bernard. Probably by the time she found any recognition at all, she'd be so old her acting career would be about over anyway. And then too, there was Marcus. She was really beginning to depend upon his friendship.

As sunlight began to creep across the floor, Mil heard kitchen sounds. Mama and Tata were awake. She slipped into robe and slippers and joined them. Mama and Tata looked surprised at her early arrival.

"What you do so early, Dziecko?"

"Couldn't sleep, Mama."

"Humph." Tata grunted at her from behind the morning paper.

Mil kissed them both.

"I'm thinking about Billy's offer. It sounds so glamorous. I'd like to do it...but..."

At that point, Tata's fist slammed down onto the table, rattling coffee cups and spoons, startling her as well as interrupting her.

Mama rushed to his side, straightening the table arrangements. She fussed a little longer, then began patting Tata gently on the shoulder.

Mil watched them. She was confused. She'd never witnessed a scene like that before. Sure, Mama and Tata must have had arguments, but if and when they did, the rest of the family never saw or heard. Sometimes, Mil felt tension between Mama and Tata, but that was all. Now, Mil wondered if, and began to suspect, that this disagreement had to do with her...maybe with Billy's proposal that she join his act. Mil wasn't sure what to say next...how to broach the subject again. Then, she had an idea.

"I think I'll call Billy in a little while," Mil said.

She expected Mama to ask why, and then they could talk some about the good and bad of the offer, instead, Mama turned to her with blazing eyes, and Tata stomped off to the window and looked grimly out at nothing in particular.

"Mama, what's the matter?" Unaccountably, visions of the red-head and the man swept before her mind's eyes.

"No!" Mama almost shouted, "You no can go mit Billy! Tata und I, we say."

Mil was totally unprepared for such an outburst. She'd never had a reaction like that from her Mama. And it was uncalled for. What in the world was really behind it? Mama and Tata both knew that she talked on and off about becoming an actress...ever since she was little. Mama always seemed to go along with the idea. Frustration began to build within Mil. It grew. How dare they, she thought angrily, and before she realized what was happening, words tumbled from her lips.

"Mama, what do you mean...I *can't* go. You and Tata have no right to order me around. I'm a woman. I earn my own living! I've had a husband and a baby!"

"Ya, und you want to lose baby, und you do lose baby."

Mama's words stung, like a sudden slap in the face.

The look on Mama's face, the tone of her voice...both triggered an onslaught of violent feelings that literally propelled Mil forward. Raising both hands she shoved Mama back against the stove. Horrified at her own actions, she felt completely out of control.

Then she saw Tata spring at her...felt herself hit the floor...cringed from his look...his unexpected violence.

"Never!" he spat, "never, you touch your Mama in madness."

With crimson face, bowed head and straight form, he loomed over her like a life-threatening giant.

"What kind of girl are you now? God is nothing...church is nothing. Now, like tramp, you will go with Billy? No!"

Metal pellets, those words were, hurting more than his actions. Tears of rage ran down her cheeks as she echoed Tata's words, shooting them back.

"Like a tramp? What are you talking about, Tata? What do you know about it anyway? Billy just asked me to be part of his act. That's all! Nothing more."

"You think Billy will stay here...in neighborhood? Billy will go. He will go far, and you will go too."

"Well, what if I do?"

"Billy is Catholic?"

"You know he's not. What difference does that make? You didn't care before.

"Is Billy ask you to marry?"

"I don't want to marry Billy."

"So, you go like tramp. No, not in this house."

Mil scrambled up off the floor, gulping sobs, strangling them in her throat. She ran to her room and slammed the door.

Going to the closet, she tore one of her dresses from its hanger, hurriedly wriggled into it, grabbed her coat and ran from the house.

If only it weren't so early in the morning. If only Marcus were at the store. Emilia wanted so badly to talk to him. If only she'd thought to take money, than she would have taken the streetcar to Marcus' house. He would help her, Marcus would. Stupid "if's". As things were, there was no way she could see Marcus right now.

Mil wondered around the neighborhood, up one street, down the next, rejecting the idea of stopping at Ludmilla's or Helcha's. She wouldn't tell them about the scene with Tata and Mama. She couldn't.

Inadvertently, she'd gone down Lawndale, and there was the church. Haha! Mil raised her fist, shaking it to the steeple...to heaven itself.

"You...You...God! Again you've made trouble for me. What kind of loving Father are you, anyway?"

Suddenly Mil felt cold, colder than she'd ever felt. She wrapped her coat more closely around herself, hurrying past the church steps so she wouldn't be tempted to fly to the top and seek shelter in the warmth contained behind the great oak doors, so she wouldn't be tempted to apologize to God out of fear that He would somehow strike out at her as Tata did...maybe even strike her dead.

Then the church doors opened. People were coming out of the great oak doors. Mass must have ended. Oh, if she could only believe that the God who was housed in that temple, that he was a loving Father, if she could only believe that, then things would be better for her...maybe...easier. But even Tata, Tata who'd prayed for her when she was sick, even he didn't love her anymore. If he did, he wouldn't have called her that name. He wouldn't have hit her. No, he didn't love her anymore. Again, tears ran down her cheeks. Then, she remembered. If Mass was over, then Marcus would soon be coming to the fruit store. He would be unlocking the doors...Oh, Marcus, she thought. "I need you so much. I need your help more than I've ever needed it." She stomped along, as quickly as she could, in the direction of Belmont Avenue. She heard someone call.

"Emilia, is that you?"

Without turning, she knew it was Elinora Steech. Then, the woman was puffing along beside her.

"What are you doing here girl? Were you in church?"

"I'll never go inside that church again!" Mil shouted.

Elinora looked at Mil's tear-streaked face, her shaking hands, and wondered what had happened to cause such an outburst, but she asked nothing. She merely walked along beside Emilia. Then she put her hand on Emilia's arm, slowing the pace a little, so she could speak to Mil.

"My Jan, he says..."

"Your Jan...your Jan! Elinora, your Jan is dead, just like my Frankie...only you saw Jan's dead body. I never saw Frankie...never saw him dead...but I know...they told me...so I believe it. Why can't you remember...believe? It's crazy that you don't believe Jan is dead!"

Elinora stopped and pulled Emilia to a stop beside her. She searched Emilia's face.

"Emilia, is better for you? The way you believe? You are crying; I am not. The church, it says we have souls, and the souls live. So, my Jan lives still...in my head...in my heart. I remember his words good...all the things that we talked of...in my memory, he is still real."

Elinora paused, looked sadly into Emilia's eyes.

"Is that bad, Girl? Is that so bad?"

Emilia couldn't stand the pleading look in Elinora's eyes. She put her arms around the woman and hugged her. Then she turned from Elinora and hurried on down the street toward Belmont. She would go crazy if she didn't talk to Marcus soon. As she ran, Elinora's words haunted her. But Mil knew she'd go crazy if she kept remembering Frankie.

When Emilia reached the store, Marcus already had a fire going in the pot bellied wood stove. Its radiant warmth was an invitation to Mil to sit close beside the small stove. She hadn't said good morning, she hadn't removed her coat, nothing...she merely entered, then seated herself. Next she looked about; no customers...no Peter. She sighed with relief. Though Peter hadn't been opening the store since his illness, Emilia feared today might be the day he would decide to do so, and at that moment, she wanted no one but Marcus.

For his part, Marcus could see something was very wrong. Emilia looked disheveled. Her lips were blue with cold, face tear-streaked; he couldn't imagine what awful thing had happened. He had expected that today, she would be in a very cheery mood. After all, he thought, not often did one see a friend starring in vaudeville.

Aha...that must be it. Something with the show...or with Billy...maybe with whatever it was he asked her afterward. Perhaps, after all, he had asked her to marry him. No, he didn't think she would be so upset over a proposal of marriage.

He went to her side, unbuttoned her coat and turned her so she faced the stove. He rubbed her hands vigorously. When she showed signs of becoming more herself, he asked her what was wrong. She poured her heart out, crying again, as she relived the scene with Mama and Tata.

"So, you think they don't love you, because they are angry at you."

"We've never had such an argument as that."

"And Emilia, when you heard of Frankie's death, and you told God you would exchange the baby's life for Frankie's. Were you angry?"

"Of course!"

"So that means you didn't love Frankie or the baby?"

"But I did! I've never stopped loving them! Oh...I still love them. I need them so." Again she cried. Then she thought of something else. "It's God I've stopped loving. I don't need Him and He doesn't need me."

They sat quietly together until Mil spoke again, telling Marcus about passing the church and railing against God...against the trouble He was causing her once more...against the kind of Father he was...

Marcus interrupted.

"Did God say those things to you this morning in the kitchen? Did God push your Mama?"

"You know He didn't, Marcus, but..."

"Emilia, you can't have it two ways. You just told me God didn't do those things to you." Marcus paused, fearing he might say too much and in Emilia's present state, she might not be able to grasp the real meaning of his words. Then, gently, he continued, holding onto her hands all the while.

Softly, he said, "Emilia, *you* pushed your Mama. I think you caused your trouble this morning." He waited. "Didn't you?"

Emilia nodded and began to cry all over again. Marcus soothed her, told her to lie down in back for awhile. He spoke gentle words as he led her to the cot in the back room. Then he said, when she was ready, to come out again. Maybe if she worked on something...the accounts...she would feel better...she would occupy her mind with other things.

Emilia did as Marcus suggested. After lying down with a cold cloth covering her head and eyes for what seemed to be a long while, she rose, splashed her face with water from the little sink in the corner, then straightened her hair and clothing and headed toward the counter where Marcus had just completed ringing up a sale. She took the account cards and the ledger book - spread them out before herself.

She tried to keep her mind on the accounts, but to no avail. Her mind kept wandering back to the early morning scene with Mama and Tata. They hadn't even given her a chance to explain, to talk about her ideas. They didn't even really know if she had made up her mind to join Billy, which she really hadn't, but now, now she decided she would. Though she hadn't really wanted to leave the family, and although she thought she would be awfully nervous if ever she were on stage, (just watching Billy was too much) still, she now decided she would accept his offer. She would not be told what she could and could not do with her own life now that she was a woman. Yes, she knew what she would do. She would call Billy in a while, and tell him that she would be his partner in the act.

Marcus, thankful for the cold weather and the lack of customers which gave him time for Emilia and her problem, watched carefully from the corner of his eye as Emilia worked. He saw how hard she was thinking. He guessed she was debating with herself and he wondered who was winning, but he knew better than to ask. Emilia had had too much advice for one morning, especially now, now that she was so determined to become her own woman. He continued to busy himself, again feeling thankful for a slow day.

Soon Emilia put her pencil down and spoke to him.

"I've made up my mind, Marcus."

"Good! And what did you decide?"

"I'm going to join Billy."

Marcus looked at her defiant little face. It didn't seem to hold any excitement over the prospect of becoming a star. Her face showed only defiant resolution. Of course, she'd had a bitter experience this morning. Maybe she was covering her enthusiasm. Marcus decided to try to find out.

"You'll be a beautiful actress, Emilia."

"And will you come to see me?"

"I'm sure I will...while you're performing around here."

"Well, this is the only place I'll perform."

"I see."

Emilia said nothing more, she turned again to the accounts. Marcus could see she wasn't working.

"But, just suppose more offers come in and you go to...say...New York...you and

Billy. That should be very exciting, shouldn't it?"

"Umm." That was all she said.

The phone rang. Marcus left to answer. Emilia's mind went to work once again.

New York, she thought, was very far. It was also very big, much bigger than Chicago. But, she would see the Statue-of-Liberty. That would be exciting.

But all of her family would be so far away. Nieces and nephews would grow up and she wouldn't even know them. There would be births and deaths and she wouldn't be here to witness them. Where would she live? How would she learn to get around in a strange big city like New York?

How would they travel about together..she and Billy...without being married. Hm...married. Would she want to marry Billy? He was handsome. He was a good person too. He was a good friend. But he was very different from herself. He enjoyed her family, but he wouldn't *marry* them. Family would play second fiddle to the stage. Yes, they really were very different, she and Billy. No...no...she couldn't marry Billy...or anyone else for that matter, until she stopped loving Frankie. Humph...then maybe she never would marry anyone else, because she didn't think she could ever stop loving Frankie.

Marcus returned. Emilia put the pencil down again.

"Marcus, I don't think I'll do it...go on the stage with Billy. I think I've changed my mind."

Marcus smiled at her.

"I know you'll do the right thing, Emilia. The right thing for you, that is."

She ran to him and hugged him. "You help me so much."

"That's good. Now what about your mama?"

"Oh, she must be terribly worried. Or, maybe she doesn't care at all. If she did, wouldn't she have come here to look for me by now?"

"No, but she might have telephoned to see if you'd come here."

They laughed.

"So, that was the phone call you answered while I was pretending to work with the accounts."

Marcus nodded.

"Did Mama sound mad?"

"Upset, I think."

"Oh, Marcus, what can I say to her? I don't think I can face Mama or Tata."

"Are you sorry you pushed her?"

"I'd give anything to change what happened this morning."

"Then, why don't you go home and tell them that?"

"Do you think they'll forgive me?"

"Have you forgiven them?"

"Oh, Marcus...you and your questions!"

Again, Emilia hugged him, then cleaned the counter, grabbed her coat, and left for home.

When Emilia entered the house, she was surprised to see Tata there with Mama, that he hadn't gone to work. That really frightened her, for she could count on the fingers of one hand, the few times Tata had ever stayed home from work. Only very serious matters kept him home. She noted, however, that neither Mama nor Tata looked angry. Mama had been crying, she could see that. Tata? He didn't look angry... maybe serious.

She ran to Mama, flinging her arms tightly around Michalina's neck. All the words she'd rehearsed on the way home had left her mind. All she could say was, "I'm sorry, Mama...so sorry. Tata, please forgive me."

"Ya. Dziecko, ya. We, too, are feeling sorrow."

But that was all Mama said. Tata said nothing about the morning's happenings, or about Billy, or about acting, or about anything else. The air still hung heavy with unspoken words, but Emilia was too fearful to speak them herself.

Silently, Emilia went to her room, changed clothes, and rehearsed what she would say when she went back to the kitchen. Nothing sounded right. She loved Mama and Tata, but she didn't want them to think they'd frightened her into changing her mind about Billy's offer. No, they needed to understand that the decision was hers, but she didn't know how to tell them that without starting another argument.

After changing and combing her hair, Emilia went back to the kitchen. It was three o'clock. She thought about Billy. He ought to be awake, and at home. Maybe she would call him. Yes, that was it. She would call him, and then Mama and Tata would hear her. They would know, they would hear by her words to Billy that she'd made up her own mind.

Without saying anything to them, Emilia picked up the phone. She gave the number to the operator and waited to hear Billy's voice. The kitchen was unusually silent.

Mil started the conversation directly and matter-of-factly by telling Billy exactly what she'd decided. Then, she told him a lot about what she'd been thinking through at the store all morning...mostly about the fact that she didn't want to leave home and family...and that...somehow...she had to be here, because she just wasn't finished with waiting for Frankie...strange as that sounded...even to her.

She'd never forget how Billy took it. He guessed it was in the cards, he said. He hoped they'd still be friends, and that she'd continue to come to his performances... even thought he could get her in free every now and then...and if ever she changed her mind...he'd always find a spot for her.

Then she had to ask...was he hoping for a "big offer" some day? Like an offer from New York or Hollywood?

Of course he was. That was the whole idea.

Yes, she understood that, but no, she would have to make her fortune some other way. She didn't know how. But she would have to. She didn't think it would work for her...living in New York...or Hollywood...no, she didn't think it would work.

When she hung up, Mama and Tata pretended to be busy.

"Come on," she said. "I know you heard."

They smiled and hugged, each thinking separate thoughts about the same subject.

"Ach," Mama thought. "What is comes next now? How Emilia looks for fortune?"

Tata sighed thinking that was the American spirit...how to get rich...and it was good...if Emilia stayed to be a good girl.

Emilia, herself, remembered what she'd decided not too long before...that fame and fortune should be for "their" kind too. All that remained for her now, was to figure out the right road to take. Someday one of them would, someday...she was sure, but she began to doubt that she would be the one.

## CHAPTER 34

"There's nothing like an evening in May for a stroll, is there, Emilia?"

"It is a beautiful night, Marcus. How I love the smell of all these lilacs."

"Yes, Emilia, and do you plan to have lilacs of your own someday, my Emilia?"

"Maybe, someday. Who knows."

Marcus looked down at the delicate hand resting so lightly on his arm. He would have liked to claim that hand as his very own, but somehow, he was never sure of Emilia...of her feelings. Of course, he knew she still loved Frankie, but how long could she go on with her devotion to a ghost? On the other hand, what about Billy? They were still friends, and it was possible Billy's present successes at the GRAND would influence Emilia. Perhaps she would change her mind about Billy's initial offer. Now that his star was rapidly rising, maybe Emilia would decide to go with him as a part of the act, and then if she did, mightn't they decide upon marriage.

Marcus looked up at the clear sky. So many stars. Would one of them point Emilia's way to Billy? He was behaving like a fool. He should confront the situation. Why not ask Emilia outright. But it was that May-December difference. That's what frightened him into holding back. Still, hadn't he told Emilia many times, that anything truly worth having was worth every reasonable risk? He should follow his own advice.

"What are you thinking, Marcus?"

He looked into Emilia's eyes and saw genuine interest and concern. That gave him courage. He knew what he must do. He began.

"That was a wonderful show we saw tonight, wasn't it?"

"Oh, yes. But I'm prejudiced. You know how I love to go to the GRAND."

"Of course. Your friend, Billy. And he is good."

"Oh, he's made wonderful progress. He really has quite a following already, doesn't he, Marcus?"

Again Marcus studied her face. So enthusiastic. So alive. He couldn't stop now. He had to know.

"Emilia, are you sorry?"

"For what?" She looked genuinely astonished.

"That you didn't take Billy's offer?"

"Marcus...that's...silly. I enjoy Billy's performances...always, but I also enjoy the wonderful movies they show at the GRAND. Why tonight, for instance, wasn't Marion Davies just breathtaking? She sure is beautiful."

"Yes, she is." Marcus looked down at the ground. He wanted to say more. He must gather his courage. He cleared his throat. "Yes, Marion Davies is beautiful..." Marcus's voice trailed off as he turned to Emilia. She looked back at him quizzically. Then he continued, "But no lovelier than you, dear Emilia."

She was touched to tears, not overflowing tears, merely to scarce pools of water that confined themselves to her eyes.

"Why, Marcus, that's the sweetest thing anyone has ever said to me. Thank you."

They walked a little further in silence. Soon Emilia's house would be visible to them. Marcus felt the atmosphere was right. He must pursue this subject that consumed his thoughts so often. He must try to speak before the mood was gone.

"About Billy, Emilia. You didn't really answer my question."

"I don't understand. What question?"

"Would you like to be up on that stage with Billy? Would you like to call him and say you've changed your mind about his offer?"

Marcus held his breath for a second after that, fearful of her answer.

He saw that Emilia frowned and seemed to be considering how to respond. It seemed to him that a long time passed before she spoke, but he knew it wasn't really. He told himself he must pay close attention, in every way, to her answer.

"Sometimes, Marcus, I think, dream really, about the fame, and the glamour...and the money...that could come to me from a career on the stage. Maybe even that the stage would lead to the movies, like it did for Marion Davies. In my mind's eye I can see myself as the star of "The Restless Heart" or some other wonderful movie, and I think...yes...that's what I want...fame and fortune..."

Her voice trailed off and her dreamy eyes seemed to fix themselves upon some distant spring eve vision.

"Then you are sorry."

"Not really Marcus. I don't know how to say it, but I guess I'm only sorry in my dreams. Do you understand?"

When she turned her face toward him, so pretty with its furrowed brow, its look of concentration, he wanted to take her in his arms...to hold her, and protect her, and love her...but he couldn't. He was so much older. He just couldn't do it.

"You see, Marcus, I think it's only the idea of being on the stage that I like. I don't want to leave Mama and Tata...the rest of my family...this place...my friends...you..."

She smiled at him, brightening his evening like a star fallen to the earth, but he saw she wasn't finished.

"And besides all that, I'd only want to *be* on the stage. I wouldn't want to practice for hours, or help to write material, do the planning, none of that part. So, I'm not really sorry. No, not really. Only in my dreams. Is that wrong, Marcus?"

"Wrong to dream? Not if you know it's only a dream. Everybody needs a dream.

Besides, maybe you'll find something, or somebody who will replace that dream with another."

"What somebody? What other dream?"

"Somebody like me, Emilia. I could offer you lilacs."

Emilia's lips parted just a little. What was she hearing? Her eyes searched Marcus's face. The humor lines, so deeply etched at the corners of his eyes, were still there, but they weren't crinkling. No, his face was serious. Marcus meant what he said. But did he mean what she was thinking he meant? Was her friend offering her a proposal of marriage?

Marcus pulled her to a stop. He held both her hands tightly in his own. He searched her face. She wasn't laughing at him. Emilia's face told him she was turning his words over carefully. He dared not breathe.

"Marcus? Did you just offer me a proposal of marriage?"

"I did, Emilia. Will you have me?"

They stood still for what seemed a long time. Then, Emilia moved closer to Marcus, resting her head on his shoulder. Her arms crept around his neck.

"Oh, dear, dear Marcus. My dearest friend. Do you love me?"

"Child, how can you ask? I have feared for so long that it showed."

"Perhaps I haven't been looking."

"Well, Emilia...will you marry me?"

"Dearest Marcus, I think you know that there's much of Frankie still filling my heart, don't you?"

"Yes, Emilia, I know that. But the heart is a muscle that expands. I think yours will expand with my love."

"Marcus, dear, I'm not at all sure that I deserve someone like you."

"I am."

"Then, how can I say anything but, yes, my Marcus."

Marcus folded his arms around her and let his tears mingle with the golden strands of her hair.

They stood that way in the middle of the sidewalk until Emilia decided they ought to rush home to tell Mama and Tata.

"Marcus," she asked, "what time is it?"

He withdrew his pocket watch.

"Near midnight."

"Late. I think we'll have to wait until tomorrow to tell Mama and Tata."

"I think you're right."

They walked on farther, holding hands. Then Emilia thought of something.

"Marcus, will you come to breakfast in the morning? We can tell Mama and Tata then, together."

Instead, they decided that maybe morning coffee would be better, about ten o'clock, and afterward they would go for a drive in the Poulis brothers' car. Peter usually used the auto on Saturdays while Marcus used it on Sundays. Emilia was excited by the prospect.

When they reached the door, Emilia searched through her purse for the key, then handed it to Marcus, but he merely dropped it into his pocket in order to have both hands free.

Then, very tenderly, he took her into his arms and kissed her the way he'd always longed to do.

Emilia was surprised at her response. Marcus's gentle love had touched all of the tightly bound feelings which she'd labeled "Frankie", the feelings that she'd carefully stored away in a deep recess of her heart. Now, she clung to Marcus urgently, and returned his kiss. She felt both excited and frightened. It was exciting to know that hearts could expand, but frightening to think that she might someday completely forget how much she had loved her Frankie. No, she wouldn't allow herself to forget. She would share that love...with Frankie's memory, and with the person of Marcus. Having decided that, she gave herself up completely to another kind of excitement...tingling and physical.

In a little while, Marcus unlocked the door for her.

"Go, my Child. Sleep well, for my love goes with you."

"I know, Marcus. Good night, my dearest friend."

As Emilia readied herself for bed, she cherished the memory of Marcus's arms, of his parting words. What a wonderful man he was. She wanted never to hurt him. She vowed she never would.

## CHAPTER 35

On Sunday morning, Emilia woke with the sun, and couldn't fall asleep again. Instead, she lay in bed thinking. It felt good to lie there thinking pleasant thoughts. She had so much to be thankful for this May of 1919.

There was Marcus, of course. Dear Marcus. Marcus her friend, and Marcus of last night. The very thought of their time together last night, made her feel delicious. She'd lain there remembering for quite some time. Yes, last night's events made her feel very good, and feeling so good led her to feel thankful for other things too.

She felt sadness only for Frankie, but *that* she pushed far back from her mind, concentrating instead on the rest of their people who had come home now from the war. Most were safe and sound. Only two had been physically wounded, but their wounds were not so serious as to interfere with their normal activities.

Of the two, Frankie's brother, Ed, had been hurt the most seriously. He'd developed a bone infection after being hit in the leg. He was in the hospital for months afterwards, and though he was now limping some, and would probably do so for the rest of his life, the treatment was successful enough to keep him alive, and to leave him without great disability. He didn't like limping, and at first he felt very self-conscious, but the passage of time had helped him to accept his disability, and to realize that it really wasn't as obvious as he first felt it was.

Billy, too had been wounded in the leg, but he was completely healed now - had been since he first introduced himself to Emilia. She smiled to herself, remembering that introduction and her resistance of Billy's friendship, but how she now included Billy with family members. Everyone else did too. It was natural, of course, since he had no family of his own. Yes, they simply adopted one another...Billy and the whole family. Maybe Marcus would think of him that way too, now that she'd accepted Marcus's proposal.

"Proposal". It struck her as a strange sounding word...but wonderful, she thought, as she repeated the word to herself several times. What would Mama and Tata say? Would they be surprised? She thought, they would be. For some reason that thought made her shiver with delight.

Then, she led her mind back to family members and the men who'd returned from the War.

Kate's Hank was home...untouched...handsome as ever. They celebrated their first anniversary, a little late, but celebrate they did. Mil felt happy for them, in spite of the little nagging darts of envy that pierced her heart each time she saw Kate and Hank together. They had no baby yet, but maybe that was good. They seemed just to be enjoying one another, even though they had limited space and privacy to do it in, because they too were living with Mother J. However, Lily and Joe were moving out soon; they'd found a place of their own. And, of course, Busha was gone...and Frankie...but still, there was Mother J., Ed, and Kate with her Hank. Well, as long as they were happy.

Finally, there was Ludmilla's Frank. He was home, not wounded, but they were having a very hard time. Frank was so nervous. He couldn't talk of what he'd been through, but he dreamed much about it. Ludmilla said he suffered from constant nightmares. Each time he woke from one of those terrible dreams, he'd not be able to fall asleep again. The doctor said that lack of sleep was part of the reason for his nervousness. However, Frank was lucky in one respect...he'd found a job when many of the returning boys couldn't. Even that good fortune was adding to his nervousness, for he feared losing the job because of his condition. His employer, however, was a fine man who understood the problems of returning soldiers. Frank was very lucky that way. But, of course, a newspaper company would understand these war veterans because many of the reporters had been overseas themselves, covering the news of the war, so they knew what it was all about. And maybe help was coming sooner than any of them thought, for Ludmilla had recently talked Frank into seeing Dr. Noshkins, and submitting to a new treatment. Dr. Noshkins also drew Frank into conversation, so he was better able to talk about some of the horrors he'd seen. Already it seemed to help. Now, Ludmilla cried less, feeling as she saw progress, that there was more hope.

Well, so Ludmilla had her Frank, and Kate had her Hank. Emilia was the only one who'd lost her love.

Ah, but no, she wouldn't think that way anymore. She not only wouldn't allow it, she wouldn't have to think about being alone anymore. She had a wonderful, loving friend in Marcus Poulis. She really learned last night how much Marcus cared about her. Even now she could feel his love, here in the quiet of a Sunday morning in her sunny room.

She loved spring...sunshine...May. Maybe she and Marcus would marry in May, not this year, of course, but next. How would Marcus like that she wondered. Perhaps today, they would talk about a wedding date when they went out driving.

How many women, she wondered, were married twice by her age. Here she was, soon to turn nineteen and already considering...no...planning a second marriage. Life was strange. Or God was strange. He made peculiar demands upon people, although, she figured He would begin to make fewer demands upon her, because she was grown-up enough now to recognize that she didn't need Him and He didn't need her. Yes, God could pick on someone else now.

Mama, Tata and Emilia were sitting in the parlor reading the Sunday papers when Marcus rang the doorbell. At the sound of the bell, Emilia rushed to the door. When Marcus entered, the two stood for a moment, looking into one another's eyes, silently communicating. It was as though Marcus were asking if Emilia broke the news and she was responding, telling him that she hadn't.

Michalina watched the exchange, and she wondered about it. She thought there was something "special" in their greeting this morning. She also thought it unusual that Emilia hadn't mentioned that Marcus was coming, though it was obvious she had expected him.

Tata looked up from the paper. He said nothing, but his eyes narrowed.

"What is..." Mama thought, "What is..."

Then Emilia took Marcus' hand and together they approached Michalina and Caspar.

"Mama...Tata...Marcus would like to speak to you."

Emilia's mouth felt dry. She looked imploringly at Marcus.

"Michalina...Caspar...I would like to marry Emilia. I have asked her. She has said yes. I hope now you will grant us your permission, and give us your blessing."

The mantle clock loudly ticked the seconds away as Emilia waited for someone to speak.

"Tata," Emilia said, "Marcus is my dearest friend...and I think he loves me very much."

Tata grunted in reply; said no more.

Emilia studied his face. She was impatient. "What does that mean, Tata?"

"Marcus is good man. I think, too, he loves you. I think, he will be good to you...but..."

"Tata, what? What...'but'?"

Tata cleared his throat. "You are young, Emilia. Will you, too, be good to Marcus?"

"Tata!" Emilia's feelings were hurt. Hot tears burned her eyelids.

Then Mama spoke quickly. "Tata think maybe you are too young for Marcus. He think maybe such marriage no can work."

Mil turned to Marcus. Admiration flowed from her eyes, washing Marcus with a very special feeling.

Still studying Emilia, Marcus said, "I think we are ready to make such a marriage work. I think Emilia truly cares for me, and I know that I carry in my heart enough love for both of us."

"So," Tata said, "you will marry. I wish blessings on your heads. I wish for you much happiness."

Mama said nothing, but she thought much. In ten years, when Emilia was twenty-nine and Marcus fifty, then what? And what of children?

"Ya, ya," Michalina muttered softly. "Little children is little troubles. Big children is big troubles." Aloud, she said, "When you will do this?"

"Marcus?" Emilia's face was bright with anticipation. "What do you think? Would you like to marry next May?"

Marcus's face showed disappointment, but he merely said, "If that's what you'd like, Emilia."

"Ya," Mama thought. "Is long for him." But she determined to say nothing. As God willed, so it would work, she thought.

******************

Emilia loved sitting in the auto next to Marcus. Already, she felt as though she were special, as though she really "belonged" again. What a wonderful feeling that was. They drove happily out of the city, down blossoming country lanes, breathing the fresh air spiced with wonderful spring aromas. They laughed and talked of buying a house of their own. Wouldn't it be fun shopping for furniture? And dishes? Linens? Oh, a home of their own! What a wonderful dream...no, a plan.

Marcus was thrilled by all the excitement and enthusiasm generating from Emilia's face. She looked lovelier than ever to him. When he could stand it no longer, he pulled off the road and gathered her to himself, covering her with gentle kisses, marveling at the wonder of it all.

Then Marcus decided it would be a good idea if Emilia learned to drive the car. She shifted over to the wheel while Marcus stepped out to turn the hand crank. The car coughed and sputtered and Marcus hurried to jump in as the auto seemed to leap away with them. Emilia squealed in fright, but Marcus placed a guiding hand on the wheel, directing and encouraging her all the while, until Emilia finally felt confident enough to try by herself to actually drive. Again she squealed...this time with delight, for she felt like a conquering heroine.

"Oh," she thought. "How good Marcus was. How kind and patient. Thank God for Marcus! Oh...she'd gone and done it again...thanked God. Well, she decided, that was merely a figure of speech."

Much later that evening, a while after Marcus had left the house, the phone rang. On the other end, Emilia heard Kate's excited voice.

"Emilia, I'm going to the doctor tomorrow."

"Oh, Kate, is it...are you..."

"I think so. In fact, I'm sure. I believe you're going to be an aunt again."

Emilia was thrilled. A baby was something Kate had wanted for a long time. They talked awhile, and Emilia expressed her complete delight, then she spoke again.

"Kate...I too have something to tell. I hope you'll be happy for me."

"What is it, Emilia?"

"Kate, Marcus Poulis has asked me to marry him...and Kate, I've accepted."

Kate didn't respond. There was silence between them that seemed to last forever. The silence became a strain. Emilia broke it.

"Kate? Are you angry?"

Kate stammered her reply, but assured Mil she wasn't angry.

"Then what is it, Kate?"

When Kate failed to answer immediately, Emilia continued, feeling a need to explain her actions.

"I can't live alone forever. I'm only nineteen. And Marcus really loves me...I can feel it."

Still, Kate was silent. Emilia felt hurt. She couldn't understand what seemed to be Kate's rejection...disapproval...of her news. Finally, Kate spoke.

"Mil, I'm sorry I seemed so...so stunned. Of course you're happy and of course I'm surprised, that's all. I'll go now, Mil, and I'll tell Ma all about it." Then she added hastily, "I'll talk to you tomorrow...after the doctor."

And Kate hung up.

Emilia replaced the receiver...puzzled. What was wrong with Kate? Would all the Jagiens be angry at her? Emilia sat down to read again, seeing nothing of the words on the pages. She reread them. It was no use. Something was wrong. She didn't know what, but something was very wrong. She looked at the clock. Too late tonight to call Kate back. Tomorrow she would find out exactly what was wrong, what the real trouble was.

## CHAPTER 36

Emilia woke early Monday morning after a troubled sleep. She was eager to call Kate, but it was too early. Instead, she would go to the fruit store as usual. She would see Marcus. Besides, she didn't wish to be late for work simply because she was now engaged to marry one of the store owners. She wouldn't take advantage of Marcus and Peter, though she knew they wouldn't think of it that way.

Right after breakfast, Emilia hurried down to Belmont. It was going to be a lovely day in May...a lovely day to anticipate greeting the man she would marry. The man she would marry. How strange that thought struck her. How strange were the ways of life.

With that thought still on her mind, she entered the store. It was empty, except for Marcus. With a smile and a furrowed brow she ran to him, kissed his cheek quickly.

Marcus knew something was troubling her. Taking her hand, he pulled her into the back room, just as Peter was entering the shop. Peter saw them and winked knowingly at his brother. Tactfully, he remained in the store, leaving the quiet of the back room to Marcus and Emilia, remembering how exciting it was to be newly engaged.

After gently kissing Emilia and rubbing her troubled brow, Marcus questioned her. Emilia told him about her telephone conversation with Kate. Marcus reassured her, tried to convince her that there was no need to worry, but worry was on her mind, so she transferred her worry to Marcus.

"Oh, Marcus, dear...aren't you tired of hearing my troubles? Especially my constant reference to Frankie and his family?"

"Emilia, Emilia, you can't deny any part of your life. You were married to Frankie and now his family is your family. I understand that my child. I also understand that you must put all of your fears behind you before we can be happy together."

She hugged him tightly.

"I told you I didn't deserve you."

Marcus kissed her again before responding. "Now, go home. Call Kate...do whatever you must do. I'll see you later."

Mil ran all the way, and still out of breath, she placed her call. The Jagien's phone rang and rang, but no one answered. Several times she tried to call - without any luck.

She threw herself into a chair. her stomach churned. The house was so silent. Tata, of course, was at work, but where was Mama? At Ludmilla's, probably. She grabbed an apple from the bowl on the table next to her. Between munching, she kept trying the Jagien's number. Still, no response.

Why should she be so bothered? Kate promised to call back after her visit to the doctor's; surely she would do that and then the mystery would be cleared up.

After all, why shouldn't Kate be surprised? Marcus was a much older man, though a good one. No doubt the Jagiens hadn't considered remarriage for Emilia, since she hadn't mentioned anyone in particular, and they probably wouldn't have thought she would marry a man so much older. Of course it was a surprise. Why shouldn't it be? Emilia was surprised herself. Still, no amount of self-reasoning would calm her stomach. Way down deep, she had an uncomfortable feeling that something was very wrong. But what in God's name could it be?

Oh...she was doing it again! God, God, God. Why didn't she leave Him out of it? Her constant silent praying was a real source of irritation to her. She didn't need God, so why did she keep calling on Him? Emotions. Hers were very fickle, she decided.

Trying to take her mind off things, Emilia busied herself around the house until noon. Then she ate lunch and read a magazine. Then the mantle clock chimed. It was one o'clock. Still early. A thought struck her. Why not go to Mother Jagien's? If Mother wasn't home, she would surely be at the tailor shop. In fact she probably would be at the tailor shop, but since the streetcar stopped directly across the street from the Jagien house, she might as well check there first. Emilia decided that was a good idea. She would make the trip. That way, she wouldn't have to worry and wonder. If there were anything at all to be concerned about, Mother J. would tell her. Mother J. was like that. And what concern could there possibly be? If they were upset with her plans to remarry, surely she could make them understand her thinking...her need. Yes, and she could better make them understand by talking to them personally. Yes indeed. She would go to them. It would help her; it would help them. Besides that, it was a beautiful day for a streetcar ride.

Emilia didn't bother to change. She left a note for Mama, phoned Marcus and told him what she planned to do, grabbed her sweater and purse, and set out for the streetcar stop.

As she walked toward Belmont, Emilia saw Elinora coming from the opposite direction. Elinora stopped and waved. Emilia waved back. She saw that Elinora was waiting for her, so Emilia stepped up her pace a little.

"You are going to the fruit market, Emilia."

"No, not now. I'm going to Frankie's Ma's house."

"Oh."

That was all Elinora said, but Emilia thought she sounded funny, as though there were some meaning behind the one little word that Emilia didn't understand. She wanted to question Elinora, but the streetcar was coming and she didn't want to miss it.

"Go, go." Elinora waved her on. "I go to market. Jan wants bananas."

Then, after taking note of Emilia's expression, Elinora spoke gain.

"No, I go for bananas because I feel very hungry for their taste."

Then she smiled at Emilia as if to say, "See, it's only my game. I know that my Jan is dead."

Emilia smiled in return and hurried up the streetcar steps, thinking that the woman wasn't nearly as crazy as she pretended to be. Maybe Marcus had a lot to do with that too. He was so good at listening to Elinora, conversing with her, gently prodding her memory in the direction of Jan's death. So, maybe now she really was beginning to accept it.

As the streetcar screeched to a halt before the pile of rubble that once was the mustard factory, Emilia remembered how Frankie used to tell her of his morning game, the one where he'd try to time his jump from the streetcar in order to bring him right in line with the front door of the factory. She wondered how many times he actually succeeded. Then she wondered how long it would take to clear away the last of the factory rubble. Maybe the hospital would enlarge and they would be rid of the eyesore. That would probably please the whole Jagien family, though she didn't know, since they never mentioned anything about it...probably didn't even notice. Between working at the tailor shop, and taking care of the house, they probably had no time to think about someone else's rubble.

Emilia crossed the street and knocked loudly on Mother J.'s door a number of times. As she expected, no one responded. She hoped now that it wasn't foolish on her part to have made the trip, for Mother J. might have gone with Kate to the doctor, and in that case, she wouldn't even be at the shop. However, she told herself, that wasn't likely. Mother J. wouldn't have closed the shop early just to sit in the waiting room. No, Emilia would probably find Mother J. behind the sewing machine, feet working hard at the treadle.

Emilia hurried down the steps toward Paulina Street and the tailor shop. It was now after two and the sun was hot. Emilia stopped to remove her sweater. As she struggled out of it, she dropped her purse. Emilia turned around to pick it up. Back down the block, she saw a couple crossing the street...slowly, carefully. The woman had gorgeous red hair. Emilia had seen that hair before. Of course...Busha's wake. She looked again. Another memory was triggered...Billy's starring performance...the woman with red hair...the man who looked so much like Frankie. Emilia stood and watched. It was the same couple, she was sure. Had she seen a cane jutting out from somewhere behind the woman's skirt? She couldn't tell. They were too far away. Then they were out of sight. Maybe the red-head's companion was an aging father? He walked slowly. Well, it was hard to say. She couldn't see them very well at all. It was only that gorgeous red hair. That, she could see. Emilia shrugged and moved on.

When Emilia reached the tailor shop, she saw the door standing open as if to welcome her. She smiled at her imaginings. The door was open because of the sun-warming heat on this beautiful afternoon in May. Fortunately, there was still a lack of bugs in the air. Well, it was good to see the open door, even if Mother J. couldn't possibly be expecting her.

Emilia peered inside. Mother was tending a customer. At the sound of Emilia's footsteps, Mother J. looked toward the door, her almond eyes peering over her glasses. An expression of surprise which quickly turned to consternation flickered across her face.

Kate told Mother about Marcus, Emilia thought, but she wasn't expecting me here today.

The customer soon left and Mother J. crossed the room to Emilia, taking Emilia's hands in her own, quite seriously, it seemed. Then they hugged, clinging longer than usual, Emilia noticed. Mother seemed to be struggling with something...making some decision...maybe deciding what to say.

Emilia broke the silence. “Kate told you about Marcus and me, didn't she?”

Mother J. nodded solemnly.

“You don't approve.”

Though Emilia intended her words to be a question, they seemed to formulate a statement.

“I don't know how to tell you, Emilia.”

“It doesn't matter how you tell me. Your disapproval is very painful to me. I can't bear to have you think I'm deserting Frankie...his memory.”

“That's not what I'm thinking.”

Emilia was surprised. "Then what?"

There were tears in Mother's eyes. Emilia had never seen her mother-in-law with tears...never...not even when she came with the news of Frankie...no, never before. She couldn't imagine what was so wrong as to bring tears to Frankie's mother. She felt cold...suddenly cold.

"Come, Emilia. Let us sit down."

Mother led Emilia to the straight backed chairs which lined the wall beneath the big store windows at the front of the shop. The windows were clear...not at all steamy on this day.

"Sit down, Emilia. Please."

Emilia looked out the window at the fresh green patches of city grass, and the baby leaves swaying gently on the tree branches. Then she looked down at Mother's pleading eyes. On a day like this, what could Mother possibly say to upset her? What could be so awful? Mother had already given her the most terrible news in the world...ages ago...a lifetime ago. Again, Emilia looked out the window. No news could ever do to her what that dreadful announcement of Frankie's death had done... especially not on a day like this. Nevertheless, Emilia stood a little longer, relishing the greens of spring, wishing to postpone what she instinctively felt to be the inevitable.

"Emilia, you mustn't marry Marcus."

Emilia didn't take her eyes from the view outside the window. She stood, turning Mother's words over and over in her head. She waited for some further explanation. None came.

"Why? Why mustn't I marry Marcus, Mother? Why do you..."

Emilia's thoughts were interrupted by what she saw from the window. The red-head and the man. They were across the street, still moving slowly...so slowly...the way she'd seen them on that cold evening...outside the theater. Yes, it was that same couple...the red-head and that man. And she was leading him, like she did that night. His arm might be linked through hers...his hand resting on her forearm. He wore a cap. The visor hid his face. They continued walking...passing the front windows. Emilia watched the swaying of her skirt...the man's tense movements. That walk again. Emilia knew it from some distant past. She knew those broad young shoulders. There was no doubt now in her mind. She knew who that man was.

Emilia ran from the store. She ran across the street, disregarding the vendor with his horse as they clomped down the street, disregarding the oath he uttered loud enough for her to hear as she ran in front of him.

She screamed. "Frankie!"

Only once she shouted his name, but the command in her voice stopped the couple. The red-head turned around to look at her; but not the man...he continued to look straight in front of him. His shoulders slumped forward...his head drooped a little.

Emilia stopped short behind him, waiting for him to turn, but he wouldn't. She knew now...without any doubt whatever...it was Frankie..:but he wouldn't look at her.

"Oh...you Devil. Truly you are a Devil." Emilia's voice dripped venom. "What have you done? How could you do this to us?"

Still, he didn't turn.

Vera placed her hand on Emilia's arm. "Mil, I can explain," she said.

Emilia shook her arm free of the contamination.

Again, she hissed, "Look at me, you Devil man. Turn around and look at me!"

She screamed the words again, completely oblivious to the vendor and the several passing ladies who moved past them...shopping bags swaying from their forearms. The people stopped...stared.

Slowly, Frankie turned, pointing himself in the direction of her voice. He pretended to see her, but she knew he didn't, for his gaze was fixed just to the side of her face. Emilia looked down at the cane which was now so plainly visible. She covered her face with her hands. Now she knew. Her Frankie couldn't see her. He was blind.

## CHAPTER 37

It was dark as Emilia stepped down from the streetcar. Emilia pulled her sweater tighter to her chest. She'd never felt so cold...so miserable...not even when she believed Frankie to be dead.

She wasn't worried about Mama and Tata. They'd already called Jagien's, but she wouldn't allow anyone to tell them the truth. Emilia had merely told Mama that she was spending the night with Frankie's family. She couldn't tell them the truth, because she needed time...time to sort out the awful happenings of the day. She needed time alone to go over and over the scenes from the dreadful afternoon, an afternoon that she never would have believed possible. Never did she think anything could be worse than the news of Frankie's death, but now she knew that always there could be something worse than even the worst.

She hated them all! All the Jagiens had conspired against her. But most of all, she hated Catherine, Frankie's Ma. How could she have kept such a secret? What right had she to do it! Oh yes...she was helping Frankie...hoping for a miracle...praying his eyesight would return...that God would make everything right for all of them. Emilia could never forgive her for this terrible deception.

And those prayers! Such craziness. What made Catherine believe that God heard anything? That he cared about anything? Anybody? Most of all, about Emilia?

Emilia pressed her fingers to her temples, wanting to run somewhere...anywhere. Perhaps this was the ultimate nightmare. Maybe she would awaken soon and find that none of today had happened at all. Maybe she was still sick and when she awoke from her delirium she would find Frankie lying beside her...in their wonderful bed...on the back porch. Oh, please God...let it be that way...delirium... nightmare...but no, it wouldn't be because God didn't care. He wouldn't help her.

And Frankie, what of Frankie? If he had really loved her, wanted to be a husband to her, then he would have come to her...as soon as he returned from the war... even if he was blind...even if he was blind...yes, even then, he would have come to her...if he loved her. Instead he'd turned to Vera, proving that he didn't care about her...didn't love her as a husband should....didn't trust her enough to think she would stick by him. Now, he wanted a divorce, because he had Vera, because as he said, he'd been "living with Vera."

Emilia felt she couldn't breathe. She stopped to lean against a building. The pain she felt in her chest...everywhere...was unbelievable. As she stood there, eyes closed, Vera's beautiful red curls seemed to dance before her. She waved her hands around, trying to erase those curls, but she couldn't...and then she knew. It was simple. Why shouldn't he want Vera? He'd turned to her, and she'd been there for him. She was lovely, healthy and vital.

Emilia traced her name along the brick wall...Vera. Then she traced that other word...the awful reality of Frankie's demand...divorce. No one in the family had ever been divorced. She'd only known one person in all her life who'd experienced divorce; that was Elinora Steech. She didn't wish to be in any way like Elinora Steech.

Emilia whimpered to herself as she heard the approaching shuffle of one of the corner drunks. If Mama or Tata came and saw her here...this way...they would be furious. She must get away. She must hurry...but not home. She needed more time.

Looking farther down the street, she saw lights reflecting from the fruit market. Marcus. Yes, she would go to Marcus, for he would be there...waiting for her... knowing instinctively that she needed him. Of course....of course, Marcus knew that because he loved her. In her misery, she didn't think of that. Marcus loved her...and he deserved to be told of all this.

She began to run toward the fruit market...to Marcus. Yes, he wanted to marry her. That was her answer...her refuge. Yes, to hell with them all. Frankie wanted a divorce? Well, he could have one. Why should she care about Mama and Tata...their feelings? Why should she care about God or church law? None of that mattered anymore. If Marcus would still have her, she would marry him. She would show them all.

As she ran, Emilia's hurt took on a new dimension. The effort of running fanned her pounding hurt until it flamed red...turning into hot anger. Her sorrow shriveled... tears dried...there was nothing left but hate and anger.

Then suddenly she was there, standing before the store window. Lights from the big windows beckoned to her, spilling out to spread a warm carpet of gold for her to step upon.

She must hurry inside. She couldn't wait to see Marcus. He was sensitive... needed her...wanted her. Marcus would never hurt her the way Frankie had. No, Marcus was a man...a real man.

She pushed the door open. There he was...Marcus...head bowed over the books. He looked up, lightening her heart with a warm smile.

"Dear, dearest Marcus."

Emilia's voice...a passionate groan...startled Marcus, alerted him. He steeled himself, anticipating the worst. What it could be, he didn't know, but tragedy was written all over his darling child.

Marcus took her into his arms, protected her from her awful cold feeling like a warm blanket. Still Emilia trembled, her body quaking with fury and unshed tears.

After a few minutes, Marcus released her; looked into her face. He saw blazing eyes...flaming cheeks; they told him much...none of the story...but much nevertheless. He knew above all that they were facing a serious crisis. Marcus feared this fury in Emilia, more than he would have feared hysterical sobbing. Yes, something very stirring happened to Emilia, something very stirring indeed, and it happened at Jagien's.

"All right, my child, tell me. What happened to you?"

Emilia tried to pull herself together, to tell a coherent story, but with each sentence, she became more frightened. She'd never seen Marcus angry, but now he sat before her, dark skin blanched, black eyes snapping as he pounded his fist upon the counter.

Marcus said nothing as he tried to organize and control his speeding thoughts and emotions. How dare they play God, those people...for any reason! His heart was bursting. Emilia's hurt...his own...there were no words to express what he felt. How could he...they...deal with this? A dead man...alive...blind...living with some whore. How could anyone accept...understand such deception? And now this foolish young man wanted a divorce? How big of him! Were they to feel gratitude for this *favor*? What was all this lying about? What was it really all about? And then he heard Emilia's tearful pleading.

"Please, Marcus...please...you will marry me, won't you? In spite of a divorce?"

Emilia's pleading eyes were destroying him. If he had Frankie Jagien now, within his reach, Marcus would have killed him. but Frankie wasn't there. Instead, Marcus felt the warmth of Emilia's body pressing closer and closer to his own. He felt her nearness as he'd never felt it before. He was holding her closer than he'd ever dared, wanting so much to take her into the back room...to lock the doors...to lay with her...to make her his, so neither of them could turn back...but he wouldn't. He loved her too much. He wouldn't take advantage of her fury and confusion. No, he had to be certain of her *love* for *him*. He had to be certain that Emilia wanted to be Mrs. Marcus Poulis because she loved him, not because she wanted to get even with Frankie...or his family...or maybe to show everyone what she could do.

"Oh, damn them all," he muttered, "for putting me in such a position...for causing me this pain..."

Marcus turned away from Emilia. She studied him with wide eyes. His shoulders shook a little. Was her Marcus crying? She went to him...timidly placed her hands on his shoulders. Marcus faced her again.

"Emilia, Child, I love you so much...and I will marry you...but first, we must take care of some things."

"What things, Marcus? What do you mean?" she asked as he led her to the cot in the back room.

Marcus took a bottle of root beer from the little ice box he kept for storing the makings of lunch or dinner. He poured a glass for each of them, wishing he had something stronger, but he didn't dare keep alcohol around now...not with Prohibition. The local cops would have his hide...money too.

Emilia watched him. Still, he looked so strained...no, more than that...anger lines drew the corners of his mouth down in a way she'd never seen before. This unfamiliar look on his face frightened her.

Marcus handed her the glass of root beer. He made a conscious effort to smile.

"Take this, lovely Child, you need energy."

When he called her 'Child', Emilia felt tense all over...angry again, but she reached for the glass as she continued to study his face.

"You always call me, Child. Don't do it anymore."

"That's merely my term of endearment."

An unnatural silence came between them. Marcus swirled the root beer in his glass, watching it intently as though the action would help him to know what to do next...what to say...so that Emilia would understand, because he felt she didn't...not completely. She was too hurt and angry to really understand how miserable he felt... how furious...how unbelieving.

"All right, Marcus. I'm waiting. What things...what must we take care of?"

Was she throwing the gauntlet? Daring him to continue loving her?

"Well, to begin with, my Dearest, this divorce...you don't have it yet. Also, after you begin the process, it will take at least a year to become final."

"So long?"

Marcus smiled ruefully. "Even the law doesn't take divorce lightly. Civil law in our state requires that enough time be given for you to be certain that this is what you want."

"That's crazy! I don't want to wait that long. I can't! I won't be Mrs. Frankie Jagien for one minute longer than I've already been."

"You'll be Frankie's wife in name only...just as you have been for most of your married life."

Emilia's eyes flashed back at him.

"Don't tell me that! Don't you understand? I feel dirty...used..."

Emilia began to pace back and forth, wringing her hands.

"Marcus, I hate him! His Busha was right to call him 'Devil'. That's what he is. He's just like his grandfather."

Marcus let her go on. She needed to do that. He studied her face...listened to her words. Still there were no tears, but there was much fury. Several times, she'd mentioned hating Frankie, but somehow Marcus thought, he would have preferred that she said she didn't love Frankie anymore. Somehow, that would have meant more to Marcus, for as he watched her, he wondered if she were really saying, "I love him so much that I hate him for disappointing me...for hurting me...for deceiving me...for turning to someone else."

Watching her, he'd felt his own anger dissipate...drain from his body. He sighed. Soon, he would walk her home. Probably, in a year's time, things would straighten out in spite of them all. How...he didn't know, but nothing ever stayed the same...things always changed. There was only one thing that he could be certain of. Someone was going to be hurt by all of this...maybe more than one. They'd had no right to do it..the Jagiens...but now it was done. Now..they must wait...and see.

## CHAPTER 38

Marcus thought it better not to go inside with Emilia. She agreed. Telling Mama and Tata what had happened wouldn't be easy, in fact, she didn't know how she would do it, but she did feel it would be good to be alone with them when the words were spoken. There was no use subjecting Marcus to another scene. She remembered not long ago, vowing to herself that she would never hurt Marcus. Now, in the light of what happened, that notion seemed pretty funny. How could she ever hurt Marcus more than she had tonight? Was she destined in this life to break every vow she made? Maybe the secret of a happy life was not to make vows. Well, thinking about life wouldn't postpone living it. She must go inside and she must tell Mama and Tata that Frankie was alive...alive and blind. Emilia shuddered, still hoping she'd dreamed it all up...that she'd waken from this terrible nightmare.

"Ach, foolish girl," she thought. "No, no girl," she mumbled. Not long ago, she'd declared herself a woman. But if this was what it meant to be a woman, God help her.

Again she did it...God...oh well, better to move inside and finish with it all. Quietly, she slipped into the kitchen.

"Milia?" Mama called from somewhere.

"I know I'm late, Mama."

"Ya, Dziecko. I call Jagien's again...making sure you be all right when you stay, but Mrs., she say you comin' home. She worry...thinks you be home already. She say to call when you come."

"You call her, Mama."

"Something is wrong, Milia?"

The phone rang before Emilia could answer.

From Mama's end of the conversation, Emilia knew that Frankie's Ma was on the other end of the line.

"Keep it short, Mama," was all Emilia said, but Michalina knew something awful was wrong. Listening to Emilia...looking at her...she knew. Michalina quickly said goodbye and replaced the receiver.

Tata had wandered in from the parlor. He eyed her speculatively, but said nothing.

"Dziecko, I make coffee for us."

"Never mind, Mama. Just sit down."

Without further conversation, Mama, and Tata also, took their customary chairs by the big table. They watched Emilia begin to pace. her face was now pale... her eyes wide. Michalina felt more and more fearful.

Emilia decided there was nothing to do, but to say it. There was no easy way.

"Frankie's alive. He's blind."

"Jesu kochanji."

To Emilia, Michalina's voice sounded very loud in the silence of the room. Emilia looked at Tata. His face was grim...jaw set tight.

"How this can be?"

"Frankie was hit by shrapnel. He stumbled and fell, unconscious, over the body of his friend. Frankie's pay book and identification must have fallen from his pocket. Later, it was found near the body of his friend who was killed. That buddy of Frankie's, the one that was killed, he was badly torn up, and when they finally were able to get to him, the only identification they found was Frankie's. The ambulance crew, well, they turned in those papers, and Frankie was reported dead."

"But, why he doesn't tell later?"

"He was unconscious for quite a while, and when he did come to, he couldn't remember anything. After awhile, his memory came back, but not his eyesight."

Emilia sat down. She was so tired. She felt so empty, that even anger couldn't sustain her. Emilia folded her arms on the table and lay her head down upon them. Then floods of tears came...tears she felt would never stop.

"Ach, Dziecko." Mama ran around the table to her baby. In awhile, Tata came to her other side, and lay his hand tenderly upon her shoulder. He puffed at his pipe, thoughtfully.

"But...Mama...Tata...the worst is that none of them...not Frankie's Ma...not any of them...ever told me Frankie was alive." Between sobs, she continued, "If I'd known, if only I'd known, Frankie wouldn't be with Vera now."

"Ach...ach...ach..." Mama said, looking at Tata and nodding her head. Now she understood the heaviest hurt of all that Emilia was bearing.

"He doesn't want me...and he doesn't need me..." Emilia tried to pull herself together. "Frankie wants a divorce. He's living with Vera now."

"Coffee, Mama," Tata said. "Milia, you go...put water on your face...cold...you feel better. Then come, coffee be ready and again, we talk."

Reluctantly, Emilia rose from the table, heading toward the bathroom. In the middle of the hallway, she stopped and turned toward them once again.

"You know," she said, "I should be happy that he's alive...but I'm not. All I can think of is that now he has Vera instead of me...and she has him...and none of them ever told me he was home...alive. Lies. That's all they did...they lied...all of them... even Frankie's ma."

With shoulders bent and arms hanging limp at her sides, Emilia turned away from them and went into the bathroom.

******************

The clock in Emilia's bedroom told her it was early...seven a.m....very early considering she'd barely crawled into bed, however, it would do no good for her to try to sleep any longer. She couldn't.

Emilia raised the bedroom shade. It was a dreary day...no sun. She may as well dress and go to the fruit market. She would feel better there. Marcus cared about her. He cared about her very much...and he would want to know how Mama and Tata reacted to her news.

They reacted all right. And Harry! Tata had to restrain him. Her brother wanted to go right over to Frankie's last night. Poor Harry. He didn't know what a mess he was coming home to. He looked so happy when he came in. He and his girl must have enjoyed their evening together, and then he came home to that.

But what had surprised her more than anything, was the kind of support Mama and Tata gave her. She was so sure they would tell her she couldn't even consider divorce, instead, they weighed all the pros and cons with her, deciding that divorce was her only alternative, under the circumstances. Harry said so too.

After she told them about the things Frankie had said to her...that he no longer cared about her...that it was too late...that she'd never been there when he needed her...that she'd never really been a wife to him...then they knew.

And when these words...these accusations that Frankie made...when they turned her anger to guilt and she began to plead with him, begging for understanding...humiliating herself in front of Vera, who, Frankie insisted must stay...that was when he said the most awful things of all. Then, he told her that she had killed their son...that she deliberately fell, causing herself to miscarry because she didn't want to have his baby. At first, as she listened to his words, she fell apart...completely shattered...but then, all guilt and anger left her, and only hate remained. Then she ran from the house.

Of course, what she hadn't told them, because in all her misery it didn't even seem important, was what Frankie's ma had done.

After Mil had stopped Frankie and Vera in the street, they'd all gone into the shop. That's where Mother J. had insisted they go, and there they talked...long... late...and Mother insisted that Vera leave, but Frankie wouldn't let her. Oh, it was a terrible scene. She hated even remembering it, but the one thing that really stuck in her mind now, this morning, was how Catherine had followed Emilia as she ran out of the door, after Frankie made those terrible accusations about the baby...and told her he wanted a divorce, and she screamed back at him that she did too, then Catherine grabbed her arm and said, "Emilia, sometimes things are not what they seem. You must think about the terrible things Frankie has been through."

Emilia remembered then that she shook herself loose from Catherine's grip, thinking that she didn't care about what Frankie had been through, because she'd been through her own hell but no one seemed to care about that at all. She began then to run while Catherine called after her, "Emilia, Emilia, my dearest...be careful. Do not do anything foolish!"

Catherine had shouted something more, but Emilia didn't hear it as she ran toward the streetcar stop with her hands clasped tightly over her ears. Now, in the light of morning, she couldn't help wondering what it was that Catherine had been shouting, though it probably didn't matter. Nothing could change all the terrible things Frankie had said to her.

Mama and Tata and Harry were right last night. She should give Frankie his divorce, and she should marry Marcus, and then she should seek an annulment. There must be a way to do that, not for her sake, but for Mama's and Tata's. Surely, under these terrible circumstances the Church would grant her an annulment. She was called Mother Church, and no Mother would exclude someone forever.

As far as she was concerned, an annulment wasn't important. She didn't think God cared enough about her one way or the other to worry about whether or not she sought an annulment, but it was important to Mama and Tata. Though why that should concern them so gravely was more than she could figure out. Emilia was the one hurting...no one else...not really...except maybe Marcus. So, why should anyone else care? It was easy for others to give advice. Mama and Tata, they had one another...always...as long as she could remember. They'd been married more than forty years. What did they know about being alone? Why they'd never been alone! They'd always had one another to turn to. Yes, advice was easy.

"Oh, Emilia," she admonished herself, "you are getting crazy. Now, you're even angry at Mama and Tata."

Quickly, she finished dressing, even before washing. She would do a quick job of her toilette this morning. Marcus was the one she needed today. She had to hurry down to the store.

## CHAPTER 39

Emilia pawed through her closet searching for something cool to wear on a hot fourth of July morning, something casual for the outing she and Marcus had planned. Despite her feeling of lethargy due to the typical Chicago summer humidity, she was eager to go. Emilia loved the lakefront, and surely it would be cooler there. Emilia decided to pack her bathing suit in the picnic basket, along with their lunch. She was excited, really looking forward to a pleasant day. Maybe she would call Marcus and remind him to bring his bathing suit along...maybe, if she could reach the phone without disturbing Mama.

It was good of Peter to let them have the car for the day. Maybe she and Marcus would get a car of their own if they married. If? Now, why did she say "if"? Of course they would marry.

Anyway, maybe Marcus would let her drive a bit. She really relished the feeling of freedom and control that driving bestowed upon her. While driving she felt like a woman...not a child, though she'd come to accept the fact that Marcus would probably always call her child.

In her cool voile dress, Emilia slipped out of the bedroom and hurried into the kitchen. She heard Mama downstairs at the washing machine. Good, maybe she didn't hear Emilia moving about. They'd had another argument last night, but it wasn't really Mil's fault. Mama and Tata had to learn to stop pushing her. Everyday, they asked, no insisted, that she see a lawyer. They wanted her to finish with divorce proceedings so she could look into annulment. That's all they seemed to worry about... that annulment. Why *she* didn't even care about it, but they pushed and pushed. They were so fearful of God and the Church. They weren't nearly so concerned with her happiness as they were with everything being right with the Church. She was sick of it all.

She slapped mayonnaise on a couple of slices of bread and made sandwiches. Marcus didn't push her the way they did, and he was the one most concerned. He was the one who would marry her. Marcus was the bright spot in her life, she thought, remembering the way he always looked at her. He made her feel whole.

Suddenly, she felt like crying...for no reason. Well, she simply wouldn't do that. Hastily, she wiped a few errant tears, as she heard the Poulis auto roar to a stop in front of their house.

Hearing Mama's footsteps hurrying up the stairs, she quickly assembled her belongings and went to the door, but not quickly enough.

"Milia, Dziecko...come. You no even say good morning."

"I don't want to talk about it anymore, Mama. If I decide upon a divorce, I'll get one. That's that."

Mama shot a surprised inquiring glance at Emilia.

"What you say...IF...? Frankie live somewhere else...with 'nother woman...und you say 'IF' now?"

Then Mama slapped her. It was a sudden blow...unexpected. Emilia flinched, but she did nothing in response.

"Stubborn, you are! You don't care about nothing...only yourself! You no care about how you hurt your Mama...your Tata...nothing!"

"Hurt YOU? What about me, Mama? I'm the one who's hurt! I'm the one who's going to decide!"

Emilia yanked the door open and ran down the front stairs without a goodbye.

"Go!" Mama yelled after her. "Go, already! Next you say you will go to be with Marcus!"

Mama slammed the door and gave vent to her anger in a few strangled sobs, something she rarely did, as she stomped down the basement stairs once again. She would finish the washing. It would feel good to finish something...to make something clean.

Emilia slid into the passenger seat next to Marcus. He looked at her sympathetically.

"Child, you are fighting again with your Mama?"

"No, Marcus! Mama's fighting with me!"

"So, relax, my Child," Marcus said as he pulled away heading the auto toward Belmont Avenue and then in an easterly direction toward the lake.

They rode in silence for awhile. Marcus wanted to ask questions, but decided against upsetting Emilia further. He pretty much knew what the problem was all about anyway, it was just that Michalina's parting comment surprised him somewhat, but angry people frequently said surprising things. Instead of questioning Emilia, Marcus thought he might try to distract her. She seemed calmer now, as she sat quietly next to him observing the world around them.

"Would you like to drive, my Emilia?"

She looked at him with a bright smile and nodded. He pulled over and they exchanged seats. Emilia felt freer immediately. As they rode along in silence, Emilia let her mind wander. Then she began reading the various posters which decorated store front windows. There was an old campaign poster urging people to vote for Wilson. Well, it worked, she thought. He was elected, poor man, though she wondered now if he thought the Presidency had been worth all the struggle. The newspapers claimed the President was suffering from depression. Not long ago he had returned from Europe without much hope for the success of his proposal for the League of Nations.

Soon they passed Barney's tavern...now, turned "restaurant". Despite the picture of Carry Nation in the window, leading the Temperance League, the picture looming large as the woman herself, all six feet and 175 pounds of her, Emilia wondered if the "restaurant" now served only food, coffee and soft drinks, or whether the startling huge picture was a cover-up for the usual activities. Emilia's brothers certainly didn't think much of Prohibition. They said it simply gave the hoodlums excuse to become better organized so they could make and sell "moonshine".

On the next block, Emilia spotted the GRAND THEATER, better known in her own mind as "Billy's Palace". He still worked there, intermittently, between the many other places which clamored for his talents. He was becoming quite famous. Emilia was glad she had decided not to go with him. She would have been away from home a great deal. Emilia squinted, trying to focus her eyes better, wanting to see what movie was playing. Maybe she and Marcus could go there tonight. Then they were close enough to read the bold lettering which announced the "Birth of a Nation" by D. W. Griffith. That was an old movie, maybe three or four years anyway, but it was touted as the greatest movie ever produced. She's missed it the first time it came around, and she had really wanted to see it. She craned her neck to read better the names of the stars... Henry B. Walthall and May Marsh. Now she remembered. She also remembered reading that it was a Civil War spectacle. Should be exciting to see...especially on the Fourth of July. She remembered reading at the time it was very expensive to produce...$100,000...or some such huge amount.

"Marcus, may we go to see that tonight? She pointed at the theater.

He read the advertisement. "It'll be there a few more days, Emilia. I would rather go tomorrow night, or the next, if you don't mind too much."

"Oh," she said, grinning at him, "and the reason is...?"

"Jack Dempsey is fighting Jess Willart tonight for the world title. I would really like to listen to that on the radio."

Emilia looked disappointed.

"Do you mind very much?"

"Yes. But it's all right...if you promise we go to see this before the picture leaves the GRAND."

"My promise is golden." He bowed his head to her.

Again they rode along in silence as Emilia continued driving. Then she changed course. They were no longer heading east Marcus noted. He looked at Emilia. He wasn't sure she was even aware that she'd changed direction. She seemed only interested in noting all the advertisements around them. Marcus started to call her attention to the change, then thought better of it. He would sit back and see how far out of their way she would take them before noticing what she'd done. After all, it was a nice holiday for them, this Fourth of July. They had nothing more to do this day than to enjoy themselves.

Again, Emilia turned, and with a start, Marcus noted that she'd inadvertently turned down North Avenue. Was she really not aware of it? He thought not. Mentally, he made a bet with himself. They would be passing Frankie's house shortly, he was sure. Marcus began to wonder what Frankie's house looked like. To his knowledge, he'd never seen it. Actually, he hadn't been in this particular neighborhood at all... nearby, sometimes...when going to the city market, but other than that he had no reason to be here.

As they drove along a little further, Marcus noted a change in Emilia's expression. He thought she'd suddenly become aware of where they were headed. Her hands tensed as they gripped the wheel.

Soon, he saw her face blanch. She caught her breath. She sped the car up as much as she dared, and then Marcus caught sight of Frankie and his red-headed Vera sitting on the front steps of an older house. There was a factory on either side of it. Marcus remembered Emilia mentioning that fact to him several times. Nevertheless, he noted a certain charm about that house. He couldn't help noting also, Vera's beautiful red hair and her figure. Even sitting down, he could see she was a well built woman. He didn't think they, or she, saw them. But then, who would be expecting Emilia to *drive* by.

They passed and Emilia began to cry, not loudly, but Marcus saw a few glistening droplets slide down her cheeks. As he continued to watch her, he was certain of only one thing. Emilia's heart was hurting.

Then she pulled over and asked Marcus to relieve her of driving. He was glad, seeing how upset she was.

"Marcus," she began in explanation.

"No, Emilia. Don't say anything. I know what you saw. Later we'll talk. Now, we'll enjoy our holiday.

She reached over to pat his hand. "Thank you."

"Dry your tears, now. We're going to enjoy a picnic."

The lakefront was crowded, but Emilia and Marcus found a lovely spot of shade on a patch of grass where they sat enjoying an occasional cool Lake Michigan breeze. Though they changed into bathing suits, neither felt like swimming, or talking much. They simply sat together, companionably, each thinking private thoughts.

In the later afternoon, they watched a Company of Doughboys, newly returned from overseas, parading down the Avenue, their wrapped leggings and booted feet tapping rhythmically down the street. The sight of them caused Emilia to cry once again.

Marcus held Emilia closely until the Parade passed them by. Then he said it was time for them to talk.

They did, long and passionately, and though Emilia tried very hard to convince Marcus that all she wanted in the world was to marry him, he thought he knew better.

Marcus had been weighing all the observable evidence that Emilia so often unknowingly furnished. He thought that if he and Frankie were to sit in a pan on either side of a balance, that Frankie's side of the scale would somehow weight more in Emilia's favor. One thing he definitely knew. He knew there would be no happiness for Marcus and Emilia until his dear Child confronted Frankie once again...alone and on her own terms.

So, together they decided...at the insistence of Marcus...that Emilia would take the automobile within the next few days, and unexpectedly she would pull up to the Jagien's, and she and Frankie would go for a drive. Alone and away from everyone else, they would settle, once and for all, the future course of their lives. They would decide, once and for all, whether or not there was any future for them as a couple. This was something Emilia didn't wish to do, but as Marcus finally pointed out, she owed that much to him. Marcus loved her. He wanted to wait no longer. Now, he wanted either to be her lover, and then her husband when she was free, or he wished to be merely Marcus Poulis, neighborhood fruit store proprietor. He would no longer be merely, her good friend.

Emilia understood this need, and so she agreed. Of course, they would need Mother J.'s assistance. Mother J. and her assistance were something that Emilia would rather not need, but she understood the necessity...her predicament...the predicament that patient Marcus was in. Marcus had been more sorely used than even she, herself, had been, and he didn't deserve such treatment. Emilia knew he'd been extraordinarily good to her, and he didn't deserve the treatment he was getting.

And so, Emilia agreed. She would go about enlisting the aid...the assistance of Mother J. in the morning.

## CHAPTER 40

The next morning, Marcus drove Emilia to the tailor shop. He had no intention of letting Emilia face that ordeal alone, knowing as he did, how she dreaded seeing Frankie's ma. So, once again, Peter took over in the store, while Marcus and Emilia set out in the automobile.

Emilia was nervous enough to consider abandoning the plan, but Marcus wouldn't allow it. He reminded her of their agreement and why it was necessary that she confront Frankie, so early the next morning, much to Mama's regret, they started out. Mama had no idea where they were going thus she was fearful of this early morning trip on a workday, because she thought Emilia might be planning to run away with Marcus. Emilia did nothing to quell Mama's fears. She was tired of trying to convince Mama that things would work out properly, and she was tired of all this sudden suspicion. Before, it was like Mama and Tata thought she could do no wrong, and now suddenly, they seemed to feel that everything she did was wrong.

As Marcus and Emilia drove along, they conversed very little. Then, all too soon for Emilia's comfort, they'd reached the shop. Marcus waited in the auto while Emilia went inside.

Mother J.'s surprise at seeing Emilia was very obvious, even to Marcus who did his observing through the store window. Soon, he saw Frankie's ma grasp Emilia's hands...then fall to her knees, as though begging forgiveness. Marcus couldn't see Emilia's face, but he imagined that she was very much surprised.

Inside the shop, Emilia's emotions were fast tying into knots. After the terrible things they'd all said at their last meeting, Emilia anticipated the possibility of being thrown out. Instead, there was proud Catherine kneeling at her feet. Emilia's heart began to soften, until she quickly remembered what Catherine and the others had done to her...to Marcus. Then she tried to pull loose from Frankie's ma's grasp.

"Please, Emilia, please...don't. Listen to me."

Emilia's energies were drained. She stopped fighting Catherine.

"Please forgive me, Emilia. Forgive us. We didn't know...not about your Marcus. You never mentioned him. We thought that surely, before you became entangled with anyone else...well, the doctors assured us...insisted that Frankie would see again...that his blindness wasn't physical...so we thought...in a matter of months maybe that Frankie would be whole again."

"But you...none of you...trusted me enough..."

"Oh, yes, Emilia, yes. We trusted too much. We knew, all of us...that you would stand by Frankie no matter what happened. He said he wouldn't have that."

"Are you telling me he still loves me?" Emilia's heart began to pound until she thought even Catherine might hear it.

"I believe so."

"Then what about Vera?"

"Oh, Emilia...I don't know...I don't know what to say..."

"Then I must find out...for myself...my own sake..and for Marcus..."

It was then that Emilia told Mother J. why she had come.

Mother J. thought the confrontation plan was a good one, and she agreed that Marcus deserved this consideration. So, it was decided that on Friday, Mother J. would request Vera's help in the tailor shop, because on that day Kate was going to the doctor, and then Frankie's ma would insist that Frankie stay home to wait for a package delivery that Kate was supposedly expecting. At the appointed time, Emilia would ring the doorbell and tell Frankie his mother wanted him to come to the tailor shop, and that she would drive him there. Emilia knew she could disguise her voice well enough to fool Frankie into thinking she was a customer of his ma's, for awhile anyway, long enough to lure him into the automobile. Then she would drive away, and they would find a place to talk.

After planning this, Emilia called Marcus in to meet Mother J. It was a strained meeting, punctuated by halting conversation, still Emilia had the feeling that they sincerely liked one another.

Within an hour after their arrival at the shop, Emilia and Marcus were on their way home again. Emilia felt much better now that the first step in the plan had been accomplished, that of enlisting Mother J.'s help. However, she began to feel more and more anxious over the next step. What if Frankie wasn't fooled by her disguised voice? What if he wouldn't go in the auto with her? What would she do then? Marcus convinced her that if such be the case, Emilia would have to talk fast right on the front porch with Frankie. Though she agreed, Emilia still felt very uneasy.

When Marcus and Emilia returned from the tailor shop, they went directly to the fruit market, for Emilia didn't wish to return home to Mama's questions. The less Mama knew about this particular episode, the better it would be for all of them. Of this, Emilia was certain.

Later in the day however, Michalina went shopping. She "needed" onions. When she saw Emilia sitting with the ledger books, she was vastly relieved.

******************

Back at the tailor shop, Catherine Jagien worked furiously, and when Kate came in a while later, she was surprised to see what her mother had accomplished in those few morning hours...and in the heat. Catherine merely said she felt ambitious, for she felt it best not to mention any part of the visit or the plan.

Her reluctance to talk about it, was due to her feelings of confusion. Catherine felt an instant liking for Marcus Poulis. In fact, Catherine thought he would make a wonderful husband for Emilia, even though he was much older. It bothered her considerably that she thought this. She should have disliked Marcus Poulis immensely, under the circumstances. Liking Marcus and admiring him made Catherine feel very disloyal to Frankie, her own son, even though she did harbor a frustrating feeling of resentment toward Frankie right now. And why shouldn't she? After all, Frankie had convinced her to lie for him...telling her he needed to be whole to be worthy of loving Emilia...but then, why did he really turn to Vera? Catherine, at first had been certain that Frankie really loved and wanted Emilia...still, no one truly knew the heart of another human being, not even when that human being was a son.

But in any case, Catherine had deceived Emilia...and Marcus...and Emilia's whole family. That deceit hadn't been right, no matter what the reason. Lies always came out. Of course, it was easy to reason that out now, because hindsight was always better than foresight.

Funny, how at the time of Frankie's return from the war, she'd felt sure that his eyesight, which the doctor's diagnosed as "hysterical blindness", resulting from shock, that that eyesight would return, that Frankie would again become and feel whole. Now, she wondered about that, and she wondered as well if he would ever return to Emilia. Vera seemed to love him very much and he was dependent upon her. And what of Emilia and Marcus? No one had any idea that they would come together. Certainly they had no idea that Marcus would turn out to be such a fine person. How could they know these things? More importantly, how could she, Catherine, have known?

No wonder it was hard to forgive herself. Probably, it was as hard for her to grant herself forgiveness, as it was for Frankie to forgive himself for being alive, particularly after they heard of his cousin Stash's death.

Poor Stash. He'd survived the sinking of the Lusitania, then felt a need to join an American army unit, only to be killed in battle shortly after.

Frankie, on the other hand was alive, but felt only half whole...blind...deceiving those he loved...deceiving Emilia, whom he didn't wish to contact in his blindness. No one had been able to convince him that Stash's death wasn't a factor he could control.

Then, of course, there was the death that he'd seen all around him. He talked of the many boys he'd seen "splattered" to use his word, just before he, himself, went down. Yes, Catherine guessed, these were the reasons her sensitive boy could not now see.

Still, thinking about all of this, understanding it, none of that was helping anyone. Now, there were many hearts aching, and one of those many...either Frankie's or Marcus's or both, would suffer greatly. She couldn't help wishing that in some way things would turn out so that no one suffered. But of course, it wouldn't...because it couldn't.

And so, while thinking all these thoughts, Catherine had accomplished much work in the tailor shop, but she wasn't about to explain that to Kate. In due time, very soon in fact, Kate would know all about it anyway.

******************

On Friday morning, Mil woke very early. Mama wondered why. Emilia said it was impossible to sleep in the heat. Mama said nothing, but looked at Emilia as though thinking it was no wonder Emilia couldn't sleep. Many things there were to settle in her life and nothing was Emilia doing about them.

Emilia thought, "Little did Mama know. Little did she know."

Emilia washed and dressed carefully that morning. She chose her prettiest voile dress, for the heat seemed unbearable already. Finally, she chose her perfume...very carefully...for though Frankie couldn't see, he could smell, and Emilia determined that she would smell very good to him...possibly irresistibly good to him.

Then, with the curling iron heated to just the right temperature on the gas stove in the kitchen, she arranged and curled her hair to perfection, she thought.

All dressed, she spun before the mirror. Yes, her reflection said she'd done everything correctly. If there was any hope of winning Frankie back, she would certainly fan the fire of that hope today. For even though he couldn't see her, she knew how pretty she looked and it gave her the confidence needed to carry out the plan.

Then, in the middle of a pirouette, she stopped short, realizing that mentally, she'd already made her choice between the two men. All her talk of hating Frankie because he'd deceived her and lived now with Vera, that was all mere talk. She had just dressed for the battle of the sexes. She wanted Frankie back again, to be her husband. Yes, and she knew why. He had been her first love...married her when she was dying, just so she would fight harder for life. He was the father of their baby boy, the man who went to war because he loved her too much to keep away from her. She owed him a debt...no, more than that even...she owed him her life...her constancy...her love. There was no choice for her. Frankie had to be her man.

Emilia's eyes were alight with self-admitted knowledge, as though someone had stealthily turned on some switch in her head, flooding it with that understanding which shone now from the windows of her mind...those bright blue eyes that sparkled back at her from the mirror.

As she nodded to herself in understanding, she caught Mama's reflection in the mirror also, standing behind her own reflection, hands on hips, eyes asking unspoken questions like, "Why you dress like this?"

Emilia's face flushed as she turned to her mama.

"Marcus and I are going out to lunch today," she lied, averting her own eyes.

Mama said nothing in reply, she merely returned to the kitchen as Emilia, purse in hand, left the house.

******************

If Emilia weren't feeling so nervous, she would have been exulting in the feeling of complete freedom she could have experienced while driving the touring auto around the city all by herself. Never could she have imagined doing such a thing. Marcus was so good to her. She owed him so much. That's what she'd said to him before she left. He nodded and smiled and took her in his arms, but she saw sadness in his eyes. He'd guessed that she'd made her choice. Of course, Emilia knew he was no fool. He must have known it the moment he saw her so beautifully dressed and smelling so special. Yes, he was so wise and sensitive, that's why she would always love him too. That's why she wished as she removed the engagement ring from her finger and pressed it into his hand, that she could have two men in her life. That somehow, she could be married to them both.

So, now, she was truly free from any other commitment, and now in that freedom, she was able to tell herself that it was necessary to win Frankie back. But it was frightening, this knowledge. What would she do if he didn't have her? Fear and tension caused her to clutch the wheel until her knuckles shone white, and then she realized that she was there...at the appointed hour. She was keeping her date with fate.

"Oh, please God," she muttered, "Please."

Realizing again that she'd prayed, Emilia uttered an oath under her breath. Then, head held high, she ascended the front steps of Frankie's house.

Emilia reached for the doorbell, but pulled her hand back again. She turned as if to leave. Then, once again she reached for the doorbell and this time, she pressed... waiting. No sounds came to her from within the house. She pressed again. Then she heard them, the footsteps...soft...shuffling...the footstep sounds of an old man.

"Oh, my God," Emilia muttered. "That can't be my Frankie."

When the door opened slowly, she saw him, her Frankie...still young...handsome...dark hair already laced with gray threads. He was now not a boy, but a handsome man, though a blind one. Oh, how she wished he could see her. But he could smell her, she knew. He took a deep breath and his face lit up. Emilia took courage.

Emilia followed the plan. With pounding heart, she disguised her voice and led Frankie to the automobile. How strange it felt to open the door for him, to hold it as he climbed inside with her help, and then to close it for him. Carefully, she kept a reasonable distance from him. He mustn't touch her, for then he would know. She was sure of it.

Once in the auto and on the way again, Emilia felt much better. Somehow, she knew she'd captured him once more and wouldn't let him go until everything was settled to their satisfaction.

They had been driving for five...maybe ten minutes. Emilia was heading nowhere in particular. They were traveling the main streets which were crowded with shoppers. She thought a busy route might be best, offering less opportunity to escape, for Frankie mustn't escape. Emilia wanted so much to speak to him, but she didn't know what to say.

Finally, Frankie spoke. "Where are we going?"

Emilia responded in the delicate high pitched voice she'd used at Frankie's front door.

"To the shop."

"No, we're not. The shop is a minute's drive from the house. The shop is on a quiet side street. There's too much traffic here."

Emilia didn't respond.

Frankie turned to her as though he could see her.

"Who are you?" he demanded. "Where are we going?"

Emilia searched for the right words. She couldn't find them.

"Where are we?" he demanded...angry...determined. "Stop this automobile and let me out. Now!"

Her heart ached for his blind confusion. She reached one hand out and lightly touched Frankie's.

"Frankie's. It's me. It's Mil."

"Jesus Christ," he said, almost prayer like. "What damn fool thing are you doing?"

"Frankie, please."

"Can't you understand? I don't need you. I don't want you. I demand a divorce."

"Frankie, I won't listen to you. I won't! And I won't consider a divorce."

"It doesn't matter to me. Vera will have me just the way things are now. If you don't care, neither do I."

"Frankie...I love you."

Mil watched his face as she said this. She saw his jaw tighten, a shot of pain momentarily fly across his face. Now she was sure. Frankie did love her, so much that he couldn't bear to be bound to her in blindness. Mil smiled triumphantly. She was certain now, that nothing could make her give him up. There would be no divorce.

"Mil, stop this auto. I'm getting out."

"Frankie, don't be..."

Mil interrupted her own words with a gasp. What was she seeing?

Frankie sensed fear in her. "What is it, Mil?"

Before she could tell him about the two men who'd just run out of a jewelry store, faces partially covered by kerchiefs, the air around them seemed to explode.

Guns were shooting...people shouting and screaming...running. A man in the doorway of the jewelry shop clutched his chest and fell to the ground.

Mil tried to speed the car up, fearing they might become victims themselves. Somehow, instead of pressing the gas pedal, she'd applied the brake, slowing the car to a near stop.

The two masked men dashing across the street in front of the Poulis automobile, saw what Mil had done. Before she could speed up again, the masked men split, one to each side of the auto, grabbed onto the doors, and held fast as they mounted the running boards. Then, pushing guns inside, they aimed directly at Mil and Frankie and ordered them to get going. Fast!

"For God's sake, Mil, what's happening?"

"Sit still, Frankie,or they'll shoot us!" Mil screamed.

Frankie's sightless eyes opened very wide, though he said nothing more. The muscles in his jaw worked tensely; Mil tried to read his mind. What would he do to save them if he were driving.

Her scattered thoughts were interrupted by more exploding sounds as one of the men shot into the air over the crowd. Again people scattered. Mil knew the only help they could count on would have to come from her.

Unconsciously, Mil's old prayer habit came forth again, and God-pleading words flooded her mind.

"Please, please, God, what should I do?"

As though in answer to this unconscious prayer, a thought struck her like a bolt of lightning.

In response, Mil suddenly pressed the gas pedal down to the floor. The auto lurched forward. The men on either side of the auto teetered violently but didn't fall. Instead, they tightened grips. The one on Mil's side, growled at her as he pressed the gun muzzle closer to her temple.

"Don't try that again, sister. Just keep this crate moving fast, and no more funny business or we'll blow your brains out. His, too."

Mil began to cry.

"Shut up!"

On the other side of the car, the gunman leaned his face closer to Frankie's, then he yelled to his partner.

"Jake, this one can't see nothin'."

"Well...well..."

"Oh, Lord, God," Mil prayed again, as she consciously turned to God. Maybe God was all she had left. "Please, please help us."

She sped along, following instructions, looking for some opportunity that wasn't coming along. Suddenly she realized what these men were doing.

"My God," she thought, "they're leading us out of the city. They plan to kill us."

Soon, Mil was ordered to pull into a tree lined drive. It was long and curving...and desolate.

Jake ordered Mil to stop. She looked around for some means of escape. There was nothing, just an old white farm house standing in front of them...clothes poles to the side of it...many trees...a barn toward the rear of the house. No people, it seemed. If only Frankie could see, maybe they could make a dash for the barn, but what good would that do? There was no place to hide. There weren't enough trees in the little woods alongside of them to offer any real protection.

"Oh, dear God, we're dead," she thought. "I know it."

She began to sob, and then Frankie's voice stopped her.

"Where are we?" he demanded.

"Never mind, Buddy. You got nothin' to say."

The one called Jake ordered Mil out of the auto. He shoved her toward the house.

Jake yelled to his partner. "Hey, Duke, take care of him." Then he laughed. "I'll take good care of her."

"Please God, help me. Don't let him touch me. Help me get to Frankie! Please. I'll do anything, God!"

Again Jake shoved Mil.

"C'mon, sister. You're comin' inside with me."

"Wait!" Frankie yelled desperately.

Mil heard the click of Duke's gun. She turned, wild-eyed. Jake turned too. Duke's gun was pointed at Frankie's head, his finger on the trigger.

"Oh, my God! No!" Mil screamed.

Like a cornered tigress, she leaped, hurling herself at Jake.Taken by surprise, he toppled, discharging his gun. Someone groaned. Mil prayed it wasn't Frankie. She looked again at Jake sprawled on the ground, still clutching the gun. Instinctively, she stomped her heel into his hand. He yelled in pain, releasing the gun at the same time. She kicked it aside, spotted a good sized rock, reached for it, then plunged it down on Jake's head. The sound of the dull thud, the sight of blood spurting through her fingers, forced a piercing scream from her lips, just as a gun shot broke the air behind her.

Oh, God, no! Had Duke shot her Frankie? She scrambled for the fallen gun near her feet, grabbed it, jumped up and wheeled around in time to see Frankie on the ground with Duke standing over him.

Without hesitation, Mil pointed the gun at Duke's back and fired. Duke clutched his side and fell to the ground.

"Oh, Jesus, God, I've killed two men," she whispered.

Though she was very frightened, she knew she must push that fear from her mind. Frankie needed her. She went to him, saw blood trickling from an ugly gash on the side of his head. Please Lord, don't let him be dead. She was so frightened, but she continued to pray as she lay her head on his chest. As though in answer to her prayer, she felt Frankie breathing. And then she saw blood coming from his left arm, soaking his shirt. She thanked God that at least he was alive.

Mil wanted to tend his wounds right away, but knew she had to first insure their safety. She forced her attention away from Frankie as she tried to decide what must be done.

She looked from Jake to Duke. They were both bleeding, but Jake, at least seemed to be alive and breathing. She wasn't sure about Duke. Should she kill them and have done with it? Perhaps, and then she could drag Frankie to the auto. Well, she would do that if she had to, but there must be another way.

Frantically, she scanned their surroundings. Clothesline hung from one of the poles.

She untangled it, and then used it to bind Jake as tightly as she could. Then, with a knife from his own pocket, she cut what was left of the rope and started toward Duke. Frankie stirred and groaned as she passed. Thank God! She needed the reassurance that he was still alive.

How she wanted to go to him, but she mustn't. First, she had to tie Duke. She thought he might be dead, but she couldn't be sure, in any case, she needed to be sure he was safely tied and couldn't possibly harm them before she tended to Frankie. As she looped the last knot and pulled it as tightly as she was able, she heard Frankie mumble. She listened carefully before getting up to move.

"Jesus Christ. I must be in heaven."

Was he delirious?, she wondered. Then, she crept to Frankie's side.

His eyes were open. She leaned over him. He reached up and touched her face.

"Mil," he whispered. "It's really you...alive...golden hair...just as I remembered it..."

His voice trailed off. He began to cry.

Tenderly, Mil raised his head, and wrapped her arms beneath him. Frankie felt limp, still he spoke as though his open eyes were seeing her again. Did she dare to hope? Did he speak from memory, or did he really see her once again? He continued to smooth her hair, and their tears mingled. With his right arm, he tried to pull her down upon himself, but the effort caused him to wince.

She straightened, looked again at the bleeding wounds. Something must be done. But what? She attempted to pull his shirt loose, but that caused him pain. Her petticoat...that's what she must use. Raising the skirt of her pretty dress, she pulled hard, managing to rip out the hem of her petticoat. She ripped a strip free from the undergarment.

Tenderly, she touched the wound on Frankie's arm. It looked so ugly, but maybe it wasn't too serious. Apparently, Duke had somehow shot Frankie. The wound was still bleeding, so she couldn't tell how deep it was. With one of the satin strips of cloth, she bound his arm tightly, but she hoped not too tightly. With the other piece of cloth, she wrapped his head as well as she could, hoping to keep the gash on Frankie's temple from bleeding too heavily.

Then, drained and exhausted, she lay next to him, needing not only to rest, but to feel the physical presence of her Frankie, even for a brief moment.

Frankie's eyes were closed again. They didn't speak. Soon, Frankie looked at the sky through very heavy eyelids, trying to reassure himself of what he "saw"...trying to reassure himself that the brightness stabbing through the tree limbs above, was a real shaft of sunlight.

Mil watched him closely. She was afraid to ask, but when he turned toward her once again, his face radiant, she knew.

"Oh, Frankie, my darling. You can see, can't you."

He wrapped his good arm around her, unable to answer.

For a few more moments, they lay together on the ground, close as a pair of attracting magnets, blotting out their surroundings, until Frankie regained enough consciousness to press Emilia for details of what had happened. Yes, he could see, but he couldn't quite remember what had just happened to them. His mind was fuzzy and his vision gauzy. Emilia gave him the details very briefly as she helped him to struggle to his feet.

With her continued help, they struggled to the automobile and drove away.

Frankie's vision seemed to clear a bit more as they drove along, and though still not perfect, he was at least able to recognize where they were. After what seemed to be an eternity, they reached the city limits where they were able to hail a traffic cop. Excitedly, they reported what had happened to them, and though the telling was disjointed, they were able to make themselves understood well enough so the cop could call for help. Then, Mil was taken back to the farmhouse, while Frankie was taken to the hospital for emergency treatment.

At the farm, the captors, now captives, still lay where they'd been left. The astounded policeman then took over, promising to handle everything for Emilia. The worst was over. Mil collapsed.

## CHAPTER 41

It was late when Mil and Frankie were released from the hospital...well past nine o'clock..and getting dark.

Mil reached for Frankie's hand. "I love you, Frankie."

"Oh, my Mil." With his good arm, he pulled her close.

She mumbled into his shoulder. "Thank God, you had the hospital call Noshkins."

Emilia squeezed. Frankie winced. He was still mighty sore, but nevertheless highly energized. He could see again, his wounds were bandaged and not too serious, and his wife, Emilia was with him, close to him. Momentarily, he was forgetting everything that had happened to him in the past few years, except that he and Emilia were together.

Emilia was thinking how funny it was that such a short time ago, she'd been exhausted, yet now, with her head on Frankie's shoulder, she was feeling wonderful.

It was cool in the darkness that had quickly gathered around them. She looked up to see stars sparkling down at them like flirting fireflies. They stood out here, alone now, and together.

Frankie began to kiss her, covering her with kisses, as his hand moved gently over her body, making a silent statement of his love...as though reaffirming an old claim.

How amazing it was...the feeling she had, as she melted into his warm body, clinging so close to him. Despite the heat of their bodies, the wetness of their mingled perspiration...all of the human animal elements...how wonderful their closeness felt.

"Let's go home," Frankie said, his voice husky with emotion.

"Oh, Frankie..." Emilia's unfinished thought played through Frankie's brain like the sounds of a melody, played in a minor key, a melody that ended with a note of pleading.

Emilia *was* pleading, for she didn't wish to be surrounded by family and questions, and explanations, not until they'd had an opportunity to be lovers once again. How long it had been.

Across the street, lights beckoned from the elegant lobby of a small hotel. Emilia looked from Frankie to the hotel lobby. Her eyes asked an unspoken question, then arm in arm, they crossed the street and requested a room.

Though the astonished night clerk made no comment, his surprised face asked many questions.

Frankie said they were newlyweds who'd been in an accident and couldn't go any farther...and they needed a room for the night...to rest up so they could continue their trip in the morning.

The clerk sympathized heartily and gave them a room.

Emilia muffled her giggles until they entered the elevator.

"Frankie," she laughed, "we can't stay all night. Marcus will wonder about the car."

"Call Mama from the room. Tell her we're honeymooning tonight, and ask them to call the others."

Emilia objected until she saw the room. It was perfect for a honeymoon. Besides, neither of them had ever stayed in a hotel before. Oh, it was elegant. Such a beautiful bed...soft lights...their own bath.

Again, they melted together. Then, Emilia pushed Frankie away. He winced. Gently, Emilia kissed his sore arm...shoulder...neck...then she stopped and backed away.

"I'd better call. They'll all be very worried."

"You'd better hurry," was all Frankie said in reply.

Emilia did just that, though it wasn't easy, for Mama didn't understand at all, but finally, she agreed to call Mother J. and Marcus, however, she demanded some sort of explanation in return. Emilia decided not to mention Frankie's eyesight or the robbery, fearing that she'd never be able to leave the phone. Instead, she told Mama only that she was with Frankie and that they were fine, also that they owed much to God, who was indeed a loving Father, and that Emilia would never stop thanking God herself for all He'd done, but that there wasn't time to explain any more. She assured Mama that Marcus had known about her visit with Frankie. Then Emilia said she was hanging up the phone, but she promised that Mama and Tata would know everything the next day.

When Emilia replaced the receiver, she thought what a good inspiration that was, to tell Mama about God, but she really meant it. She would never stop thanking God for this night. When she turned to see Frankie lying on the bed with his good arm extended to receive her, she forgot everything else.

"I haven't washed," she said.

"Later," he answered as love subdued pain.

They lay side by side, content at long last. Emilia knew for certain that it was right for them to do this. They needed this time to be alone together. Now she knew they would always be together, for now they knew what real love was. She was sure Frankie thought this too, and she felt that neither of them could ever live without the love of the other again.

Frankie's deep breathing told her he was asleep. They'd been through a great deal that day...he, more than she.

What was it that Noshkins had said to her just a short while ago at the hospital? Yes, he said that God had certainly helped them, that He heard their prayers, and that what happened this night was truly a miracle. Then Noshkins reminded her that once he'd told her she was destined to be a survivor...and she was. Emilia had survived...and she'd helped Frankie to do the same, just as he'd once helped her.

Emilia breathed deeply, encouraging her own body to succumb to sleep. She smiled as she began to doze, thinking that they never did bathe in the beautiful bathroom.

## CHAPTER 42

Morning brought sunshine...and reality. Such wonderful reality.

Mil yawned and stretched, turned on her side to see if Frankie was really there, but found herself alone in the bed. His half was empty! The cold hand of panic tried to squeeze the very life out of her heart. Mil jumped to her feet. She reached for her clothes, trying to unscramble the tangled pile. Then the bathroom door opened, and there stood Frankie...cleaned and refreshed...left arm still lightly bandaged. She ran to him clinging...reassuring herself of his presence.

Frankie came to Mil and held her. He felt her trembling.

"I'm sorry I frightened you. Did you think I would leave you? My foolish angel."

Mil clung to him. Then she spoke.

"Frankie, it's just that...well...all this time, so many things have gone wrong for us. We've had so little time together. I think for awhile I'll feel frightened...afraid that something...maybe someone...will come between us."

She looked into his face in time to see it clouded by concern.

"Frankie?"

He smiled at her. "Go. It's a beautiful bathroom."

When she came out, bathed and feeling cooler, she saw that Frankie hadn't yet dressed. He was waiting for her...on the bed. Once again they loved. How happy she felt.

Afterward, they lay together quietly, resting, then Mil spoke.

"We'd better leave, Frankie. We promised."

"Ummm." He seemed preoccupied.

"What is it?" Again, Mil began to tremble.

"Nothing, my Angel."

"It's something." She pushed herself upright...searched his face.

Frankie shrugged.

Suddenly, Mil knew what it was.

"It's Vera, isn't it?" Mil's voice was demanding.

"It'll be hard for her, that's all."

"What do you mean by that? *I'm* your wife!" Mil's voice rose a little.

"Mil, don't. Surely you can understand how much she did for me...even though I couldn't....you know..."

"No...no, I can't understand. What did she do for you...other than allow you to paw her...to "lust" after her?"

Emilia's hands, clenched tightly shut, shook violently; her face flamed.

Frankie rose from the bed and began to pace.

"Lord, Mil! When I was blind, she stood by me..."

Mil interrupted him, her voice sharp as cut glass.

"Only because you didn't give *me* the chance."

The room was ominously silent. Neither of them moved. Then Frankie turned and faced her.

"*I'm* your wife," Mil said, poking her chest with her own finger, "Me... Emilia...the one who thought you were dead. The one who broke a kind man's heart to return to you. The one who asked God to exchange your son's life for yours. I'll never be able to forget that. Don't tell me Vera stood by you. When you're gone, she'll find another...like that..." and Mil snapped her fingers in his face.

Without saying another word, she pulled her clothes on, picked up her purse, and slammed out of the room. She was furious enough to get into the car, and drive away...without Frankie.

Emilia was stomping toward the elevator when she heard a door open and close. Then she heard Frankie's voice calling her. She stopped. He caught up to her. She felt his hands on her shoulders.

"I'm sorry, Emilia. You're right. We'll work it out."

She turned to him and wiped away his tears. They stepped into the elevator, then out into the sunshine. But in the deepest chamber of her heart, Emilia knew and understood what it was Frankie felt for Vera. Then she thought of Marcus.

## CHAPTER 43

Their drive home was beautiful, in spite of the already sultry day. Nothing could mar the happiness Emilia and Frankie felt...a couple at last.

Once in their own neighborhood, Emilia detoured around, stopping the auto first in front of their Church...St. Wenceslaus...the church of their marriage. She would begin right now to show God how thankful she was.

When Frankie looked at her in surprise, she explained that to him.

How elated Mil felt to be walking steadily into the quiet dimness, holding her man's arm, this time not for support, but simply holding onto him because she wanted to...because they shared a feeling of belonging...one to the other.

The church was empty. Mil was glad. She didn't wish to have to explain Frankie's real live presence to anyone they knew. Not before they reached home...Mama...Tata.

Together they knelt in the back pew, bowed their heads, and prayed.

Over and over again, Mil whispered one phrase...thank you God...thank you God. She guessed Frankie was doing the same. How, she wondered, had she ever been so hateful toward God...so angry? Time and again, He'd only helped her...been a good loving Father to her. She thought about all that God had done for her...helped her to live...to conquer the 'con'...to survive the loss of her baby...to bring Frankie back to her in spite of the poor odds of war and battle. And now...now...He'd not only returned Frankie to her, but God had even restored Frankie's eyesight. And finally, He'd saved them both from death at the hands of the gangsters. But most of all, He'd allowed them to love one another...to become two in one flesh...to know something of what heaven must be like. Thank you wasn't enough to say to God, but it was all she knew how to do.

Emilia vowed never to doubt God again, for now she knew how much she needed God. Yes, she decided, and God needed her too, or He wouldn't have allowed her to live.

Emilia felt eyes. She looked at Frankie. He was watching her...love spilling from his tender gaze.

"Ready?" he asked.

Together, they genuflected and left the church.

******************

The fruit market was only a few blocks from the church. Emilia drove very slowly.

"Mil, you can drive a little faster," Frankie urged.

"Oh...yes..."

Despite her answer, Mil couldn't bring herself to hurry the auto along.

Frankie studied her face. He saw tears lurking on the lids of her eyes. He turned away, thinking of how she must hate to face Marcus. He understood that because of his own feeling for Vera's hurt, still he didn't like it at all that Mil should feel so strongly about Marcus. Had there been more between them than the intention of marrying? For the first time, he began to think about that...to wonder. He felt jealous of her concern...jealous of what he began to suspect. He vowed they wouldn't stay long in that neighborhood. Just as soon as possible, he would see about returning to his old job, and finding a flat away from here...before they had any more babies.

Emilia stopped the auto in front of the big store window, where as usual, fresh fruits and vegetables seemed to wink in the sunlight. Frankie saw her knuckles...hard and white against the wheel. He reached over to her, laying his big hand over hers.

"Come," he said, "take the keys. You go in and return them. Then we'll walk home together."

"Come in with me?"

Frankie's heart ached at the small sound of her voice, knowing how she dreaded going inside and facing Marcus. Nevertheless, in reply to her question, he shook his head from side to side. Feeling as he did about the situation with Emilia and Marcus, he felt it better for everyone that he didn't go into the store with Emilia. Besides, Emilia would have to face Marcus sometime, and it was probably better sooner than later.

No, he was not ready to face Marcus. Why risk even the possibility of a scene? He knew Marcus meant no harm to anyone, the man simply fell in love with Emilia. How could anyone blame him for that? But though Frankie didn't blame Marcus, he wasn't feeling very forgiving either.

The fact was, Marcus had literally steered Emilia back to Frankie by insisting she meet him and talk things over. Frankie was glad for that, and he had to admit, grudgingly, that Marcus deserved some respect for that. However, in his heart, Frankie also resented Marcus for that, for now Emilia would always hold a soft spot for "good, kind, understanding" Marcus.

No, Frankie wasn't ready to go in and be civil to Marcus. Maybe Frankie would never be ready for that. He shrugged in reply to his own thoughts.

As Emilia and Frankie stepped from the auto to the sidewalk, they looked in the store window. Marcus looked back at them from his stance near the counter at the front of the store. He must have been watching them, and now Emilia saw him incline his head toward them in greeting, but there was no smile on his usually happy face. He didn't wave either. His arms were folded across his chest, as though he were protecting himself. Emilia couldn't remember ever seeing him look like that. She wanted to cry. She swallowed hard, hoping to forestall any hot tears.

"Damn it to hell," she thought.

Elinora was in there too, standing a little apart from Marcus. Why did it have to be everything at once? Well, let Marcus tell Elinora all about everything, if he hadn't already. In any case, she couldn't.

"And please, God," she thought, "When I go in, please don't let Elinora mention her dead Jan." For some reason, Mil knew she couldn't cope with that too. "And, excuse me, God, for swearing," she added.

Once more, Emilia reached for Frankie seeking his reassurance, but he was no longer beside her. Then she saw him standing beyond window range, so neither he nor Marcus would have to endure unnecessary exposure to one another.

Emilia entered the store to the jangle of the merry little bell. She tried to look pleasant...noncommittal...however, the uncharacteristic stoop of her shoulders belied her true emotional state.

Emilia tried to speak, but only tears came. She extended her open palm to Marcus, offering him the keys to his touring auto.

Marcus understood her pain. His heart went out to her. Of course, even though he understood what she was going through, the understanding made it no easier for him. His heart was also heavy, and in addition his pride was sorely wounded when he looked out the window at the broad shouldered young stallion who'd taken his place. Blind or not, Emilia had chosen Frankie.

"Who said," he wondered mentally, "better to have loved and lost than never to have loved at all."

Marcus wasn't sure that was true, but maybe in time...maybe then it would be.

Again, he looked at her tears, her unhappy face.

"Child," he said, "at least it's all settled."

"Oh, my dearest, sweetest Marcus. I wish...somehow..." but she couldn't finish.

Instead, she found herself rushing into the arms of Marcus, the kindest friend she'd ever know. He held her, patting her back, reassuring her. She lay her head on his shoulder and let the tears finish themselves. At the sound of Elinora's voice, Emilia straightened.

"Ja, Girl. How hard it is...having feelings for more than one man."

Elinora stood there, thoughtfully nodding her head up and down.

"Ja. You ask Elinora. She knows."

Then, in characteristic fashion, Elinora slapped her thigh.

"But, I tell you this, Girl. You don't worry about Marcus. Elinora will take care of him."

Elinora then winked slyly at Marcus. He laughed, more uproariously than usual, Emilia thought.

"Go ahead, Emilia Child. Frankie is waiting for you."

She started for the door, as he called after her.

"And by the way, if you need a job..."

That was all she heard as she rushed out the door.

## CHAPTER 44

Emilia's hands were ice cold. She and Frankie had been through so much in the past few days that facing Mama and Tata should be like reading the happy ending to a dramatic romance. However, it wasn't like that for Emilia. She gripped Frankie's hand very hard with her tense fingers, as they walked up the front steps of the solid, red brick, two flat.

"Well," she thought, "at least they know Frankie and I are together again. They know we've spent the night together. Some of the shock will be gone, even if they don't understand what's happened."

"Mama..Tata..." Emilia called as she and Frankie pushed open the front door.

Emilia heard voices coming from the kitchen. She ran toward them, pulling Frankie behind her, eager now to put this last hurdle behind them.

As soon as they entered the room, Emilia and Frankie stopped short. Mama and Tata weren't alone. Seated around the table were Walter and his Lydia, Harry, and Mama and Tata. The room turned silent. All thoughts of continued discussion seemed to have vanished. The group at the table stared at the hand-holding couple, with an air of aloofness, Emilia thought.

Emilia felt her mouth go dry. She ran her tongue over her lips. That didn't seem to help.

"Mama...Tata...Frankie can see!"

Murmurs bubbled up from the tight little group. Then, as if on command, they all rose from their seats and went forward to greet Mil and Frankie. Questions were flying and hands were pumping congratulations.

Matching questions with answers, while satisfying everyone's curiosity, became an almost humorous and impossible situation, but soon the babbling died down. After Mil finally disclosed the details of her "plan" with Mother J. and the adventure that resulted from it, as well as the amazing return of Frankie's eyesight, then everything settled down some.

Then it was time for Mil and Frankie to receive news. Walter told them of his plans...his and Lydia's...their plans to marry.

Harry, listening to all the bubbly talk lost control of his usual staid sophistication and wept for joy. Finally, came the reckoning. It was Tata who asked the sore question.

"You haf seen Marcus?"

That was all Tata said as he fastened his steely blue gaze upon Emilia's face.

She nodded and cried.

Mama scooped her baby into an embrace as though she were a child again. She pulled Emilia to a chair and settled her daughter upon her lap.

"Tata," she said sternly. "Co cie tam?"

Tata grumbled in reply.

"You must know is worry to Milia and Frankie," Mama continued.

She rocked her girl and crooned to her.

Emilia dried her eyes.

"It's all right, Mama. We might as well tell you everything, huh, Frankie?" She looked at him for confirmation.

Frankie nodded back to her.

Quickly, Emilia explained about Marcus and her feelings for him, and how he understood..mostly, understood, anyway. Though it was a brief explanation, she felt exhausted afterward as she lay back against Mama's bosom.

Then Tata turned to Frankie.

"And your woman that stayed with you? What you do with her?"

"Tata, Mil and I have talked about it. It'll be all right."

"Tata!" Michalina looked at her husband with reproving eyes. "Frankie fixes. Milia say so."

Tata looked at Frankie severely, and ignoring Mama's statement, continued to make his point. "Only one woman you can keep Frankie."

Frankie nodded to his father-in-law. "Only one woman I want, Tata."

Frankie walked over and pulled Emilia from Mama's lap. He pulled her out to their old bedroom on the porch, but their furniture was gone. His look of surprise brought laughter to everyone, and eased the tension.

Emilia pointed to their new room.

"We're tired," Frankie said. "See you all later."

He settled Mil on the bed and closed the door firmly.

"We're not staying here much longer Mil."

"You need a job."

"I'll have one."

Mil traced her finger tip from his forehead down to his chin.

"What do you think Kate and Hank will have?"

"A baby, I hope."

"And us?"

"A baby...someday."

"Not now?" she asked, blushing a little.

"Not now. But someday."

They lay side by side, looking out the window, watching Mil's beloved poplar tree wave its branches at them, as though sending a cooling breeze their way.

Each of them thought private thoughts...thoughts of the future.

Frankie wondered where they should look for a flat, and how much money he needed to make to support them. One thing he knew. They needed to start a private life of their own. Another thing he certainly knew. Emilia would never work for Marcus Poulis again...no matter how good he was.

Mil lay dreaming about the home they would have...hoping to be near Mama and Tata. She thought about Walter and Lydia and their coming wedding...about how much she would miss having Harry around all the time...about how she'd miss being his baby sister.

Then once again, she thought about Kate and Hank and their coming baby. She hoped she'd have a baby soon too...maybe a little girl..and then a boy...but not a boy first. It wouldn't seem right to replace their lost baby boy with another boy right away.

Yes, she thought, and right after they rested, they must go to Frankie's house... tell Mother J. and all of the Jagiens about what had happened. But they needed to rest first before going through all that again. Besides, now it was their turn...the Jagiens... to wait, like they'd made her wait. Though Mil felt angry still, she was beginning to understand Catherine's reasons for holding back the truth. But she wouldn't think about all that now. It only made her angry.

And wouldn't their Ludmilla be surprised, she thought, about Frankie's eyesight coming back. How strange it all was. Never before had she heard of a bump on the head being a good thing to have happen. Oh, she couldn't wait to call Ludi.

Emilia began to feel dozy tired. Her eyes really felt heavy.

"Oh yes," she whispered. "And God, please remember. I'd like that first baby to be a girl."

She smiled, thinking she'd heard a whispered "yes" as though in answer to her prayer. She smiled again. Those whispering poplar leaves could always make her believe anything. Still...well...time would tell.

Breathing deeply, she allowed her heavy eyelids to close. Then, turning on her side, she threw her arm around Frankie, encircling him, literally and figuratively with her love - a woman's love, the love that might wax and wane like the rising and receding tide, but a love that would never end. How could it? She would pass it down to her daughter one day - just as Mama had passed that ability to love down to her, and so on it would go...just as God had intended...until the end of time.